HUNTRESS

A Royal States Novel

SUSAN COPPERFIELD

HUNTRESS
A ROYAL STATES NOVEL
BY SUSAN COPPERFIELD

Like the other men in Prince Kelvin's line, only the love of another can free him from his family's curse, but it's hard finding the perfect woman able to love him despite all his flaws—and his tendency to transform into an animal during the spring. To survive and reclaim his humanity, he must find someone who would turn the world upside down for him, not because of fame, wealth, or power, but because he has earned her trust and love.

When he develops an unhealthy case of infatuation for the huntress wanting him as her next trophy, his curse may be his salvation, if he can convince the wild woman of the woods to see him for who he is rather than the beast he has become.

Copyright © 2017 by Susan Copperfield

All rights reserved.

No part of this book may be reproduced in any form or by any electronic or mechanical means, including information storage and retrieval systems, without written permission from the author, except for the use of brief quotations in a book review.

Cover design by Rebecca Frank of Bewitching Book Covers by Rebecca Frank.

ONE

Gail had loved the idea of marrying a prince.

A LONG TIME AGO, someone I wished I could've loved dubbed me Rose because I smelled too nice to be an onion. My closest friends and family still called me Rose to tease me, but they didn't know the truth.

Gail had loved the idea of marrying a prince.

She hadn't loved the prince.

I would've given her the spring wedding she had desired. I would've given her everything.

Had she loved me, my family's curse wouldn't have stolen my humanity on the first day of spring as always.

I waited for summer deep in the forest, avoiding man and beast alike. I terrified other turkeys; at almost double their size, they had reason to fear me. The persistent hens had learned to run from me; I drove them away with warning pecks whenever they came too close. On rare occasion, I was forced to use my claws and spurs, which I always regretted.

It wasn't their fault I was human. One day, I would find someone who loved me more than my rank. Until I did, the family curse would take hold every spring, proving once again I hadn't earned a woman's love.

If I'd inherited my father's animal, I would've enjoyed spring at the castle.

My father became a lynx.

My grandfather became a lion.

My great-grandpa became a bear, a mean old grizzly who refused to do us all a favor and die.

My uncles turned into wolves, and all four of them loved harassing His Royal Majesty, the King of Illinois.

I became a turkey, a white one with silver barring on my feathers, which meant my entire family, assorted cousins included, viewed me as dinner. If they ever learned what I became, I'd be grateful if they kept their teasing to calling me Rose.

None of them knew what I became in the spring, and I meant to keep it that way. As the only prey species in a long line of proud predators and scavengers, I'd become the family shame the instant anyone learned the truth. My father would toy with me because he was a cat, and that's what cats did. My great-grandpa would solve the shame problem by eating me and leaving the few bones he didn't devour for my uncles. I had no idea who would inherit the throne; none of my sisters suffered from the family curse, eliminating them as possible heirs. None of the women in the family line had ever suffered from the family curse.

Had my father been wise, he would've named Grégoire his successor instead of me.

In a few days, the cycle would begin again, and I wondered if anything would change. Miracles could happen. One had when Montana's king had found a queen. I gave it a few years before that woman ruled the world with an iron fist. She'd humanized the world's most feared monarch. A woman like her existed for a man like him.

She gave me hope someone existed for me, too. I just had to find her before I ended up a trophy on someone's wall.

No matter how I looked at it, I was doomed.

A HUNTRESS STALKED me through the woods, leather-clad and armed with a bow. A pair of swords hung from her back, their hilts sticking up over her shoulders. If she moved the wrong way, they'd smack into the back of her head. I'd never seen someone like her before, and I'd risk life, limb, and feather for a chance to meet her while human.

She glided through the forest, her steps quiet.

Her confidence worried me. That the swords glowed a ghostly blue and fire-bright orange licked at the arrowhead transformed my worry into dread, especially since the bow was pointed in my direction.

"Aren't you a pretty one," she drawled, exposing her as having come from somewhere in the south although she lacked the flair I associated with Texas and other south-eastern kingdoms.

Great. I'd found a trophy hunter. My family would be expecting me to drag my ass home tomorrow, but I'd be decorating someone's mantle.

I gobbled my disgust.

Running would earn me an arrow in the back. Not running would earn me an arrow in the chest. Of the two, I'd rather face death with dignity.

An Averett fought to the bitter end.

Most Averett men had flesh-rending claws and fangs.

Fighting was a lot easier with claws and fangs. I'd have to make do with my wings, which could break bones if I landed a lucky hit. My beak could do damage. My claws weren't a match for a real predator's, but I could draw blood with them if I worked at it.

I'd give the huntress a fight she wouldn't forget, and if my luck turned in the right direction for a change, I'd escape with my life. Shit odds annoyed me. Assuming I wasn't killed by the huntress who'd dared to invade *my* forest dressed in an outfit I wanted to strip her out of, my sisters would cackle over my misfortune until I died from embarrassment.

I blamed my family for my interest in women who looked like they could kick my ass if given an excuse and five minutes. My grizzly great-grandpa, in particular, held the most responsibility. The harder my great-grandmother beat him for his stubborn stupidity, the happier he got.

It was no surprise, really, why I had so many relatives. My great-grandpa's genes had corrupted my grandfather and father into loving feisty women. Unlike my great-grandpa, who'd limited the number of children to a reasonable number, the rest of my family bred like rabbits.

Charging the woman and beating her with my wings was rude, especially when I didn't bother with any of the warning signs natural animals offered before attacking. I needed to spare my breath for my run for the hills.

The woman yelped, and the burning arrow left the bow with a twang. Heat seared across my side below my wing.

I screamed because it hurt. I had no idea why she screamed; while I managed to smack her with a wing, I hadn't hit her *that* hard.

Since shooting me hadn't been bad enough, she adjusted her grip on her bow and clubbed me with it. In good news, the bow's string broke. In bad news, the murderous gleam in her eyes was familiar. When I'd been thirteen, someone had tried to kidnap me, and my grizzly of a great-grandpa had taken offense to that.

The palace staff had used a mop and bucket to clean most of the mess up after my great-grandpa had finished working his temper out on the man.

Averett men were often brave and stupid, but we weren't suicidal. I ran like I meant it, and should my sisters ask, I'd tell them the truth: I'd pissed off a woman and valued my life.

MY ATTACK BOUGHT me enough time to get a head start, and years of living in the forest every spring gave me the knowledge I needed to make distance. Despite my pale feathers serving as a distinct disadvantage, there were many ways a white turkey could disappear without a trace.

The waterfall where the river branched into two streams offered the ideal hiding place. The cascades ran white and mist rose from the stones surrounding a deep pool. Most never realized there were ledges behind the falls large enough for an industrious—or desperate—animal to hide. The water would beat me black and blue, but I'd become invisible.

Best of all, the shores were of weathered

stone, which would minimize my tracks and keep her from hunting me easily. A plunge through thickets too dense for her to pass through bought me enough time to clean my feet in the stream before running to the falls.

Fortunately for me, she hadn't found me far from the waterfall, and I hoped going around the thicket would slow her down enough for me to pull off my disappearing act. A ten-foot block of pale granite formed the foundation of the falls, and I dove into the spray, pressed against the rock, and waited.

Within minutes of hiding, the gash across my side flared, reminding me I'd barely dodged becoming a trophy. The water helped numb the injury, plastered my feathers to me, and ensured I'd spend the first days of summer sick and miserable on top of bruised, battered, and bleeding. In the worst-case scenario, I'd have to wait until I involuntarily transformed to leave, resulting in a naked hike to my nearest stash of clothes several miles away. From the stash, I'd have another five-mile adventure to reach my wallet, phone, and its solar charger, which I'd use to either call a cab or contact the RPS for pickup.

My family really hated when I called a cab for a lift home after an entire spring out in the woods.

Maybe if I didn't have to put up with new RPS agents every summer, I'd be more willing to call them. My spring disappearances drove my agents off each and every time. Runaway royals didn't bother them—not usually.

Runaway royals they couldn't recover drove them to the brink of insanity. Most quit and found saner jobs. Others requested transfers to a different kingdom. A rare few stayed in Illinois, transferring to a different sector of the RPS.

The day I found even a single agent capable of dealing with me, I'd do everything in my power to keep him—or her—from quitting my detail.

None of it mattered if I didn't evade the woman hunting me. I hunched in my spot, kept quiet, and mourned for the loss of my typically quiet turkey life, which involved foraging for food and convincing the local wildlife to leave me alone.

I was in for a long, miserable wait, but it beat becoming a trophy on a huntress's wall.

THE WOMAN FOUND THE WATERFALL, but judging from her cursing, she'd lost my trail. I'd seen plenty of temper tantrums from my sisters, but they'd done theirs in the prettiest fashion possible, as princesses couldn't allow themselves to be anything other than picture perfect. I found that mentality ridiculous, but the first—and last—time I'd mentioned that, the entire lot of them had gone on a rampage aimed in my general direction.

Had the women of my line been cursed, too, I would've had at least a quartet of grizzlies, a pair of wolves, and a lioness hot on my heels ready to separate my head from my shoulders. I'd earned my beating, accepting what they'd refused to believe since the day they'd learned to talk.

My sisters weren't very good at being princesses.

The huntress spewing profanities along the shore wouldn't make a very good princess, either. Maybe that's what I liked about her. Few would accept her based on appearances alone. She didn't need beauty; she wore leather like she'd been born in it, something I found too appealing for my good.

Had I been wise, I wouldn't have found her awe-inspiring or attractive. Her vocabulary alone would offend every elite in the kingdom, something I didn't mind in the slightest. If I let her loose in the castle, I gave it a day before she'd turned the entire place upside down. The list of reasons why she wouldn't fit in made me want to catch her, take her home with me, and release her to see what would happen. I'd give up my claim to the throne for a chance to be part of the chaos destined to unfold if she set foot in elite society.

Such mayhem only happened once in a man's lifetime.

Had I known there'd been a woman like her in the world, I would've spent the past two years looking for her rather than attending charity auctions trying to prove I wasn't stuck on Gail. The one in Texas had been the worst; everyone had gotten caught up in the wedding frenzy. The next year's, in Maine, hadn't been much different, although instead of a wedding frenzy, people had wanted babies instead.

I'd hated the false sympathy, the sly looks, and the whispers behind my back when the gossipers thought I couldn't hear them. It all boiled down to the same thing.

They believed I'd been ruined. They believed the direct royal lineage in Illinois would end with me.

I wasn't ruined, but I'd learned an important lesson thanks to Gail: money couldn't buy anything of value.

More howled curses drew my attention back to the huntress. Had I said even one of her profanities, my mother would've washed my mouth out with soap. Hell, she would've done worse for just thinking them. My father would find the whole situation hilarious, my mother would take offense, and given a few hours, I'd be at risk of having yet another sibling.

Averett men weren't the brightest. I suspected the curse deducted at least twenty IQ points from those unfortunate enough to be saddled with it. There was no other explanation. Not only did we lose IQ points, it all came from the sections of our brain responsible for the development of common sense. Nothing good would come of my interest in a woman who viewed me as a trophy to be hunted and stuffed.

I wanted to take her home with me. With a woman like her in my life, I'd never get bored. I had doubts I'd survive the experience, but it didn't matter. Until she'd hunted me, spewing curses like a geyser when she'd lost my trail, I hadn't known a woman like her could actually exist. I'd heard rumors of bounty hunters and game hunters, and some of the rumors even included women, but I hadn't met any personally. Maybe I wasn't a predator like the rest of my family, but in all other ways, I was just like them.

We were stupid. We were brave, too—a part of what made us stupid.

Instead of returning home and dealing with the drudgery that built up during my three months of living life as a turkey, I'd be working on a new mission, one I'd enjoy far more than the ins and outs of running a kingdom. After I gave her the slip and headed home, I'd do a little hunting of my own. It was only fair.

She'd started it. It was my family's fault. Living with a bunch of predators tended to skew reality. Maybe I had a turkey's body a quarter of the year, but I had the same drive as the rest of the Averett men.

We loved impossible challenges, and one perfect for me stomped along the shore, glorious in all her flaws, in her strong features incapable of traditional beauty, and her filthy mouth.

She'd make the long, chilly wait huddled beneath a waterfall worth every scrape and bruise—and I'd pay her back for the gash across my side. How remained a mystery, but I'd enjoy solving it. My situation reminded me a lot about my father and his inability to resist a challenge.

My father's head of detail should've known better than to claim a lynx couldn't take on four wolves at once. The resulting disaster had trashed an entire wing of the castle and landed me on the throne for a week while my father recovered from breaking his wrist and arm.

My uncles had emerged relatively unscathed.

It had taken my father three years to finally get the jump on all four of them at the same time. That stunt landed me into the unwanted position of throne warmer for another two weeks. I still wasn't convinced my uncles had been the ones to try to beat sense into him.

My great-grandpa remained my top suspect, but since no one was brave or stupid enough to accuse the grizzly, the source of my father's concussion remained a mystery.

If I brought the feisty huntress home with

me, it would be beautiful chaos, mass destruction, and general confusion. I settled in to wait, spending the time plotting and scheming how to find the woman after I returned to my human form. Even facing a mountain of work and scrutiny, I had the feeling I'd enjoy my summer far more than I should.

NIGHT FELL, and the glow of the woman's weapons betrayed her presence. Like a good predator, once she settled in and stopped cussing at everything, she had patience. I disliked her decision to remain, likely some gut instinct she listened to, wise considering I was right under her nose.

Freezing my feathered ass off waiting for her to leave wasn't my idea of a good time, but I had too many plans to ruin them becoming a mantle ornament. Shifting my weight from foot to foot did no good; once I emerged from hiding, I'd be limping—or flopping, incapable of walking until I warmed up.

My father would be so happy when I showed up half-dead, plagued, and limping.

I glared through the gaps in the water and haze, willing her to go away. Instead of obeying, she sat by the shore, removed her weapons, and lined them onto the rock beside her. She restrung her bow, gave it a few test pulls to confirm I hadn't done more than break the string, and polished it. Then, to my bemusement, she unstrung it, rendering it useless if she discovered me. The weapon was still dangerous even unstrung, something I'd have to be careful to remember later. She'd club me with the damned thing again if I gave her a chance, which intrigued and annoyed me.

Yep, I was definitely my father's son.

After she finished with her bow, she cleaned her swords, examining the blades before returning them to their sheaths. She kept the swords together, covered them with a blanket, set the bow aside, and stretched out on the ground, using the pile as a pillow.

It took me a moment to realize she used a cloak as a blanket. Where the hell had she gotten a cloak?

Within minutes, she slept on the cold, damp stones, and her snores drowned out even the waterfall. I'd have to do something about that snore if I took her home with me or she'd keep the entire castle awake all night.

It would be a challenge, and I couldn't resist a challenge.

Under the cover of her thunderous snores, I limped out of my hiding place and headed downstream to rendezvous with my clothes and wait for the first day of summer.

WELL AWARE I'D be hunted if I wasn't careful, I ignored my hunger, crammed into the hollowed trunk of the tree I'd stashed my plastic-wrapped clothes within, and waited for the dawning of summer. As was often the case, I transformed while I slept, and the tree made a tight, uncomfortable hiding place. To my relief, I had enough room to check myself over, grimacing at the sluggishly bleeding gash across my side. Worse, an orange stain surrounded the wound, a promise of trouble in my near future. Until I figured out what the stain meant—or it went away on its own—I couldn't afford to waste much time thinking about it.

I had bigger things to worry about, including returning to my home and my inevitable demise courtesy of my parents. Grégoire could continue the family name probably better than I could.

Whining about it wouldn't do me any good. My sisters might indulge me if I moped enough, but I wasn't going to hold my breath. I'd pass out long before they took mercy on me.

I clacked my teeth together and got dressed, grimacing at the stiffness deep in my bones and the twinge of my bruises, which would hurt more later. They always did. Fortunately, most of the splotches were hidden beneath my clothes, but I wouldn't dodge the royal physicians for long.

A sneeze tore through me, a painful reminder my immune system would retire for a few weeks as it always did after so long trapped in a turkey's body. While tempted to dodge the castle until the bruising faded, I resigned myself to my fate.

Delaying would do me no good, so I began the long, painful hike to my wallet and phone.

A THUNDERSTORM ROLLED in and hammered me with rain, and when the rain didn't kill me, the sky opened fire and pelted me with hail. I'd welcome a tornado if the damned thing put me out of my misery. The cut across my side throbbed with each step, and spending the entire spring in a tree hadn't done my clothes or shoes any favors. The first blisters made their presence known within a mile, promising I'd regret every choice I'd made in my life before I reached my phone.

On the bright side, I could blame the hail for my bruises. By the time I reached the castle, no one would be able to tell what had caused them, and hail could tenderize anybody in a few minutes. Hiding the gash and orange stain on my skin would take more work, and I had no idea what excuse I'd make —if I needed to make an excuse at all.

Falling on a rock and battering myself bloody wouldn't work; what sort of rock would turn my skin orange? My family would lock on that like the predators they were, first to catch me in the lie, and second to discover if there were any rocks that could turn someone orange.

They loved a good mystery almost as much as they loved driving me up the nearest wall.

No, they'd annoy the truth out of me eventually, so my best defense was to stick to the truth and omit important details. They didn't need to know a huntress had shot me with an arrow. I could claim it was a dispute with a woman I found attractive.

My sisters might not buy it, but every last man in the family would. They *all* pissed off women, especially before they'd broken the curse and gained control over their shapeshifting abilities.

No matter what, I couldn't let them know I'd been shot. If they figured it out, I was confident they'd chain me in the castle next spring, ending a decade of secrecy and destroying what remained of my pride. After they laughed themselves sick, I'd have to rely on my sisters, mother, grandmother, and great-grandmother for protection against the rest of my family.

Heaven help me, I'd discovered the truth about hell. It wasn't a place after death, but the reality of a worry-wart family of predators discovering their favorite food might be a blood relative.

The entire hike to my phone, which was

punctuated with cracks of thunder, blinding flashes of lightning, wind-whipped rain, and hail with a few moments of respite tossed in, I questioned if I really needed to return home at all. My family had grown accustomed to wondering if I'd turn up each summer. As he did every year, my father would remind me every other Averett man ruled over the castle as a beast while seeking his perfect woman. Grégoire enjoyed his stints as a wolverine, teasing the castle staff whenever he visited. Maybe if I asked nicely, my father would make my cousin the heir.

Grégoire would enjoy his hunt for his wife, whereas I'd given up the search after Gail had proven what I'd suspected all along.

It would take a miracle to find someone who could look beyond the title to see the man. I still wasn't sure how my father had won my mother, but from what I'd pieced together, she hadn't known he was the heir until it was too late for her to run away. Sometimes she ran to rile him up, but she never meant it.

She just wanted him to chase her.

What should've been an uneventful albeit painful walk turned into a nightmare the instant the storm front passed. Out went the cold, in came the heat, and with the heat came the humidity, leaving me drenched in sweat before my clothes had a chance to dry. I blamed the family curse. Transforming screwed with my immune system, trashed my ability to cope with temperature fluctuations, and billed me for my general stupidity over the entire spring.

Annoyed at myself for whining, I took aim at the nearest rock, borrowed a few of the huntress's curses, and punted the damned thing. It bounced off a nearby trunk with a satisfying thump. My toes paid the price for my temper, and after a few deep breaths, I straightened and resumed my march.

What should've taken me a couple of hours at most took the entire day. My wallet, phone, and solar charger were where I'd left them, hidden within the trunk of a dying tree near a granite outcropping of stone. Unless my phone had miraculously held some of its charge, I'd be stuck waiting for dawn. To my amazement, it turned on, and the battery indicator claimed I had a quarter charge to work with.

I hadn't thought enough sun would've been able to reach the spot, but I was pleased my precautions had born fruit.

Of my options, calling my father would stir my family's ire the most and send someone the fastest. I dialed his personal cell number and faced my impending demise with pride.

"Well, well, well. It seems I still have a son," my father answered.

"Question—" I sneezed so hard I dropped my phone and scrambled to pick it up, checking the display to make sure I hadn't broken it or hung up. "Sorry. You still have a son. His name's Alan. Please tell me he's grown a fur coat."

"I regret to inform—"

Another sneeze tore through me, but I managed to keep my hold on my cell.

"You caught another cold playing outside, I see."

"Yeah. Sorry. I could use a lift, as I've caught this cold from playing outside." Why did my father insist on accusing me of playing outside rather than spending three months of my life avoiding predators and keeping persistent hens away?

Oh, right. I hadn't told him my species or my destination.

"All right, kiddo. You're always incapable of handling anything like a normal adult for a week after you turn up, so tell me where to fetch your lanky ass. While you're at it, please tell me a cold is the only thing wrong with you this time."

"But you taught me I shouldn't lie."

"Kel!"

Lying through omission might save me—maybe. "I pissed a woman off. She won the dispute."

"You're supposed to be convincing a woman to love you, not pissing her off."

"I was trying a new strategy," I lied. Well, it wasn't really a lie, was it? I'd never beaten a woman with my wings before attempting to get her attention.

"If you want a beating, ask for one. We'd have to draw a lottery to see who got a chance at you first and then form a line."

"Thanks, Dad."

"Where are you?"

"My phone is on and has a quarter charge. Make the RPS figure it out."

"You have no idea where you're at, do you?"

I snorted. "I have a vague idea of my current location."

"Well, that woman couldn't have beaten you too badly. Your awful sense of humor is still intact."

"Give me a sec." I used my phone's display for light and checked my side, which didn't look any better since I'd shifted back to human. "A little cut, a lot bruised, and I'm suffering from a severely damaged ego to go with the plague."

My father sighed. "Do you need stitches?"

"I'm unqualified to accurately answer that question."

"Kelvin."

"I'm not bleeding to death, Dad. It's a cut, not a severed limb."

"Never can tell with you. Sometimes, I think you're a grizzly just like my grandpa, so you lumber off to prevent the fights."

Me? A grizzly? I laughed so hard I hiccupped. "You're being absurd."

"I'm in a good mood. You mother's off to some movie premier with the rest of the pack, which means I get to go with the RPS without anyone annoying me about it. Christian's already got a lock on your location, and they're picking an SUV for some off-roading to get to you. I think they're looking for a waveweaver and earthweaver to go with us so we don't get stuck."

"It's a bit muddy," I admitted.

"Of course. *You're ten miles deep in a park!*" my father bellowed.

"Huh. I'm impressed I have reception."

"Your phone's in satellite mode, Kelvin."

"Oh." I winced, as I'd been beaten over the head for years to keep the damned phone with me so I could be tracked. "Right. I forgot."

"It'll be better in a few days. Try not to catch your death out there, all right? We can get to you in about two hours."

"I'll be careful."

"Good. Don't wander."

"I won't."

"And Kelvin?"

"What?"

"If you run into another woman, *don't piss her off.*"

My father hung up on me, and I rubbed my ear, already regretting my decision to call home.

TWO

I see you're feeling lively.
___

AN ENTIRE SPRING living as prey contributed to my wariness and unwillingness to stay on the ground. I climbed the nearest suitable tree to wait. To kill the time, I used my phone to research the news, beginning with Montana. When something big happened in Montana, everyone talked about it, and I'd learned the hard way people expected me to know what was going on despite the three-month 'vacation' I took every year.

Until I could control my talent, I didn't view myself as a true contender for the throne despite being the heir.

It made finding a woman my parents believed suitable difficult at best.

My mother had her heart set on Gail despite everything, and my father went with what my mother wanted rather than listening to my repeated refusals to revive my relationship with my ex. I expected the growing rift between my mother and I would become a serious issue soon, another problem I didn't want or need.

Within twenty minutes, I came to the conclusion all was quiet in Montana, a miracle all things considered. A few news outlets speculated Her Royal Majesty was pregnant again, something that didn't surprise me at all. She'd had a reputation for being the motherly type from the day she'd showed up in the Texan congress with her firstborn on her hip. His Royal Majesty seemed like the type happiest with babies underfoot.

Anyone who was taken by surprised by the pair breeding like rabbits needed their head examined and a hefty dose of common sense administered. Then again, I came from a family prone to breeding like rabbits, too.

I blamed the curse. I refused to admit I enjoyed having babies around; they brought cheerful mayhem wherever they went. I'd probably find them less appealing when I was the father losing sleep, although I had my doubts. I'd lost plenty of sleep during my life helping my parents with my younger siblings, and I hadn't minded it at all.

Under no circumstances could I let my parents know I'd lost count of the number of sisters I'd helped raise, the youngest of whom was a precocious five and spent a terrifying amount of time with my nieces.

I had at least five nieces and a nephew between my four older sisters, the ones I believed would've been wolves if the curse had landed on them.

Another realization dawned on me, one that changed nothing while changing everything: Gail wasn't the motherly type, not like Her Royal Majesty of Montana was. She'd always been the kind to focus on herself first, backpedal when she realized she sounded selfish, and pretend to be the family type. With that in mind, she'd done me a favor when she'd chosen to sleep with another man while dating me.

I could work with that. It'd also help me with my search, too.

I wanted someone who wanted to be a mother as much as I wanted to be a father.

Was the huntress the kind to like children? I worried for my sanity if she were. She'd never meet society's standards for beauty, but that wasn't a disadvantage to me. A pretty face wasn't required to rule a kingdom. A steadfast heart, courage, and a certain amount of pride certainly were, and from the little I'd seen, she'd had those traits in plentiful supply.

The real problem would be finding her. With that southern twang in her voice, I pegged her as a visitor to the kingdom—or the daughter of someone from the south. While I could recruit the RPS to help, I rejected the idea.

When I found her, it'd be because of my efforts.

Another thunderstorm and a couple of hours later, headlights in the darkness announced the arrival of my father and his RPS team. I identified my father in the darkness easily enough; he emerged from the SUV as a lynx. I rolled my eyes and considered throwing my phone at him.

Screw it. I needed a new one anyway.

To my satisfaction, my cell cracked into my father's thick skull before plopping into the mud.

Christian, the head of my father's security detail, slid out from behind the wheel, shook his head, and said, "Good evening, Your Highness. I see you're feeling lively."

"I don't know what my father told you, but I probably only have a cold and I'm not bleeding to death. I have a cut, not a gaping gash or whatever other nightmare scenario he concocted on the way here."

"He'd worked his way up to probable dismemberment and was considering decapitation as a viable diagnosis."

"Please sedate him."

My father prowled closer, growling.

"He was intending to track you with his nose, Your Highness. Was throwing your phone at him necessary?"

"Considering I'll have to deal with new RPS agents tomorrow? Yes, it was necessary."

"Very well. Is there a reason you're in a tree?"

I pointed at my father. "I didn't want to be pounced by a lynx."

"Fair enough. Do you need help getting down?"

"No, but I do need the lynx to become human so I'm not pounced. I don't want to be pounced today, Christian."

For the next week or two, I expected my tolerance for being pounced by a bunch of overenthusiastic predators to be minimal at best until I worked the worst of my damned turkey's instincts out of my system. With luck, my family wouldn't press me too hard about it.

It amazed me they hadn't guessed I was a prey species from my general reactions to them in the early summer.

"Your Majesty, please shift so we don't have to fetch His Highness from a tree by force."

Not even my mother could get my father to do anything without a fuss, but Christian's suggestion got him moving back to the SUV where he belonged. He jumped inside, and a few moments later, he growled, "Get your ass in the car, Kelvin."

I considered myself fortunate he hadn't started calling me Rose yet. It hurt, but I eased out of the tree without crashing to the ground. Christian hovered nearby, shaking his head and clicking his tongue in blatant disapproval.

"I want to say this isn't my fault, but it is."

"It's common enough knowledge your family's talent creates difficult principals at best. You did exactly as you were supposed to. You survived. To be fair to you, the rest of the royal line is spoiled; *they* stayed comfortable and safe in the castle during their three-month stints each year. They've been worried. Your brother has developed a moderately strong lightningweaving talent, and we're confident he won't be shapeshifting."

"Not waveweaving?" I asked, my brows rising. Most who could wield lightning were a variant of waveweavers who called storms. In classes, they'd been referred to as stormweavers, a nicer name for the hell they could unleash. True lightningweavers were few and far between.

"Pure lightning," Christian confirmed. "He'll be easily ranked as either a high elite or a royal in his own right with his talent. I thought it was wise to warn you: he currently has poor control." I glared at the RPS agent for his choice of words, and the man held his hands up in surrender. "His words, not mine. Beat your brother later if you want. I think you've been injured enough for one week. This mysterious woman of yours gave you quite the beating. Were you aware you've got bruises all over your face?"

"Most of that's from the hail. That didn't help."

"Of course not. I have convinced His Majesty you should have the choice of how to handle your care. Do you need to go to the hospital?"

"No. I'm bruised and have a cold. I'm not dying." I hesitated. "And the cut isn't that bad."

"Very well. Be prepared for a heavy dose of fatherly affection."

"Are you sure I can't steal you for my detail? Your first task would be to keep my father on his side of the SUV."

"I'm afraid not, Your Highness, but I have suggested you directly help with the recruitment of your future agents."

Would a woman like the huntress be interested in a job in the RPS? Hunting the hunters was something women like her might appreciate. It'd be more of a challenge than hunting a white turkey through the forest—and a great deal more frustrating. I smiled at the thought. "I think you need a raise, Christian."

"Thank you, Your Highness. The sentiment is appreciated."

Without a way to prevent or delay the inevitable, I strode to the SUV, climbed inside, and braced for the onslaught of fatherly concern.

SOMETIMES, I hated cats. As I'd been warned, my father clung to me, determined to invade my personal space. Turkeys didn't have the intimidating warning growls the rest of my family enjoyed, so I borrowed from my great-grandpa.

When growling didn't work, I went for his throat.

The resulting brawl required all four RPS agents to break up. Before they separated us, I managed to blacken my father's eye and split his lip, taking advantage of his unwillingness to add to my collection of bruises.

"Really, Your Majesty? Could you avoid provoking His Highness? I don't want to explain to Her Majesty you found the limit of your son's patience," Christian complained, cramming between us to keep the fight from resuming. "Her Majesty should be arriving at the castle soon. Convincing her not to worry will be difficult enough. Once those bruises you've earned show, she'll have a turn with all of us."

"But I didn't do anything," my father protested.

"You annoyed him and invaded his personal space after he clearly stated he didn't want to be pounced by a lynx. That's you. Please remain on your side of the vehicle. Should you fail to comply, Your Majesty, you will be sedated."

"You didn't bring any tranquilizers," my father crowed triumphantly.

"I was planning on using my fist to sedate you, Your Majesty."

When Christian issued threats, he meant them, and I had no doubt it would escalate into a lynx-vs-human battle to unconsciousness if I let them start a fight. Christian would win, my father would whine, and I'd have to deal with them both annoying me for weeks. "Please stop."

"It's your choice. If you stay on your side of the vehicle, we won't have to fight, Your Majesty."

"Fine." My father crossed his arms and grunted. "Be that way."

"Thank you. Please leave His Highness alone until he takes a nap. As long as you don't wake him, I don't care what you do."

"Thanks, Christian," I muttered, worried what my father would do if I made the mistake of closing my eyes.

"I recommend against falling asleep, Your Highness."

I sighed. "Please just get us to the castle without any accidents, Christian. Please. I've had enough excitement for one day."

I CLUNG TO CONSCIOUSNESS, determined to avoid more of my father's affection. When I wasn't coughing or sneezing, I mimicked his growls, which did a good job of destroying my voice. I could still speak, but I sounded like I'd done significant damage to my throat as a result.

"I'm impressed," my father announced. "We haven't even made it home yet and your voice is gone. Just go to sleep already."

I shook my head.

"You're going to be stubborn about this, aren't you?"

I nodded.

"Please leave him alone, Your Majesty," Christian grumbled. "Do not make me pull over and deal with you."

"He was supposed to take a nap!"

"Your Majesty, he's no longer an infant. He's not going to take a nap."

"Infants don't nap really, either," my father admitted. "It's a trap—they're just waiting for the adults to nap to carry out their ruthless schemes."

"Your Majesty, will you please relax? He's obviously doing fine. He comes home with a cold every year. You should be grateful he called instead of hitchhiking back to the castle again."

"I am grateful."

"Then act like it. Give him the next thirty minutes of quiet before he's mobbed."

"Fine."

My father lasted almost ten minutes before asking, "Did you get that woman's number before she beat you?"

"No, Dad," I croaked. "Please shut up."

"But it's a matter of utmost importance. She could be your one and only."

"Your Majesty, would you please leave him alone?"

"If he wanted me to leave him alone, he wouldn't have left home!" my father howled.

Screw it. I wound up, stole Christian's idea, and sedated Illinois's king with my fist. If I was executed, I'd consider it a mercy. My father slumped, his belt preventing him from falling off the seat. I shook out my hand and grunted my satisfaction.

The RPS agents gawked at me, and Christian pulled over so he could join in. "What the hell have you been doing all spring to learn how to punch like that?"

I hated my life sometimes. Instead of answering, I glared at him.

Christian held his hands up. "I tried to stop him."

I sighed. "Please take us home before he wakes up, Christian."

Much to my surprise, the RPS agent obeyed.

MY GREAT-GRANDPA WAITED at the front doors of the castle, a hulking brute of a man who enjoyed tricking the world into believing he was an old teddy bear. I knew better, but I valued my life so never said anything.

"Kiddo," he growled, opening my door. Stopping, he peered inside, his gaze focusing on my unconscious father. "I'm sure there's a reason for that."

I nodded.

"What is the reason?"

"Please forgive His Highness, sir. His throat's bothering him, and he's pretty hoarse from arguing with His Majesty, who insisted on being annoying."

"Well, he is a cat. Continue."

"His Highness sedated His Majesty with his fist. Good, single hit. I'm sure he'll be fine, but I can take him to the royal physician if you'd like."

"Leave the brat, he deserved it. I'll drag him to his wife and let her knock some more sense into him. Good job, kiddo. What's wrong with you this year beyond your usual cold?"

"He got beaten by a woman," Christian announced.

"That sounds promising. Where is she now?"

"He refuses to tell us anything about her, sir."

"Harass him until he does, bring her here, and we'll lock them in the dungeon together for a while. We haven't tried that tactic yet."

I wished I could get away with sedating my grizzly of a great-grandpa, but he'd laugh at my attempts and toss me into the nearest stream until I cooled my temper.

"I have the feeling he's making plans of his own, sir. I've never heard His Highness sound so offended over anything before. Perhaps we should let him try his new method before we interfere."

My great-grandpa patted my head. "Good kiddo. You run on in and go to your room. Get cleaned up. I told your mother and the rest of the family to give you some space. If you're not feeling well enough to drag yourself home, you don't need to deal with unnecessary fussing tonight."

"Who are you and what have you done with my great-grandpa?" I demanded.

"I've been doing some thinking, and I had an idea about how to help you find your perfect woman."

I should've known. "Maybe I've already found her."

"And she beat you up?"

I shrugged.

"You're the damndest stubborn kiddo this castle's ever seen. March to your room and get some rest. I had someone take some soup up for you. Try not to throw it up."

As arguing would earn me more bruises, I replied, "Yes, sir."

Obeying the cranky grizzly didn't count as running away, although I had to fight my initial instinct to hurry to get out of his reach. The trick to dealing with predators involved avoiding acting like prey. I could do that. In the wild, few sane predators toyed with an overgrown turkey. It didn't take them long to figure out I liked to aim for the eyes and used every dirty trick in the book to survive.

Too bad my tricks didn't work on my family.

AFTER A SPRING OF LIVING OUTDOORS, nothing beat soaking in my tub while sipping chicken noodle soup from a mug. I cranked the jets to maximum power, not caring if they added to my bruises. The warm water eased my bone-deep aches, which helped me see the bright side of things. Even better, the cut from the huntress's arrow had stopped bleeding, and if any of the orange stain remained, I couldn't tell due to the bruising beginning to show. I'd annoy the royal physicians with my current state, but as long as the bruises continued to darken, I'd be able to avoid unwanted scrutiny.

It was one thing for me to earn a beating from a woman, but it was another entirely if her talents were brought into the picture. The protective side of my family of hard-headed predators came out when they felt I couldn't defend myself. As I had no confirmed talents outside of the family curse, when it came to magic, I was a liability.

Since I'd first shifted during a family camping trip and developed a reputation for running off and doing exactly what I wanted unsupervised, it'd been trivial to keep my secret a secret. I'd shifted while taking a nap in a tree, which made it easy to flap to freedom, leaving my clothes for my family to find.

I'd spent most of my first spring in the wild attempting to come to terms with my new shape. My first summer officially cursed, I'd sulked whenever I thought no one had been watching.

My first shift had sealed my fate as the heir of Illinois, and my family had been thrilled.

Every year since, they'd searched for me, and I'd evaded them because they looked for a predator's scent marker when they needed to search for prey instead. As a turkey, my scent changed so much I couldn't be identified, but I hadn't understood that for a few years until my human nose had grown more sensitive.

Now I could scent my family members before they otherwise made their presence known, a useful trait for someone who didn't want found.

Someone knocked at my bathroom door, and I muttered a curse over my loss of privacy. "What is it?"

My voice sounded worse than terrible, and I hoped it dissuaded my visitor from bothering me.

"You all right?" my mother asked.

Nope, nothing on Earth would dissuade my mother, so giving in to the inevitable would save me a headache. Hopefully, she'd lose interest and leave sooner than later. I doubted it. "I'm enjoying my bath. Everything's fine."

"You're not dying?"

I was related to unforgivably lovable idiots. "No, Mother. I'm not dying."

"Are you taking a bubble bath so I can come in?"

I was the fool for hoping there'd be any privacy or restraint in my family of predators who often lost their clothes when they shifted. My mother had seen so many naked men in her life she'd become desensitized to nudity. Unlike my father, uncles, and every other Averett male, I refused to start flashing unsuspecting castle employees post-shift. Groaning, I reached for my bottle of shampoo and dumped some in. "Are you going to bring me more soup?"

"I can."

Soup would make her invasion worthwhile, and bubbles would defend my modesty sufficiently against the saner of my parents. I figured she'd put up with fourteen hours of labor to bring me into the world, so if she wanted to see my bruised chest, I could deal with it. "You bring me soup, I'll make bubbles, but you're the only one allowed in."

"Your grandma—"

"No."

"But—"

"No."

My mother huffed. "Fine. She'll see you in the morning, then."

"I can work with in the morning."

"I'll be back soon with your soup."

Knowing my mother, she'd probably stolen a slow cooker from the kitchen and had set it up in my bedroom so I'd have a ready supply. If she hadn't, she'd yell at the poor cooks until she was confident I wouldn't starve. After she conquered the kitchen, I pitied the physician she'd corner. Every sneeze would trigger a wave of parental concern until I contemplated asking someone to dose my mother with something to calm her down.

Several minutes later, she knocked, let herself in, and set a steaming mug on the ledge beside me. I marveled at how such a tiny woman could handle a man like my father—or have children at all. According to her, I'd just about killed her with my big, egotistical head.

I'd never figured out how a newborn could be egotistical, but I'd learned not to question my mother about such things.

She narrowed her eyes, her attention fixed on my shoulders and upper chest. "You look like you were on the losing end of a bad brawl."

"True enough," I acknowledged. "No matter what any idiots tell you, I fully intend on dealing with the woman responsible personally."

"Dare I ask?"

"Please don't."

"Are you going to do something I'm going to regret?"

"Not intentionally."

My mother grunted and sat on the tub's ledge. "Very well. How was your spring?"

Most of my favored words to describe my spring would result in my mouth being washed out with soap, so I replied, "Annoying."

"I'm sorry, baby. Are all those bruises from this woman you tangoed with?"

"Not all of them. The hail contributed."

"I see."

"I'm surprised Great-Grandpa let you in here." One day, I would sock the traitor grizzly in the nose for selling me out so soon.

"I drew the short straw to give you the latest news, and I refused to tell you if I had to wait until tomorrow. I won. It's about Gail."

I scowled at the mention of my ex. "What about her?"

"She's cancelled her wedding and is telling everyone leaving you was the worst mistake she's made in her life. She wants to make things right with you, and she's not shy about working the court to get you. To be fair, she's also cancelling her wedding because she learned her new man was cheating on her with her sister."

After several years of freedom from my

ex, she was still haunting me. I questioned why I'd returned home. "No. Just no. I don't want to deal with Gail. No, no, no."

"You're fond of that word tonight."

"I thought 'over my dead body' was a little rude as an opener."

"I take it I'm correct to assume that you're against any ideas involving her visiting you?"

"I'm going to drink my soup and hope you poisoned it. That would be preferred."

My mother arched a brow at me. "Some believe she'd be a good queen."

My mother was one of those some, and I believed she needed a trip to the royal physician more than I did to have her head examined. I took a sip of soup. Unfortunately, my soup seemed free of poison, and I survived several sips without incident. "Pass."

"Are you sure?"

What did I need to do to convince the world I wanted nothing to do with Gail? "Mother, my brother and sisters call me Rose because I was too complicated for Gail, and the only good news is I don't stink. I don't care what people think. The answer is no. I don't love her, I won't love her, and frankly, I'm completely unsurprised Donald cheated on her. She would've seen the writing on that wall if she'd ever paid attention to any of the court gossip floating around. I lost count of the number of women Donald cheated on before he had graduated from high school. Why would anyone believe he'd change after graduation?"

"Are you sure? You might fall in love with her."

"I'm moving to the next phase of this conversation. Over my dead body, Mom. She left me because of grass is greener syndrome. Anyway, our family's talent is not one she'll ever approve of. I'm not stupid. I'll never love her because I'll never be able to trust her."

"Drink your soup and rest your voice, Kelvin. I'll tell your brother and sisters they'll face the mean old grizzly if they keep calling you Rose. If you're not interested in Gail, you're not interested. Since we've gotten that out of the way, let's start going over what you've missed."

My mother was definitely up to something, and it involved Gail. Arguing with her wouldn't do any good, so I drank my soup as ordered and waited.

"You've been invited to New York to meet with a princess."

Somehow, I'd returned home to hell. "Please, no," I whispered.

My mother chuckled. "It's not what you think. Princess Abigail of North Dakota is touring the Royal States, and she expressed interest in visiting potentially, but she wanted to meet with you first. I told her you're always sick this time of year due to complications with the family talent, but she was welcome to come stay with us for a while. As such, she'll be in residence for the next two months, and she'll be arriving next week. As you seem to have no interest in your former girlfriend, I thought it might be entertaining if Gail served as lady-in-waiting to Princess Abigail. Princess Abigail isn't looking for a husband right now, not after the troubles her family has faced, but she *is* looking for alliances and friends. You do friends with other royalty quite well. You liked Princess Abigail growing up, too."

"Could you not invite Gail to the castle, Mother? I have no objection to Princess Abigail staying here, but my ex? You may as well bring me a gallon of turpentine. Or arsenic. All her being here will do is spread more rumors that I'm stuck on her. I'm not." My throat itched with the need to cough, and I drank more of my soup to suppress it.

"You used to tolerate her."

"I'll never love her. As such, there's zero point in keeping her around and pretending something is going to happen when something isn't going to happen."

"Your father used to hate me. I changed his mind."

"You're a crazy cat lady who figured out you could have your own on-demand lynx. First, he didn't hate you. He was playing hard to get to entice you, the crazy cat lady, to pick him, the cat. That's what cats do."

"Close enough."

"Moving on. What real news do you have for me?"

"Princess Abigail visiting *is* real news."

I glared at my mother. "Mom."

"Fine, fine. Congress is getting edgy because you're not married yet. They're going to be pushing you hard this year. By pushing you hard, I mean they've made a long list of eligible ladies they hope will interest you. There was even an hour-long debate about dumping you on an island with a few candidates."

"I refuse to be marooned with a bunch of women."

"I thought it was a good idea."

"There will be some new rules. One: if Congress—or anyone—throws Gail or Princess Abigail at me, I'm abdicating in favor of Grégoire. Two: if anyone maroons me on an island with a bunch of women, I'm abdicating. Three: if uninvited women show up in my room, I'm abdicating and possibly murdering my parents along with the entirety of Congress."

"I'll let them know you're uninterested. Wait. Are you interested in someone and haven't told your dear old mother yet?"

"I'm definitely not interested in Gail."

"Fine. I'll find someone else to be Princess Abigail's lady-in-waiting."

How would the huntress who'd tried to shoot me full of arrows handle a princess? The thought of it was enough to make me grin. If I could find her, could I entice her into accepting a position at the castle? The first half of my battle would be luring her close. The second would be netting her and turning the tables on her.

Success came in so many forms, and I could readily pick one job she'd thrive at: security.

"I'm not sure I like that expression, Kelvin. That expression's trouble. What are you scheming?"

I smiled. "I have an idea. Why not let me pick a lady-in-waiting for Princess Abigail?"

"There's no way this is going to end well, but fine. Try not to shame the poor woman. She's had a rough enough time of it lately."

I wouldn't tell my mother picking my ex counted as the worst shame of all. "Don't worry, Mom. I'll make certain she knows she's welcome here in Illinois without any pressure from me."

"You're definitely scheming something."

I nodded, maintaining my sweetest smile.

"All right. You win this time. Finish your soup and get to bed. Heaven knows you'll be a mess in the morning. And don't think I didn't notice you trying not to cough."

"You're the one who invaded my bathroom. If you hadn't invaded my bathroom, I could've coughed in peace."

"True enough, but I would've heard you through the door anyway. Get out and get some rest. No woman except your poor mother's going to fall in love with you when you're looking like the victim of a bad beating."

"The hail won."

"I'm sure it did. Now that you've been warned of the trouble on the horizon, you get some sleep. The rest can wait until morning."

THREE

The truth grated on my nerves.

CATCHING up on the news ultimately waited for four days, which was how long it took me to kick the worst of my cold and recover from my beating. The bruises took longer to heal than I liked, but the real problem was the cut. The injury was all but gone, but a bright orange stain in the shape of a stylized flame betrayed where the huntress had scored her hit. Most would believe I'd gotten a rather nice tattoo.

As it often did, the truth grated on my nerves.

My foul-mouthed devil of a huntress wasn't just a flameweaver. She had a strong illumination talent, one that would let her track me at her leisure. Most called it a brand, and hers was prettier than others I'd seen, too.

She'd spent a great deal of time honing her skills, and I'd have a hell of a time ditching her unless I had it removed. Had I wanted to ditch her, I'd consider it a problem. As I wanted her to come straight to me, the brand was the best lure I could hope for. After I learned who she was, I'd have it removed—if removing it served my needs.

I'd have to do some research. As far as I could recall, if either one of us had a leeching talent, the brand could become permanent.

Being a stereotypical Averett man, I had no problem with the brand leading to something more permanent. I could make a relationship with a foul-mouthed huntress work. Hell, half the fun would be the chase, and I bet she'd start running the instant she realized she'd almost skewered a prince.

Then again, she could be a bounty hunter. Talented trackers made excellent bounty hunters. They didn't lose their prey. If that was the case, no wonder she'd lost her temper. She would've known I'd been nearby but hadn't been able to find me. One of the first safety rules I'd had shoved down my throat was to have any brands immediately removed.

I regarded my side with my mouth twitching, wondering how long I'd be able to hide the truth. Until I had a dedicated RPS detail, I might escape scrutiny, but once I had a security team breathing down my neck, I'd be sunk. Someone would notice, Christian would find out, and he'd use brute force if necessary to ensure my cooperation.

I needed to lure her somewhere public and safe for me, find out who she was, start tracking her, and only then get her brand removed.

I frowned and poked at the tender skin, considering my options. Would makeup cover it? I didn't resort to makeup often, but everyone in the royal family had some for public appearances. I suspected the magic would show through, but it might buy me time to turn the tables on her—or at least learn her name before I got taken down by my father's RPS detail and stripped of her magic.

A wiser man would've had the brand removed without taking any risks. It wasn't unheard of for bounties to be placed on royals, resulting in someone being tagged for relocation. I hadn't been successfully taken, but my family never got tired of reminding me about my father and the time the South Dakota royal family had invited him for an unexpected visit. Unbeknownst to us, it'd been a planned joint venture performed by the RPS of both kingdoms to test the effectiveness of the tactic.

I hadn't been born yet but was grateful he'd been tagged and bagged, as the trip resulted in my mother and father marrying. My father swore he'd murder anyone who involved him in any relocation scenarios in the future, but we ignored him.

Christian made sure he was tagged and

bagged once a year because he could, and we loved it. The bagger was usually my mother, which ensured no one was actually murdered.

It was only a matter of time before the RPS started toying with me, too. If my mother got a say in it, she'd probably start repeating history and sending me to other kingdoms during scenarios to see if I found someone like my father had.

I was in so much trouble, and I didn't even know how to begin digging myself out of it. I'd already started thinking of the huntress as my wild woman with a foul mouth, which reinforced my desire to set her loose in the castle to watch the mayhem. Had she been part of the RPS wanting to drag me off, I'd have a difficult time saying no.

Damn it, I was like a puppy but worse. I deserved to be called a feather brain for even thinking about cooperating with someone who'd cut open my side and hunted me for a trophy. To her, I'd been nothing more than a beast.

Once she figured it out, she'd probably continue to view me as nothing more than an animal. A royal lineage wouldn't protect me from the prejudices. My family escaped scrutiny because we could, once we gained full control of our talent, shift at will. Some, like my father, never quite mastered the art of transforming his clothes along with his body.

My uncles liked showing off, although I doubted I'd ever get used to hearing a wolf ring. Where in his body was the cell phone, and how did it still work?

Until I found the right woman, I wouldn't know if I'd leave my clothing strewn across the castle every time I shifted or if I'd ring while in my feathered, bird-brained form. If I had a choice, I'd prefer my father's problem of having to find clothing after his shifts.

The real problem was dealing with my huntress's awareness of my second form. When we crossed paths again and she sensed her mark on me, she'd know my secret. What would she do with the knowledge? Was she the type to take a shapeshifter as a trophy? If she showed up wearing leather, I'd be tempted to let her take me as a hostage with minimal fuss.

Those who wanted shapeshifters as trophies wanted live trophies. As a general rule, the laws prohibited the hunting of shapeshifters, which kept most from actively killing those with talents similar to mine. In the case of my father's adventure in South Dakota, captured shapeshifters were used as bargaining chips or tools, and such kidnappings had personal motives.

My mother, true to her crazy cat lady ways, had discovered my father was a cat and wanted him all to herself.

My father hadn't stood a chance.

Was beating my huntress in the face with my wings and evading her talent enough to prick her pride and force her to hunt me? If she exposed my secret, I'd be in a world of hurt from my family. I had no idea what the rest of the world would do beyond laugh. Laughter I could deal with if I had control of my shapeshifting. Turkeys weren't great flyers, but I had a lot of power in my wings when I unleashed them. Add in my claws, spurs, and beak, and I could make a human regret crossing me.

It didn't hurt I dwarfed even domesticated turkeys.

I paced my bedroom at a loss of what to do about the woman I wanted to meet again. Her ability to brand and track made her ideal for the RPS *if* I could convince her to join. I'd break every rule in the book pursuing an agent as my future queen, but it wouldn't take much to get around those rules.

In Illinois, the queen's past meant nothing. Peasant or princess, it didn't matter who she'd been before ensnaring an Averett man. She earned her worth proving she was a woman capable of taming the man and the beast.

I'd have to get into a fight with the RPS about it and endure the inevitable scolding for encouraging a relationship with an agent. If she, by some miracle, was *my* agent, she'd be transferred to a different kingdom, put through training again, and possibly fired. I'd chase her, create an international incident and, assuming she didn't murder me for putting her job at risk, I'd take her home while deflecting the annoyed RPS agents inevitably chasing me.

The whole plan was a mess, but I'd have a great deal of fun pushing my luck.

Having fun had never been part of any of my plans. With Gail, I'd been more focused on getting to the next day with my sanity intact. I expected similar struggles in my near future for new reasons—better reasons. If anyone discovered my interest in my huntress, I already knew what I'd tell them. She had a way with words I couldn't ignore. Under no circumstances would I admit I meant to pursue her due to my case of instant lust for her in leather. Then again, maybe I should admit it.

Since age twelve, when I'd discovered girls were interesting, I'd tried founding relationships based on what I thought love should be like and had women like Gail to show for it.

It seemed absurd to hope for better luck pursuing a woman so wrong for me I had no idea how we'd make a relationship work. Did it count as a relationship if I ran while she tried her best to kill me?

Desperation made me an idiot in need of a psychologist. I'd heard stories about my father before he'd met my mother. If the rumors were true, he'd resorted to prostitutes in hopes of finding love.

No, I would not stoop to my father's level of desperation, but if a certain leather-clad woman wanted to kidnap me for a while, I'd go along for the ride to see what happened.

Part of me wanted to spend the whole day in my room contemplating how I'd catch a huntress who'd almost killed me. Breaking the curse had always been a top priority, but something had changed.

Her arrow had done more than leave me branded and bleeding.

I touched the mark, wincing at the bruising beneath. As a child, I'd believed it couldn't be too hard to find a woman who could love me and not my rank. I'd been wrong.

I understood why my father hadn't shattered my delusions as a child. Some lessons were best learned through experience.

Without a good excuse to hide for another day, I dressed in a classic black suit with a boring tie to limit how many noticed my presence. People would notice me no matter what I did; word had already spread of my return. A mountain of paperwork awaited my attention, and someone had left a foot-thick pile of papers on my coffee table as a not-so-subtle hint. The briefings could be dealt with in my office on the other side of the castle, and I anticipated I'd be invading my parents' offices for clarifications.

The real problem was my lack of permanent RPS agents. Had either one of my old agents stayed through the spring, one of them would've been standing near the door, a living statue keeping a close eye on me so I wouldn't escape without someone knowing I'd left.

With so many RPS agents around and my lack of interest in leaving my room, it didn't surprise me I hadn't been saddled with replacement agents yet.

I snatched part of the pile and hiked across the castle to the working wing, muttering a few of the curses I'd learned in the woods. When I met her, I'd have to ask what most of them meant. The staff hurried about their business, and I adopted my favorite tactic of looking busy to dodge unwanted interaction.

"Hey, Rose," my cousin greeted, falling into step with me. "You came out of your suite early."

I swallowed all the curses I'd picked up, resisted the urge to feed my cousin a hefty dose of my knuckles, and fought to restore my patience. Fuck it.

I was done with Gail, her fucking nickname for me, and everyone's enjoyment of taunting me with it. "Keep calling me Rose, Greggie." To add a little extra insult to my choice of name for him, I faked a French accent and glared at him.

He twitched. "When you do that, you remind me of Great-Grandpa."

"I'm tired of that idiotic nickname. My name is Kelvin, but you can call me Kel if you'd like. If you want a ridiculous nickname, you can be Gail's next rebound. I pass."

"When Aunt Sarah said I shouldn't test my luck, I thought she'd been exaggerating. I see she wasn't."

I'd risk the gardener's wrath and steal a bouquet of flowers for my mother; the higher the risk of getting them, the more she appreciated the effort. "What do you want?"

"Apparently, I want to apologize for being rude and inconsiderate."

"I see they're serving ice water in hell today. What do you actually want?"

"Can't I be concerned for my cousin?"

I laughed. "You're only concerned you might have to take the throne. For what it's worth, I think you'd do a good job. Actually, I hazard you'd do a better job than me."

"I think you hit your head and didn't tell anyone. You'll feel better about things in a few weeks, after you're caught up. In good news for you, I've been recruited."

"As what? A distraction?"

"Your assistant."

I halted, blinking as I tried to come to terms with my wolverine cousin putting up with me for more than a few minutes at a time. "Dad must be cranky with us both."

"His Majesty is distraught." Grégoire rolled his eyes. "Everyone else thinks it's hilarious. There's a betting pool on your species going on, by the way. The current theory is you're either a grizzly like our great-grandpa, a lion, or a honey badger."

"You've been goofing off on the internet again, I see."

"It's funny. You'd be a hilarious honey badger. Honestly, you wouldn't be a very good one. You have too much patience. A real honey badger would've gone for my throat by now."

"It's really not funny."

"Come on, Kel. What's meaner than a grizzly, lion, or honey badger?"

"Me if you call me Rose again."

"Well played. Point taken. You're obviously not heartbroken over your ex."

"I don't know why everyone thinks I want her back in my life. We all know she only wanted the crown. It's pretty obvious."

"You were pretty upset when you two split."

If Grégoire knew the truth, he would've understood why I'd reacted as I had, but I left Gail's reputation intact. I hadn't told anyone I'd caught her sleeping with another man. "Of course I was. I did my best to love her, and it was an unmitigated disaster. Mom cried for a week, claiming the royal line was doomed to die with me. I told her I gave it a few years before you started competing with Grandpa for most kids."

"I'm delightfully randy, it's true."

"I didn't love her then, and I definitely don't love her now."

"Why date her for so long, then?"

"Couldn't find out if I could love her if I didn't show up and try."

"That's fair. What about this woman you met?"

I laughed. "Three words: she wears leather."

Snickering, my cousin shook his head. "Wrong type of love, Kel. That said, I approve. Unwind, have a little fun. Nothing in the rules says you can't dip your toes in the water and see if a little time between the sheets can't lead to better things. I'm pretty sure every man in our line has resorted to that a time or two."

"Two charity auctions," I reminded him, not that I'd taken any of the girls I'd met to bed.

"Rumor has it you were a perfect angel, much to the disappointment of the princesses who wanted to find out if you're a beast in bed."

"Just for the record, if you relay any part of this conversation to my parents, I'm telling Great-Grandpa you were the one who broke his rocking chair."

"This is why you're the better choice for king. You're ruthless."

Shaking my head and wondering why I hadn't just stayed in the woods to become a hermit, I shouldered into my office to discover my father sitting at my desk. "Finally got demoted?"

"How do you find anything on this computer?" he complained, clicking at my mouse while his eyes remained locked on my monitor. "This is not logical organization, Kel."

Like hell it wasn't. After having seen the organizational disaster that was my father's office, I doubted he'd be able to find something set right in front of him. "What are you looking for?"

"Your little black book of ladies. I was thinking of inviting them to a ball."

"Dad."

"You're no fun today. I'm looking for last year's audit report you compiled about Chicago's police force. The commissioner's trying to tell me we didn't do the report. It's screwing with his budget."

"Have you tried the report folder, Dad? Report is a six-letter word starting with r."

"Don't you get smart with me. That's too obvious. Anyway, why would I do something like look in the obvious place first?"

"Because you hate me and enjoy annoying me. Give me a break. What are you actually doing with my computer?"

"I really did need a copy of the report, but I'm also updating your file access. Rob made us change all the passwords a few weeks ago, and he hadn't gotten around to doing your system."

"Is there a reason Rob can't do it?"

"Rob has the day off. Honestly, we didn't expect you to stop playing hermit for a few more days, but I'd gotten warning you were looking restless and likely to emerge. How are you feeling?"

Sometimes, I hated the nosy palace staff. My father had probably gotten a report every time I'd coughed since coming home. "I'm fine." I set my files on my desk and considered how best to evict my father so I could get some work done. "I was planning on going over this stack of paperwork left in my room, so I probably won't need updated file access yet. Why are you dodging work?"

"South Dakota wants to make an official visit."

"Oh!" If South Dakota made an official visit, my grandparents would tag along for a chance to annoy us all. I loved it. Everyone else didn't, with the exception of my mother. My mother would be over the moon for at least a week before and after their visit.

Behind closed doors, I'd enjoy visiting with my aunt and uncle, who were refreshingly sane people I could relate to.

"Don't look so happy about it."

"Are you still mad at Grandmother?"

"Eternally."

As the hatcher of the plan that'd gotten my mother to target my father, I had a special appreciation for my grandmother, who did what she wanted, when she wanted, and how she wanted. Better yet, she got exactly what she wanted, and like my mother, my grandmother was a crazy cat lady to the core. With my father's luck, he'd end up collared, leashed, and forced to endure being petted by my mother's side of the family.

"When?"

"Too soon," my father groused.

Given a chance, my father would whine over the royal visit for hours, and until he decided he was done with my computer, I'd be stuck with him. I considered the problem and decided there was only one man capable of saving me. "Can I borrow Christian for a few hours to deal with agent recruitment?"

My father grunted, reached over, and snatched my phone from its hook, dialing a number. "Christian, come to the royal brat's office. I have a question for you."

After he hung up, I sighed and said, "He's going to kill you one of these days, Dad."

"Nonsense. Christian adores me. I'm the best principal he's ever had. Anyway, I'm sorry we haven't replaced your agents yet. There's been a general detail monitoring the hall, but until you come out on your own, you're a bit of a bear."

"I just don't want to be smothered."

"That's what your mother said. Take pity on us. We've been worried about you."

"Why? Obviously, I turned up. It's pretty

clear to me that Grégoire doesn't want the throne, not that I blame him. You can stop worrying. I just need a few days to get used to being around people again."

"You mean people who don't want to beat you up."

I arched a brow. "By default, that means I don't want to be around my entire family."

"We don't want to beat you up. We're toughening you up so you can rule without faltering."

A knock on the door saved my father from a beating, and Christian stepped inside my office. "Good morning, Your Majesty. Your Highness."

My father resumed his work on my computer. "Christian, take the royal brat somewhere quiet and start reviewing his requirements for a detail. Prioritize locating someone who'll stick around when he's off being a reclusive idiot. It's about time he had a stable RPS crew protecting him."

"I can do that, but is there any reason we can't use His Highness's office?"

"I'm busying fixing his computer right now, and I don't want to hear it. He'll have ridiculous requirements I won't like. He always does."

Christian sighed. "Where are your agents?"

"I fed them to the grizzly."

"You know what, Your Majesty? One of these days, I'll—"

"Hold that thought, Christian," I ordered. "Dad, please don't break my computer. Grégoire, if he breaks my computer, deal with him."

"Violently?"

I chuckled at my cousin's hopeful tone. "I don't care at this point. It's not like I haven't had a few stints pretending I'm the king because my father utterly lacks in common sense."

"Kel," my father complained.

"Don't break my computer, don't rearrange my office, and don't buy me new furniture. In fact, don't do anything that'll annoy me—and please stop driving off your agents."

"You're being bossy today."

"Someone has to be responsible in this damned castle." I snatched my paperwork and abandoned my office. "Christian, please call in a pair of agents for His Royal Idiot so my mother doesn't murder us all."

"Of course, Your Highness. Please don't wander while I deal with this." Christian lifted his hand to his ear. "Lynx is in His Highness's office."

I rolled my eyes at my father's RPS identifier and stepped into the hallway to escape the insanity. If I let them maintain tradition, I'd be forever known as Turkey. If I got lucky, I'd be dubbed Tom. Birdbrain would be more appropriate. Within a minute, a pair of agents marched into my office, freeing Christian to deal with me.

My father's head of detail sighed. "Any preference for location, Your Highness?"

"Take me to Chicago," I ordered. At the kingdom's capital building, an hour and a half drive from the castle, I might be able to get some work done.

FOUR

Do I want to know about the state of my office?

ON THE OUTSIDE, nothing about the main offices of the Illinois government screamed it was the heart and soul the kingdom. Like the other sterile skyscrapers around it, nothing betrayed it as special or interesting, not even when a royal was present working. More than ever, I appreciated the locked elevator leading directly to the third floor, which was where I'd spend the rest of my day. If I really wanted, I could hide in my office without the receptionist being aware of my presence.

The yearly ritual of adapting back to my life began in earnest. "Do I want to know about the state of my office?"

Last year, it'd taken me a week to vanquish the dust bunnies.

"It's clean. The day after you returned, I gave unassigned agents a chance to be on your detail. Those interested handled the cleaning so you could return to work with minimal hassle."

"How many were interested?"

"Ten."

"That many?"

"For nine months of the year, you're an excellent principal. It's the other three months that cause issues."

As the rest of my family was at the castle where they belonged, the office was empty and quiet. My office, as promised, was clean and free of dust, but my old couch had been removed and replaced with a leather one. I flopped onto it, discovering it had the ability to eat princes at its leisure. With a satisfied groan, I stretched out. "Feel up to becoming my conspirator?"

"Should I be concerned?"

"If you're conspiring with me, I'm probably not going to surprise you. I thought I was being considerate."

"All right, Your Highness. What are you scheming?"

"I want you to open a few RPS slots for women on my detail, and I want to train with them."

"Training with them is necessary, Your Highness. There's also never been a rule barring from women serving on your detail."

Training with my detail was necessary, but there was an automatic wall between principal and agent to maintain priority and keep business to business. I'd seen it plenty of times before; agents had a completely different dynamic with each other. If I managed to lure my huntress to the RPS, I needed the sort of relationship with her agents shared with each other—and I'd have to figure out how to break down the wall dividing agent and principal.

It would be a challenge.

"No, I mean I'd be training as a prospective agent with them."

"You'll be recognized, sir. You're a distinctive man."

I appreciated he used distinctive over pretty, however true. I preferred handsome, but my father pulled off handsome. I was too lanky for handsome, so I was accused of being a model or gorgeous. I didn't care too much either way, although it made me embarrassingly popular at the charity auctions.

I sighed. "That's a problem, true. With my face, we'd have to completely cover it for me to be anonymous. We could work with masks. Silk ones, because obviously, it would be a tragedy if my pretty face was marred by a bad mask." Shaking my head, I kicked off my shoes and launched them in the direction of the door. "I need the training and exercise. I'd also like a chance to work with the agents and get a feel for them."

"What's your goal?"

"You mean beyond exercise?"

"Yes, Your Highness. Beyond exercise. You do not plan exercise unless it's crucial to something else you're planning. While this is a refreshing change from certain members of your family, I'm concerned."

"All right. And you swear secrecy?"

"You know the routine, Your Highness. It's secret as long as it doesn't impair our job to protect your wellbeing."

"Fair enough. I'm looking for a woman *I* can love, and she's the type who'd likely work well in the RPS. I'm trying to find someone, and I'm tired of the standard bullshit shoveled in my direction. I have a list of criteria you can use to find her."

"This might be a good time to remind you agents don't form relationships with their principals."

"But they *do* form relationships with other agents. Anyway, I'll convince her to retire and accept a new position. I'm looking for a queen, Christian. I don't want a lackey. I don't want a delicate flower like Gail. I want someone strong, someone who can kick my ass, and someone who can take care of herself. The RPS is perfect. If she can handle RPS training, she meets those criteria—and she'll learn a lot about politics on the job."

"Let me see if I understand this. You want me to hire a woman capable of kicking your ass so I can train her to be your agent, so you in turn can convince her to marry you and become your future queen."

"That sounds about right."

"Do you have a specific woman in mind?"

"I might."

"And if we can't find this specific woman?"

Next time I cooked up a plan, I needed to think it through *before* telling my conspirator about them. Thinking on my feet gave me a headache as often as not. "I'll have a strong team I've worked with extensively, and in the spring while I'm out of the castle, I'll have you send them out of the kingdom for a special training session coupled with paid vacation. That way, they're not worried about me, their principal, as I'll be under lock and key with you—or so they believe. Sure, the older agents will know I pull a vanishing trick every year, but the new recruits will think they're being rewarded for hard work and going through training. In the worst-case scenario, you place a few phone calls and we have some exceptional agents for a few queens. In that case, I'll try again next year. Ideally, I'll find her this year. *If* this works, I'd like to use the method for the long-term to build a better detail."

Christian stared at me, his jaw slack.

"Christian?"

"I'm not sure our current training methods are suitable for this plan."

"We'll have to change things up. You're able to deal with my family. Contact Montana or Hawaii and ask if we can secure a trainer to help. They have good trainers, don't they? And when you do, confide in a trainer you can trust to keep quiet."

"Hawaii has several women in their

training department. Texas does as well. Montana might. I expect His Royal Majesty brought a few women on board after the birth of his daughter. I have one in particular in mind who might work."

"Would she be on board with the idea?"

"With some disclosures about the nature of your family's talent, possibly, especially since you'd be willing to send some of the trained women to work with the queens. It's hard convincing women to join the RPS, though."

"Can you?"

"Possibly."

"Will you?"

"I'll think about it. You seemed to have a specific woman in mind. Tell me about her."

"She's a trophy hunter, and she has some form of tracking talent. She's perfection."

Christian twitched. "Are you being tracked, Your Highness?"

"I certainly hope so. How the hell else am I going to find her again? If she is, she's going to come straight to me. Since I'll be at the RPS training complex surrounded by agents, I'll be perfectly safe. If she's any good, she'll do whatever it takes to get near me. I'll recognize her."

There was no way I'd forget her or her foul mouth.

"Are you implying she tagged you in your animal form?"

"Maybe." At Christian's glare, I grinned. "I wasn't human."

"And she has no idea who you are?"

"No, I don't believe so."

Christian pinched the bridge of his nose, and I was willing to bet the entire royal family's wealth, prestige, and power I'd given my father's agent a migraine. "All right. I'm going to go along with this because you brought it to my attention in a timely fashion. You're going to test my patience, Your Highness."

"I can't confirm I'm still being tracked. The bruises cover the spot. Where she marked me healed well, and it's caused no discomfort. Had it, I would've had it removed."

"That's another factor. I'm going to allow you to use your judgment on this, but if I feel you're in any danger, I'm having the mark removed. Do you think it's a full brand?"

"I'd assume so. From what I saw of it, she's talented; it was a pattern with good definition."

"Color?"

"She's a flameweaver variant."

"Fire brand?"

"Flame patterned, yes."

"No obvious burns?"

"No."

"All right. I need to know if there's any discomfort or if you can spot the brand again so we can evaluate it."

"That's fair. Why are you cooperating without a fight?"

"Unlike His Royal Majesty, I still possess basic common sense, Your Highness. First, you're trusting me with a secret. Second, you asked for help with your scheme. Third, you presented a reasonable idea you've put some thought into. Deliberately challenging the fraternization law is interesting. Why go through this much trouble? Most women would appreciate a chance to come to the castle to meet a prince."

I chuckled. "And that just leads to the same old problems. For this to work, she needs to love me enough she's willing to risk her career to be my partner. The rules state exile. A rule I'll have immediately overturned," I warned.

"In the case of your familial circumstances, an overturning would be a swift process, although I hope you would convince her to retire before it reached that stage. She'd probably be sent to a different kingdom temporarily while her discharge processes."

"And I'll follow her until the exile is overturned, as she'd need to know I'd give up everything for her, too. There's no middle ground here, Christian. All or nothing. That's how it is in my family."

"You're playing a dangerous game, but you already know that, don't you?"

"Yes, I do. It's not a game to me. I'm tired of yearly exile."

"Self-imposed," he reminded me.

As I'd already revealed one secret—one even more important than my shape—to my father's agent, I rolled off the couch, grabbed a notepad from my desk, and wrote my species on it. "If anyone learns of this, I really might kill you. Understood?"

"The same rules apply for life-and-death situations."

"That's fair." I showed him the paper and waited for him to laugh.

"This explains so much. That said, you'd be at no risk at the castle, Your Highness. Your father would lose his mind if you were threatened. Your mother would murder anyone who laughed at you without hesitation. I think you're worried over nothing."

To ensure no one else learned my secret, I shredded the paper and ate it. "We'll see. So, how can we make this plan work?"

CHRISTIAN LIKELY CURSED me for adding to his work, and it didn't take him long to come to the conclusion he'd have to do a lot of research to turn my idea into a viable plan. Slipping me in among the hopeful RPS agents was only his first challenge. To hide my presence among them, he'd have to hire people who weren't familiar with the Illinois royal family, which meant recruiting from abroad. To mask my interest in a specific woman, he'd have to hire an equal mix of genders. With a little work, he believed he could double the normal number of trainees assigned to my detail, which would lead to a housing shortage at the training center.

A housing shortage would let Christian stuff me in a secured office—or give me an opportunity to return to the castle five minutes away. If everyone wore masks during training, I'd be able to participate until my duties as the heir got in the way. Assuming we could lure my huntress to the compound, I'd have the time I needed to see if the right kind of sparks would fly between us.

I'd also have a chance to prove I was her match, but I'd have to start getting into shape if I wanted to keep up with the RPS agents working hard to earn a place on my detail.

All in all, I'd made quite the mess for myself.

I sneezed, cursed, and hoped my cold stayed manageable enough during the interview process. Christian took over my desk while I stretched out on my couch and flipped through my briefing papers.

By the third page of palace staff adjustments, I lost my will to live. By the fifth page, they bored me straight into unconsciousness.

"What the hell did I do to deserve the flightiest damned heir on the planet?" my father roared.

I hit the carpet with a startled squawk. Papers scattered, fluttering to the floor around me while my heart pounded so hard I worried it might burst out of my chest and make a run for it. "Damn it, Dad!"

A coughing fit caught me by surprise, and when the worst of it subsided, my father offered me a glass of water, which I guzzled. I caught my breath, got to my feet, and placed the glass on my desk so I wouldn't smash it into my father's head.

"You all right?"

"Despite you trying to scare me to death, I'm fine." Mostly. Maybe.

"You ran away from home again," my father complained.

Why wasn't it legal to murder my father? I sighed and bowed my head. "Coming here isn't running away. And if I was going to run away, I wouldn't bring Christian with me. It's his job to return me to the castle."

"You were inaccessible. Same difference."

My father was an idiot. "Christian?"

"Your Majesty, he made it to page five before he passed out. I left him to sleep. We've made good progress on arranging his next RPS detail. Perhaps you should give him some credit. He's been taking his work seriously. He's still recovering. I've been with him the entire time."

"Maybe if you're still not feeling well, you should tell us." My father dropped onto my couch, arched a brow, and stared at me. "Or at least tell me you're leaving the castle. That would be nice. I spent two hours searching the castle for my heir."

"Why didn't you call Christian?"

My father's head of detail chuckled. "He did, Your Highness. I told him you were fine."

"Well, Christian's right. I'm fine. Tired is an acceptable state. I did some work and took a nap. Maybe I should've made it further than page five before taking a nap, but that's a different story."

"You've decided what you're going to do about your RPS detail problem?"

"Yes." I hid my grin and waited for my father's patience to fray.

"Can't you give your old man a break, Kel?"

"My sisters are probably so very happy they're girls. You just baby them."

"I've been told I'm a stalker numerous times today," he conceded.

Taking pity on him might buy me some peace and quiet, so I said, "Christian knows what I want to do about my detail issue. I'm letting him do his job without getting in his way. What's so important you came out to Chicago?"

"Gail invaded our home and is looking for you. I wanted to warn you. I don't think she's going to be accepting no for an answer anytime soon. The girl's lost her mind. Grégoire lost his temper with her and made a scene—and he made it clear she only wanted you for your title. Let's just say that didn't go over very well. She claims you still love her."

"That's just what I need. Why now? I've barely spoken to her in two years. Why would she even think that? I would've thought my policy of avoiding her whenever humanly possible would've been enough to convince her we were over."

"I don't know, but she wants to get near you."

"Christian?" I asked.

"Yes, Your Highness?"

"Extend Gail an invitation to join the training session. If she can't keep up, she's obviously not going to meet my standards—and I expect she'll wash out fast. Present it as a chance for her to prove herself."

The Gail I knew had an allergy to hard work and exercise, and she opted to stay thin by starving herself whenever possible. I gave it three or four days before she gave up. Better yet, if she couldn't recognize me in with the RPS agents, I doubted anyone could.

"That's rather ruthless, Your Highness."

"It is, but I don't care. In case you've forgotten, she left me. I don't have anything to prove to her. She's up to something because Gail is always up to something. The only question is what."

My father grunted, narrowing his eyes. "Risk assessment, Christian?"

"I'll look into the situation and do a full evaluation, Your Majesty. I'll also make certain there's a team present when she's on our turf."

I rubbed my forehead and willed my growing headache to take a hike. "Perhaps people could stop extending her invitations to the private wings of the castle. She's not my girlfriend. At no time in my future will she ever be my girlfriend again. If people other than me would figure this out, I would be very appreciative."

"His Highness seems to have developed a preference for athletic women who can cross the street without his assistance," my father's head of detail stated.

I admired his neutral tone.

"He's finally acknowledged he has a type?" my father blurted.

"Maybe if you'd stop bothering me so much about it, I'd be more willing to give you updates whenever I find a woman attractive. Actually, no. I won't. You might lower yourself to relocating her at your leisure. Kidnapping is illegal unless you're a principal of a bunch of asshole RPS agents determined to marry you off."

Christian snickered.

"Kid, you haven't been much of a talker since the day you were born, and exactly no one was surprised when your first word was no. I hope you have a child just like you."

"There won't be if I waste all of my time dodging Gail," I pointed out.

"Harsh. Point taken. I'll make sure her access to the private wings of the castle is revoked. Any other demands?"

"Don't scare me awake."

"I was testing if you'd shift. Fear is an excellent trigger. That's how I figured out I'd gained control of my talent."

"Dad, for that to happen, I need to meet the right woman. I'm trying something, so could you please keep your nose out of my business for a change?"

"It's really hard to keep my nose out of your business when you say things like that. You should know better than to say things like that to me. I'm a cat."

"Please give me a break already."

"I'll think about it."

I sighed.

FIVE

I'm sorry, ma'am, but you can't bring swords into the building.

MY FATHER HAUNTED ME, refusing to leave me alone until I surrendered to his demands and agreed to return to the castle. To make it clear I wasn't dead, I headed downstairs so the general public could see me up and about. Christian muttered curses over the lackluster security but went along with the idea, forcing my father to cooperate.

In the lobby, several security guards argued with someone, their bodies masking the subject of their interest. Aware Christian would take me out like a sack of grain if I got into any trouble, I angled closer to hear what was going on.

"I'm sorry, ma'am, but you can't bring swords into the building."

Had sweeter words ever been spoken by a guard? A woman with swords caught and held my attention. I grinned and edged closer, hoping the mark on my side had led my foul-mouthed huntress straight to me.

When Christian followed but didn't interfere, I strolled closer. "Is there a problem, gentlemen?"

The security guards jumped, turned, and snapped salutes. I caught myself before rolling my eyes. With them focused on me, I was able to get a view of the woman they'd stopped.

I liked my huntress in leather but jeans did her justice. While she'd never fit in with the higher castes in her worn-out t-shirt, the logo faded beyond recognition, I liked how comfortable she looked in it. Her swords hung from her hips, and a faint blue haze leeched from the tops of their sheaths.

"It's a basic security issue, Your Highness," Piers, the senior of the lot, replied. "She's hesitant to turn her swords over for safe keeping until she's finished in the building."

Her eyes widened, and I savored her stunned expression. To mask my interest in her, I focused on her weapons. "All right. Swords are weapons. You planning on stabbing anyone with those, ma'am?"

"Fuck no."

My father's sigh almost broke my resolve. If I started laughing, I'd start coughing, and if I tried to cough and laugh at the same time, I'd end up on the floor again. "I'd hazard a guess that a lady like you wouldn't be bringing swords here without a reason. Part of your talent?"

"Who the hell you callin' a lady?"

If I could listen to her make such exclamations every day for the rest of my life, I'd die a happy man. "You."

She looked me over like I looked her over. "And you're a Your Highness? Did you hit your head?"

I probably had, but I'd keep hold of some remnants of my pride. "An unfortunate accident of birth. You take your swords everywhere?"

"I guess."

"While stabbing me might be tempting, would you show me your blades without cutting me to pieces?"

She hesitated, glancing at the guards. "Sure?"

"Unless she cuts me to pieces, just ignore that she has swords," I ordered.

Christian and my father sighed, and I wondered which one of them would crack first. Piers chuckled, shook his head, and raised his hands in surrender. "If anything happens, I'm blaming you, Your Highness."

With a shrug and puzzled expression, she drew one of her blades, turned it, and offered me the hilt. Up close, the blue light radiated from streamers of flame enveloping the steel from guard to tip. The leather wrapping the hilt warmed my hand. Taking a few steps back, I tested the weapon's heft and weight like I'd been taught. I'd never expected to need the lessons, but I appreciated the chance to look somewhat competent.

I'd handled some nice swords, but I hadn't seen anything quite like it. I turned to my father. "I think I need one of these for Christmas, Dad." Satisfied I'd expressed my appreciation of the blade's craftsmanship, I gave my huntress my undivided attention. "Do you know the smith, ma'am?"

She nodded. "Yeah, I do."

"Any chance I can get your contact information so we can talk about your swords?"

"You really must have hit your head."

I laughed. "Probably. It's a bad habit." Reversing the blade, I offered her the hilt. "Thank you for letting me look at it. It's an exquisite weapon. Christian, please get her information—I'd love to see those swords in action. If possible, can you arrange a demonstration? This blade is far too beautiful to hide."

After she reclaimed her sword, I thanked her, dipped into a bow, and headed for the elevator. My father followed, waiting until we turned the corner to ask, "What was that about?"

"I was curious about something."

"Like what? How to get stabbed in a public place and cause an incident?"

"What sort of woman is gutsy enough to bring swords into a government building? That's definitely part of it. And look. I didn't get stabbed. It's like she doesn't actually have it out for me."

"She's probably a lost tourist."

I laughed at the thought of a tourist running around Chicago with two swords. "Probably."

At least I could trust my father to readily accept my excuse; for the next while, he'd approve of anything that restored his sense of normality, and an interest in sharp, pointy objects counted.

"Was it a nice sword?"

"I don't know where she got it, but I want one." While true, the swords' wielder interested me more. She'd never polish into a queen most expected, but I had no doubt she'd keep me on my toes. If anything, my interest in her fulfilled a family tradition of odd choices of queens.

Most had no idea a family curse picked the queen, and she was never what the kingdom needed. She was always what the king needed to conquer his beast.

She was what the king needed to thrive. Had I been wiser, I never would've clung to Gail for so long. Everything would've been different.

It took ten minutes for Christian to return, and he glared at me. "Are you really certain about this? That woman is absolutely uncouth."

As I had no doubt she'd filled Christian's ears with vocabulary he'd rather not hear, I asked, "But did you get her information between the bursts of profanity?"

"She thought the idea ridiculous, but yes. I

have her information. She's leaving the kingdom soon."

That would put a kink in my plans. "Do a full evaluation so my father won't whine as much."

"You're overly optimistic on your odds of that happening, Your Highness."

"If you leave my father's det—"

My father clamped his hand over my mouth. "Absolutely not. Ignore that suggestion, Christian. You're not leaving my detail to join his. No."

I tried to bite him without success.

"Your Majesty, please be nice to your heir."

He lowered his hand. "I spent years looking for you. My son can't have you."

"Since I can't keep a detail, give the lady with the swords a chance. She can't possibly be any worse than agents who won't stick around."

"No," my father snapped. "Wait. She's a woman and you haven't run away yet? I've changed my mind. Yes."

My father must have been dropped on his head as a baby. I closed my eyes and wondered how to encourage him without looking like I was encouraging him.

When I opened my eyes, my father was halfway back to where the woman stood near the security guards. "Miss? Miss? A moment of your time, please?"

"What the fuck do you want now?"

The sight of my father taking on my foul-mouthed huntress, who was likely out for my blood, would be a cherished memory for the rest of my life.

ACCORDING TO CHRISTIAN, my huntress's name was Evangeline, and her conversation with my father was doomed from the beginning. Either she had no clue he was the king or simply didn't give a damn, but within five minutes, she went to the security guards informing them of a harasser and probable imposter.

At that point, I started laughing and couldn't stop. Between coughing fits and gasping for air, I snickered and chortled. Christian hovered, sighing while debating which royal to protect. He stuck with me, as my father earned having his ass handed to him by the woman he was annoying. "This isn't promising."

"It's perfect." I sucked in a breath and fought to control myself. "Look at her. She has zero care he's royalty. She might even face off against Montana without hesitation. RPS agents need that quality."

"As do queens," he conceded.

"If we do a trial contract, we can strike the fraternization rules from her paperwork. Then, if I flirt with her, I'm the only one who gets into shit for it."

She was already a good influence on me, and I liked it.

"We'd also have to strike the language rules."

"If we—"

"Are you fucking mad?" Evangeline demanded so loud everyone in the lobby stopped and stared.

I moaned my laughter, leaned against the wall, and struggled to stay on my feet. I had no idea what my father said, but she flung her hands in the air and marched straight for me.

I was about five seconds from collapsing into a manically laughing heap, but I straightened and struggled to contain my mirth.

"Hey, you. Tell this menace to stop fucking bothering me already, would ya?"

"I've been trying my entire life without success." It amazed me I got the entire sentence out without choking, coughing, or bursting into another fit of laughter.

"You poor bastard. Do you need a rescue?"

"It's entirely possible."

Evangeline glanced over her shoulder with a scowl. "Is he really a king?"

"Unfortunately."

"Does that mean I can't hit him?"

"If you work with the RPS for me, I'll have it to your employment papers you can hit him at least once during training scenarios."

"And you? How about you? Do I get to hit you?"

"It's a part of the job. The agents get to take turns tenderizing me."

While that wasn't quite true, it would be for however long she was involved with the RPS. Christian would not be happy with me, but I figured I'd emerge better equipped to withstand a beating—and better trained in avoiding beatings in the first place.

Evangeline thrust out her hand. "Deal."

I foresaw much pain, suffering, and trouble in my future, but that didn't stop me from shaking with her. "I look forward to working with you."

She turned to Christian, and in a solemn tone, she said, "I'm not sure I can beat sanity into either one of them, but I'll try."

"I wish you the best of luck with that, Miss Evangeline. You'll need it. Having dealt with both for many years, you'll find His Highness is the most pleasant of the royals here."

Evangeline tightened her grip before releasing me. "Interesting. What the fuck do you fucking folks want with a bitch like me?"

I had so many reasons, but I decided to go with the third on my list. "You're not afraid of my father. That's a good reason on its own. You're comfortable with yelling at him. It usually takes months to get new agents comfortable using their authority on royalty. I expect you'll get to yell at us often. My father gets yelled at daily."

"And you?"

"I'll try to keep my misbehavior to reasonable levels, but I wouldn't want to deprive you of a chance to scold me."

"And how much does this pay?"

"Christian will be the one to negotiate your salary, but the kingdom-wide entry minimum for new RPS agents is sixty-five thousand a year."

"Paid training?"

"You're not trained unless you're hired, so yes."

"Bonuses and hazard pay?"

Was there anything lovelier than a practical woman? I thought not. "Agents receive both."

"I'd need a visa to work here."

The kingdom's immigration system would discover I could be as annoying as my father if there was an issue with her paperwork. "Where are you originally from?"

"Nevada. I have a weapon carry permit and a hunting license for Illinois."

"Christian, arrange a formal interview," I ordered. "And get Dad's schedule arranged so she can face him on the mat during the interview."

"Well, that'll make it worth dealing with some damned interview," Evangeline muttered.

"Excellent. I look forward to seeing you again, Evangeline."

She shook her head and sighed. "You're a nutter."

I was, and I planned on enjoying every moment I spent testing her mettle.

SIX

You sweet, sweet boy.

I WANTED to concentrate on Evangeline, but reality was a cruel mistress and work couldn't wait. Finding a lady-in-waiting for Princess Abigail would be easy, and I'd get to hit two birds with one stone. I could think of no better person to give the princess some tender loving care, and I'd get to yank my father's stubbed tail at the same time. By putting so much effort into avoiding my mother's mother, he made an easy mark for me, a son interested in securing some harmless, fun, and effective payback.

The instant we returned to the castle, I locked myself in my office, snarling threats of death to keep my father out, and dialed the switchboard for South Dakota's royal family.

"How many I help you, Your Highness?" a woman answered by the third ring.

"Can you connect me to my grandmother, please?"

"One moment, Your Highness." There was

a long enough wait that I expected I'd have to call back when the line clicked and the operator said, "Connecting."

"It's not like you to call me so early in the summer," the wavering voice of my grandmother declared. "What do you need?"

"How's your relationship with North Dakota right now?"

My loaded question might land me in a hot water; with the overturn of the royal family, something I hadn't seen coming at all, I feared I waded into choppy political waters. That the former royal family had married into the new royal family hadn't been a surprise.

Some things were meant to be, and I was grateful the pair had been reunited. It would take years before the kingdom recovered from its short but explosive civil war. I sat tense in my chair, waiting for my grandmother's answer.

"Those poor dears. We're amiable with the new monarchs. Why?"

"Princess Abigail of North Dakota will be visiting in the near future. She needs a lady-in-waiting, and I thought it would be a nice for her if I asked you. It would give you a chance to escape my aunt for a while and pester Dad."

"You sweet, sweet boy. When?"

"She'll be here for a few months, and I believe she's arriving in two to three weeks. Mom has the details. I just offered to make the arrangements for someone to fill the spot."

"It's been a long time since I've had a good vacation. Count me in. Little Abby does like my cookies, and she needs some tender loving care. And how about you, dear? How are you doing? Have you found a special lady for yourself yet?"

"I'm working on that. It'd be a lot easier if I had a really nice grandmother around to drive my ex off. She keeps pulling stupid stunts destined to make my life even more difficult."

"I think I can keep that waif of a girl off your back. How was your spring?"

Any other year, I would've grunted something to brush off the conversation. "Annoying until a woman beat me black and blue. After that, I had a nice time. Still fighting off a cold, though."

"As always. I see you're a little like your father. A feisty lady is in your future, I expect. And don't you deny your mother's status as a feisty lady. I raised that girl to be a little feisty. How else was she going to tame herself a haughty cat?"

I couldn't imagine myself without a feisty woman in my future. "Well, I certainly hope I'll find someone at least a little feisty."

Evangeline had clued me into several benefits of partnering with a woman who wasn't afraid of anyone or anything.

"That's progress. And here I was hoping to

stage another kidnapping. I had so much fun with your father. The pipsqueak here isn't nearly as entertaining."

"Uncle Carl isn't letting you kidnap him for fun, is he?"

"I'm banned from creating any RPS scenarios for a whole year because I broke two SUVs. I even offered to replace them. It's not my fault the agents were overenthusiastic in following my directions. *I* didn't break the SUVs specifically. Others did. They were just following my scenario. They got creative! It's not my fault when the RPS agents get creative during scenarios."

I loved my grandmother as much as my father loved avoiding her. "I might let you help plan some training scenarios for my new detail with a few conditions."

"You must really miss your old grandma to offer such a wonderful bribe."

"Or I just really hate my father," I countered.

"There's that, too. What's bringing this on, dear boy? This is not your normal style. Your normal style is carefully planned. This is impulsive enough I'm concerned there's more than your fair share of your father's genes in your blood."

"Gail's been a pest, and I've decided to do extensive RPS training. She might find some way to interfere."

"That was foolish of you, leaving her an opening."

"I wasn't feeling all that well when I came up with the idea," I confessed.

"It's all right, Kel. Now, if your daddy had the sense to call for help, he wouldn't have gotten beaten so bad when he faced off against his brothers. Don't you worry about that ex of yours. I'll make sure she won't bother you. I've a few boys in mind who can keep her busy. With that out of the way, tell me about this lady you're interested in."

"Lady is a bit of a stretch."

"Commoner, then?"

"Don't know, don't care."

She chuckled. "That's my boy. Is she pretty?'

"She's too strong to be traditionally pretty. Mother won't approve."

"Ignore your mother. You'd be miserable if you had to defend your lady from those ruffian relatives of yours. Get me all the details while I handle things here." My grandmother's exasperated sigh warned me of trouble. "Kel, baby, your uncle wants a word."

"I didn't do anything this time, I swear."

She snickered. "Here, sonny. Don't you go talking the poor boy's ear off. He's not feeling well."

The phone exchanged hands, and my uncle laughed. "Hey, kiddo," His Royal Majesty of South Dakota greeted. "I hear you decked your old man for annoying you. Good job. Any luck on convincing your old man to retire so he'll stop bothering me?"

"Not yet, sorry."

"Don't be sorry. You father had a rough go of it, too. Your aunt's been pestering me about helping you find a woman you might actually like, so I'm under threat of death to offer any help you might want."

"I'm trying something new this year, but if it's a miserable failure, sure. It can't hurt at this point."

"I'm so glad you opted against hiring prostitutes."

"Unlike the rest of my family, I have standards."

"It'll be a shock to the entirety of Illinois when they learn they'll one day have a sensible monarch."

My uncle liked the direct truth, and all denying it would do was earn me an extra dose of reality. "Out of familial obligation, I'm required to say Dad's not *that* bad."

"Oh, he's that bad. He's a cat. He can't help it. I'll let your aunt know she gets her turn next year. Expect insanity. She's just like your mother."

What had I done? My aunt might be worse than my mother, but I wasn't brave enough to tell anyone that. "Please no marooning me on a deserted island. I'm spoiled."

My uncle laughed. "I'll make sure to inform any planners of next year's activities that you are not to be marooned anywhere. Your grandmother ran off cackling, so I'll let you get back to catching up. If you need to escape, give me a call. I'll whip together a relocation scenario with Christian so you can get some peace and quiet."

Given a month, I'd appreciate the offer. "On the off-chance things go well, let's say I wanted a relocation with specific company…"

"Give me her details. I'm game."

"If needed, I will."

"Good on you for taking a page out of your mother's book. Just expect your lady to be pretty cranky afterwards if you don't tell her about the relocation prior to it happening."

"Well, let's just say she'd be in a position where I'd be doing it to see her in action."

"Dare I ask?"

"If I need help, I'll fill you in," I promised.

"Remember, outside of planned scenarios with mostly willing participations, kidnapping is illegal and bad. If you want your lady involved with the relocation, she needs warned there's an RPS scenario going on and that she may become involved."

"Not going to be an issue."

"Good. Go get some rest, Kel. You sound like hell." My uncle hung up, and I wondered how I'd survive my family's matchmaking ways.

WITH THE ISSUE of Princess Abigail's grandmother-in-waiting handled, I had a mountain of other work to contend with before I could give Evangeline my undivided attention. To pull off my crazy scheme, I'd have to live two lives. The observant agents would figure out who I was because of my voice and build unless I used magic.

An illuminator might be able to help disguise me for a while.

The problem was handling my royal duties while training with the RPS. If I spent every waking minute catching up, I might be able to delegate enough I only had to work a few hours a day. On the days I didn't train with the RPS, I'd catch up instead of resting. I'd have to work with the trainers to situate the schedule so I, as the prince, wouldn't be involved for several weeks.

At best, I'd have a month before my ruse was exposed—and that was only if I got enough work done before the interview process began. I camped in my office to make the most of every minute. Within forty-eight hours, I'd plowed through most of my to-do list. My cold lingered, but I'd expected that. If I could get more rest, I'd conquer it faster, but time wasn't on my side.

I had one chance to catch my huntress's attention, and I couldn't afford to waste it.

Sometime after I should have gone to dinner, something I'd missed two nights in a row, my phone rang. "Kelvin speaking," I answered.

"You're very casual for a Your Highness,"

my huntress replied. "Who knew? Some dude in a suit gave me this phone and said I needed to talk to you about the interview."

The dude in a suit needed a raise and an immediate promotion. "How can I help you, Evangeline?"

"Ugh. Eva, please."

She was no flower, and I loved it. "All right, Eva. What do you need from me?"

"Your schedule, apparently. The dude in a suit doesn't have it, and he needs it to plan your father's beating."

"Tell me when and where, and I'll be there."

"Hey, you! He wants to know when and where. I told you he wouldn't be picky. Jesus Christ with a bucket of puppies. Get the man a secretary or a fucking calendar. Isn't a Your Highness supposed to have lackeys? No wonder he's scrawny and in need of a self-defense trainer. You probably work him half to death and forget to feed him."

I laughed because it was true.

"Well, at least *someone* here has a sense of humor."

Yep, I'd fallen in love with an irreverent, fearless woman with a foul mouth and an interest in inflicting bodily harm on members of my family. My father would be so proud when he found out. "Please tell them I'll adjust my schedule as needed, Eva."

"Hey, the Your Highness wants me to tell

you dips he can adjust his schedule as needed."

I bit my lip so I wouldn't start chuckling.

"The dude in a suit wants to know if you can be in Chicago tomorrow at one."

"Consider me there." I'd head over first thing in the morning, work while I waited, and make certain my father showed up through a clever use of taunts and threats of running away.

"He says yes. Anything else I need to tell the Your Highness?" She sighed. "That's such a dumb question. Hey, Your Highness? The dude in a suit wants to know if you could dress casually. I think he doesn't want me to mess up your pretty suit."

"I'll bring sweats and expect a workout. I need the exercise."

"There's hope for you after all. Hey, dude. He says he needs the exercise. I told you it would be fine. Lord alive, you all act like he's a girl. Just because he's pretty doesn't mean he's a girl."

I gave it less than ten minutes before the RPS hated everything about Eva. "Thank you, Eva."

"Don't hold your breath waiting for any other compliments, Your Highness. It's never happening."

My resolve to hold back my laughed cracked and one slipped out. "How good are you with a calendar?"

"I have a phone and can count up to thirty-one. That covers the basics."

Whatever. I'd make it work, I'd just make sure I didn't plan anything more than thirty-one days in advance ever again. "If you're willing, I have something to ask of you. Not a favor; you'd be paid for the work."

"What the fuck could you possibly want now?"

"Stick around, and once every twenty-eight days, you can beat my father, but you'll have to add dates to a calendar, track his beatings, and when I need scheduling help, you'll need to deal with it some."

"Maybe. What's the frequency of calendar additions for Your Highness?"

She might kill me, and at the rate I was going, I might let her. "Well, I did tell you I need exercise. How often would you recommend?"

"You're pretty scrawny, so three days a week might work. Maybe."

"You drive a hard bargain. Sold. Tell the dudes in a suit you'll be partially managing my calendar as a part-time job in addition to any work you're doing for them."

"I'll really get paid to schedule your beatings? Damn, that's a nice perk."

"We're all about employee satisfaction here, Eva."

"Nice. All right. I think the dudes in a suit are done wasting your time, Your Highness. Try not to eat lunch right before showtime.

It'd be tragic if you were to vomit on my fucking shoes." She hung up.

How the hell was I going to convince her I was good enough for her? That she didn't care what others thought of her promised success on the political battlefield. Lies and rumors wouldn't bother her like they bothered my mother. The first few curses she dropped would scandalize the court, but I didn't care.

I needed a challenge, and she was that and so much more.

But how could I win her attention? That was the problem. I sighed and prayed I'd figure something out soon.

SEVEN

Sending the appropriate email without a mouse would be a challenge.

ACCORDING TO MY COMPUTER, Armageddon began at five minutes after ten in the evening, and my father started it. My father storming into my office warned me I had trouble on my hands, but my mother's presence ensured I wouldn't survive through the next fifteen minutes without an intervention.

"What the hell do you think you're doing?" my father bellowed, slamming a file on my desk so hard my mouse bounced to the floor and broke into several pieces.

"Getting a new mouse, it seems. What did my mouse ever do to you?" I picked up the pieces, shook my head, and wondered how'd I get a replacement before I needed to get some sleep and head for Chicago in the morning. Damn it, I'd have to ask Christian to make arrangements.

Sending the appropriate email without a mouse would be a challenge.

My father spluttered. "That woman is a menace."

As my mother glared at me, I assumed he wasn't talking about her, which meant he'd found something out about Eva or had learned my grandmother would be paying him an extended visit. I picked up the folder, flipped it open, and discovered Eva's background check had come in.

Her history as a law-abiding, no-kill bounty hunter didn't surprise me. The long list of marksmanship championships did, and she held a black belt in jujitsu. The two-page summary of her martial arts exploits included several trips to Japan, and she'd emerged a regional champion once, an international champion three times, and had a rap sheet of fifteen counts of self-defense leading to arrest.

"Well, I certainly won't be worried when she crosses the street. What's the problem, Dad?"

"She's a bounty hunter."

"And? She has a good record, she's law-abiding, and she's obviously skilled. The no-kill clause on her contract is excellent. She has morals."

"She curses worse than a sailor!"

I stared at him. "Are you serious? Deal with it, Dad. Mother, I already informed Eva she'll have once-a-month sessions with Dad. I'll need to know a good time to schedule him in. With this much practical experience, she's priceless."

"I told you," Mom muttered. "Kelvin, do you really think it's wise to bring someone like that into the castle?"

As a general rule, I never called my royal relatives on my cell to theirs, but I made an exception, and I thumbed through my contacts until I found my grandmother.

She answered on the second ring. "Kelvin, sweet baby boy, what's wrong that you're calling me direct this late at night?"

"I'm putting you on speaker. Kindly remind your daughter what she was doing at the age of fifteen."

My mother blanched. I set my phone on my desk, enabling the speaker function. "It's on speaker now."

"Sarah, why is that dear boy of yours resorting to this? You know full well you were wading knee-deep through cow shit working the manure line because you couldn't figure out how to count to ten without a calculator."

"Mom!" my mother wailed.

"Don't you throw stones in a glass house, little girl. Knee-deep through cow shit. You might be a queen now, but you sure didn't start that way."

"But Mom…"

"Don't you even. Knee-deep through cow shit. How many times do I need to repeat it?"

"But this hussy's a bounty hunter!"

I stiffened. "Excuse me?"

"Now you've done it, little girl. You've gone and offended your sweet little boy. Do you have proof she's a hussy, or are you mad you've been outclassed?"

I flipped through Eva's file, disliking what I found. "No, she's not a hussy, but she's faced charges—since written-off—for self-defense. She hospitalized two would-be rapists. She has a count of obstructing a theft with violence, which resulted in a broken window. She used the thief's head to break the window. She paid a fine of five hundred for the damages."

"I'm not seeing the issue."

"Neither am I," I snapped, closing the folder.

"Have you listened to her talk?" my mother demanded.

"Yes, I have."

My grandmother cackled. "Does Kelvin's little lady have colorful language?"

"She's foul!"

"Knee-deep in cow shit, little girl." When my grandmother issued warnings, the wise listened. "I'll be there the day after tomorrow, and I expect both of you to be nice to that young lady. Am I understood?"

My parents froze, their eyes widening. While I'd made arrangements with the palace staff regarding my grandmother's arrival, I'd forgotten an important detail. "Oh, right.

That reminds me. Grandmother will be Princess Abigail's lady-in-waiting. I thought she'd like it."

My mother clapped her hands to her mouth, and her eyes watered. "Oh, Kel."

"If your sweet little boy wants a foul-mouthed lady who can cross the street without help, let him have her. His heart has always been in the right place, even though you can't see that. Hell, she'd be a fine queen for him from what I'm hearing, and I haven't even met her yet. When you've got a heart of gold on one side, you need a sharp sword on the other to protect it. Our sweet baby boy here's a lot of things, but he's no warrior. You two leave him alone about her, apologize for being mean, and let him figure things out without you meddling. Behave!"

My grandmother hung up.

"Kelvin," my father growled.

I wasn't going to survive to attend Eva's interview. My father was going to kill me. My only hope was to distract my parents with discussion of Abby's upcoming visit. "Princess Abigail has always loved Grandmother. Should you as much as even think of criticizing my choice, maybe I will just pass the crown to Grégoire so I don't have to deal with it—and if Grégoire doesn't want it, I'm sure Uncle Tim would love to be saddled with the job."

"That's not funny, Kelvin."

"Good, because I wasn't joking. I really don't care if you're scared shitless of my grandmother. I also don't care if Evangeline isn't the typical RPS applicant." I picked up Eva's file and slapped it against my desk. "First, she's competent. Second, she's not afraid of royalty. Third, she's unafraid of the RPS. She calls them dudes in suits to their faces. I'm tired of people throwing women like Gail at me. I'm tired of meeting expectations. As such, I'm going to surround myself with people who have turned their weaknesses into strengths. She's done that."

"But she could be dangerous," my mother whispered.

"I'm not concerned about a no-kill bounty hunter with a serious case of ethics. Sure, she's no princess, but I don't need a princess."

"What do you need then?" my father snapped.

"Someone who won't run away screaming from a bunch of predatory shapeshifters? How about someone capable of taking care of herself? Let's not be idiots about this, Dad. I have a hard enough time taking care of myself, which is why she'll get to beat me three times a week compared to your once a month."

My mother sighed. "He has a point. If he survives that, he can probably survive anything. But why a bounty hunter?"

"Well, another bounty hunter won't get

past her, and neither will most assassins. But that's not going to fly with you two, is it?"

"No," Dad replied. "It won't."

"I'll allow it as a pro on the list. That doesn't excuse the rest."

I loved my mother, but I needed to make it clear where I stood, and it wasn't with her. "No one asked you to excuse anything, Mother. You just need to deal with it. Preferably quietly."

"Fine. Give him what he wants. If he's kidnapped, maybe we'll just name one of the girls the heir. Supposedly, this is when we should be grateful he's being assertive."

"Babe," Dad complained.

"I had to resort to kidnapping to get you. Maybe he's just walking in your footsteps." My mother scowled. "You're ruthless, Kel. Calling my mother like that!"

"I certainly wasn't going to win otherwise."

"You haven't won this yet," my father reminded me.

He was right. I hadn't. Until I had a chance to find out if I could have a profane-ever-after with my plucky little huntress, I was in the loser category. "She's a no-kill bounty hunter. Not an assassin. Not some common criminal. She's skilled, and that's what the RPS needs. I'm looking for people who'll stick around this time. If I can't keep a detail for more than nine months, what makes you think I'll have any luck finding a wife?"

My parents stared at each other. When they remained silent, I slapped the folder against my desk. "You're going to have a round with her on the mat at one in Chicago, Dad. I'm going to have a round with her on the mat, too. If you're worried, invite my uncles and the rest of my menacing relatives. I'm sure Great-Grandpa would love to watch you get beat by a woman."

"You're going to regret this, son."

"You're joking, right? I invited myself to a beating and promised her three sessions a week as a bribe to keep her from leaving Illinois. If she doesn't beat me into submission, no one can."

"Why do this, then?"

"If I can't keep a stable RPS detail, at least this way I'll be able to protect myself. This file tells me one thing: this woman knows how to protect herself."

EIGHT CAME EARLY, and aware of Eva's warning, I ate a big breakfast and planned to avoid lunch altogether. Either worried I'd abdicate or curious, my father accompanied me to Chicago. I could've lived without his presence, especially after his commentary about Eva. A hefty dose of the silent treatment might impress upon him my parents had crossed a line with me. Taking advantage of the fact I refused to pay him a single grain of attention, I read over the daily briefing and confirmed I'd finished catching up on what I'd missed over the spring.

"Your Majesty, please leave His Highness alone," Christian requested. I'd heard the man make similar requests already, but I'd gotten good at tuning out my father—and I hadn't bothered counting the number of times Christian had gotten annoyed over the situation.

I checked out the window and sighed at the maze of streets we still needed to navigate to reach the office.

Closing my folder, I returned it to my briefcase. "What do you want now, Dad?"

Well over an hour of ignoring him wouldn't win me much in the grand scheme of things, but hopefully he'd remember I wasn't going to let him keep badmouthing Eva.

"Why are we doing this?"

"I'm out of shape and need exercise. You're an asshole who needs a reminder being a cat won't save you from someone better armed and better trained. As I'm unable to keep a reliable detail, I'll learn from the type of person who'd trouble the RPS if she were out for my blood. I'm tired of the bullshit. Unless you want to choose a new heir, I suggest you leave me alone about it. I wasn't joking about the possibility of abdicating. I'm getting old enough where another option for the next king might be the wise choice for the sake of the kingdom's stability. And don't try to play stupid with me. Why else would the congress start pressuring about my marital status?"

"You don't have to abdicate for being slow to marry. You just—"

"Haven't been looking for a wife in a parent-approved fashion."

"Kelvin!"

"It's true. And until I have a stable detail, I refuse. If I can't get a stable detail, my wife would go unprotected, too. No. My way or I'm taking the highway on this one. I'm not the last of the line, and Grégoire isn't my only cousin dealing with the family curse. The rest just stay at home because they can."

"Fucking wolves," my father growled.

"It would be tragic if a cat had a dog for his heir."

Christian snorted. "Your Majesty, it's worth pointing out Miss Evangeline's resume and background are ideal for RPS work."

"What's her last name?" I asked.

"She doesn't have one, sir. She was disowned and did not opt to have a new last name issued."

I cringed, and as expected, my father pounced on the information. "What rank?"

"We expect her talent evaluation to come back as a low to moderate level elite. She's disclosed parts of her bloodline for talent inheritance purposes but asked we leave it out of any official paperwork. I agreed due to circumstances."

"Risk factor?"

"For His Highness? Nil. For Miss Evangeline? It's a possibility, but from my understanding of the situation, her family lacks the general resources to pose much of a threat. Her joining the RPS would offer her protections she does not currently enjoy. Due to her disowning, she's been wandering the Royal States since she was fifteen. Since eighteen, she's been accepting government contracts in order to maintain her visas legally. Her work record's good. Her specialization is in tracking and recovery, with a few relocation runs with acceptable circumstances for her hire. She's in Illinois on a valid hunting and fishing visa, and we've verified she's a conservationist. For the uninformed, she only kills what she'll eat and releases the rest. Her trophy shots are of tranquilized targets, which she monitors during their release. She's made a substantial amount of money tagging endangered species for tracking for kingdoms."

I huffed over the confirmation of my initial thoughts, pleased she avoided unnecessary killing. It offered me the hope she'd been tracking me to make certain I hadn't kicked the bucket rather than to turn me into a very large but delicious dinner. "Got a gallery of her trophies?"

"If you ask her, you'll lose several hours

without seeing the entirety of it," Christian warned.

"That's no issue."

"Yes, it is," my father grumbled.

"Dad, I was not joking about abdicating to Grégoire if you can't remain civil. I can have the paperwork finished by this evening if you can't at least attempt to cooperate. So help me, try testing your luck. Congress isn't far from here, and I have zero problems with making an appearance, informing them I'm abdicating, and making arrangements to leave Illinois. And I'll cite you *and* their efforts to marry me off as the cause. No."

"You signed me up for monthly beatings."

Christian cleared his throat. "Before this escalates further, I would like to remind Your Majesty that His Highness is completely within his rights to forfeit his claim on the crown and invoke the law to secure an immediate transfer out of kingdom. That is his right, and as a member of the RPS, it is my legal duty and responsibility to see that happen if he requests it."

"I understand the law," my father snapped.

"Then take this seriously. His Highness has obviously been provoked, and unless you *want* to lose your heir, perhaps a change of course would be prudent. As for Miss Evangeline, His Highness has presented a very good idea which the RPS will be implementing. After discussion, which included Miss Evangeline, we have decided on once-a-week sessions, and these sessions will also include Her Majesty and the rest of the royal children. To begin with, she will do one-hour sessions in the evenings following typical RPS agent training sessions. Considering His Highness's difficulties maintaining a detail, this is the safest course of action. Miss Evangeline has the experience most in the RPS do not: she's been taking care of herself without the benefit of a bodyguard for the entirety of her adult life and much of her teenage years."

"You, too?" Dad complained.

"Losing your heir to prideful stupidity is not beneficial to Illinois."

"You're really siding with him."

"Yes, sir, I am."

"I've been demoted now, too?"

Christian chuckled. "Should you fire me, I intend to apply to His Highness's detail."

"Absolutely not!"

"Then perhaps you should be more considerate towards His Highness's requests, Your Majesty."

"It's a conspiracy," Dad muttered. "Fine. If she hurts you, Kelvin, I'm killing her myself."

Why did *I* have to have the psychotic overprotective father with feline tendencies? "Bruising and injuries sustained during training don't count."

"Damn it."

I allowed myself to smile. "I see she's already being a good influence on you."

"You're a spoiled rotten little shit, Kelvin."

"Forgive His Majesty, Your Highness. It's always tough on a father when his baby boy becomes a man."

I snickered at Christian's comment. "My sisters, my *older* sisters, are just going to love hearing about this."

"No," Dad stated.

"Yes. I think I'll call Suzette tonight. Think she might be game for dinner after my scheduled beating, Christian?"

"I'll check her schedule after you're settled in your office, Your Highness."

"My son may be a little shit, but you're something else, Christian."

"You appreciate having someone around who'll nudge you when you're wrong. That's why you haven't fired me yet."

"I'm never allowed to fire you. The wife would kill me."

"Her Majesty is wise—usually."

Usually was the key word, and I had my doubts my mother would ever approve of Eva no matter what I said or did. The sooner I accepted that, the better off I'd be.

The truth hurt, and I supposed it was yet another stage of preparing to become a king in my father's stead. Neither of my parents needed to approve of her.

They didn't even need to approve of me.

I just needed a chance to discover if Eva was what I needed—and if she'd accept me despite everything stacked against the possibility of there being an us.

The news of her disowning worried me, for she had every reason to resent my existence and no reason to trust me.

I'd have my work cut out for me, which meant it was just another day in Illinois.

EIGHT

You recognize there need to be rules.

WHILE EVA WAS MY GOAL, I needed a solid detail of people I could trust. If things went as I hoped, half of the people I recruited would ultimately protect her. If I could prove we could be partners in all ways, I'd sleep better at night knowing my partner could protect herself from anything anyone tossed at her.

The problem of finding a good detail left me with a large stack of paperwork and an older woman who looked me over with open disapproval. Christian left me alone with her, returning to his duties protecting my father, which led me to believe she was some form of RPS agent. I eyed her as much as she eyed me, sat behind my desk and pulled the files closer.

"I've been briefed on your familial circumstances. In any other situation, I would never condone a plan of this nature. However, Christian's work is well-respected, and he's not one to exaggerate a situation. Your problems with your detail concern me, an obvious issue relating to your specific talent. So, here I am. I'm Meredith Scarson, and I'll be acting as the head of your detail until a suitable candidate is found and trained. I'll also be managing your potential relationship with Evangeline, as I've been informed you're hopeless."

I relaxed, flipped open the top folder to discover a stats sheet of a potential RPS agent, and considered my options. If I wanted to keep Meredith on my side, I'd have to handle her carefully—something I rarely worried about with Christian and the other long-term agents. "That's fair. What are the rules?"

"Good. You recognize there need to be rules. Some fledgling monarchs don't understand this concept. You will keep your relationship with Miss Evangeline clean. No sex, no holding hands, no sneaking kisses in a closet. Throughout the duration of training, which will not involve masks of any nature, and until it's determined a relationship can progress, you will act like a professional at all times. *If* this woman is the one for you, she must want you for you. Not your rank or face. And I strongly recommend against displaying any signs of affection. She's a professional, and that would be a quick way to ruin any chance you might have with her. I'm not convinced you will be able to break the barriers of her professionalism, frankly."

"I can work with that. I'm hoping my initial bribes have earned some good will."

"Yes, I heard about that. Monthly beatings for His Majesty at her hand, as he annoys her. That was a sly move, and yes, you have caught her attention with that stunt. He's a lynx shapeshifter and the definition of annoying. Shapeshifters usually are. They're too much like their beast. That, too, will be an issue you have to overcome. Miss Evangeline is of the opinion shapeshifters sacrifice much of their humanity to be what they are, and her opinions of your family are colored by this. She is aware you're from a line of shapeshifters. Christian has notified me he knows your form but is under oath to keep it a secret unless it is a life-or-death situation."

"That's correct. If you're still here in the winter, I'll consider sharing the details with you under the same terms. As I can't shift at will, it's a non-issue."

"That's fine. I was informed your talent is linked to your future wife. This is something I can work with. I trust you will notify me if you believe it becomes an issue."

"If it becomes an issue, I'll notify you," I promised.

"Thank you, Your Highness. I can work with this. Now, onto business. I'm significantly concerned about your interest in covertly training with the RPS. However, an experimental program where the principal openly trains with the agents may work. To begin with, I'm willing to set up an intensive one-month session. During this, you will remain with your detail at all times. You'll be expected to also attend to your full duties. This is to train your agents to identify and deal with royal fatigue. It's expected you'll succumb to general exhaustion and stress within one to two weeks." Meredith's mouth twitched, then she smiled. "It may be embarrassing."

"I'll pay you if you plan a relocation scenario meant to antagonize my father."

She arched a brow. "While the offer is appreciated, I'm already paid to plan all types of scenarios. Your team will be expected to protect you from numerous relocation scenarios."

"My grandmother will be visiting the kingdom and would enjoy helping."

"I've been briefed about Illinois's unique relationship with South Dakota's royal family. I'll inquire."

"What do you need from me for this?"

"During training, act as you actually do. If you'd indulge in cat-like behavior because of your father's contribution of genes, do so. Behave normally. Anything else will hurt your team's ability to protect you and monitor your whereabouts."

I thought about it. "If you run me into the ground, I'll probably try to run away when I finally snap," I admitted.

"Then please do your best when you run. It's a good training exercise."

"If I start drinking, I expect an immediate intervention. I drink twice a year: Christmas and my birthday."

"No other holidays?"

"No. I'm the adult supervision the rest of the year."

"Consider it noted. You'll be expected to get drunk once for training purposes."

I wrinkled my nose. "When you're stocking the drinks for this party, I like girly drinks because they taste better than the straight shit and get the job done faster."

"You're not a fan of the taste of alcohol, are you?"

"Not at all. I just like to pretend I'm an adult of legal drinking age every rare now and then. What do you think of Evangeline?"

Meredith's smile worried me. "I wish you the best of luck, Your Highness. You'll need it."

Every year, the candidates to join the RPS were similar. Young men used to being the best applied to continue being the best. Meredith observed from beside the door, which put her in the best position to take out anyone who might come in. My desk would act as a barrier to slow intruders down, buying my agent sufficient time to protect me.

All in all, I was torn between relief I had

an agent again and annoyance that I needed one.

Complaining about it wouldn't do me any good, so I did the only thing I could. I directed my attention back to the problem of finding agents who'd stick around for a change. "Have you gone through these, Meredith?"

"I have, sir."

"Do any of these actually have potential? Don't get me wrong, they look like the cream of the crop, but this is the same type who can't deal with my yearly transformation in the spring."

"I have my doubts."

"Do we have candidates with promising talents and skills from the lower castes?"

"I have a foot-tall stack of such applicants, sir."

"And these are applicants who've already gone through base review?"

"Yes, sir."

Interesting. I'd have to remember there were far more viable applicants than I'd believed. "Take the best five from this pool and fill out the rest of the roster from the lower caste applicants. To make it clear they're here on merit, we'll ban all caste badges from trainees. Washouts will be replaced by random draw."

"Random draw, sir?"

"They wouldn't have gotten to this stage if they didn't pass muster with someone.

They've been reviewed, which I assume means they've passed their background checks and basic competency checks. Random draw is a fair method of picking replacements. I think I've already established that picking the best of the best won't work in my situation."

"Why include any of them, then?"

"The lower caste recruits need a chance to work with elites. It'll take them time to figure out how to interact with them as equals."

She smiled, and her approval startled me. "Any other requests?"

"I want the trainees to be a fifty-fifty split of men and women, even if it means we need to recruit from outside of the kingdom to find ladies willing to take on the job. My top requirement is that they must be able to work well with Evangeline."

"You mean to train her detail along with yours. I would like to remind you that you're not even certain if she'll accept you as her partner."

Partner was a good way to consider her; I wanted everything. But being her partner was ideal. I wanted to become her husband. I wanted to become her everything. I doubted I'd ever find someone like her again. The thought of losing my chance to prove I could be a good partner for her created a tight ball in my chest.

I inhaled, held my breath until the tension in my chest peaked, and released it in a sigh.

"If they can work well with Evangeline, they'll be able to work with anyone. We can run scenarios where agents take turns being the principal. Evangeline should excel in that role just from her experience living on her own and her skillset. She's used to taking care of herself. She'll have the same issues royals do working with their details. She's headstrong. Should we be able to partner together, she'll be ready to take her place as my queen. Better yet, her detail will be ready, too."

"The agents may not approve."

"If she's playing the role of principal often, she'll be perceived as a principal rather than a fellow agent. She'll also be respected due to her skills and abilities."

"That's a gamble, sir. RPS agents are all the same breed; they are competitive and take their work seriously. Everything she does will be scrutinized when she's working in the role of the principal. The agents will not forget she's supposed to be one of them."

While I acknowledged Meredith had a point, I also couldn't force myself to agree with her. "Doing things the safe way hasn't done me any good yet, so I need to gamble. I'm okay with gambling. I can deal with failure. I expect failure. I expect my attempts with Evangeline will result in an unmitigated disaster, and it's entirely possible I'll spend years trying to convince her to forgive me. Abdication might become a requirement, and it's not just due to this issue."

The real reason my father reacted as he had wasn't because of Evangeline, it wasn't even because of my lack of a stable detail.

The reality of what I faced likely sank in for him.

Meredith waited, her brow arched in silent questioning.

"There's unrest in the congress. I can't rule without a queen. This might work—and it might buy me time. Unfortunately, it might confirm I'll live a cursed life."

"Abdication is a serious step, Your Highness."

"I can't rule without a queen, and I've already made up my mind." My next words might condemn me to a shortened, feathered life, one that would inevitably end in a forest unable to return to human form. "Where Evangeline goes, I'll follow. My father's crown means nothing to me if I have to rule his kingdom as part man, part beast. She knows me for what I am. If she can't accept me for all I am, I can't expect anyone else to."

"She knows your animal form?"

"Yes, she does."

"That was not in her file."

"Christian's aware. I told him. I'd rather that information didn't spread, so I don't want it written down anywhere."

"Is it true she marked you? And that you refused to have her brand removed?"

"It's true."

Her cheek twitched. "I'll allow the brand

to remain, but only because it'll allow her to protect you better. Your circumstances are also a part of the reason why I'll allow this. In any other situation, I would be having it removed immediately, even if I had to subdue you to have it done."

After having subdued my father with my fist, I had no doubt Meredith would stoop to similar levels to have her way.

RPS agents were required to protect their principals, and nothing in their rulebook stated they couldn't get rough if their royal put up a fight.

"Thank you."

"Now, with that said, I need to disclose the potential consequences of a long-term brand. Depending on her talent, it could become a permanent bond. If she has any latent healing talents, it could form a life bond."

I'd heard of leech bonds, but not life bonds before. "You've lost me. A life bond?"

"Should she die, you'll die. That's a life bond."

Enlightenment struck me, and I fought my urge to laugh. My family's curse came bundled with such a bond, or so I believed. I wondered if Meredith could confirm it, so I said, "My great-grandma is a hundred and thirty years old. She looks like she's fifty. Is that what you mean? If so, we just consider that a part of the family curse."

Meredith's eyes widened. "Oh."

"My great-great-grandparents are still alive, too."

"You're serious? They are? They weren't in any of the paperwork."

My great-great-grandfather's fate would be mine by the time I was thirty if I didn't get my act in gear and find someone to keep me human. Confessing the truth of the family curse hurt, but it offered a sense of freedom and release, too. "He's no longer human. He hasn't become a human since before I was born. He's the start of our line, and a living reminder of what we face if we fail to control our magic."

"And your great-great-grandmother?"

"She found a way to join him. I suppose he sacrificed his humanity to share his magic with her. If I don't find my partner, that's my fate. One spring, I won't return to being human. I'm on a time limit, and if I get too close to it, I'll have to abdicate. I can't rule as an animal. I don't even know if I'll remember I'd ever been human."

"Has it happened to anyone else in your line?"

"Yes, it has. I have between roughly two to five years. None have made it beyond thirty without shifting to their beast and remaining a beast for the rest of their lives. I'll abdicate in the winter after I turn twenty-seven at the latest."

I had two more years, and if things didn't work out with Evangeline, my grandmother's scheme to match me with someone would be my last hope of staying human.

"Christian implied this was a serious situation, but I hadn't understood how serious. With this in mind, I'll move forward with your idea to ease Evangeline into acting as a principal for the majority of your training. I'll even look the other way if you win her over enough for some illicit activities to take place. However, I will expect you to keep me updated. If your relationship with her does develop, I need to know immediately."

"I really don't expect it will. Perhaps I can convince her to give us a try, but she's a professional at heart. No, your initial rules and assessment were correct. If I want any hope of becoming her partner, I need to respect those boundaries and convince her despite them. I'll be honest with you, Meredith. Until Evangeline, I didn't think I'd actually have a hope of finding someone who might want me for me. I'm not like the rest of my family. They're predators. They live for the hunt. I don't."

"You're a prey species, aren't you?"

"Yes, I am."

"This complicates things."

"Welcome to my life, Meredith." I sighed. "Welcome to my life."

AT TWELVE-THIRTY, I changed into a pair of

sweats and stretched in my office, grimacing at the lingering aches in my muscles.

"Are you sure you're up for this? She's not going to hold back."

"I expect she'll attempt to knock the sense back into me. It'll hurt, and next session, I'll work harder so it hurts less. Eventually, I might escape relatively unscathed. I won't improve unless I try."

"This won't be easy on you."

I appreciated Meredith's blunt honestly despite her words stinging my already battered pride. "I didn't expect easy. If I thought this would be easy, I'd walk onto the mat, ask her to marry me, and be done with it."

The new head of my detail laughed. "If you're going to attempt that, I recommend you wait until right after a particularly hard hit, one that leaves you breathless on the floor. That might leave a positive impression. Otherwise, I'd recommend against it."

"I will if you think it's wise. As I said, I'm hopeless at this."

Not only was I hopeless, I was running out of time. I had a guaranteed year or two left, and after that, it'd be the toss of a coin if I could return to my human life in the spring. No matter what I said to convince everyone I could approach the family curse at a leisurely pace, it was a lie—a lie everyone ignored because no one wanted to deal with the reality of my situation.

Christian had warned my father about

testing his luck, but my father would lose his heir one way or another if something didn't change soon.

"You're going to receive a hard rejection if you ask her after she floors you, but she'll remember you appreciated her efforts. It could also backfire. Why knows? Maybe it'll work. But don't hold your breath."

"I won't."

"Good. Stretch your left leg more; you're pulling your stride. You need it looked at after Evangeline tenderizes you on the mat."

I obeyed despite the stretches bordering on being painful enough I wanted to crawl to my couch and give up for the rest of the day.

"As I thought. You're really a mess, aren't you?"

"There's a legitimate reason I signed myself for torture sessions, Meredith. It's not just because I'm interested in Eva."

"I may have to reevaluate my training schedule if you're still moving like a cripple in two weeks. I'd planned to have a tolerably healthy principal."

"They don't get to choose when I'm limping. Neither do I, really. It's good practice for them. You'll also be able to sift out the ones with too much of an ego. If they can't deal with me when I'm out of shape and bruised to hell, they can't deal with me when I'm healthy, either."

"That's an interesting way to look at it."

I shrugged. "I may as well make the most

out of my condition. It's nothing new. I have these problems every year. In a few months, I'll be all right."

It had gotten a little harder each year to get back into shape, and I was prone to getting sicker and staying sicker for longer, but I'd try my best to keep my deteriorating health a private matter. The royal physicians weren't concerned, and while I recognized there was something wrong, I couldn't do much about it.

What they said went, and I could complain all day long without it changing anything. Ever since I'd turned fifteen, complaining about the yearly flu and general malaise earned me nothing but scoldings for whining.

It wasn't worth making a fuss over, especially when I was already running out of time.

I'd be doing my father a favor if I abdicated; he'd be able to find a stable heir who had a few extra years before the family curse kicked in for good.

"And this is a yearly issue?"

"Indeed." To appease Meredith, I did an extra full round of stretches. "I'm used to it. It's everyone else who has a problem."

"Have you seen the royal physicians about it?"

"Yes, of course. They know. They say there's not much to be done about it. They deal with the myriad of viruses I bring home every summer. The bruising and soreness is my problem."

"They're being assholes because they can." The anger in her voice made me pause, and I considered the situation.

Christian had found a perfect agent, and I didn't get to keep her. Could my luck get any worse? I assumed so, and I assumed my family would have something to do with it.

"That, too. I inconvenience a lot of people. It's not worth fighting."

"It's willful neglect."

That someone finally understood would've made me a happy man in the winter before I'd shifted for my yearly stint as a white and silver turkey. "It's okay, Meredith. I'm used to it. If I thought it was a serious issue, I'd recruit someone to help. I can take care of myself."

"That's unacceptable, Your Highness. You're the heir. How can anyone expect you to fulfill your duties if you're in a constant state of pain and illness? You're moving like it hurts, and you're moving in a way meant to hide that it hurts."

Damn it. I'd have to be more careful around her in the future. "You're definitely a more aggressive agent than I'm used to. I'm not sure what to tell you, Meredith. I've been dealing with this since I turned fifteen. It's part of why I've threatened to abdicate. It gets worse every year. Add in the family curse, and I'm in a downward spiral. It's best for the kingdom this way. I just need the excuse at this point."

"Please excuse me, Your Highness."

Meredith stepped outside of my office, and when the screaming started, I chuckled, shook my head, and gathered my things, stuffed them into my briefcase, and waited for the fireworks to end. Ten minutes until the interview was scheduled to begin, the argument hadn't stopped. I meandered to the elevator and headed for the gym so I wouldn't be late.

Meredith could catch up once she was done eviscerating Christian over my health and threat to abdicate. Arguing wouldn't change anything. She couldn't change reality, and no matter how much I wanted to hide or deny it, a simple truth remained.

I was tired.

Trouble waited for me in the gym; the entirety of my family, uncles and great-uncles included, lined the gym's walls to watch my beating. I supposed they could've been present to watch my father get a taste of just desserts, but I doubted it.

I hadn't broken the family curse yet, and too much hinged on me doing so.

Eva waited on the mat wearing a martial arts uniform of some sort, stretching with far more grace than my pitiful efforts. "Well, at least one of you isn't late. That's fucking something."

"You can blame me if His Majesty is late.

There's an agent-on-agent debate going on upstairs, and he usually won't wander off when there's free entertainment to be had."

"Whatever. Tardiness results in a harder training session. As you were here on time, you'll get a standard spar. Put that fancy leather purse down and get your ass on the mat. We don't have all day, and I want to see what you're capable of."

I tossed my briefcase to Grégoire. "Beat any overly caring royal idiots into unconsciousness if they interfere."

"You got it. Hey, lady? Please don't kill my cousin. I don't want to be the next king."

"He can't pay me to beat him if he's dead. Are you a moron?"

"Yes, I am, ma'am."

Eva sighed and stared me in the eyes. "What would I have to do for a chance to beat that one, too?"

"Not much. He could use the exercise."

"Not cool, Kel. Not cool."

I allowed myself a grim smile. "He's a scaredy cat like my father."

"All right. Get your ass over here. To start with, I want to see how you move. Your job is to try to hit me. I don't care how you do it, but try to hit me like you mean it. If you can. I can learn a lot about what you know by how you move."

I foresaw a great deal of pain in my future along with a close introduction to the mat. "What's off limits?"

"Nothing."

Every man in my family snickered, my mother scowled and sighed, and I expected to be screamed at for hours if I hit Eva anywhere inappropriate. I'd be aiming to hit whatever I could and expected to fail, but my mother would never learn that from me.

Had any member of my family asked, I would've bluffed or just aimed right for the face like I had with my father. With Eva, she'd get the straight-up truth. "I basically have no idea what I'm doing, but okay."

"Do your best."

Had I not heard her talk, cuss worse than any sailor I'd ever met, and seen her background record, I might've believed her to be a compassionate woman ready to dish out the encouragement.

I knew better.

I doubted I'd be able to beat her using speed. Hell, I doubted I'd be able to touch her no matter what I did. With few options, I adopted my father's tendency to stalk his prey, circling and keeping an eye on how she moved. Feathers on a breeze had nothing on her, and if I managed to brush her clothes with my fingertips, I'd consider it my win.

"You're never going to hit me if we spend all day dancing."

"I'm pretty sure you're faster me, and I have no idea where to even try to hit you," I confessed.

She pointed at her breasts. "If you can hit

my center of mass, you have a chance of unbalancing me with a little work and some tactics. For example, if you destabilize my leg and throw me off balance at the chest, you might be able to knock me over."

I'd seen tactics like that in the movies, but I'd always believed it was choreographed and wouldn't work in reality. "You mean like in the movies when someone spins into a kick and whips his arm at his opponent's chest?"

"I hate those stupid, inaccurate movies. But yes, the idea is similar, but please don't try that. You'd kill yourself and the whiners along the wall would get pissy."

"I'd try that and fall on my face. You might be able to pay me to try it, but it'd have to be a damned good bribe." Laughing, I stepped forward and whipped my arm at her side. As expected, she whirled away without me touching her.

If I wanted her to flatten me so hard I begged her to marry me in front of my entire family, I'd have to do a lot better. In an endurance fight, I'd lose. I'd lose in any sort of fight. After I recovered from my yearly illnesses, I'd have a decent chance of outrunning her, but I wasn't going to hold my breath for that, either. She'd just wait until I tired, track me using her brand, and win anyway.

I'd never enjoyed the thought of losing before.

I lunged as I had before, waited for her to spin, and dove for her. In a perfect would, I would've touched her before she cracked her arm into my chest, flipped me onto my back, and drove the air out of my lungs.

Three months in the wild and fear of death kept me mobile, and I rolled to escape any additional pummeling.

Eva chuckled. "Catch your breath and try again. This time, I'll stand still for you."

If she didn't dodge, I'd have a better chance of hitting her and vastly better chances of being flattened so hard I'd humiliate myself with the world's worst proposal. If I wanted to get a hit in on her before she flattened me, I'd have to do something unexpected. She likely believed I was a royal gentleman like the rest of my family; I rarely cussed, I did as most expected from those born with a silver spoon crammed up their asses, and I'd been taught my manners.

Hitting a woman in the face simply wasn't done.

In the slim chance I landed a hit, I hoped she'd forgive me. I grunted, got to my feet, and shook myself off, waiting until I no longer gasped for air. "All right."

"This time, pick your target but try to watch how I move. Self-defense is all about reading your opponent and maximizing non-lethal pain to buy yourself time to escape. In your case, lethal pain is also acceptable, although we'll keep all of our sparring to non-lethal tactics."

"This is going to hurt, isn't it?"

"You better fucking believe it, princess."

As she'd already invited me to hit her chest, I'd enjoy the view while I gathered the courage to walk into my next beating. I had two hands. I'd use my right to aim for her perfect breasts and my left to target her face. I'd try to avoid her nose and mouth; making her bleed wasn't on my list of things to do.

Black eyes healed better than a broken nose or a split lip.

Expecting pain without reward, I dove into the fray.

I WOKE on the mat to Eva batting my cheeks and holding fingers in front of my face. "Count 'em, princess," she ordered.

Sometime after trying to grab her chest and hit her in the face, Eva had smacked me down so hard I remembered nothing.

Meredith was right. One option stood before the rest, and a wise man didn't allow such an opportunity to escape. "Please marry me."

"Please marry me is not a number."

I squinted at her blurred hand. "I'm going to need a few minutes on the number. I'm not sure I could give you my phone number right now."

"You're not slurring, your eyes are mostly focusing as far as I can tell. You're not going to die from that. Blink a few times, take a few minutes to catch your breath, and walk it off."

"That's always good news." I blinked a few times as ordered to discover Eva was flipping someone off, and I didn't think it was me. "It's one finger. Your middle one, and I think you're pointing it at some member of my family, so my initial statement still stands. Please marry me."

"You're a nutter. Go to the wall and take a breather while I beat the idiot growling at me for knocking the sense out of you."

"I expect there are a lot of growling idiots in this room. Please feel free to beat as many of them as you'd like."

"That would take all night."

"Perhaps we could discuss future beatings over dinner?"

"Deal. You need a better diet and a trip to the doctor, by the way. You're at least ten pounds underweight. We'll discuss what you should be eating over dinner along with an exercise regime to get you into tolerable shape. I can't work you properly if knocking you over is going to knock you out." Eva scowled, and her attention focused on someone other than me. "Which one of you assholes is responsible for this Your Highness's general health? You're at the front of the line, and you deserve every fucking bruise I give you."

I sat up and grimaced at the throb centered in the back of my head. "Those would be the royal physicians, and I think Meredith's already out for their blood, but please feel free to share with her. Dad's the one who hired them, so he should go first."

"Any other culprits?"

"My mother would be second."

"Kelvin," my mother snapped.

"Go sit with your agent, Your Highness. I'll take care of this mess."

As I was sometimes a wise man, I retreated to Meredith, sat at her feet, and hoped she wasn't going to have a round with me, too.

My agent crouched beside me and gave me a companionable pat on the back. "You hit her. She deflected your right hand. You booped her on the nose with your left."

"Booped? I did what?"

"You tapped her just hard enough she knew you'd caught her flatfooted at her own game. Then she took you out like a lion after a three-legged gazelle. I figured you don't remember any of that. You hit the mat hard. In good news, you weren't out long."

"I don't remember that."

"It's not uncommon. Good use of humor with your marriage proposal. Your entire family heard you. Expect trouble."

"You were right about the rejection part."

"All she did was tell you 'Please marry me is not a number.' That's not a rejection. And she agreed to have dinner with you tonight. That's definitely not a rejection."

"That's only so she can beat me more efficiently later."

"Take what you can get, Your Highness. It went much better than I thought it would, truth be told. I'm surprised."

"Why are you surprised?"

"She just doesn't seem like the type to leave such a proposal open. She's crude, but she doesn't toy with people. Not like that. Every time someone has come into her comfort zone, she's been very aggressive about making it clear she's not interested."

"She's probably distracted and pissed my health is messing with her plans to evaluate how useless I am in a fight. I tried to tell her I know nothing."

"You're probably right. Most royals have rudimentary training."

"I can hold a sword, barely. I missed the rest of the training."

"Please tell me you've done some RPS scenario training."

"There's zero chance I'll meet your standards on this. I've done the basics, but I've never had a stable or cohesive detail. It's hard to do anything beyond the basics when the detail can't hold together."

"It's like they want you to be killed," she muttered.

"Why waste the effort? Everybody here knows what'll happen in a few years, and it's not like there aren't plenty of other options in this room. And when I'm realistic about it,

I'm not going to win any popularity contests. I'm private and known to be erratic. I'm unsurprised. Hell, I'm only the heir because I'm the only child with the right talent."

"Your brother doesn't have it? I noticed he isn't here."

I wanted to think better of my mother and father, but I had no doubt my little brother was at the castle or being shipped off to boarding school so he wouldn't be exposed to Eva and her inevitable corruptions. "Don't worry about it. It's only to be expected."

White turkey, black sheep. In my family, it was one and the same. While I wanted to rest all my hopes on Eva, I couldn't help but wonder if I'd do Illinois more justice in surrendering to the inevitable rather than stirring royal trouble on a maybe.

I'd think about it after dinner.

NINE

I'd made it clear I'd drawn lines.

MY GREAT-GRANDPA BROKE Eva's arm and flattened her with one hit, and my plans to think about my actions after dinner came to an abrupt halt. After spending his entire long life learning to control his strength, the truth stared me right in the face.

He'd hurt Eva on purpose. Depending on how her arm healed, she might never be able to hold a bow again. I rose to my feet. Instead of the heat I expected, fury turned me to ice.

If they wanted me dead, if they wanted the curse to take root and leave me stuck as an animal for the rest of my unnatural life, they were going about it the right way.

It made my decision much easier to make.

Illinois needed someone reliable, and I'd leave my human life with my pride intact.

I lifted my chin, taking my time looking at each member of my family in the eyes before locking onto my father. He stared back, his expression neutral. Waiting.

He'd been warned, and he was about to find out his son had more steel in his spine than he'd like.

"Meredith, please accept my apologies, but your services are no longer required. I hereby abdicate to Grégoire, effective immediately."

Maybe another day, if I had more days in my life than I expected, I'd regret my choice. Then again, I wouldn't. It'd be unlikely I lived long enough for it to matter.

The silence hung heavy, and it fueled the fury freezing my blood in my veins.

I'd always been taught silence was assent, and I saw no need to believe otherwise.

"Agent Scarson, I would be appreciative if you could see Eva's arm tended to properly. It seems your thoughts on certain matters are accurate. I'll fill out the paperwork and submit them to the congress myself. I hereby invoke the self-disowning clause and cut all ties, also effective immediately."

It would take a miracle, an approved order from the congress, and my signature to undo my words, but I no longer cared.

They could all rot in hell for all I cared.

"I'll see it taken care of, Mr. Averett."

If I ever saw Meredith again, I'd have to thank her. By stripping me of my titled, witnessed by Christian, she confirmed my edict and would fulfill her duties from the RPS side of things.

Someone tried to say something to me, but my heartbeat throbbed in my ears and drowned out the words. If my luck held out, Meredith, Christian, and the other RPS agents stationed in the room would uphold the law.

I had an hour to leave the building. It would take me less than that to change, print out the appropriate forms, and sign them. I'd leave them on my desk for someone else to deal with, a final jab at the royal family for having betrayed me one last time.

I'd made it clear I'd drawn lines, and they'd crossed them without care.

The congress would have to live without a personal delivery of their precious papers and deal with the fallout of my abdication on their own. Most would rejoice.

I marched out of the gym, and once I stopped looking at my father, I refused to acknowledge any member of the royal family.

In my office, I filled out the forms, signed them, and dug through the bottom drawer of my desk for the spare key to the car I had parked in the garage but rarely used. Tucked in the very back behind some files was a roll of twenties I kept around when I wanted delivery.

The four hundred and twenty would take me as far as I needed to go, and once I'd gotten far enough, I'd dump the vehicle for someone to find later.

One change of clothes later and with fifty-two minutes left on my countdown, I left the building, shaking with rage.

Unlike most of the royal family, my personal car was as common as dirt and a boring gray. Its tags marked it as a government vehicle. No one would look at it twice. It was one of many in Chicago, but once I left the city, it'd be a novelty.

No one associated dirt cheap, common cars as property of a former member of the royal family. In a few days, my father could take my vehicle and shove it up his ass for all I cared. My great-grandpa wouldn't have acted without my father's encouragement—or my mother's. Either way, my parents held the majority of the blame.

My father had known I'd issued an ultimatum, and he'd given me his answer using my great-grandpa.

As I expected someone would track my movements, I left the garage and headed in the direction of Congressional Hall, but instead of delivering the papers I hadn't brought with me, I kept going.

Driving helped cool my anger, but it didn't change anything else. I could come up with a hundred different reasons why my great-grandpa would break Eva's arm. None of them were for my sake. The betrayal cut deep, and I hoped they'd finally gotten what they wanted.

Had my parents been behind the royal physicians discounting my yearly illnesses and the prolonged time it took for me to recover? I'd tried to tell them, but I'd given up.

Had it been on my parents' orders?

Either my father hadn't believed I'd abdicate or he'd taken advantage of the opportunity to be rid of me. It didn't matter.

Not anymore.

My hope Eva could've been my one and only broke apart, a hope as fragile as her arm beneath a grizzly's blow. The bone had snapped loud enough I'd heard it. I wanted to forget the sound of it breaking and the thump of her body striking the mat.

Both haunted me.

My own family had sabotaged my last hope for a future, and they'd done it in a way meant to hurt Eva the most. It would've been kinder to kill me off to get their way. But no. That would've ruined the royal family's reputation. They could call Eva's injury a training accident.

I'd been as much of the target as her. I'd made my stand. The inevitability of the family curse hung heavily on my shoulders, and it dictated where I drove.

What was the point of fighting against the inevitable I'd spent years struggling to ignore? I'd run out of reasons why. My family had been my reason to keep putting one foot in front of the other.

News of my abdication would cause the royal family trouble, but the kingdom would enjoy the stability Grégoire could provide. Unlike me, he was more aggressive about finding the perfect woman for him. I gave it one or two years before he settled down. His queen would unlock his ability to control his talent, and life would go on.

He had the extra years I didn't to find someone. When the weight of his future crown came crashing down, he'd have every reason to do as the rest of our bloodline had. One day, if I lived long enough for it to matter, I might even feel guilty over leaving him to do my job.

I needed to stop being overly optimistic about the future I had left.

Every spring, I picked a new forest to occupy, although I'd avoided the larger ones, wary of venturing too deep into the woods to make it out on my own. My old rules no longer applied; becoming lost no longer factored into my choice. Of the forests within Illinois's borders, Huron-Manistee provided everything I needed to disappear without a trace. Not even the royal family could search a million acres with much hope of success. If Christian told them my secret, they'd need more than luck to find a turkey, assuming I stayed off the radar and survived until the spring.

Living for that long would be a challenge, one I wasn't certain I could overcome anymore.

The drive to Huron-Manistee took me five hours, and I parked in the public lot after paying ten dollars in penance at one of the automated machines to keep the vehicle there until nightfall without anyone paying it any attention. Sometime after dark, someone would run the tags and report my car's presence. They might tow it for safe keeping, but my registration information would come up.

They'd know who owned the vehicle.

I didn't have much time to venture into the park and lose myself among the trees.

If all went as I expected, the royal family would delay announcing my abdication for as long as possible in the hopes of a reversal, one I had no intention of signing.

They might get away with it for months if they opted to leave the forms on my desk. In theory, they might even find some loophole to stall the legalities.

I refused to waste my time on the details. With almost a million of acres to search, there'd be only one way for them to find me. I wished the royal family luck convincing Eva to help them after breaking her arm.

Eva had no reason to use her magic for their sake. She hadn't wanted to interview for the RPS job in the first place. If her arm didn't heal well, she'd lose everything she'd built through her hard work.

Guilt, as always, ate away at me. After a quick check of the trail map, I picked a spot as far off the beaten path as I could, and I walked.

THE WEATHER SOURED AT NIGHTFALL, the temperature dropped, and the skies opened. Rain hammered the trail, transforming it into a muddy mess, one that promised hell to anyone foolish enough to remain outdoors. An hour and a half of hiking hadn't put me far enough into the forest, but it would have to do.

There was no way I'd gone more than a few miles down the quiet trails. In the time I'd started my hike, I hadn't run into anyone at all.

Sane hikers would've checked the weather and gone another day, I supposed.

A few miles would have to do to satisfy my sole criteria of becoming lost. If I went west, I'd hit Lake Michigan eventually. Heading east would take me outside of the park at some point, which wouldn't work for my needs. If I found the lake, I'd follow it north before making the hike deeper into the forest.

If I'd done everything as everyone else wanted, I would've married Gail. The truth would've been exposed faster. Averett men didn't divorce. Till death was a vow taken seriously, and when they gave their vow, death itself was defied. No, marrying Gail would've only led to my death a little faster.

If I couldn't love her no matter how hard I'd tried, I had no hope of living a day beyond thirty.

I wondered if my family remembered that when they'd taken the spar a step too far.

My doubts chilled me almost as much as the downpour. Leaving the trail would likely be one of the last things I did. For a long time, I stood and thought about it. Lightning flashed across the sky, and the thunder boomed as though urging me to make a decision one way or the other.

Every day of my life, I'd tried to live up to their expectations only to fail time and time again. Even my species, something I had no control over, couldn't meet anyone's standards. The truth hurt, but I faced it as I should've long ago.

Had I been wise, I would've abdicated the instant I'd returned to being human after my first spring as a turkey. Prolonging the inevitable hadn't done anyone any good.

In the end, the fault was with me and my cowardice. If I hadn't kept the truth hidden, everyone would've been able to accept I'd never be what was needed.

Every year, I'd worked hard to make up for my failings. Had my father refused to believe me when I'd promised to abdicate? Christian had, and the RPS agent would hold himself responsible. He'd tried to tell my father.

My father hadn't listened.

My parents had probably filled my great-grandpa's ears with some twisted version of the truth meant to turn him against Eva—and ultimately against me. I just didn't understand why.

Eva hadn't done anything wrong.

Why had I wanted to stay human in the first place? As a beast, survival trumped all, and I'd learned how to cope with the solitude. As a man, the solitude chased me into crowded rooms. The fault remained mine.

I'd allowed myself to believe I had a future, and I'd tried too hard.

I was so tired of being human. I was so tired of living a half life, fearing when someone would learn the truth.

No matter what I did, I'd never be good enough to stand equal among predators. I'd always disappoint.

All things considered, it amazed me I hadn't given up sooner. I shook my head and stepped off the beaten path, wondering how long I'd wander before I finally stopped.

When I couldn't take another step, the storm still raged through the night, and I sat beneath a proud oak to listen to the drain drumming through the leaves.

HAD I been taking better care of myself, if I hadn't been fighting off the remnants of my yearly cold, things might've been different. The fever hit hard and fast, but I lacked the strength or will to do anything about it. Instead of seeking fresh water and buying myself a month of survival, assuming the cold didn't kill me, I stared through the trees and waited for dawn. When the sun rose, the rain eased to chilly mist. Noon brought clear skies, but the sun couldn't warm me, not when the fever made way for chills.

At some point, I went from thirsty to exhausted. The realization sank in—Eva had been right to line people up and start beating sense into them.

Had I been healthier, it would've taken a lot longer than twenty-four hours for me to reach the point where I understood if I closed my eyes I might not open them again. I found cold comfort in the fact I wouldn't take anyone with me when I went. By my own words, I'd condemned myself to having nothing.

Had I done things properly, I would've filed the official paperwork, and citing medical malpractice I suspected would be easily verified, I would've been awarded a large enough settlement to buy me a few years of comfort before I slid into life as a null stripped of all rank and privilege, all evidence of my heritage erased.

In reality, the settlement wouldn't have needed to last long, so I spared everyone the hassle. There'd be questions, but I'd pulled the cord as painlessly as I could.

I'd tried.

I was so tired of trying.

I hadn't needed their approval to pursue

Eva, but I couldn't win against betrayal and obstruction. Others could stand fast time and time again. Some could climb any mountain dumped in front of them. Some never found their limit, enduring despite the odds stacked against them.

Fighting year after year had worn me thin, and every summer I stayed sicker for longer. Had I listened to my body, I would've understood sooner I lived on borrowed time.

Maybe my weary heart and body knew best of all my time ran short.

With nothing left to do, I waited.

TEN

> Well, at least you're man enough to admit it.

NOTHING WENT RIGHT, not even death, but I appreciated the hallucination of Eva. I'd conjured her without a broken arm, safe and sound, perfectly grumpy, and spewing curses. Any other man would've flinched at her disapproving expression. When she noticed me watching her, she announced, "You're a fucking idiot."

I opened my mouth to discover that it and my throat were so parched it hurt to breathe. I nodded.

Appeasing the hallucination might keep her around a bit longer before she bludgeoned me back into the black void death was supposed to be.

"Well, at least you're man enough to admit it. A broken arm isn't that big of a deal. They heal. This? This is just stupidity. Are you trying to catch your death out here? And while I'm at it, it wouldn't have hurt for you to eat something on route to your ill-planned camping trip, you feather-brained dunce. I've never seen one man create so much drama in my entire fucking life."

By some miracle, I forced my tongue to cooperate with me. "You obviously haven't met my family."

"They're fucking assholes. They're sorry fucking assholes, but they're still assholes. I'd be dramatic, too, if I had to put up with such a bunch of shit-brained, inconsiderate lowlife scum suckers!" She shot a glare over her shoulder. "Useless man whores, all of them."

For some reason I couldn't fathom, I felt the need to defend them. "They were only man whores before they got married."

"If women can't ditch the slut rep, neither can the prissy princesses pretending they're men who are incapable of minding their own fucking business. Was it really necessary to hike ten miles into this wet hellhole? Because seriously, how the fuck did you even manage that when you're in as shitty of a condition as you are? Then you have the fucking nerve to skip dinner?"

I should've known my subconscious would punish me for skipping dinner with Eva. "Please blame the royal family populated by fucking assholes."

"The one's only a minor asshole. The others can go fucking rot in hell. Apparently, they seem to believe I can convince you to negate your abdication and exit from their asshole family. Why the fuck would they think I'd encourage you to go back to that sort of shit? I told them they could go fuck themselves with a stick. They aren't good at listening."

As I wouldn't want to hallucinate my family coming near me anytime soon, I came to the conclusion I'd failed to meet my end in the forest. I coughed, which sapped the little energy I had left. "They really aren't."

"They haven't turned in your fancy piece of paper in the hopes you'd change your mind. Those RPS agents? Total dicks, dude. I ain't ever seen so many pissed off dudes in suits before in my entire life. The lead dude in a suit is a master of the silent treatment. The ruler assholes can't even take a shit without earning his disapproval. It's pretty hilarious, actually. There's so much drama in this family I'm surprised they haven't choked on it yet." Eva twisted around. "You all are worse than teenagers!"

"Don't insult teenagers," I chided. "They're so much better than my family. I want to say I have the weirdest fucking hallucinations, but this isn't a hallucination, is it?"

"I have some bad news for you. You're not hallucinating. Unfortunately, neither am I. There's a damned pack of wolves, a goddamned lion, and a runty, brain-dead cat back there all pissed their precious, superior noses couldn't track you while I could. I'm not fucking talking to the grizzly right now.

If he comes within ten feet of me, I swear I'll shoot the mangy fucker."

"I'm sorry he broke your arm."

"Oh. That. Bad angle. He didn't hit me that hard. No, I'm pissed the fuck off because he fucking licked me."

"He what?"

"He licked me."

"I'll help you kill him," I growled.

"You couldn't kill an ant right now, you feather-brained dipshit."

I needed to figure out how to get her to cuss at me all the time. For the rest of my life would be good, however long or short that was. "You're probably right."

"I know I'm right. Here's what's going to happen. The dudette in a suit is going to come over here and talk to you. You're going to play nice and tell her you'll put a thirty-day stay on your abandonment of the shit ship that's your family. Then you're going to take a nap for a while. I'll settle with a nod if you're not up for talking. Until you do, those furry busybody idiots and their dudes in suits can't do jack shit. The dudette in a suit can because she was part of your detail."

"Loopholes," I grumbled.

"Lifesaving loopholes, dumbass. You've impressed upon the dudes in suits you were completely correct regarding the situation with your detail. The dudette in a suit is pretty pissed at the whole lot of fuckers."

Dealing with Meredith seemed like a lot

of work when I struggled to handle Eva alone. "Can't I just tell you?"

"I'll try to convince them you authorized it through me, but no promises. Fuck, they should be grateful. I'm surrounded by damned morons. I'd say stay, but you're not going anywhere without an intervention. Look on the bright side. You won't be conscious for the embarrassing part, which involves figuring out how the fuck we're going to get you out of here."

I hated she was right, and too tired to argue with her, I surrendered without a fight. I only meant to close my eyes for a moment, but exhaustion dragged me into darkness and refused to let me go.

THE NEXT TIME I wanted to avoid a confrontation, unconsciousness worked well. If Meredith had tried to talk to me, I remembered nothing of it. The details of leaving the forest and arriving at a hospital remained a mystery, and when coherency reluctantly returned, Meredith stood guard near the door.

An older woman in a doctor's coat clucked her tongue at me, and I wondered what I'd done to earn her disapproval. After ten possibilities, I gave up trying to pinpoint a singular reason.

The only good thing about my situation was the fact I didn't recognize her.

"Good afternoon, Your Highness. I'm Dr. Hampford, and I'm in charge of your care for the foreseeable future. You've been here for three days undergoing treatments for a mild concussion, pneumonia, a rather persistent cold virus, and malnutrition. If your lungs sound better in the morning, it's possible I can authorize your discharge to a nearby hotel for the remainder of your recovery, which will take a minimum of one to two weeks. I've been informed you're familiar with the routine."

I croaked something she interpreted as an acknowledgement, nodded, and offered me a cup of water with a straw. "Drink slowly."

The first few sips didn't make it to my throat. Once I felt almost human again, I croaked, "Pneumonia sucks."

"It certainly does. We had you on a ventilator for two days; your breathing was inconsistent, resulting in low blood-oxygen levels. From what I can tell, you've had viral pneumonia for at least a week prior to admission. Stress triggered and exposure worsened your condition. Instead of a fairly simple treatment, I've had to do extensive work to make sufficient progress to safely remove you from the ventilator so I could finish an otherwise basic procedure."

The thought of trying to explain my yearly illnesses tired me.

Meredith cleared her throat.

"Go ahead, Agent Scarson. Now that your

principal is coherent enough to verify your observations, I can consider them."

"I watched a physical evaluation in a controlled environment, which was the triggering element of this dispute. Neglect from the royal physicians is probable. I'd be comfortable witnessing in court there was evidence of substantial physical strain prior to his concussion. In my short time with him, he's had every critical marker of psychological strain. I acted in what I felt was his best interests at the time. I was unaware the situation was worse than I'd suspected."

"I'm not faulting you for your choices, Agent Scarson. An abdication can be overturned, as can a willful familial severance. You had no reasonable way of knowing the severity of the situation, nor can you be held responsible. Others are the guilty party in this. That said, there are serious health issues that will need to be addressed. If these issues aren't addressed to my satisfaction, I'll block any and all attempts to officially reinstate my patient as the heir of Illinois."

"Understood, Dr. Hampford."

"Now, if you could convince His Highness to put in a year's notice on a conditional abdication due to his health, the kingdom would be grateful. This will settle unrest issues and give His Highness time to handle his current situation. The paperwork involved would allow for a year extension of his notice if his general health improves. This also gives the royal family sufficient time to train a new heir should it be required."

Meredith sighed. "Your Highness, Dr. Hampford is a royal physician employed by Montana for viral and contagious illnesses, brought here at my request. I cited concerns of deliberate intent to harm you. You shouldn't have been in the condition you were, especially not when there's evidence you'd been in the care of royal physicians." Meredith scowled. "I took the liberty of barring visits from all members of the royal family until an evaluation has been done to determine if they were involved in your mistreatment."

"As other agents are supporting this claim as well, the royal family has zero recourse. You'll be left alone to recover in peace and quiet until you're ready for a formal meeting with them," Dr. Hampford added.

"Is this formal year notice in writing?" I asked.

"Montana drew it up on your behalf. It's awaiting your signature." Meredith stepped away from the door, picked up a briefcase, and handed it to Dr. Hampford. "There are conditions for your full reinstatement as the heir, guidelines for you leaving the kingdom should you not be reinstated, and conditions for the extension. I've read over it. It's sane. It lays out your royal responsibilities until the first day of spring, at which time you'll absolved of all such duties due to the circumstances of your talent. It will resume again on the first day of summer and hold until either an extension is approved or you leave the kingdom. Due to the circumstances, Montana has proposed that there will be an exemption of status loss, and he will personally review proposals for you to join another royal family. The circumstances of your talent will be made known to your adoptive family, so in the worst-case scenario, you will have a suitable caretaker. His Royal Majesty of Montana is insistent you will be treated with dignity."

"I've made quite the mess, I see," I mumbled.

"You were sick, stressed, and exhausted. Add in a serious case of provocation, and no one in the RPS is surprised the situation escalated as it did. Christian told everyone you'd notified His Majesty of the possibility of abdication. You're at no fault for following through." Meredith returned to her post near the door. "I believe the two days you spent in critical condition in ICU sufficiently corrected misconceptions regarding the severity of the situation."

Dr. Hampford cleared her throat. "I feel it's important you understand that your hike into a park only sped your illness. It's probable your condition would've deteriorated to critical in the span of several days to a week at most."

"Damned cold."

"Viral pneumonia," she corrected. "All

things considered, should I authorize your release for tomorrow, it's strongly recommended you stay in bed for the vast majority of the time, else you'll be back here in intensive care again." Dr. Hampford set the briefcase at my feet, opened it, and offered a thick stack of paper to me along with a pen. "Read this and sign if you agree to the terms."

Like the well-trained gopher I so often was, I did as told.

INSTEAD OF ESCAPING from the hospital in the morning as Dr. Hampford hoped, I spent two weeks in the hospital battling setback after setback, most of them involving my lungs. Meredith upheld the family visitation ban, not that I was in any condition to care if anyone visited. I spent as much time in ICU as not.

It took Dr. Hampford a week to discover the cause of my illnesses and the reason for my slow recovery year after year. Unbeknownst to me, I'd been fighting against an immune disorder, and in a lucky roll of the dice, I'd developed one she could cure rather than combat with treatments. It took a specialist with the right talent and a volunteer to donate a substantial amount of bone marrow to replace my defective marrow so it would stop producing cells preventing my immune system from functioning properly.

To ensure my body didn't replace the donated bone marrow with defective cells, the first stage was to purge my body of as much of my natural marrow as possible, a painful procedure destined to keep me in the hospital for at least a month. Only after the faulty cells were killed off to Dr. Hampford's satisfaction was the donor's marrow introduced into my body.

It hurt like hell from start to finish, and I spent the month in the hospital in a special ward typically reserved for chemotherapy patients to prevent me from catching any illnesses I'd be unable to fight until the donor's marrow was established and confirmed to have taken root in my bones with the assistance of magic.

The procedure worked, and in what I counted as a miracle, I graduated from the hospital to bedrest at a nearby hotel with frequent visits to the hospital for monitoring.

Seventy-eight days following my initial hospitalization, Meredith delivered the good news: I was free and clear to resume my normal life on a light regime with monthly checkups. "If you were going to relapse, you would've done so by now." My agent smiled at me, and I wondered if she ever slept—or if another agent stood in for her while I slept.

Probably the latter.

Meredith liked reassuring me she wasn't going anywhere anytime soon, something I appreciated.

"In better news, I have one hell of a medical file supporting the probationary period, which reminds me. No one has told me how the congress reacted to the filings."

"It was entertaining. It's been recorded for your enjoyment if you'd like to watch the sessions regarding your condition. Montana thought it'd be wise if everything was handled in as open a fashion as possible, and as you were physically unable to attend any of the sessions, they were recorded for your review. I delivered the documentation when you were in surgery preparing for your transplant."

"Do you ever sleep?" If she didn't, I'd worry—and I'd have to find some way to contact Christian to get her some help so I wouldn't lose her before the year ended.

"I do. Please don't worry, Your Highness. I've had assistance with my duties; I've brought in a few friends from Texas and Hawaii, and we've begun building a proper detail for you. Everyone hired has read a copy of your transitional paperwork and understands most will be transferred to your replacement's detail. There will be several permanent positions on your detail, as you will be entitled to four agents following the end of the probationary period should you not remain in Illinois."

The question I feared most nagged me until I asked, "And Eva?"

"I was wondering when you'd work up the

nerve to ask. She's in rotation in the night shift. She had two weeks off to handle personal matters, but she is typically here when I'm not."

"Ha, so you do sleep."

Meredith chuckled. "I do. When Agent Evangeline isn't on duty in here, she's enjoying her second job, which involves making certain none of your family pays any unrequested visits. She's had several altercations with the grizzly, but she's emerged the clear victor every time. They're developing a rather odd relationship. Under the circumstances, I thought it wise to encourage it."

Before I got too angry, I'd try to be reasonable. "They're developing a what? Why?"

"The grizzly enjoys physical conflict and doesn't mind an earned beating. He tests her boundaries, she beats him until he leaves her territory, and this daily routine makes them both happy. The grizzly is staying at a hotel several blocks away. This ritual has drawn a certain amount of media attention, and whenever clips of their disputes are played, ratings increase."

I groaned. "He's letting her beat him up?"

"I believe he's trying to earn her trust through tolerated violence."

The world had turned upside down on me without appropriate notice. "Why would he do that?"

"Well, he did trigger your abdication, and Evangeline was the one who'd gotten her arm broken. If he can earn Evangeline's trust, he's hoping he can earn back your trust. I expect he'll have an easier time compared to the monarchs. Your grandmother on your mother's side is a very vocal woman."

I'd forgotten about her visit right along with Princess Abigail's stay in the kingdom. "I'm such an idiot."

"Why?"

"Princess Abigail was supposed to come to Illinois to get away from all this."

Meredith chuckled. "You have nothing to worry about. She's joined forces with your grandmother. They're having a splendid time. The only ones bothered by your filing are your immediate family and the congress."

"What do I need to look out for from the congress?"

"Expect pressure. Your hospitalization for a serious health issue has triggered a landslide of lawsuits against several of the royal physicians. As it only took Dr. Hampford a week to identify the base issue and a total of two months to complete treatment and prepare you for physical therapy, there's zero excuse for your condition. This should have been treated years ago. Also, no members of the royal family have been indicted although His Majesty has undergone a great deal of scrutiny over the progression of the disorder. From what Dr. Hampford can tell, you've had the disorder since your first shift. She suspects the deterioration of your bone marrow is the consequence of your family's unchecked talent and may be what triggers the irreversible shift. Upon discovery of your syndrome, several younger men in your family have been tested, and they all show evidence of bone marrow degradation."

"Grégoire?"

"Has been confirmed to have the syndrome but to a much milder extent. The current theory is your talent requires a compatible individual to rewrite certain biological processes. When you'd mentioned the age of your living relatives, I asked Christian. He agrees with my speculation, and Dr. Hampford has likewise contributed similar opinions. Men of your line seem to require a life bond to counter the syndrome."

"And the bone marrow transplant?"

"Dr. Hampton believes the procedure will reset your biology to your first shift. Degradation will likely resume at the same rate, which means you'll have ongoing problems with illness and require a transplant every five to ten years until you bond with someone."

I took my time thinking it through, and I realized Meredith had been relaying most of the critical updates about my progress rather than Dr. Hampford for the past week. "Why isn't Dr. Hampford telling me this?"

"Dr. Hampford has been running around like a chicken with its head cut off. She's currently at an appointment with the marrow donor. As this is new territory, the donor's health is being carefully monitored."

"Who is the donor?"

"I'm not at liberty to say at the donor's request. The donor wishes to remain anonymous. The only people who know the identity of the donor are myself, Dr. Hampford, and several other doctors and nurses at the hospital."

"Well, I'm appreciative, if it's possible to pass along the word."

"I'll tell the donor."

"Thank you." As though I didn't have enough problems to contend with, the subject of my uncertain future refused to leave me alone. As I'd run out of excuses and doctor's appointments to delay the inevitable, I asked, "What happens next?"

"Physical therapy, which will likely be done at the RPS training center. An office has been set up for you at the center so you won't need to go to the castle. As you've filed, this will begin the transition process. Grégoire is undergoing training, but it seems he lacks the appropriate temperament for rulership, so frustration levels are high. As I said, expect pressure. This incident has been a wake-up call for many, as they'd dramatically underestimated the amount of work you do."

"Someone had to do it."

"Indeed. With a treatment plan and monitoring, Dr. Hampford speculates you'll have as much time as you need to find a solution for your talent's limitations. Without a life bond, she does theorize the disorder will run its full progression by the time you're fifty. Repeated transplants will be hard on your body, and it's likely you'll die from pneumonia, as that seems to be the point of failure for your immune system. She hasn't figured out the biological reason for this yet."

"Compared to the rest of my family, I'll die young."

"Yes, you will."

"Pleasant thought."

"It's generally accepted your abdication will be a quiet way for you to retire and die in a peaceful environment." Meredith's expression darkened. "There are few who can do the transplants required, as it does require magic to do successfully."

"Which means I won't be able to have it done once my abdication is finalized." While I'd spent my life as a spoiled royal, I'd done enough budgets for various departments in the kingdom to have a realistic idea of how much people made. I'd never be able to afford treatments requiring specialized talents.

"That's correct. With your history of contracting pneumonia, it's more likely you'll die from illness rather than undergo your family's typical final shift. Dr. Hampford wanted you to be able to make an educated decision, and she thought I was the best one to discuss the options with you."

"She's probably right. Where does this realistically leave me?"

"A lot depends on you."

"What's your opinion?"

"While I won't judge you from sticking to your guns, Agent Evangeline has made progress forming a functional relationship with a grizzly."

"They're beating each other up."

"Loudly, with much cursing. I believe they enjoy it."

"He's not the king, Meredith."

"No, he's not. Resentment is to be expected. Ideally, you'll be able to work around the rest of the royal family. They've received the message that they've spectacularly burned bridges with you. It's been made clear their actions almost cost you your life. That's a difficult pill for parents to swallow."

"They should've left Eva alone."

"No one is arguing that point. You're an adult. If you want to hire an army of prostitutes, you can. Honestly, I believe you'd have plenty of women volunteer to see if they're compatible with you." Meredith's tone turned wry. "On your behalf, I've politely declined those invitations citing your health."

"Invitations? What invitations?"

"At last count, there were twenty-six royal invitations, and I lost count of the ones from elites in Illinois and abroad. Most of these invitations were issued by women around your age interested in pursuing a more serious relationship. The rest were from royal families interested in potential proposals for you to join their family."

"Thank you for declining."

"Until you're done with physical therapy, it's not an option. When you're prepared to handle a meeting with the royal family, it would be wise to set that up. Part of the probationary period does include an effort for a proper resolution."

"I make no promises I'll speak to them."

"If Agent Evangeline can handle talking to them, you can, too."

Eva was talking to my parents? I scowled, struggling against my surge of temper. "Why is Eva talking to them?"

"In Agent Evangeline's words, I'm 'an insufferable fucking bitch with a shitty sense of humor.' I assigned her to handling updates on your condition to the royal family and the congress. The last congressional session she attended, she only said fuck twice, which is a marked improvement from her first session. That woman can strip paint from the wall with her vocabulary when she wants. I've been teaching her a well-timed curse is a more effective tool in her arsenal. I suggested she invest in a dictionary to find eloquent ways to insult people to their faces."

I foresaw a hilarious disaster in my future. "That's an interesting solution. And Eva's relationship with the monarchs?"

"I've been highly entertained. They

haven't been nearly as entertained. It's a controlled disaster. In good news, most people who have met Agent Evangeline like her." Meredith chuckled. "Agent Evangeline's primary flaw is her honesty. No one doubts how she feels about something, and once she picks sides, she doesn't change her mind. She's not going to budge until the monarchs have groveled sufficiently. I expect Her Majesty will cry. If you could convince Agent Evangeline to stop tormenting the queen, it would make the rest of the RPS happier."

"Eva's bullying my mother?"

"Not quite. If anything, I'd say Her Majesty is the bully. Whenever Her Majesty makes a jab at Agent Evangeline, she fights back. She doesn't start anything, but she does finish it."

"Can we just make Eva the queen?"

"That would involve you agreeing to resume your duties and marrying her, Your Highness. You also would need to convince her to accept your proposal."

"Did she tell you why she agreed to track me?"

"The queen was sobbing because the tracker on your car wasn't functioning. Agent Evangeline, fresh from having her arm set and hopped up on painkillers, pointed in the right direction and gave an approximate distance."

"She's that good?"

"Her margin of error is less than half a

mile. She's phenomenal. I have no idea why her family disowned her; she might qualify as a royal-level talent. If her accuracy remains consistent and if her range exceeds a thousand miles, she qualifies. She was formally notified by Dr. Hampford about the potential consequences of maintaining her brand on you. Agent Evangeline is rather intent on leaving it in place. In her words, you're nothing but trouble."

"I'm not going to argue with that."

"I didn't think you would. If Dr. Hampford clears you tonight, unless there's something you want to do, the next stop is the RPS training center to begin physical therapy."

Meredith's words confirmed life did go on. I just didn't know what to expect in the aftermath of everything that had happened.

ELEVEN

I should just accept now I've been tricked, shouldn't I?

HAD I GOTTEN MY WAY, I would've left for the RPS training center without fanfare or fuss, but Eva wanted me to watch her beat my great-grandpa. Meredith supported the idea, not that she needed to. Eva's glare promised a world of misery if I refused to cooperate. To delay the inevitable, I adjusted my tie for the third time. "Why are we doing this?"

"Just accept the damned bear's apology already. My arm's fine. No loss of mobility, and I was back to archery within a week. It only took an extra week or two to be back in top shape. Best of all, the damned bear paid the bill. I got the fancy treatment, too. He's not going to bite you, but I'd expect hugs. I'm not rescuing you from any hugs unless he's not gentle. He'll be gentle. I also refuse to promise any protections from relocation if he's the one relocating you."

"Meredith," I complained.

"I think she's right. Your great-grandfather understands parental visits are still barred, but this is a start. This period *is* to give a fair chance of reconciliation. It's my job to make certain that happens. Of course, there are outside factors. It's very difficult to control the monarchs when they decide to do something, so you may as well accept a meeting will happen. When, I can't tell you. But it's coming."

"Christian's warned you, hasn't he?"

"He's been warning me for the past week. It is much easier to keep them out of the hotel. Once we leave the hotel, it'll be much more difficult to prevent them from paying you a visit."

I sighed. "It's been a miracle they've left me alone this long. I should just accept now I've been tricked, shouldn't I?"

"Yes," both women replied.

During my recovery, I'd dealt with the aches and pains from the transplant, and my lengthy inactivity had reduced me to a tired mess physical therapy would address. The walk to the lobby would be challenging enough without adding arguing with the women to it. I gave it fifty-fifty odds I took a nap the instant I reached the vehicle destined to cart me back towards the Chicago area. "Let's get this over with, then. And Eva?"

"Yes?"

"Kick the fucking bear's ass."

"That's the idea."

Since I was being bossy and she hadn't put me in my place yet, I added, "Cuss more, too."

Meredith scowled. "Your Highness."

"Let the woman curse. Until I sign a piece of paper overturning it, it's not like I plan to fucking stick around, so while she's assigned to my detail, if she wants to tell Congress to fuck off on public television, great."

"I told you," Eva informed Meredith. "Expecting him to be charitable over this bullshit is unreasonable."

"Try to limit the vulgarity to tolerable degrees, both of you."

"I'll think about it," I replied. "It's part of my strategy to ensure my future freedom."

Both women rolled their eyes, and Eva prodded me in the chest with a finger. "Stop being a fucking baby and march your ass downstairs, Your Highness."

"I can't promise marching. How about a slow plod?"

"I don't care, just don't fall on your fucking face. I will drag you by your foot to the car."

She would, and I was tempted to fall on my ass to watch her strut her stuff and haul me around. As I had no doubt there'd be reporters waiting to catch such a moment, I'd refrain. "A low bar I hope to meet. What do I need to bring with me?"

Meredith snorted. "Yourself. You're going to have a difficult enough time managing the walk to the car."

"While true, I don't have my wallet, keys, or phone."

"They're in your briefcase, which I'll be carrying it," Meredith replied. "Your personal vehicle is also waiting for you at the RPS training center, but it's in need of some repairs."

My car needed to be repaired? Damn it. "Was it impounded?"

"No, of course not. They ran the plates and notified the RPS your car was in the lot and asked us what we wanted done with it. It stayed in the lot overnight before Christian arranged for someone to take it back to Chicago. You may want to consider a new vehicle."

"What happened to my car?"

"The brakes went out on it," she replied. "I've been told you don't drive often but take good care of the car. It's being investigated, but it looks like an issue from sitting around so long without the brake fluid being replaced. We'll be notified if it's more than a maintenance issue."

"Seriously?" What could go wrong did go wrong, and if someone had screwed with my car, I'd have Eva teach me every dirty trick in the book so I could deal with the culprit personally. "Eva?"

"What now?"

"You can use a replacement car that won't try to kill me as ammunition in your skirmishes with the royal family."

"Nice. Preference?"

"Surprise me. If I pick, I'm going to the nearest dealership and picking the cheapest, most boring car I can find."

Eva shuddered. "I can do better than that without thinking about it. Two seater or four seater?"

Any other day, I would've said a four-seater, but I remembered if I picked a two-seater, I could take Eva and leave everyone else behind. "If I have a two-seater, we can ditch Meredith and make her chase us in an inferior vehicle."

She chuckled. "I'll figure out something with enough under the hood its pride won't be hurt when armor plating and bulletproof glass is added."

RPS agents. I could always trust them to find ways to complicate things for me. "Use your judgment."

"Your Highness, this is a matter of your kingdom's future prosperity," Meredith reminded me. "What do you want done with your vehicle?"

"Since Eva will be using a new vehicle for me as ammunition, have my car repaired, find a family on welfare who needs a vehicle, and give it to them. Make sure any trackers are stripped off of the vehicle and do a full inspection to make certain there wasn't anything added I'm not aware of."

Meredith pulled out her phone and

tapped at the screen. "I'll make certain it's done, Your Highness. Anything else?"

The list was too long to bother with, although one thing stood out to me more than the rest for the immediate future. I plucked at the sleeve of my suit jacket, which had been a snug fit prior to my hospitalization. "Clothes that fit might be a good start."

"Better fitting clothing is on the agenda. You'll put back on muscle and weight in the next few weeks. If it's any consolation, you look fine, and only those who know you really well are going to notice." Meredith returned her phone to her pocket and retrieved a briefcase from near the door. "We can discuss your wardrobe on the way to Chicago."

Eva smirked, and her playful expression captured my attention. "If he's not grabbed by the bear."

One day, maybe I would understand why everyone in my idiot family loved when the women they loved enjoyed themselves at our general expense. I was a chip off my father's block, however much I hated to admit it.

"You're enjoying this possibility too much," I complained.

Eva's smirk widened into a grin. "Relocations are fun, especially when they're harmless and I get to laugh at the participants. The RPS has so many options I can work with. It's wonderful."

Meredith laughed. "You only have yourself to blame for this, Your Highness. You wanted the bounty hunter with a tracking talent on your team."

Yes, I had. I still did. I always would. Despite everything that had happened, I refused to regret it.

AS I'D BEEN WARNED, my great-grandpa waited in the lobby, and his eyes widened when he spotted me. "I'll be damned."

A lifetime of dealing with my family and grumpy politicians gave me all the tools I needed to survive through the next few minutes with some of my dignity intact. The first rule of survival involved keeping my tone reasonable and maintaining a cheery demeanor. Politicians jumped on surly moods like wolves on a lamb. "It's hard to decline an invitation to a public brawl between a woman and a mangy bear."

"Deserved," he conceded. "You're scrawny."

Where had he been all my life? I'd been scrawny from the day I'd been born, although before I'd been hospitalized, I'd balanced scrawny with decent muscle definition. As my great-grandpa seemed inclined to keep things civil, I tossed the first rule out the window in favor of direct honesty. "Shit happens."

"Shit that could've been avoided. I had no idea your idiot father had taken leave of his senses due to immature jealousy. He wrongly perceived a threat. For that, I apologize."

Letting go was much easier than holding on, and while he'd done more than his fair share to contribute, Eva enjoyed her bouts with him. For that reason alone, I'd put aside my anger. "All right. Accepted, but there's a condition."

"What condition?"

I pointed at Eva. "She sets your beating schedule. I get to watch whenever I want, and I will shoot you if you break another of her bones. Fair fighting. Accidents happen, but it better be an accident."

My great-grandpa chuckled. "You're letting me off light. That's a fair condition. For how long?"

I shrugged. "Ask Eva."

"Agent Evangeline?"

"However long he decides to put up with the royalty shit."

Her immediate reply amused me. Had my terms been so predictable? Probably, but I didn't care. Her answer implied if I stayed, she'd stay.

"That's slightly concerning."

I frowned. "Why?"

"You're joking, right? This lady hits harder than I do."

"Has she broken anything yet?"

"My pride and delicate sensibilities."

Standing around and talking was enough to

wear me out, and I wondered how long it would take before I could live like a normal person again. "I'm too tired for any bullshit, so if you're pulling any relocation stunts, get on with it."

My great-grandpa glanced at Meredith.

"He's grumpy about his car, sir. He's also grumpy I have his wallet, keys, and phone. Just grab him, stuff him in the SUV, and get on with it before the reporters decide to shove their cameras in his face. He doesn't need the extra stress right now."

With a low chuckle, the grizzly pointed at the lobby doors. "Move it, kiddo. You're too scrawny to hand over the RPS for detail training. You'd break and end up in the hospital again. A few solid meals and some exercise will do you a world of good."

I recognized a pre-planned transition when I saw one; Christian often did it to my father. "This was part of your plan all along, wasn't it, Meredith?"

"His vacation home makes a suitable neutral ground for a tentative meeting with the monarchs on a purely parental level."

My great-grandpa put his hand between my shoulders and nudged me towards the doors. "I'll bribe you, kiddo, but for the sake of the entire kingdom, please make the crying stop."

I could easily see how Eva could make my mother cry, and I could also understand how my mother would set herself up for it, too.

"Maybe if Mother would leave Eva alone, Eva wouldn't fire back."

"I tried to tell her that, but she's stubborn. No matter what anyone tells her, she refuses to believe she's wrong."

Of course. I had a hard time imagining my prim and proper mother wading through manure before meeting my father. "Knee-deep in cow shit reminders might help."

"Those are my favorite," Eva said with a smile. "She hates when I use dated insults on her, too. If she didn't make it so much fun, I'd stop."

As I obviously couldn't trust Eva or my great-grandpa to give me a straight answer, I turned to Meredith, digging in my heels, not that it stopped the grizzly from propelling me along. "How bad is it really?"

"It's probably worse than you think. Please go to the car, Your Highness."

Had I been left alone, I probably would've wasted five minutes trying to figure out which black SUV she meant, as there was a collection of them on the street, some new, some old. My great-grandpa solved the problem, guiding me to one of the newer ones waiting at the curb. I gave up trying to delay the inevitable, but he wasn't taking any chances; he snagged me by the back of the neck. "This way, you can complain over how cruelly you were treated during this relocation. Your father will love it."

My father would have a fit if anyone took

a picture of my great-grandpa manhandling me into a black, unmarked vehicle. For that reason alone, I cooperated. "That only works when my RPS agents aren't in on it," I reminded him.

Eva gasped. "Oh, no. We're being forcibly relocated. Whatever will we do?" Faking a swoon against Meredith, she pressed the back of her hand to her forehead. "So tragic." She straightened and grinned. "I get paid extra when this shit happens."

I loved a foul-mouthed mercenary of a woman. "I don't get paid extra. That's not fair."

"Negotiate hazard pay as a condition of remaining the heir. If the kingdom has to pay you for incidents, they'll make sure your RPS detail is much better."

Meredith choked back a laugh. "Please stop giving him ideas, Agent Evangeline. He's already made his point. The congress is already prepared to bend over backwards to have the abdication stricken."

Before I had a chance to ask for more details, my great-grandpa shoved me into the back of the SUV.

As neither Meredith nor Eva could do anything about the source of the problem, I focused on my great-grandpa. "Get my mother to stop antagonizing Eva. Then, and only then, will I think about making the stay on my abdication permanent."

"That's a tall order, kiddo. Your mother's

so jealous she's beside herself right now. To add to the nonsense, she's convinced, as always, she knows what's best for you more than you do. Start with your father. He'll be easier to bring into line. Try to cut him a little slack. He really had no idea about your health. The royal physicians told him it was just a cold."

Eva pointed at the back seat. "You sit there. I'm with you, as Meredith thinks I'll spend the whole drive provoking the grizzly because I can. She's not wrong."

"All right." In any other situation, I would've taken the middle seat, but sitting with Eva encouraged me to break the comfort of old routines. I buckled in, grateful for the darkened windows preventing the curious bystanders from gawking. Inevitably, someone had caught a picture of my great-grandpa shoving me into the vehicle.

I wondered how the public would react. Royals weren't voted into office; the days of the United States being a democratic republic had ended shortly after magic had washed over the world and triggered the second civil war. The violence had lasted over two decades before the original royals managed to restructure society and create the Royal States from the ashes of the United States.

It had taken more than one lifetime to make the Royal States an official entity in the eyes of the rest of the world, who had watched the continent fall completely apart, although Mexico had dodged most of the conflict.

North Dakota's people had reminded the world revolt was an option, and their new king had earned the unwavering adoration of the lower castes through living among them for years before rising from the ashes of his past like a modern-day phoenix.

I'd developed unfortunate similarities to King Adam's situation. His health issues had resolved upon his reunion with his wife and queen. In a few months, they'd have their first children, and the Royal States held its breath waiting to discover how many they'd have.

The good-humored competition with Montana amused me, as they'd only announced there was more than one on the way. I found the race for most children between the two kingdoms ridiculous, but I wished the best for both couples. After what they'd gone through, they deserved happiness.

Maybe I needed to take a hike to North Dakota or Montana and get some advice from a more reasonable source.

"I don't know what you're scheming back there, kiddo, but the answer is probably no," my great-grandpa announced. "You have at least a week of low-level therapy ahead of you before you're fit enough to work with your new detail in any capacity."

Of North Dakota and Montana, North Dakota's King Adam would likely understand my situation better. "I was thinking about asking North Dakota for advice," I confessed.

"You're not up for any serious travel right now, but there's no reason you can't give them a call. Their king's royal physician might be a good resource. Agent Scarson?"

Meredith claimed the spot next to my great-grandpa. "Yes, sir?"

"Get in touch with Dr. Hampford and suggest she meet with North Dakota's team; they might be able to offer advice for our specific situation."

"I'll suggest it to her, sir."

My great-grandpa twisted around to face me. "What do we need to do to fix this mess, kiddo?"

I raised a brow. "I already told you."

"It can't be that simple."

"It is that simple. I'm not asking for much. I never have. But I'm done with being obstructed, sabotaged, and betrayed."

"Grégoire wouldn't be a good king. He knows it, the congress knows it, and even the general public has figured it out. The other options aren't any better. It's a problem."

I kept my brow raised, wondering why he was telling me what I'd already been told. "He's always been in line after me. This isn't a surprise."

"No, it's not. The surprise is how poorly he's handling the work."

Why would anyone expect Grégoire to pick up where I'd left off without bumps along the way? The insanity of the idea rendered me speechless for so long Eva nudged me with her elbow. At a loss, I said, "It's not his fault he doesn't have my training."

"It's not a matter of training. He's a wolverine. On a good day, he's impatient. No one had any idea of your absurd tolerance levels until he tried to fill your shoes and found them an uncomfortable fit."

It worried me Grégoire's trial by fire was souring so fast, but even if I wanted to jump back into the fray of handling Illinois's political matters, I couldn't. The short walk had tired me out enough I doubted a week would be enough to restore me to partial functionality. "He's burning out that fast?" I swallowed a frustrated sigh and stared out the window, unable to identify the city from its streets alone. By necessity, we were likely near Huron-Manistee, but no one had told me the specifics, and I hadn't asked. "Grégoire's always been helpful with taking the load off before."

"There's a huge difference between helping out and taking the reins, kiddo. Your father's beside himself at this point. Your filing has made it clear they need to get their ducks in a row."

"Having heard this analogy many times before, their squirrels are at a rave, too. Correct?"

"And they're rabid," my great-grandpa added.

"I suppose hospital-grade drugs count as something you might get at a rave."

"I'll play the rabid squirrel," Eva volunteered.

I grinned, and when Meredith turned in her seat to look at me, I arched a brow at her.

"Don't look at me. I'm not getting involved with ducks, a rave, or rabid squirrels."

My great-grandpa laughed. "I don't know where Christian found you, but I'll bribe you to get you to stay."

"Texas, sir."

"You don't sound like a Texan."

No kidding. Every time I spoke to the Texans on the phone, I felt like I needed a translator. His Royal Majesty did it on purpose, while Queen Jessica only slipped when someone had annoyed her enough.

"I travel extensively, sir. I was trained in Hawaii. Now, I go where I'm needed, but I'm officially attached to Texas."

"How'd Christian lure you here? We can't figure it out."

"That's a private matter, sir. Christian acted on behalf of His Highness and contacted me. I reviewed the situation and accepted his request. That's all you need to know."

My great-grandpa watched her with the intensity of a predator ready to pounce, and I tensed, holding my breath.

"It's up for negotiation. I've already informed the Texan RPS I won't be leaving until matters are resolved here. I've come to the conclusion I might be here a while."

Eva snickered. "Sucker."

"Keep talking, Agent Evangeline. I control your schedule."

"As long as I get to beat the royal bastards, I don't care."

My great-grandpa sighed. "Let me see if I understand this correctly. If we want to keep you for Kel's detail, we have to stir up just enough shit so you don't feel comfortable leaving. Agent Evangeline will be easier to entice into staying, I see."

The woman I wanted to marry and keep close the rest of my life snickered. "You're getting senile, bear."

"I haven't forgotten anything. I'm not senile. I'm contumacious."

I scowled. "You're what?"

"Intransigent."

Eva's snickers bloomed into a grin. "Headstrong, uncompromising asshole," she translated.

"You weren't supposed to know that, Agent Evangeline," the grizzly complained.

"When my boss orders me to read the fucking dictionary to expand my damned vocabulary so I can function in this shit ship, I do as I'm told."

He glared at her. "You just like to curse, don't you?"

"It's enjoyable with a bonus of easily offending small-minded people. The Your

Highness back here isn't easily offended unlike the rest of his biological family." Shaking her head, Eva stared out the window. "I don't have to curse. It's just fucking fun."

"What do you think about all this, kiddo?"

"I think I was tricked. I haven't gotten a chance to watch Eva beat you. How long will I be stuck in a car with you for?"

"Six hours. Go ahead and catch a nap. You haven't been this level of over-tired and cranky since you were five. Did that doc of yours forget your painkillers this morning?"

"I've been off the painkillers for two days," I grumbled.

"Withdrawal?"

"Fuck you, Grandpa."

"What? I'm not great anymore?"

It took Eva and Meredith working together to keep me from strangling him.

TWELVE

Are you sure he's not a honey badger?

EVERYONE EXPECTED me to drag my ass into my great-grandpa's vacation home, but I doubted I'd make it five feet before I flopped, gave up, and begged to be put out of my misery. I only had myself to blame. Strangling the grizzly would've been therapeutic if my own RPS agents hadn't insisted on restraining me.

Why had they stopped me? Strangling the grizzly would've helped in more ways than I could count.

"Are you sure he's not a honey badger? He's acting like one. Only a honey badger would go after a grizzly in his condition," my great-grandpa complained.

"I'm not a honey badger, and I go after you whenever I want," Eva replied, arching a brow. "If you agree to be gentle, you can play with him again later. But until you learn to be gentle, the answer is no."

"He'd break if I flicked him with a nail. I

remember from the ten times you lectured me about this issue yesterday, Agent Evangeline."

"If you listened, I'd only have to lecture you once."

I didn't want to know what they were talking about, which motivated me enough to get out of the car, brace myself for an embarrassing flop to the ground, and head for the porch. Meredith beat me up the stairs, opened the door, and hissed curses, rivaling Eva in general viciousness and variety.

I turned to Eva, pointed at Meredith, and demanded, "How did you do this?"

"I can't take credit, Your Highness. I didn't do anything this time."

What could have possibly triggered Meredith's departure from her calm professionalism? One option stood out over the rest, and it involved my parents in some fashion. When the king and queen decided to go somewhere, they went, and no former monarch could realistically stop them.

I sighed. "Don't worry about it, Meredith. If they tick me off, I'll have Eva join forces with the bear. That should make them both happy."

"Hear that, bear? The Your Highness over there has his shit figured out. You get to take the queen. She pisses me off."

My great-grandpa hopped up the stairs, nudged me aside, and placed his big hand between Meredith's shoulders and shoved her through the door. "Why are you two here? I made it very clear I get the kiddo for a week while he rests. I just spent six hours playing with him in the car. He's too tired to deal with your shit right now. He's definitely too tired to deal with the extra shit you've brought with you, too. And don't you two fucking look at me like that. Your title as current reigning monarchs doesn't mean jack shit to me today."

I'd have to find a way to thank Eva for introducing profanity to the Averett family. Eva shook her head and gestured for me to go inside. "There's no point in avoiding it now. They're here. And no, they were not part of our plan. Had I known they'd show up, I would've taken it upon myself to relocate you somewhere else."

I thought about it. "It's not a kidnapping if I go willingly."

"Maybe next time."

While tempted to turn around, head back to the SUV, and hide until my parents went away, I had no doubt they'd persist until they got their way. Grumbling a few curses of my own, I stepped inside.

Had my parents been alone, I might've been all right, but they'd brought Gail with them. I stared at my ex, going cold at the realization I'd have to deal with her, her infidelity, and my mother's pressure to bring her back in my life.

There was only one thing for me to say. "Are you out of your fucking minds?"

Everyone stared at me, and Eva chuckled, stepped to my side, and placed her hand against my back. "Good use of a common word," she whispered. "Next time, we'll upgrade you to something more archaic so you can impress them with your vocabulary."

Two counts of regicide and one count of murder would make a quick end to my life, and I waited until the murderous impulse faded to something more manageable, forcing myself to take slow, deep breaths to bring my heart rate back to the sane and safe. Gail inspired lust in men and envy in women, and I'd let the lust element trap me for too long. Subconsciously, I'd figured out the truth early on, taking every precaution possible to protect myself.

Had I done a better job of listening to my heart instead of my eyes and falling for the fragile shell of her beauty, things would've been a lot different.

"It's been a while, Rose."

I'd never wanted to kill another human being so much in my entire life. "Gail."

My great-grandpa growled, startling me when he came between me and my ex. Eva snagged my suit jacket in her hand, holding me in place. "The kiddo asked a very good question. You really must be out of your minds to bring her here."

"She was concerned." My mother sniffed,

so utterly fake a sound I leaned so I could stare at her from behind the grizzly serving as a shield.

After what I'd told my mother, she'd still dared to cling to Gail? Rage rooted me in place, the kind that'd driven me to Huron-Manistee in the first place.

Eva tugged on my suit to catch my attention, then she smoothed the cloth, her hand stroking my back before she tapped my shoulder. "If I lose my job over this, we'll have words."

I struggled with my anger, boxed it away, and inhaled until I could speak without snapping at anyone. "As long as those words are punctuated with inventive cursing, by all means."

"Fuck is a very inventive and versatile curse, Your Highness."

I forced a chuckle. "Before you show me the inventiveness and versatility of the word fuck, why are you worried about losing your job? You beat a bear for fun."

"I'm pretty sure I'm about to commit several fireable offenses."

I couldn't let that happen, so I turned to Meredith. "Agent Scarson?"

"Yes, Your Highness?"

"Please don't fire Eva for anything that happens in the next ten minutes, as long as she keeps any altercations non-violent."

"I'll take that into consideration, Your Highness."

As I refused to miss a single moment of Eva tearing into my mother or Gail, I stepped to my great-grandpa's side, prepared to use him as a living shield if necessary. Ignoring the women earned me glares, but I refused to be cowed by either of them, directing a scowl at my father. "Your Majesty, why did you go along with this?"

If my use of his proper title didn't clue him in he'd crossed a line with me, nothing would.

My father flinched, the only evidence I'd landed a hit on him. "Technically, I didn't. She got a rental and followed us. Your mother refused to acknowledge the profound stupidity of encouraging her to stay for your arrival."

"I'm accepting that at face value. You can be grateful for that later. Mother, since you seem to be hard of hearing, my opinion hasn't changed. No. Gail, the day you decided to fuck and marry another man, we were through. Irrevocably. I'm not a whore, no matter what rumors you may have heard or started. I've never cheated on a woman in my entire life, nor will I ever. I'm also not a therapy plan for you to develop a sense of loyalty. If you want a prince, sell yourself at the yearly auction and pray."

Gail's mouth dropped open, and her eyes widened.

The silence thickened until Eva made a thoughtful sound in her throat. "Is this what you meant with your lectures about selective cursing, Meredith?"

"Yes, it was."

"Effective. She's turning green."

Long after I expected Gail to snap at Eva or lecture me for telling the truth, she remained silent.

As Eva showed no sign of fighting my war for me, for which I was grateful, I lifted my chin and braced for the inevitable conflict. "Why did you leave the man you were supposed to marry, anyway? I never understood that. I try not to pay attention to baseless rumors. Was the one saying he cheated on you true?"

My mother paled. "Kelvin!"

"Mother, she cheated on me. Why would you ever think I'd be able to ignore that?"

"You don't know that."

"He does," Gail admitted. "He's always told the truth. It's simpler for him. That's what you get with him. Simple."

Eva stepped to my side, and her mouth dropped open. While staring at her would send a message to everyone, I couldn't tear my attention away from her shocked expression. I waited for the moment she finally snapped and said the first thing to pop into her head.

"Were you dropped on your head as a baby? There's nothing simple about this Your Highness. It's pretty infuriating, really. He's a pain in the ass, but there's nothing simple about him."

"And just who do you think you are?" Gail demanded.

"Sweetie, I'm the woman he asked to marry him because I kicked his ass so hard romance popped out."

Gail's eyes widened to the point I wondered if they'd actually pop out of her head. "What?"

The green cast to my ex's face splotched with red. With her true colors on display for the world to see, it baffled me I'd ever wanted her in my life in the first place.

"And since the Your Highness here doesn't cheat on his woman and I haven't answered him yet, you don't have a horse in this race, sugar plum. Run on home to the man you ditched; you ain't got a hope in hell with this one, dumpling."

No wonder Eva believed she'd lose her job. She took the no fraternization portion of the RPS's hiring agreement, snapped it over her knee, and then used the fact she hadn't answered me as a weapon against everyone in the room.

"My name is Gail."

"Whatever you say, sweet cheeks."

"My. Name. Is. Gail."

"Okay, skunk weed."

Skunk weed? I'd had a run in or two with the pungent plant, and it took every scrap of my will to keep from bursting into laughter.

Compared to the insults Eva flung at my ex, Rose wasn't so bad no matter how much I hated the name.

"Gail!" my ex shrieked.

"Corpse flower. Kinda pretty, but anyone with a functional nose can tell you're rotten. You're so not right for him, dandelion."

My great-grandpa leaned close and whispered in my ear, "I think I understand a little better why you don't want to let this one get away, kiddo."

I shot him a glare. "There's a reason I got so pissed, old fart."

"I see that now."

Eva turned on my great-grandpa, and I almost expected her to start hissing. "Be quiet, bear. You're interrupting."

The meanest member of my family, a grizzly with anger-management issues, snapped his teeth together and shut up.

Wise man.

"How dare you?"

At the rate Gail was screaming, I'd need painkillers to rid myself of my growing headache.

"Holy fuck, Your Highness. You must be the most patient idiot on this planet to put up with this shit. Look, Gail. His name is Kelvin. You keep calling him some bullshit name he doesn't like, and I'll be happy to remind Congress that the queen wants to put a cheating busybody on the throne. He doesn't like you, and frankly, they'll be serving snow cones in hell long before he loves you. That shit ship sailed already. Do us all a favor and leave."

"How dare you?"

"You asked that already. Unlike you, I'm supposed to be here."

Unless I wanted to watch the two women brawl, I needed to do something. Plus, with one simple question, I could make it clear to everyone present where I stood. "Eva?"

She faced me. "What is it?"

"When are you going to give me an answer?"

"I don't want to be fired today."

"But I asked Meredith not to fire you."

"Do you actually think that'll work, feather brain?"

As she had a valid point, I looked to Meredith. "A little help here?"

The head of my detail sighed. "I can rehire her in a training capacity and detail augmentation. It'll work as a temporary measure, as there's nothing in the rules stating a trainer can't engage in relationships with principals. Should you actually marry her, I'll have to fire her, not that she'd be in a position to handle her RPS duties. We can consider it a transitional period, and her skills in martial arts are too good to let go of until mandatory."

"And my pay?" Eva demanded.

I loved a practical woman who wanted to take care of herself without having to rely on me. Once she married me, I'd have every opportunity to care for and spoiler her as I wanted, although I worried she'd make work for herself until the day she died.

"Trainers have longer hours but better pay."

"Can I still beat the bear?"

"Trainers do enjoy that privilege."

"Huh. And the Your Highness here?"

"If you're going to be marrying him, I'm presuming you'll get to do whatever he'll let you do. I'm sure he'll be easy enough for you to manage."

My mother made a strangled noise. "He—"

My father placed his hand over my mother's mouth. "I love you, darling, but it's not your choice."

"It's a miracle," my great-grandpa muttered.

Eva smirked at me. "I'll marry you on the condition you land a good hit on me by the last day of winter, and I'm not going to take it easy on you."

If she'd been searching for a way to encourage me to deal with physical therapy and self-defense, she'd found it. "Never challenge an Averett man, Eva. We're too stupid to know when to quit."

She smiled. "I was counting on that. The hunt's on. Good luck. You're going to need it. Let's find out if there's more to you than a pretty face and your feather-brained ideas."

Gail spluttered. "You're not serious. You

can't possibly mean to pick some mercenary slut over me."

"I certainly don't need or want a queen who needs a manual to understand integrity or loyalty. Maybe if I hadn't caught you in my bed with another man, I might've been fooled. It's not my fault you were stupid enough to pull that shit. It's well enough you left Donald. I would've felt guilty for not warning him you two are birds of a feather. Just go, Gail. I don't want to smear you in the eyes of the court, but I will if I must."

"You've changed," Gail snapped. "And not for the better."

I understood; before, I'd been much more pliable and willing to dance to her tune on the slim hope of lifting the family curse. I had changed. I'd rather remain cursed and be with Eva than live a long life with Gail.

A short but happy life was more my speed, and she'd never understand that.

"Meredith, please make certain Gail leaves the property and doesn't return," I ordered. "Also, ensure the RPS is notified she isn't to make any unexpected visits without my direct approval. And should she seek an audience with the monarchs, I'll require notification so I can be elsewhere."

"Understood, Your Highness."

Meredith wasn't given a chance to do her job. After a murderous glare in my direction, my ex stormed out of my great-grandpa's home. I sighed my relief. "I'm too tired for this shit."

If anyone had problems with me whining, I'd deal with them after I got some sleep.

My great-grandpa gripped the back of my neck, his touch light for a walking, talking grizzly stuck in a human's body. "Come along, kiddo. It's nap time for you. You can deal with your parental pests in the morning. I've got the suite ready with three bedrooms, but for some reason, I'm thinking you'll only need two of them."

A grizzly holding my neck ensured obedience, and I glanced towards Eva. "Please don't kill anyone unless I'm watching."

Eva laughed and graced me with a smile. "Only this once, and only because you asked nicely."

"Good, because I only get one chance to watch you kill someone. But then again, if you managed to kill someone more than once, I'd be impressed."

"I won't literally kill anyone without just cause. I'll just make the teddy bear cry, and that's even better. He can cry more than once."

I didn't have to think long about it. "I can live with that."

"I thought you could. March, you. It's bedtime for you. The rest of the bullshit can wait until later."

I STAYED at my great-grandpa's place at least once a year, but I'd never slept in one of the suites. The living room couch lured me without fail, although he wouldn't let me head towards my desired spot, and he used Eva to ensure my cooperation. Once directed to the room he'd selected, I aimed for the nearest soft surface, which proved to be a couch, flopped, and passed out before I landed.

The six-hour scuffle in the car on top of everything else kept me down for twelve hours, and it took coffee, a treat banned for over two months, waved under my nose to coerce me into moving.

I regretted getting up the instant I lurched upright. Every muscle in my body screamed protest, and I considered rolling onto the floor and begging for mercy, painkillers, or both.

My current torturer waved the coffee mug in my face again. "You can't sleep forever," Meredith informed me. "You need breakfast before Dr. Hampford gets here and kills me. It's bad enough we couldn't wake you for dinner, but if you miss breakfast, too? You'll need a new head of your detail. While she said to let you sleep until now, I hold zero faith she'll have any leniency if I'm late getting breakfast into you."

I groaned and made a grab for the mug. Only when she was confident I wouldn't spill it all over the place did she relent and hand it over. "What time is it?"

"Six. You have time to drink your coffee, take a shower, and get dressed before breakfast will be ready. Just so you're aware, Dr. Hampford is dictating what you'll be eating all week."

"That's nothing new."

"Well, I'm about to disrupt your habits, as the monarchs want you to have breakfast with them. I've already spoke to both of them, and I've come to the conclusion you should expect some groveling and general begging for forgiveness. I took the liberty of recording Agent Evangeline tearing into both of them over that woman's presence."

A recording wasn't quite as good as being there, but I'd take what I could get. "Was there a lot of cursing?"

"She reserved certain words for the perfect moment, which made her barbs more effective than usual. A hesitant truce has been declared between her and the queen. The king was tenderized by a literal bear. There were minor injuries. As Christian watched without interfering, I wasn't concerned." Meredith watched me like a hawk as I sipped at my coffee and prepared to get on with my day despite being sore from head to toe. "I've been asked to make sure you sleep in a more dignified place while wearing pajamas tonight. I refused to allow anyone to relocate you in your sleep, and not even Agent Evangeline could coax you off the couch."

"I'm genuinely surprised the bear didn't come in and do it anyway."

"He tried. The resulting hallway brawl amused me. Your newly rehired physical therapist and trainer enjoyed defending your territory. We have to come up with an official title for her, but we're moving forward with the plan to have Agent Evangeline work as a principal while in her trainer capacity. Officially, there is no relationship between you. What you do off duty is your concern. However, there is the issue of that woman you had an altercation with yesterday."

"We'll talk about Gail later. Eva hasn't rejected me yet?"

"Agent Evangeline is treating her conditional acceptance of your proposal very seriously. I'd be concerned, except having gone over her physical therapy regime for you, I'm tempted to fire her and have her sent to medical school. She's thorough, has a very good eye for pushing limits, and should it work as Agent Evangeline wants, you're going to impress everyone with your general recovery. Unofficially, your status is currently involved, and the woman you're involved with is enjoying herself immensely."

In a world of kings and queens, official meant paperwork signed and legalized. My relationship with Eva would remain unofficial until the day I coaxed her into marrying me.

The uncertainty of when and how that'd happened rattled my nerves, as though I walked a wire and expected to fall at any moment.

"Where is Eva?"

"She's overseeing the kitchen staff; she currently has trust issues. I tried to convince her the bear's staff had been in service to him for a long time, as did Christian, but she's in there playing with one of their chef's knives making certain nothing's amiss. She'll settle down in a few days, I expect. The presence of that woman yesterday infringed on her territory and made her rather overprotective. I thought it wise to leave it be. It's not uncommon with newer agents, especially once they've settled into their role enough they're attached to their principal. I will say this much: your judgment on her potential as an agent was spectacular, and I might request your aid with evaluations of RPS candidates in the future."

Eva wasn't the only one with trust issues. "If you think it'll help. Honestly, I was trying to spin it to keep her around."

"That much is obvious, but your spin and judgment were correct. Every quality you listed as a reason she'd be a good agent was accurate. I'd like to see if we can find more people like Eva, who are categorized in the lower castes but meet the minimum talent rating to work in the RPS. Too often, the RPS only recruits elites."

"You won't hear me arguing. Any idea of what my parents want to discuss?"

"They're looking into options. His Majesty is the most sensible of the two, and fortunately, he has the legal right to override Her Majesty, so this shouldn't turn out to be a disaster. Drink your coffee and take your shower. It'll give you time to prepare."

I'd need a lot longer than the time it took me to shower and drink my coffee to prepare for a meeting with my parents. "They're probably going to ask what I'll do when Gail opens her mouth and starts spreading rumors." It would come, eventually. I expected the truth to be mingled with a lot of lies, lies I planned on unraveling through magic. Gail wouldn't expect or appreciate my reaction, but if she decided to slander me or Eva, the entire Royal States would learn the truth.

After two months of caffeine restrictions, I appreciated the immediate buzz, which made getting up off the couch easier.

One cold shower later, dressed in a pair of jeans and a button-up shirt that fit, I felt like a brand new and rather hungry man. My stomach growled its unhappiness over being empty loud enough Meredith laughed.

"I've been warned everyone in your family becomes growly when hungry, but it's not usually their stomachs doing the growling."

"I'm planning on an act of gluttony, one

that renders me comatose so I can dodge talking with my parents."

"With that much coffee in you? I wish you the best of luck. We're going to have to tether you to keep you from entering orbit."

I feared she was right, but I couldn't help but grin. "It didn't help I guzzled it."

"I'm impressed it stayed in the mug as long as it did. Please remember you did sign an agreement to attempt reconciliation. Using your future wife to torment the monarchs isn't a serious attempt at reconciliation."

"Conditionally my future wife," I reminded her. Sighing my dismay over the condition, I added, "I'm doomed."

It would take a miracle or a really well-planned ambush to land a hit on her. If I reached the tail-end of winter without securing my victory fairly, I'd resort to cheating. Eva had to sleep sometime, and nothing in the agreement between us stated she had to be conscious when I landed my hit. As long as I recorded my victory, I'd use it to ensure my spot as her husband.

"You'll be motivated to learn self-defense with a healthy smattering of offense. That's something."

"If I plan and stage ambushes, will you rescue me before the murder part of her retaliation happens? If I have to stoop to ambushing her, I really might die."

"She won't kill you, Your Highness. If you

plan your ambush well enough, she'll likely praise you. She understands your nature."

"Better than most," I muttered.

"That did work in our favor when establishing her new rank in the RPS. With her and Christian the only two who know your species, she's invaluable. A good thing, really. With her playing as a principal, she'll have a chance to adapt to life with protection and be able to protect you at the same time. Knowing your species gives her an edge over the other agents, and everyone knows it, especially since you're so sensitive over it."

"Is she okay with this?"

"I believe so. She was interested in how she'd help train agents in her new capacity. She's also planning your training regime. She wants you to start on the basics today."

"Today?" I'd be tired enough walking to the dining room for breakfast. "Are you sure she's not trying to kill me?"

"No. She's very motivated to get you back into tolerable shape. That woman concerns her, and she wants you to be able to defend yourself as soon as possible. Also, you didn't hear that from me."

In the RPS, agents often twisted the rules to benefit their principals, and I suspected Eva already knew Meredith would snitch about that little detail, but Eva wouldn't learn a thing from me. "Understood."

"Good. It's time to deal with the monarchs. It'll be less painful if you don't fight it."

Meredith was right. I sighed and headed for the dining room.

———✦———

WE WERE the last to arrive, and I had the dubious honor of sitting between my father and great-grandpa, two men I couldn't escape from on a good day. "I'm too tired for any bullshit."

Meredith joined Christian and my mother's lead agent, Robert, near the door. With the faintest of smirks, she settled in to stand guard.

"I second the anti-bullshit motion," my great-grandpa announced. "My house, my rules. Grégoire is a day or two from a complete meltdown, so you two need to convince your boy to stick around after he's on the mend, and that means convincing the girl to keep the boy. Good luck. You're going to need it."

In less than a minute, everyone in the room would learn just how odd I could be and how minor my demands were in their eyes. My request would be anything but minor to me, but that wouldn't matter, not to them. "The only apology I care about or need is the one owed to Eva. Get the teddy bear to do your dirty work again, and I really will be out for good. I'm satisfied neither of you believed my yearly illnesses were anything more than a persistent cold. I didn't, either.

But I'm picking my wife without help from you or the congress. I don't care if you don't approve of her. Your approval in this means less than nothing to me. I will not be sabotaged, nor will I tolerate anything done meant to hurt Eva. She worked hard to hone her skills."

"We'll talk to her," my father promised.

I expected he'd be easier than my mother, and he'd overrule her as needed, but that wasn't enough. "Mother?"

She sighed but nodded.

"I'm also stating, for the record, the instant Gail opens her mouth and starts spreading rumors or lies, I'm going to cause an incident. I'll probably cause several incidents. I'll go public under verified oath with the circumstances of our split, and I will not leave out any of the details. I recommend one of you suggest she leave quietly and keep her mouth shut. I will fight fire with fire. In this ballpark, I'm more innocent than an angel, but I'll be more ruthless than the devil."

My father arched a brow, leaning back in his chair and crossing his arms over his chest. "Are you sure you're my son? Because before I met your mother, I did laps around the block."

I shuddered at the thought. "Let's not discuss the specifics, please."

"I'm just saying you haven't even made one lap around the block, kiddo. And while your mother's a headstrong woman, while your grandma's headstrong, and your great-grandma's downright terrifying, none of them are inclined to beat on a grizzly for fun. That agent of yours wanted a second round the instant her arm was set. She's crazy, son."

"And?"

"I'm just saying you're going to be whipped within a month."

Bowing her head, my mother sighed again.

"And?"

"Kelvin," my father complained. "You'll be the king."

How many times would I have to repeat the same damned question before he understood I didn't care what he thought about my relationship with Eva? He didn't have to live my life. I did. "And?"

"Kings shouldn't be whipped."

I rolled my eyes so hard I held hope I might knock myself out. Unfortunately, the coffee intervened and kept me conscious. "Kings can certainly be happily whipped by his queen. As the one who would be whipped, I have no problems with that. Happily whipped is preferable to unhappily single. My masculinity, such as it is, is not threatened by a competent and capable woman."

The grizzly leaned back in his chair and howled his laughter. "You just lost this fight, grandson. As a translation, he's saying he's in no way belittled by having a strong woman backing him. She's had a round at me most days for almost three months. Let the kiddo do things his way. The main issue remains: his health currently bars him from doing his full duties, but if you three can figure out how to function, the majority of the load can be shifted off Grégoire."

"I can delegate the work better in a few days after I've had a chance to go over the briefing files," I promised. "I'll take what I can handle, I'll assign Eva some material to ease her into the work, and I'll recruit Meredith to find me capable personnel that can handle the non-sensitive material. What's left will go to Grégoire as usual, so he'll be able to work in a capacity he's comfortable with."

Eva cleared her throat from right behind me. Leaning back, I tilted my head until I spotted her. "I can handle your training regime and some paperwork."

"You think you can. When I'm not making certain you eat, you'll be exercising and moving around."

Reading while walking wouldn't be an issue; I'd done it plenty of times at home. "I can read while I walk, and if I have to use a stationary bike, I can read while doing that, too. If I don't stop exercising for a little while, I'll expire."

"I have no issues with dragging you to bed after you faint."

She would, too. I had no doubt of it.

"At least I won't be left somewhere to sleep it off."

"That's one way of looking on the bright side of things. Eat as much as you can, but don't make yourself sick. Once you're done eating, we're going on a walk. We're going to evaluate how you do taking it easy."

"Sounds good, but I make no promises how long I'll last."

"If you make it an hour, I'll be happy. Realistically, I'm expecting thirty minutes at a leisurely plod."

"I think it should count at any pace."

"If you're reduced to crawling to last an hour, so be it."

It was going to be a long day.

THIRTEEN

Eva didn't play fair.

EVA JOINED forces with Dr. Hampford to maximize how much they could torture me in a week. I questioned every decision I'd made in my life, yet again, especially the one where I wanted an exercise-obsessed, martial artist lunatic for my wife. She approached her exercise regime like a demon possessed, so ruthless I would've admired her if I weren't her target. Dr. Hampford used her talent to speed my recovery so Eva could run me through the gauntlet again and again.

Despite my complaints, their method worked. By day six, I could run again, something I hadn't expected for a few weeks at the earliest. I made use of my regained health to bolt at every opportunity. Most of the time, Meredith either clotheslined or otherwise tripped me.

Sometimes, when she was tired of aborting my escape plans, she sent Eva after me.

Eva didn't play fair. Eva also belonged on the football field, as she could take me out faster than any one of my predatory family members.

It took until the evening of my last night with my great-grandpa to give Eva and Meredith the slip, and I retreated to the last place I thought they'd look.

My great-grandpa wasn't impressed with me hiding under his desk, but I didn't fit under his bed.

"I see you've finally had enough of your babysitters. Dare I ask how you escaped from them?"

"I waited for them to start planning my next torture session, flopped onto the ground and groaned near the hedge, and crawled away when they determined they'd worn me out. Once out of earshot, I ran."

"That explains why you're covered in dirt and leaves."

"They mentioned a treadmill. That's code for an imminent near-death experience."

"Heart monitoring?" my great-grandpa guessed.

"At a run. For thirty minutes. I think they want to confirm if I can handle a full day of being chased, tossed around, relocated, and otherwise tenderized without any prior training on surviving these things."

"I see Meredith is restarting you from the ground up. You'll get a week of that, and then you're on a twenty-four-hour schedule. If Dr.

Hampford approves, you'll be sedated at least once. That'll happen when your fatigue levels hit the maximum your detail is comfortable with. Honestly, that's the best part of training. Once you're sedated, your job is to sleep as much as you want, and if you play it cool and take naps at their request, they'll only sedate you for the first relocation."

"I've dealt with enough sedation for a lifetime."

"You're just going to have to deal with it, kiddo. Half of all incidents involving royals are for live capture, and your health problems make you an ideal target."

"That doesn't even make sense," I complained. "Royal families won't pay ransom."

"No, but you know a lot about the inner workings of Illinois, and how better to destabilize a kingdom than to take one of its rulers? There was plenty of upheaval over your health situation. You can't dodge it for forever."

"I can barely dodge three women determined to torture me."

"And you want to marry one of them."

I did, and I refused to regret my choice, not even when she tackled me into the ground and added fresh bruises to my collection. "It wouldn't be so bad if the three of them stopped ganging up on me."

"It's physical therapy, kiddo. It's not supposed to be fun. How are you feeling? You're looking better. While you're scrawnier than I like, you're starting to fill out some."

"Tenderized. How have the devils handled their eviction?"

"Parents. Not devils. They're whining, but that's to be expected. They also have updated paperwork from Montana for your review and signature. They took it upon themselves, as a peace offering, to update the terms to safeguard Agent Evangeline. Also, His Royal Majesty of Montana offers his gratitude."

"His gratitude? Why? Whatever for? If anything, I've made a mess for him."

"Your parents made the mess, and you're not to take any of the credit for the situation. We've discussed the situation with specialists around the Royal States, and the general consensus is you behaved exactly as anyone could expect in the situation. Stop blaming yourself. Your only concern right now is recovering."

I sighed, and as I recognized a battle I couldn't win, I nodded. "All right. Why is His Royal Majesty grateful?"

"His wife taunted him about your Texas auction photos before they were wed. Apparently, this sped up their reunion and marriage. I've learned it's wise to just say you're welcome and not worry about it. He's a strange one on a good day. He's a little annoyed you've picked an RPS agent to be your bride, but he's more annoyed your future queen will be terrifying and stir up trouble, thus creating more work for him."

"Great. Eva's just going to love that."

"She likely will. That woman enjoys correcting those who underestimate her."

I smiled and relaxed despite my ridiculous situation, hiding beneath my great-grandpa's desk. "She's something else, isn't she?"

"It'll take an army to take her down. I'll admit, now that I've had a chance to see you two together, she's a good match for you. You're not nearly as aggressive as your father would like you to be."

Had my father gotten his way, I'd growl more than he did and beat anyone who opposed me with frightening ruthlessness. "I can be aggressive."

"As you've demonstrated, shocking the entirety of the family."

A knock at the door signaled the end of my reign as a free man, and I sighed.

My great-grandpa nudged me with his foot, chuckled, and said, "Come on in. Your runaway is hiding under my desk as though that might actually save him. I would've brought him out after he had a breather if you hadn't found him."

"I told you, Meredith. When in doubt, hide with the bear," Eva said, laughter in her voice. "It was only some treadmill work to monitor your vitals, not an invitation to your execution. Why are you hiding under the bear's desk?"

"I hate treadmills. I especially hate them when things are attached to me. Anyway, I saw a chance, so I took it."

"You score full points for that trick. Well done. Meredith?"

"Stuff him in the SUV. If he doesn't want the treadmill that bad, we'll toss him to the wolves and see what happens."

"I think he's earned a shower and a change of clothes first," Eva replied.

Eva was taking pity on me? Alarm bells went off in my head. "What are you planning?"

"I've been informed taking over the world with you at my side is an option. I can't take over the world if you're not in your prime. Of course, when I was told this, it was under the assumption I would ignore such an opportunity. That's absurd. If I want to be able to take over the world, you need to be back in line to rule Illinois."

Someone had made a critical mistake, and when I found out who, I would start a hunt of my own. Who could stop her if she got it into her head to actually take over the world? I certainly couldn't. I crawled out from beneath my great-grandpa's desk, got to my knees, and peeked over the polished surface. "Who was dumb enough to give you that idea? That was pretty foolish of them."

"That was what I thought. I figured we could start with Montana. The head dude there looks like he needs a vacation. I suggested we relocate him for a week but was told his queen would murder him. She gets pissy if he goes anywhere without her. Anyway, I then suggested we grab them both, but they have kids. Once grabbing the kids, too, was shot down, I recommended they run away and let me take over."

"You really want to take over Montana?" I'd only dealt with a sliver of what Montana's king did on a daily basis, and I lacked the talents required to fill his shoes. "But why?"

"I've never owned a horse before. They have a lot of horses there."

I worried for the world. I also worried for me; I wanted to marry someone who viewed taking over an entire kingdom a viable method of securing horses for herself. "At the risk of sounding like an idiot, you don't have to take over an entire kingdom for a horse. If you'd like a horse, I'll buy you one."

"It's more fun to earn the horse this way. Have you been to his house? It's overrun with animals, dude. He'd thank me if I relieved him of a few."

Having been to Montana before, many years ago, I was aware the palace had more cats, dogs, and horses than should be legal in any one place. I still wasn't sure how they kept the place so clean it sparkled, and I'd been amazed at how such a beautiful place could have so many pets without any evidence hundreds of animals shared the same space.

I'd explored and hadn't found a single litter box or mess anywhere in the entire palace.

"I'm not sure he'd be happy if you stole his pets, Eva."

"Oh, they aren't all his. I'd have to leave his personal dogs along, but the rest are rescues owned and cared for by the palace staff. They won't miss a few of them, dude."

"Were you born in California?" Chuckling over the absurdity of Eva wanting to take over an entire kingdom so she could have a few pets, I got to my feet and brushed some of the leaves off my sweats.

"Thanks, kiddo," my great-grandpa muttered.

I ignored him. "If we take over Montana, we have to babysit the entirety of the Royal States."

"One continent down in one fell swoop." Eva grinned. "It's brilliant."

We were all doomed, and I welcomed the source of our destruction with open arms. "Meredith? If you get a list of places Eva plans to conquer, please share it with me. I'm going to need a lot of time to review her efforts."

"That's a moderately concerning request, Your Highness."

"No, it's not. I'm being realistic. I've learned its unwise to underestimate Eva, and if she's wanting to take over Montana so she can have a horse, who am I to tell her no?" I shook my head at the insanity, embraced it, and matched Eva's grin. "I might need a clone. One kingdom is hard enough to manage. The world will be a challenge."

My great-grandpa groaned. "Good job, Agent Evangeline. You've given him ideas. He doesn't need new ideas. He has too many of his own to last us for the rest of the year. His quota on creativity has been met."

Eva snorted and kept her attention on me. "What do you think about taking over England after Montana?"

"They're stuffy over there, Eva. You'd curse once and give the elites a collective seizure. What would we want England for?"

"The young prince they've got is pretty cute. If we have a daughter, he might be worthy of her. Maybe."

Dear Lord alive. She was already planning the succession, and we weren't even married yet.

I took a moment to think about it, and in order for her plan to work, we'd need to be married and sharing the same bed. Realistically, we just needed to be sharing the same bed.

Unable to find a single problem with the base requirements of her plan, I decided to let her have her way, although I'd have to remind her of a few critical facts of life. "He'll be too old for any daughter of ours, Eva. Anyway, do you really think your daughter would allow a mere king to dictate anything to her? They're patriarchal over there."

"You make a good point. My gene contribution will be a little troublesome, I suspect." She shrugged, and I got the feeling she didn't care at all how much trouble she caused. "A pity."

"You could just marry me, say, tomorrow. Then you can toy with your new in-laws until they figure it out. I bet the bear wouldn't mind a road trip somewhere. I also know, for a fact, if we road trip to Montana, you could get His Royal Majesty to stay quiet about it for however long we wanted. You'd have to rethink your plans for world domination for a while, though."

"But we have RPS training tomorrow."

"We can afford to be late. They can't start without me. It's a short flight to Montana. I bet the bear would enjoy the foray, too."

Eva narrowed her eyes, looking me and my filthy sweats over.

I bet she debated if I was worth delays in her plans for world domination.

"What do you say, bear?"

"The kiddo is an adult. If he wants to go to Montana and elope and toy with the rest of the family, he can. Count me in. I can arrange transport if Meredith can handle securing a flight authorization. It's been a while since I've gotten to fly for pleasure."

Eva hummed a merry little tune. "How scandalizing is eloping like this?"

I laughed long and loud, and I couldn't stop until I wheezed, resulting in everyone tensing and watching me. I slapped my great-grandpa's desk, gulped for air, and forced myself to choke back my mirth. "Very. Alaska's king got away with it because his queen was ill and at risk. Everyone ignores it, especially since they had an official wedding a few months later."

"And us?"

"I'm going to need a lot of popcorn so I can enjoy watching you handle any scrutiny tossed our way. I'll enjoy it immensely."

"You're hopeless. Better question. Why, exactly, do you want me?"

"You're perfect, foul mouth and all." I shrugged. "I can't say no to perfection."

"You're a nutter. You're an entertaining nutter, but you're still a nutter. It must be a genetic defect. Is this your fault, bear?"

"My father's, I'm afraid. Perhaps I should introduce you so you know exactly what you're getting yourself into."

"I've seen pictures. Let him enjoy his retirement. Someone thought a full disclosure would discourage me. It hasn't. I've already tagged you. This is just the bagging part of things. But none of that male superiority bullshit your family likes. That fucking crap pisses me off."

"I don't think that'll be a problem."

"I'm not interested in dating."

I fought to suppress another bout of laughter. "I guessed as much."

"I don't do those weird parties where people fake proposals, either."

"I already proposed, albeit rather spontaneously. I'll eventually get you a ring, but it won't have a big rock that'll get in your way."

No, Eva needed something practical, something she could wear without worrying about damaging herself or any stones.

"Good. I can work with that. I won't quit trophy hunting, either."

"I'll volunteer various members of my family to provide you with some sport."

"The bear?" The hope in her voice almost broke me.

"What do you say, bear?"

"If it means Illinois can have a stable line of succession, I'm in. I can recruit a pack of wolves for you, and I bet the wolverine would adore you for life."

Eva nodded. "Okay. Will Montana cooperate?"

"He better," I muttered, heading for the door. "I need a shower and clean clothes. Meredith? Do what you can, please."

"I'll see what I can do, Your Highness."

When the dust settled, I expected to be disowned, mauled by an angry lynx, and flattened to a pancake when my parents were finished with me. It didn't matter.

Eva was worth it.

WITHIN AN HOUR, Meredith secured a flight authorization to go to Montana. Officially, we were going to discuss paperwork. Technically, marriage contracts counted as paperwork.

Had I planned better, or planned at all, I would've worn a nicer suit. I needed a haircut, too. After I started training with the RPS, I'd ask Meredith; agents got touchy about people they didn't trust coming near their principals with sharp objects. Christian cut my hair most of the time, but it was high time I'd handled more of the basics on my own. Maybe Meredith would know a barber uninterested in slitting my throat.

"Your father fretted for almost two years before he married your mother. The year of wedding planning addled them both," my great-grandpa informed me from the bedroom doorway. "You're not wasting any time."

"I figure we can hammer out the details post marriage. She went after Gail like you do rabbits. Marriage is obviously the only correct response."

"You have no interest in confirming if she's really the one, do you?"

"Been there, done that. Gail was a mistake from the beginning, but I stuck with it because everyone told me I needed to be sure."

"That's what everyone is saying about Agent Evangeline."

I bristled. "Define everyone. I've heard the

court likes her."

"In our family."

"Our family also thought Gail was a good idea."

"This is also true. And if this doesn't work? What happens then?"

"I die by fifty? It's obvious. I'd be the most normal member of the family. I'd rather die young and be married to Eva than spend the next hundred years or longer stuck with Gail. It's a no-brainer for me. I'd rather be happy than long-lived."

"Most want to live longer."

"Most are idiots. Should my father retire before I hit the end of the line, I'll be careful about the line of succession. Grégoire's unfit, and he'll be happier in a supporting role."

"You really mean to go through with this."

"How long do you think it'll take for the rest of the family to figure out I've eloped with Eva?"

"They'll likely work to separate you two, truth be told."

"Tough shit for them. I'm a proper Averett man in that regard. She's it, and they're just going to have to deal with that."

"As long as you're prepared for the reality of the situation."

"Leaving Illinois is still an option," I reminded him. "If I feel Eva will be victimized for her association with me, I'd rather live as a penniless null with her than as a king without her. You may wish to impress that upon the rest of the family. I won't change my mind."

"But what if she changes hers?"

The thought chilled me. "I'll cross that bridge if I ever get there."

"That's not like you."

"People change, and if I want a future at all, I need to."

"Just don't become a man-whore after you're hitched."

I shrugged into my suit jacket and buttoned it, fiddling with the sleeves. It fit better than I expected, much to my relief. "Why was I born into a family of man-whores? At least none of you idiots judge my sisters."

"The first and last time your father tried, your uncles enjoyed correcting him. Anyway, we're not a family of man-whores. We're equal opportunists across genders. Except for you. Have you gotten laid since Gail? No wonder you're pissy."

"You'll hound me unless I tell you, won't you?"

"Inevitably."

"I don't do rebounds, and until Eva, there wasn't anyone I liked. Just make sure the rest of the family minds their own business for once in their lives."

"I can try, but I can't promise. Your mother is still in shock over Gail."

"My mother liked Gail and hoped for a reconciliation. She also would back off at times hoping I'd welcome Gail back. She never believed we were through, but we've been through since she cheated on me."

"If half of what you said is true, I would be, too."

"Considering I'm willing to go under oath over it, it is. I don't cheat. I don't sleep around with any interested woman, either. I sure as hell don't want Gail to be my queen. She has no idea what it means to be committed. She ditched Donald how long before the wedding? And frankly, it wouldn't surprise me if she'd been looking for greener grass just like Donald."

"A month. It's been kingdom-wide talk, too. She's been laying it on pretty thick. Some have said she might've added to your health concerns by causing more stress."

I could buy into that theory. "My mother tried to have Gail serve as Princess Abigail's lady-in-waiting, a nightmare in my opinion. I've missed the entirety of Abby's visit, too."

"Don't worry about it. Abby's not. She just wants you to get better. She's had a great time here, much to everyone's relief. You made the perfect decision to call in your grandmother. Abby needed some tender loving care, and that's what your grandmother does best."

"Along with putting my mother in her place."

"There's that, too. Ah, that is something you should know. She's been enjoying Grégoire's company a little too much for anyone's comfort."

"If he cheats on her, I'll have Eva teach me how to beat him within an inch of his life."

"He's not that stupid. If you take back your full position as the heir, he might stay in North Dakota for a while. He's pretty stressed, and she's settled him down. I'm hopeful they might make a pairing, much to everyone else's horror. They think such a relationship will end in disaster."

Great. If Grégoire went to North Dakota, especially as a suitor for Abby, I'd have to pull strings with Montana to make it happen, as he couldn't leave the kingdom until I resumed my position as heir. "Assuming I'm happily married in the very near future, I'll negotiate terms to allow him to go to North Dakota."

"Your parents will be annoyed by that."

"Good. They can handle being annoyed. Montana can help make certain Eva's prepared for the reality of being married to me. My parents wouldn't give her a fair and honest picture of life as a royal."

"For someone who hasn't had time to put a lot of thought into this, you're acting like you have."

I shrugged. "My original plan was to hire her into the RPS specifically so I'd have time to convince her to marry me. I've been thinking about it. I had no idea how spectacular she was when I concocted the idea."

"Obviously, you're incurably smitten. What caught your attention about her?"

"What else? That mouth of hers. I was charmed from first profanity."

My great-grandpa chuckled. "Why am I not surprised? You're the black sheep of the family. Of course you'd find her profanities attractive. You know what? That's good. You're unique. You're not afraid to be unique, either. Do what works for you, and I'll help keep the hordes at bay."

"Dad married a woman who'd spent most of her teens wading through cow shit to go to school. I can't claim black sheep status. He set the example."

"Ah, but she no longer shoveled manure when they got together."

"Illinois is just going to have to deal with her colorful vocabulary. I don't want her to change."

"You love her. That's why. I recommend you tell her that. In the romance department, she's dense."

Shaking my head, I retrieved my wallet, keys, and phone, putting them in their proper pockets. "You say that like it's a bad thing."

"Just make sure you tell the woman you love her before you marry her. It helps. Daily reminders help, too."

"I'll keep that in mind."

"Then again, inviting yourself to daily beatings might be just as good with her."

"There's that, too."

"Finish getting ready, kiddo. We've got a plane to catch."

FOURTEEN

This week, I escaped my detail for ten minutes.

WHEN MY PARENTS found out I flew to Montana with my great-grandpa piloting the plane, who didn't get in a lot of time flying, they'd freak. My father would do his best to take on the bear and lose.

I'd laugh.

The papers my parents had negotiated and I hadn't had a chance to read through demanded my attention. To protect Eva, they'd confirmed her position as a principal for training purposes, and the adjustment to the RPS contract gave her the same protections of a true royal.

I appreciated my parents acknowledgement of what Eva would soon become.

Nearby, Eva and Meredith discussed strategies for keeping me out of trouble, and I wished them well. They also discussed Gail, which put Eva in a sour mood. That started a spat between the two women, as Meredith refused all of Eva's solutions, which involved violence in some fashion or another.

Had I paid more attention to the paperwork and less to Eva's displays of jealousy, I might've finished reading the papers. When my great-grandpa landed at the Montana Royal Airstrip not far from the palace, I decided I'd give up trying to deal with the obnoxious stack of papers meant to keep me in Illinois.

I'd ask for a brief recap and pray I wasn't screwing up my entire life signing the documents.

Before marrying Queen Mackenzie, Montana's king had never gone out in public openly without his mask, and it took me by surprise he was on the tarmac with only one RPS agent. I climbed down the stairs, careful with my steps, as Meredith and Eva would both freak if I took a fall so close to being back in shape. The instant my feet touched the ground, Montana's king pounced, grasping my hand in a firm grip. "I love unofficial visits. I can get away without an entourage. Better yet, I get to dodge my wife for an hour."

I doubted I'd ever get used to how outgoing Montana's king had become thanks to his wife. "Thank you for agreeing to see us, Your Majesty."

"Glad to have you. You're looking much better. They've started you on physical therapy?"

"This week, I escaped my detail for ten minutes, and I made it all the way to my great-grandpa's office, where I hid under his desk."

He snickered. "That's good improvement. Tell me about this lady you want to marry."

I pointed at Eva. "Your Majesty, this is Eva. If you're lucky, she'll give you a demonstration of her vocabulary."

"Like hell I will, you nutter." Eva laughed. "You're hopeless."

"As you're saying that while smiling, I'll embrace my hopelessness happily."

Montana's king arched a brow. "Kelvin, you're worse than I was with Mackenzie, and that's a feat. If it makes you feel better, I wanted to elope, too, but a bunch of busybodies interfered."

I thought about what had happened in Texas a few years ago. "You mean the Texan royal family?"

"They started it. My daughter wanted to see her mommy in a pretty dress, and at that point, I'd lost the war. How could I tell Mireya no to that?"

I doubted I'd be able to if I had a daughter, so I nodded.

"You're a nutter, but he's a sucker. I ain't worn a dress since I was fifteen." Eva snorted and pointed at her face. "Dresses are for pretty girls, and this girl ain't pretty."

"How many dresses would it take to convince you you're pretty?" I asked. "This has somehow become important."

"I'd rather be ugly and have a horse than be painted like some doll and have a dress."

"How about one of those girl suits with a skirt? Those aren't dresses, and I'm positive you'll be beautiful in one." I grinned and stepped out of her reach. "It can be my reward for giving you the slip earlier."

"I don't own any skirts."

Providing clothes was something I could handle, and I relaxed. "I would be happy to help with that problem."

"You'll have to do better at physical therapy if you want me in a skirt. And none of those prissy little heels."

His Royal Majesty of Montana cleared his throat to catch our attention. "How about a loaned dress for the evening with a promise you don't have to wear makeup or do your hair unless you want to?"

"Loaned means I don't have to spend a ridiculous amount on a dress?"

"Exactly."

"And I won't have to take it home? Honestly, I'd destroy it within a week trying to wear it."

"I promise you won't be subjected to the dress for longer than necessary. Mackenzie got excited. I've learned to let her do what she wants when pregnant and easily provoked."

My great-grandpa snickered. "She's really pregnant again, already? Do you ever sleep?"

"Well, Geoff drugged me once last week. He's Mackenzie's primary agent. I'd figured out not to trust Alfred with my coffee after eight." Montana's king sighed. "Mackenzie made him do it. Then he took Julia to the nursery so Mackenzie could get some sleep for a change, too. She's pregnant and breastfeeding, so she can't be sedated. It's her fault. I was working hard to give her a break. She stole my birth control. She not only stole it, she looked me in the eyes and told me if I touched them again for the next year, she might kill me herself."

I covered my mouth so I wouldn't laugh.

Eva looked Montana's king over, tilting her head to the side. "Condoms are useful. Invest in some."

"She tossed them in the trash after cutting them in half. I can take a hint, especially when my queen is angling for a boy to help protect the herds of girls we'll inevitably have. If this bothers you, run while you can, Evangeline."

"I like kids, especially kids I can dump with a grizzly bear when necessary. Only an idiot threatens a kid in the care of a bear. I've eliminated the lynx as a potential babysitter; cats have bad habits. The jury is out on the wolves, but I'm not enthused about the lion. It's that issue with cats again."

"I see you've already put thought into how to protect your little ones."

"That's a matter of necessity. The Your

Highness here is going to be the overprotective, grumpy kind inclined towards violence when kids are involved, so leaving the kids with suitably trained and vicious predators will be required. I'm confident I'll have the bear toughened up within a few weeks. The Your Highness needs a lot of work, but sacrifices must be made. I consider him a long-term work in progress."

Montana's king stared at me with a raised brow. "That's a whole lot of woman to handle. Are you sure you're up for the challenge?"

"If I'm not, I'm sure she'll beat preparedness into me. Meredith might be able to keep the situation to survivable levels."

I hoped.

The agent in question snorted, which did a good job of confirming I likely had a limited lifespan.

"We can discuss the specifics in the car. While you know the ins and outs of life as a royal, I'd like to make certain Evangeline does as well."

"I come from an elite household, Your Majesty. I will not betroth any of my children to sick old perverts. Non-negotiable."

"Ah. Is it safe to assume this relates to your disowning?"

"Yes. I refused. They said I would or be disowned, so I left."

"They really tried that shit on you?" I sucked in a breath, struggling to imagine anyone stupid enough to try to control her like that.

"Sometimes, you're so fucking adorable you disgust me," she replied.

Me? Adorable? "I guess manly or handsome is a stretch, isn't it?"

"Manly or handsome are late-night descriptors used when clothes have been removed from the equation. One you have to earn, the other will be a happy accident due to physical therapy."

I recognized when arguing wouldn't win me anything, but I also understood if I didn't reply, I'd need a shovel to start digging my own grave. "I'm not going to argue with you on this one."

"That's because you're wiser than you look. Get your ass in the car so we can get the lecture over with. This Your Majesty looks like he won't be happy until he gets to do his planned lecture. I've learned it's just not worth the whining."

Considering Montana's king was used to getting his way, I had no doubt she'd profiled him with unerring accuracy. "You're probably right. After you, Eva."

Montana's king gestured to a silver SUV parked nearby. "If Agent Meredith is willing to be separated from her principal for a while, she can accompany Mr. Averett in the other car with Alfred."

The older RPS agent accompanying the king sighed.

"That dude in a suit isn't happy with that, I see. Don't worry, if I can't handle any situation, I'm sure the other dude in a suit driving this vehicle can."

"Relax, Alfred. It's a short drive, Geoff'll be with me, and His Highness of Illinois is hardly in any condition to do anything to me."

Alfred sighed. "I was more concerned about the woman who has a hobby of sparring with a grizzly bear."

"Well, I'm certainly not concerned about my safety when one of the security people in the vehicle with me has a hobby of sparring with a grizzly bear." Snickering, he shook his head. "I thought exposure to Mackenzie would've gotten you used to this by now. If it helps solve the issues in Illinois, I'll embrace the unconventional. The Royal States is turning upside down, and I'm pretty sure it's Mackenzie's fault. I married her and all hell broke loose."

"I prefer to blame New York. It's more plausible and less likely to put me in Her Majesty's sights," Alfred replied.

"Probably a wise idea. I'll be fine with the ladies and His Highness, Alfred. I'm not defenseless, and this will give you a chance to talk shop with Mr. Averett and Agent Scarson without me being in the way. We'll call it thirty before we head to the castle. It'll give Mackenzie a few extra minutes, and I told her I'd text her when we left."

"Yes, Your Majesty."

Montana's king circled the SUV and took the front passenger seat. "I'm calling shotgun so you two can sit together. Maybe if I ride in the front often enough, I'll understand why my wife likes it so much."

"It's rebellious," I suggested, happy to comply and have a chance to sit with Eva. "It also annoys the RPS."

"That's two good reasons she'd do it. How are you feeling? I noticed your doctor didn't come with you. If you need anything, I'll drag one of my physicians out of bed."

"Tired and grateful for a respite from physical therapy," I replied, taking the far seat so Eva wouldn't have to climb over me. "I'm almost to the point I don't miss the painkillers too much in the mornings."

"Withdrawal is a bitch. Mackenzie had a bad time of it after the accident. If you need any help with it, let me know. Our physicians are well accustomed with handling withdrawal. I expect you and Mackenzie will be sharing war stories about hospital stays in no time."

"Honestly, I don't remember all that much from the hospital," I admitted.

"They had him higher than a kite most of the time, and when he wasn't high, he was sedated for procedures." Eva slid onto the seat beside me and buckled in. "Dr. Hampford took the long approach with him, easing him off the painkillers to help mitigate the withdrawal symptoms. He had a slower-than-average recovery from the transplant, but that's no surprise. He was in critical condition when they brought him in."

"I've seen the medical file. It's as lengthy as Mackenzie's. While Mackenzie's injuries were extensive, they were routine trauma. Yours weren't, Your Highness. I hope you remember that during the next few months as we figure out how to stabilize Illinois and find a way you can remain heir. The others in the line of succession are worrisome."

"Grégoire is best in a support role, and my uncles are so used to diplomatic roles they wouldn't know how to take the reins if they tried at this point," I admitted. "It's an all eggs in one basket situation."

"And it's a basket no one anticipated would have any problems. You've been making waves in the Royal States. It's been years since a royal has had severe health issues."

"Alaska's queen had health issues," I reminded him. "North Dakota's king."

"Neither nearly as serious as yours and once diagnosed, easily resolved in the grand scheme of things."

"Your queen."

"She wasn't a queen yet; she was still ranked as a null officially."

"Still severe."

"While assassination attempts are severe, her situation was not nearly as problematic as yours. His Majesty of North Dakota has settled well. Alaska's queen has a ruined temple in her back yard to study, and my wife is determined to have as many children as possible. Unfortunately for you, you're the one holding everyone's attention."

"That's the last thing I need right now," I muttered.

"Your situation has made a lot of royal families consider how they handle their medical teams. That I sent one of my physicians over caused a great deal of scrutiny. For your health problems to be life-threatening and long-term? It made waves. Dr. Hampford will stay in Illinois as long as required. If she's needed here, she'll fly home or we'll go to her. She's already begun the process of recommending physicians qualified for permanent posting in Illinois."

I slumped in my seat. "Fantastic. More trouble I'll have to deal with."

Eva jabbed me with her elbow. "Stop complaining. You've reached your limit for today."

"You're probably right." Still, I'd have to deal with the problem eventually. My health had revealed a real problem, and I had no way of knowing how many other royal families suffered from similar issues. "How much paperwork are we going to be dealing with tonight, Your Majesty?"

"That depends on Agent Evangeline."

"I'm listening," she replied. "I have a low

tolerance for bullshit, though, so let's try to keep this a bullshit-free discussion."

"Mostly, you need to decide if you want to have your marriage records sealed in Montana until certain conditions are met. If they're sealed, you can remain in the RPS doing your duties with a few limitations. While you were on route here, I did some research and discussed the situation with Alfred and Geoff. Both thought this method would work and allow you to utilize a loophole we'll be closing as soon as your marriage to Prince Kelvin is publicly revealed."

"Tell me about the limitations."

"You'll be assigned a partner who will eventually become the head of your detail. This individual will know your marital status and will be in charge of your safety. As Agent Scarson has already begun implementing you as a principal for training purposes, this will work well. The real problem is the issue of your biological family. There's extra paperwork you'll both need to sign to protect your interests."

Eva tensed, and her jaw twitched. "Whatever needs to be signed to keep those bastards out of my life, I'll sign."

"And should you have children? What will happen? Custodial rights are a critical factor."

"The Averett assholes are far better qualified. My side gets no rights under any circumstances."

One day, I'd ask Eva for the full story, and

I wondered how long it would take for her to trust me with the truth. Considering how angry the thought of them made her, I expected I'd be waiting a while to hear the full story.

"That will simplify things. The next thing we need to discuss is the prenuptial agreement."

As trust was a two-way street, I had one way of showing Eva I was serious. "No prenup," I replied. "This isn't a conditional marriage. She gets the full package, rights, and responsibilities."

"Agent Evangeline?"

"I'm a feminist with a fondness of cursing as often as fucking possible. You tell me."

"Equality between the genders it is. The next item on our list: you need to be aware of the consequences of marrying him."

"You mean beyond the probable forming of various unbreakable bonds? I branded his scrawny ass from day one and refused to remove it. Once again, you tell me."

"He's a probable leech, Agent Evangeline."

Eva clapped her hands to her cheeks. "Oh, no! he might be a leech? How terribly tragic. Is that supposed to be a fucking problem?"

I laughed until my lungs burned and my sides ached. "Just because I'm not a man-whore doesn't mean I'm a leech. Magic isn't required for a man to be loyal to his woman."

"There are advantages to being a leech," Montana's king replied.

Eva snickered. "Your ass is branded, so you don't have to worry about it."

"You didn't brand my ass."

"Side, ass. Close enough. I can brand your ass, too, if I want."

I wondered what it said about me that I had no problems if she decided to do as threatened. "I'll only run when you want me to."

"Flirt," she accused. "You need to be more fit before you make satisfying prey. I want a challenge."

"You're going to be waiting a while for the challenging part."

"I'll survive."

Montana's king cleared his throat. "There's the issue of your abdication," he reminded me.

"It changes little on that front. I'll resume work as Dr. Hampford allows, and we'll see what happens in the spring. It's a safe assumption I'll be forced back into the role no matter what happens in the spring, but I have no problems with making Congress bite their nails a while."

"Well, I'm going to enjoy the spring hunt so much more than usual. Honestly, that's the only thing I care about right now."

I laughed. "You're going to make me shift even if I learn how to control my talent, aren't you?"

"That is the idea, yes. Your relatives can take turns being my prey, too. We should get that in writing. I get to have a yearly trophy hunt of the cats, the bear, and those damned whiney wolves. The wolverine gets off with a free pass; that's his thanks for covering your hospitalized ass."

"That sounds fair to me."

"I thought so. Meredith said I should be able to learn a lot about kingdom politics as a trainer playing principal, and on days we're off shift, she says I can learn a lot working in your office as part of your detail. I'll be allowed to snoop on you."

"You'll be feigning being a principal most of the time," I reminded her. "You'll be a principal in truth, too. That said, I have zero complaints if you are in my office for extended periods of time. She's right. You'll learn a lot from watching me work. Playing principal will put you in a position where I can teach you the ropes without anyone suspecting anything. The RPS agents will need to see you working and adapt to their role, so it works perfectly."

Eva grunted. "How long are we going to be sitting here? We will be leaving the tarmac sometime tonight, right?"

Montana's king chuckled. "As soon as Alfred finishes filling in Mr. Averett, we'll leave. I'll expect it'll take them a little longer to be ready. Next up is your public marriage. With your paperwork being done today, you'll have options. I recommend a full ceremony. Pull out all the stops and transform your bride into Cinderella. You'll charm the general public and make it clear you're serious, not that you'll have to work hard to prove you're serious. You might be the only prince I know of you hasn't gone to town at the charity auctions."

"I'm all right with a big wedding if my father pays for it." I shrugged. "If he's paying for it, health allowing, the abdication will need to be overturned."

Montana's king chuckled. "A simple and elegant solution to the abdication problem. I like it. It's a fairly simplistic contract. The abdication is conditional to your health, which is something the Royal States understands and accepts; it shows you're responsible and have your kingdom's interests at heart. A sick king can't do his job well. Your unobstructed courting of Agent Evangeline will be more problematic. We can make the subject of your interest anonymous in the paperwork. However, I've been warned about your altercation with your former girlfriend. She'll talk. They always do."

"I've already informed her if she talks, I will inform the entirety of the Royal States of the details of how she cheated on me in my own bed, and I'll have the truth verified."

The RPS agent in the driver's seat grunted. "He's even more ruthless than you are, Your Majesty."

"Don't mess with shapeshifters when it comes to their women. They make me look insignificant in comparison. That the family of shapeshifters didn't come to this conclusion disgusts me."

"It's an issue of species," Eva announced. "They're predators. They see the world differently than the Your Highness back here does."

"I presume that's because you're a prey species, Your Highness?"

Damn it. I shot a glare at Eva, who answered with her sweetest smile.

One day, I'd have to reveal the truth, and she'd nudge me towards doing so in a way I couldn't fight. "Yes, I'm a prey species."

"But he's a mean prey species. Honestly, he'd classify as a predator to anyone with a grain of sense, but his official categorization is prey. I can testify from personal experience that this Your Highness here has no scruples about going straight for the face. Because he's an ass. Who goes straight for the face. You went after my face twice."

Had I been sporting feathers, I would've fluffed them and showed off my tail in satisfaction over her complaint. "You started it."

"Then you dared to run off on me. Twice. You skipped dinner on me, too. You owe me dinner, a dinner where I get to plot various methods of torturing you for skipping dinner and going for my face."

"As I said. That's a whole lot of woman to handle. Are you really sure you're up for the challenge?"

"I wouldn't be here if I wasn't up for the challenge."

"Point. All right. Your relationship with an RPS agent will inevitably be revealed. If Gail doesn't do it, someone in your kingdom will expose it. Her being in a principal role handling day-to-day work for Illinois will help mitigate the damage. Her duties will be viewed as a partnership developed through close sharing of space in a position that isn't just about your security."

"I don't care what anyone thinks, Your Majesty."

"I guessed as much. I suspected you'd run out of patience with the politics of marriage around the time your abdication reached my desk along with Agent Scarson's account of the situation. Still, you have all the qualities of a good king. Your current successor doesn't. This is common public knowledge. That's no fault of his; he's just not the type. It happens. Kingdoms reliant on birth order typically overcome the shortcomings of their rulers through the congress and other legislative branches of their government. Once you impress upon your congress you have limits, they'll learn to compromise with you. That's important, but you have an advantage. They understand you had a valid reason to abdicate, and they'll see you're serious about your new wife at the same time. With the succession at much better odds of being secured, they'll negotiate."

"I was planning to go the asshole dictator route," I admitted. "I won't tolerate anyone interfering with my relationship with Eva. I'd rather not, but I'll fight if I must."

"Trust me when I say you don't want him fighting. He really likes going right for the face. After he's gotten some training, he'll be dangerous enough. He has a temper when provoked. He's just better at hiding it than his relatives."

I couldn't tell if she was criticizing me or tossing compliments my way. "Guilty as charged."

"And your thoughts on becoming a queen, Evangeline?"

"He's going to rule. I'm going to browbeat people who get in his way. I figure being the mother of a bunch of royal hooligans will be time consuming. I need to make sure they don't become hopelessly defenseless like their father."

"No matter what anyone tells you, your duties as a queen do not require you to become a royal baby maker. Ignore my wife's example. She's obsessed with babies. She tried to take home Alaska's heir the last time we visited. Don't pay attention to North Dakota, either."

"I'd correct anyone stupid enough to suggest such a thing."

Eva would, too. I'd love watching her do it.

"Considering Evangeline's talents, I recommend you propose alterations to how Illinois chooses its successor. That should help prevent future problems and create a better line of succession, one founded on the heir's qualities and not birth order and gender."

"But Montana is by birth order and gender," I reminded him.

Montana's king sighed. "And my talent is passed from father to son. I had some talents I was born with, but the important ones I only inherited when my father died. The entire family is required to carry suppressors in case the dangerous one jumps to a woman. It never has. The talent picks the ruler upon the king's death. If you strip the royal talent, I'm not nearly as powerful as people like to think. I have many abilities, but most of them aren't that strong."

"You found out your father died because you inherited his talent, didn't you?" I whispered.

"Yes. That's how I knew. How everyone found out. My talent is a dangerous one. When Mackenzie and I have a son, we'll be preparing him from birth to handle it. He'll be aware of the weight of responsibility from his first breath. He will be able to kill with a word. If I could cut out this talent and ensure it was never passed on, I would. But it will. And if I don't have a son, it'll find someone else to hit. No, it's better to prepare my future son for the worse than to allow this untamed beast to kill through someone unprepared."

"At least your talent isn't trying to kill you."

"Yes, that's something I'm grateful for. As long as I'm careful, no one is at risk from me, but I do have to prepare my children for the reality of hosting my talent. It's unavoidable."

Agent Geoff coughed. "At the risk of being fired, but Your Highness? While His Majesty does have a strong talent, he's a pussycat. He won't use that part of his power. He has other ways to kill people. That's just one element of his talent. Nothing is as it seems with him, so don't let him trick you."

"Thanks, Geoff," Montana's king grumbled.

"He's also wearing enough suppressors he could order you to fall over dead and all you'd do is faint and be unconscious for a few minutes. It's untested if he can actually command someone to die. Honestly, I think anyone who heard such a command would fall unconscious for a while, and the duration of unconsciousness would be the primary display of his strength."

"My grandfather killed with a word, Geoff."

"And there were circumstances in that case. We've done some extensive studying. The person who died was already dying from heart failure. The command triggered a heart attack. In a healthy person, I doubt it would lead to death."

Montana's king stilled in the front seat. "He had a failing heart?"

"Indeed. But it makes for a good story that helps keep people in line. No one denies or questions your family's talent has killed, but there were circumstances. We in the RPS just opt to not inform anyone of those circumstances."

"Huh. I had no idea."

"Entirely on purpose, I assure you. How better to ensure the inheritor takes no risks when he believes he can kill with a word? You'll never stop taking care with your words and your actions, so the truth isn't dangerous to tell you. But perhaps you'll stop driving us all insane when you have a panic attack because you forget you're wearing a bracelet instead of a mask."

I raised my brows, keeping quiet while the RPS agent did the one thing I'd thought impossible, scolding Montana's king without any care of the consequences.

"Mackenzie put you up to this, didn't she?"

"When isn't she putting me up to something?"

"A very good point."

"Perhaps you should focus on the issue of Agent Evangeline's lineage rather than yours," Geoff suggested.

"He's not even the head of my detail, but he never cuts me any slack."

I chuckled, understanding full well after

having been managed by Christian most of my life. Then I sobered, my worries over Eva's situation strengthening. "What's wrong with Eva's lineage?"

"That's a very good question," she grumbled.

"Were you not offered the opportunity to select a family name?"

"No, I wasn't."

"I'd like your permission to investigate the matter. It's possible the disowning paperwork was not filed properly. As far as you know, you are officially disowned, correct?"

"As far as I know, yes."

"And you were fifteen at the time?"

"Correct."

"That's young for most kingdoms within the Royal States. It might not be legal. The typical age for an official disowning is eighteen, which is the age most can be expected to realistically live without parental support of any sort. Prior to eighteen, there are rights you wouldn't have that would make life difficult for you at best."

"I'm aware."

I cringed at the coldness of Eva's tone. "Is putting her through this necessary?"

"Unfortunately. It's to protect you as well, Your Highness. I'm sorry. I'd like your permission to look into the matter, Evangeline."

Eva scowled. "If they pulled any shit about this, please light them on fire on my behalf."

"It's a safe assumption you're uninterested in a resolution?"

"Not a chance in hell. They try, you feed them to the teddy bear."

"I'll take that under advisement. There's finally the matter of adjusting the public records for your reinstatement as Illinois's heir, Prince Kelvin. If you set a wedding date officially as part of your reinstatement documentation, it'll reassure the public. And yes, that's despite your bride's identity remaining a secret. If anything, her identity being a secret will create some excellent publicity for Illinois. There's nothing gossips love more than speculating about royal weddings. It'll drive the court crazy if they can't figure it out."

"I like that. Two days before the first day of spring," Eva suggested. "That'll give us a day together before I get to hunt your scrawny ass. After I'm done with you, I want to work through the cats."

"You're not going to have any mercy on him, are you?"

"I treat beasts as beasts and men as men. Men who insist on acting like beasts are hunted for my amusement and photographed in compromised positions."

"Even if I learn to control my talent, you really are going to hunt me, aren't you?"

"Duh. You're glorious. I couldn't catch you cheating, and that's infuriating. I haven't figured out how you did it."

I laughed, pleased my ploy had worked so well. "I watched you clean your swords and cuddle with your bow. I'm prepared to sleep with your weapons as necessary."

"You were right under my nose the entire time?"

"Your tirade was magnificent, and I'm recruiting Dr. Hampford to check into your snore."

Montana's king snickered. "The issue of Evangeline's snore has already made it to my desk, courtesy of Agent Scarson. Dr. Hampford is aware and will start looking into the issue as soon as you're progressing through physical therapy. She thought it wise to have one patient on the mend before adding a second patient to her load. That said, it's probably easily resolved. It'll involve a few sleep tests. I've been through them a few times. If I snort in my sleep, the RPS busybodies want to make sure I'm not going to die."

Geoff sighed. "Your Majesty, please don't exaggerate."

"It was just a few snorts!"

"You had minor surgery to deal with a sinus problem. It was not just a few snorts. Be grateful we neglected to inform Mackenzie and did the procedure while she was in Texas."

I recognized good blackmail material when I heard it. "Just how did you manage to hide this from Her Majesty?"

"Sedatives slipped into her dinner and a late-night operation with a doctor who could handle healing the incision. By the time she returned to Montana, he no longer snored, was fully healed, and everyone was much happier. Except for him; he continues to complain we overreacted to the situation."

"I want his doctor," Eva announced.

"You have her already," the RPS agent replied. "Dr. Hampford oversaw the operation. There's a reason His Majesty sent her to Illinois. He trusts her with his life in surgery, and he doesn't send anyone he doesn't trust without question."

"We're going to up the timetable on that snore. It's bad. She was right next to a waterfall and drowned it out."

"I did not!"

"You did," His Royal Majesty of Montana replied. "He's telling the truth, which is disturbing enough I'll call Dr. Hampford and make arrangements tonight. Agent Scarson had mentioned it was bad, but I seem to have underestimated how bad."

I smirked. "Your turn."

"I'm hunting you a few extra times for that."

"You get that snore looked at, and talent allowing, you can hunt this beast to your heart's content."

"And what of the man?" she countered.

Was she kidding? I rolled my eyes and laughed. "Easy prey for you."

"Hardly. You're slippery. Whenever I take my eyes off you, something bad happens or you wander off. Troublesome man, troublesome beast. I'll enjoy my spring hunts every year."

"Are you going to shoot me with your bow again? This determines how much effort I put into escaping. That hurt, for the record."

"You'll be tranquilized, posed for my entertainment, and photographed."

"I'm not sure which is worse," I admitted.

"You're beautiful prey. I'll enjoy every minute of it."

Montana's king cleared his throat. "Please don't kill him, Evangeline, however tempting."

"I can't hunt him at my leisure if I kill him."

Geoff snickered. "I've heard this before. Mackenzie's the same way. It's hopeless. Agent Evangeline obviously lives in a different world than ours, thus we'll never have any hope of understanding her."

Montana's king sighed and shook his head. "As I'm sure you'll learn soon enough, Prince Kelvin, that's what makes her perfect for you. I've learned it's best to accept the inevitable. Who am I to judge a man willing to toss his kingdom to the curb to protect the woman he loves? I can't talk. I meddled with Texas's affairs for the first ten years of my daughter's life to protect my queen and child. It's not a stretch. Every king has his limit, and

Illinois has discovered yours. At least Illinois won't have to guess at your queen's limit. I'm sure the whole world will know when she's getting ready to snap."

"Loudly and punctuated with profanities," I confirmed.

"Best fucking job ever," my future wife muttered under her breath, and I laughed.

MONTANA'S QUEEN didn't look pregnant to me, but when we arrived at the castle, she intercepted our car before Geoff managed to park, tugged on the door nearest Eva until Geoff unlocked it, and snagged Eva by the elbow. She barked a few orders, and everyone made way.

Eva squeaked, and I added startling her to my list of things to do often.

"I'm sorry," Montana's king mumbled, sliding out of the SUV. "Next week, she'll start running."

"Pardon?"

"She's seven weeks pregnant. At eight weeks, she develops an overactive flight instinct. I'm hoping I won't have to climb too many trees this time. I've been informed Evangeline was considering taking over Montana so she could have a horse?"

"Unfortunately. World domination is on her radar for some reason. I still haven't figured out why."

"I have an older school horse, even-tempered, that might work for her. Consider it a present to put a temporary stay on her world domination plans. The mare has been on fox, boar, and deer hunts, and she enjoys trail rides. I expect your Evangeline doesn't know how to ride, but this mare will be a good teacher for her."

"I don't know how to ride, either," I confessed.

"Then it's a good thing I picked a mare for you, too. Riding is good physical therapy. I'll send a trainer through Dr. Hampford to give you both instructions on how to ride. By spring, Evangeline should be ready to hunt your family on horseback."

"Put it in the contract for my reinstatement as heir. Don't all those horse people have two each? In case one's sick or tired?"

Montana's king chuckled. "I can make arrangements to sell a second horse to you both, good animals that'll make your parents weep when the bill arrives. While Mackenzie helps Evangeline, let's handle as much of the paperwork as we can. I've been informed an unwanted party is aware of your interest in Evangeline, so I need to hear your side of the story."

"It's pretty simple. I dated Gail for five years when she decided to cheat on me at a party at the castle. In my bed. As I don't cheat and have no interest in marrying a known cheater, I quietly broke off our relationship, under the excuse of irreconcilable differences. She broke off her recent engagement and showed up at Great-Grandpa's place trying to 'repair' our relationship. Not happening."

"If she should talk?"

"I'll take the truth public, and she's aware I will. I told her that myself."

"That will create a scandal."

I snorted. "Hardly. The only scandal will be she was brazen enough to cheat on me in my damned bed. I've never cheated on a woman in my life. I haven't even been with anyone since Gail. All things I'm willing to have verified."

"But you've attended the auctions."

Sighing, I shook my head. "I bid on women who didn't want to be treated like whores and took them out to dinner. Sometimes dancing. They went home without being treated like a whore."

"Your reputation is thus one thing, reality another. And those women you bid on at the auction ultimately had a great time because you treated them well."

"Exactly."

"All right. I can work with this. I'll phrase the reinstatement documentations to link to your public marriage ceremony with the woman of your choice, and I'll set the date to two days before the spring, as Evangeline requested. That's a little short on time for planning anything elaborate, which should work well for you. You don't seem like the elaborate type."

"I'm totally the elaborate type, and I might need your help teaching Eva to ride in a wedding dress. She likes horses, and since she doesn't like her family, she can ride down the aisle if that'll make her happy."

"I'm not sure if I'm impressed or worried. I can train her horse here and have Mackenzie and Mireya help. Mackenzie is a terrible rider, so if she can stray astride, your bride should be fine."

My eyes widened. "While she's pregnant?"

"I have a tendency to hover. She'll stop riding at five or six months at doctor's orders, but in the meantime, she'll enjoy helping. If you trust me with the arrangements, I'll pick the horses."

"Please do."

"Expect to be riding as well, as only one of you riding will look strange."

"My parents' wallets are already regretting this. Excellent. I'll leave it in your hands."

"With that out of the way, onto the next item." Montana's king gestured towards the front doors of the castle, and he redirected his attention to Meredith. "Agent Scarson, if you'd accompany Evangeline, I'm certain I can keep an eye on your ward. He'll be plenty safe in my office while the ladies are preparing."

Meredith chuckled, nodded, and hurried into the castle.

"She's been here enough times she'll be able to find them with no issues. Anyway, for the paperwork issue. You're lucky. I've already drawn up a tentative proposal, and I only need to add a few amendments to make it work for what you need."

"Am I that predictable?"

"Not really. Your agent's just a sensible woman who suggested that I pretend I was you and plan accordingly. It seems we're birds of a feather when it comes to our ladies."

"No matter what Eva says, I don't want your job."

He laughed. "And there goes my hope of an early retirement. Oh well."

IT TOOK us two hours to finalize the paperwork, which I signed before I double guessed myself into changing my mind. My parents and the congress still needed to sign to confirm everything, but I expected they'd do so without debate. Their signatures would ensure they kept me as heir.

Thanks to Montana sealing the marriage license we'd be signing soon enough, they wouldn't know I'd already secured my Her Highness. They'd believe I would be securing one in the near future. A Her Highness meant the direct line would continue, the one thing the congress and my parents wanted above all else. Everyone walked away happy with the arrangement. There'd still be uncertainty, but it'd be tolerable.

I gambled on Eva, but even if my illness lingered and my talent remained rogue, I was determined to be happy with my choice. All I could do was pray I hadn't made the biggest mistake of my life. Prayer wouldn't help. It never did.

But if my talent continued to gnaw away at my bones and destroy my immune system, I'd go out content I'd chosen my own fate, even if I'd made a mistake in my choice of woman.

No, I couldn't think of Eva as a mistake. No one understood how my family's talent worked, not anymore.

No one had ever figured out the specifics of why our line needed the perfect woman so badly. Knowledge wouldn't help much, either. An anonymous donor had given me extra years, but I remembered Dr. Hampford's warning: it wouldn't last forever.

The spring would confirm if Eva was the one for me, and if she wasn't, I'd make the most of my time left with her.

It was the only choice I had.

Montana's king evened the thick stack of papers before packing them into an envelope for certified copying and distribution. "All right, Kelvin. I've received a text claiming Mackenzie is finally satisfied with her efforts."

I doubted I'd ever get used to being on a first-name basis with Montana's king. William. He preferred Will. In a conspiratorial whisper, he told me I could call him Dylan if I wanted, too. Birds of a feather needed to flock together, and he had a feeling we'd be seeking each other out to escape our wives for a while.

Strong women made wise men go into hiding when they rampaged.

"William, when you married, how much disapproval did you face?"

"About Mackenzie? Very little. She's lucky; her talent's so rare no one dares to criticize her ability. People are more concerned about my talent. If mine blends with hers, our children will be, well, terrifying. It's a lot like your family's talent. Rarity gives you rank, not strength."

"An extra-long lifespan helps with that."

"Indeed. The desire for eternal life does influence things."

"But it comes at a price." I'd been paying it since I'd turned fifteen without knowing it.

"So we've seen. Don't worry so much. You're liked across the board. You're fair to a fault, and you're so honest it disgusts people. The Royal States, as a whole, doesn't want to see an economic powerhouse like Illinois fall into disarray because of a poor monarch."

"And my cousin isn't making the cut."

William sighed. "No, he's not. He might learn over time, but he doesn't have your knack for ruling. He also lacks your charisma. Your father learned, but he was never as well-suited for it as you are."

"He's a cat. He'd rather sun himself, annoy me, and nap."

"Insist on a few years to enjoy married life before he steps down and joins the rest of the royal freeloaders plaguing your palace."

A plague of royals certainly applied in my family, although most weren't freeloaders. After ruling a kingdom, boredom set in, so most of my family found something to do. That something typically involved making money.

I needed to figure out how to get the royal freeloaders to spend more time at their homes rather than plaguing the castle all the time. "Good idea."

"I certainly thought so. I expect Mackenzie has given Evangeline a rundown of what it's like going from nothing to a queen. Honestly, I think your bride will have an easier time adapting."

"Why do you think that?"

"Evangeline has accomplished a great deal she takes pride in. Mackenzie was so terrified of losing our daughter she never was able to see how incredible she is. She still doesn't see it. One day I'll convince her. Until then, I try to reinforce when she's done yet another amazing thing. I haven't had much luck in that department, but I'm going to have spoiled children with complexes. Julia's already trying to please everybody."

"Good luck with that."

"I'll need it. Come on, then. Let's go find out if Mackenzie has scared your bride off yet."

"If you're trying to worry me, it's working."

"You're invested. I'd bet my crown you're a leech. You act like one. Add in her viciousness regarding you, she's likely one, too. Leeches are becoming more and more common. The talent likes to develop in those who want loyalty and avoids those with a wandering gaze. It sometimes surprises me Mackenzie isn't a leech. Hell, with her talent, it surprises me we were able to bond at all."

It seemed obvious enough to me. "Maybe that's why you could bond with her. Her talent only needed to make way for yours. Yours handled the rest. Both in the pair need not have the talent, right? North Dakota's queen isn't a leech."

"No, she's not. It's entirely possible. I suspect Mackenzie, had she had the leeching talent, would've latched onto me the instant she'd found out about her pregnancy if it'd been an option. Then again, I'd already bonded us together by that point, she just didn't know it. She'd gotten a hold of me from the day we'd met. She doesn't believe that, either."

"Why wasn't it an option, really? I've

heard rumors, but I try not to believe in everything I hear."

"The official reason is the real one. I wanted her to have a chance to change the world. She did. A lot of broken families have been reunited. Null rights still have a long way to go, but the castes are shifting. By the time the dust settles, I expect history will repeat itself. Civil wars will become more common as the lower castes fight for equality. Royalty will be forced to use their talents to restore order. When magic flooded the world, anarchy ruled for an entire generation. Civil war tore people apart. Montana fought to end the conflict without adding to the bloodshed, though that proved a miserable failure. Ultimately, my family's talent was used to crush the rebellion and stop the murders at the price of free will. For a time. Long enough to send the various armies home so the kingdoms could establish themselves. Montana had ultimately proposed the caste system to appease the greedy and offer some hope to those who lacked magic. I like to believe he had good intentions, but one simple truth remained: he was named the Monster of Montana for a reason. I hope change is better this time. I don't see the monarchies fading back to democracies or republics or democratic republics. Too many fear war, and for all its flaws, our system is working."

"Wars happen. Look at North Dakota."

"When a war is counted in days and the

bloodshed is minimal, everyone walks away happy. Wars just haven't happened on the scale they used to. If all the kingdoms ganged together to wage war against the rest of the world, the Royal States would be feared. No, it's better this way. Kingdom versus kingdom squabbles are far better than the alternative. I think we've worried about this enough for one day, though. Let's concentrate on something more pleasant. There'll be time enough to debate how the Royal States might collapse in on itself. Let's not keep the ladies waiting."

I'D FALLEN for Eva in leather, loved her in jeans, admired her in a suit, but the sight of her in a pale blue, floor-length dress with her hair piled on her head in perfect curls ruined me. Beauty and strength waged a vicious war, neither bowing to the other. In the end, she balanced both the same way a sword became a masterpiece of lethal art.

She stood with Montana's queen and fidgeted while I stared.

William saved me, buying me time with a bright smile. "How many did you enslave to work your magic this time?"

"You're awful," the queen complained. "If you must know, Geoff helped, thank you very much." Mackenzie's attention drifted to me, and her smile was brighter than her king's.

"You're looking better, Prince Kelvin. The few pictures in the news were concerning."

"Your Majesty."

"Yuck. Mackenzie, please. If I could bar titles in my house, I would."

William winked at me. "It took me over a year to convince her the castle really is her house."

"Dylan!" his queen wailed.

Eva cocked her head to the side, and I marveled how her curls stayed contained without the artistic wonder collapsing or becoming tangled in some horrific fashion. "Dylan?"

"My middle name. She saves it for when I'm being particularly heinous. I'm sure you'll find your own special way of expression your frustrations with Kelvin soon enough."

"I think she's covered there," I muttered.

With a roll of her eyes, Eva planted her hands on her hips. "You're both nutters."

"Is Carlos here yet, Mackenzie?"

"Armed with the paperwork we need, vital records, and all that extra crap you royals think is necessary."

William sighed. "Mackenzie, darling, you're a royal, too."

"That's your fault, and I curse you every morning for it. You could retire."

"What part of your duties has you annoyed this week?"

The queen deflated, and she pouted at her husband.

No wonder the Royal States loved gossiping about the pair; if I had to point out a couple who obviously loved each other while dancing the oddest line of conflict I'd seen in my life, I'd pick them.

"I have to go to New York next week."

"I do, too. We've both agreed this is not our favorite task in the world."

"My parents sent another letter this morning."

With a pained groan, William bowed his head. "They found out you're pregnant again?"

"Yep."

"Give me the worst news first, please."

"They want to meet the girls and us. During our visit. Next week."

Eva eased away from Mackenzie and stepped to my side to whisper in my ear, "She's terrifying. She told me I'd be wearing the heels or I'd be relocated and required to babysit for a year. Geoff looked really worried, which led me to believe she'd do it."

I peeked at her foot, which she thrust forward for me to examine. Sure enough, she wore two-inch heels that matched the dress. "I bet those would make decent weapons."

"I thought so, but my swords would be better. Or my bow."

"Still haven't talked the RPS into letting you carry them, have you?"

"Apparently, I'm terrifying. They'd feel

much safer if I just carried a gun. I think they're ridiculous."

I thought they were right, but I'd let her win for the sake of peace between us. "The weapons on your feet look lovely."

"She really wants me to keep the dress and the shoes, and she says I can get both in white. Or have these bleached. Bleach is cheaper."

"I'm happy with that dress in whatever color you want it if that pleases you. It's your dress. I'm not the one who has to wear it."

"But you're the one who is supposed to like it."

I snorted and did my best to match her disgusted expression. "Eva, you could show up in torn jeans for our wedding and I'd like that plenty. I only care you show up for the wedding. The dress is lovely on you, and you could keep it in that color if you like, too."

"Really?"

"It can be a showcase example of just how little we care for the pomp and circumstance of royal displays and ceremonies."

Eva frowned, her gaze dipping to her shoes and the hem of her dress. "I should keep the dress and the shoes, then?"

"Keeping the dress makes her happy and spares you from a month's worth of fittings, dress design, and general torture."

"Okay. I'm sold. I'll keep the dress."

"And only those of us here will know you're wearing it for the same purpose twice.

Honestly, I like that. That dress will become a favorite memory."

"You have made a successful sales pitch. But why am I wearing a dress? I don't understand how this happened."

"I don't think we're supposed to question the pregnant queen."

"You present a very good point."

I grinned. "Sometimes I do, but it's rare."

"Have I somehow agreed to marry a nutter who is also an idiot?"

"It's entirely possible."

"Well, at least I get to beat up a bear. That's a great consolation prize. Let's get this done before somebody change their mind or these shoes kill me."

A SINGLE FORM determined my marital status, and it only had one page. Check boxes confirmed the court judge had verified our vital records, and I refused to ask how His Royal Majesty of Montana had gotten hold of the required paperwork. Three additional pages confirmed I gave my wife equal status and that we refused to create a prenuptial agreement to protect my interests.

As though sensing she'd have a battle on her hands to win anything other than the dress and shoes, Mackenzie wasted no time securing our signatures following a brief lecture from the judge about our actions.

The judge seemed annoyed he had to give the lecture to confirm we knew what we were getting ourselves into, but he wasn't willing to battle with Mackenzie over it.

William's eyes narrowed with suspicion, and he looked his wife over. "You're already planning their wedding, aren't you?"

"Do they look like they want to do it?" Mackenzie lifted her chin. "I'm good at planning."

"I know you are."

"They don't want to, and I do."

I covered my mouth and struggled to contain my laughter.

"The Your Highness I just married does not have time to plan a wedding. He'll be in physical therapy, training, and doing the paperwork all you Your Highnesses and Your Majesties seem overly fond of. I have a partial stay of paperwork until the spring, but I'll be busy training him to not die in the meantime. That's important. As he very much likes the dress and the shoes, I'll wear this dress and these shoes, in these colors, to this event. I will do this with minimal protest."

"See? She's siding with me."

William drew in a deep breath and sighed, bowing his head. "No matter what I say, I lose. Have it your way, Mackenzie. Please don't traumatize Illinois's future queen. This isn't an opportunity to start another baby rivalry, either. King Adam and I are concerned the current situation will become ridiculous."

"And we both know Adam would be happy with even twenty children."

"When Julia was born, you screamed at me, Mackenzie. I clearly heard you. The words 'Never the fuck again' came out of your mouth. Repeatedly."

"I was stupid for refusing the epidural."

"Mackenzie. You didn't even last a year before you went on a rampage and slaughtered my birth control."

"It's your fault. I look at you, and then I think we need more babies."

I gulped and stared at my new wife, hoping she wouldn't kill me before I lured her to my bedroom.

She smiled at me. "I'm going to try to keep a firm grasp on reality and maintain reasonable expectations. Maybe we should pick a number?"

"I'm not a reasonable person to ask about this, Eva. My family is huge. I only have one brother, but honestly, I've lost count of my sisters."

"Well, if it's helpful, twenty seems like an unreasonable number of children."

"I'm inclined to agree with you," I replied.

"That's because you're wise and I'm right. Hey, bear?"

Crap. I'd been so focused on Eva I'd forgotten my great-grandpa had witnessed me marry her. Literally. I double checked the papers still on the king's desk, and sure enough, his signature was there as a witness.

It amazed me he'd managed to keep quiet the entire time.

"Yes, my little great-granddaughter?"

My life was destined to become very interesting.

"How long do you think we'll be able to keep this quiet?"

"With Gail and her mouth? The world will know you're in Kel's sights within a week. Enjoy any subterfuge you can."

"But I don't want to be unemployed."

"You have nothing to worry about. If you're punted out of the RPS because of being part of the family, we can find work that'll keep you busy. I'm sure Kel has a list of jobs you'd be suited for and isn't make-work."

I certainly did, and only one of them involved the bedroom I looked forward to thinking of as ours. "You'll be kept plenty busy," I promised.

"Good. I don't do bored well. I start scheming things when I get bored, or I go on a hunt."

"I'm always going to volunteer the bear if you're bored."

"I knew there was a reason I wanted to marry you."

I shrugged and laughed. "I'll take what I can get."

MY PHONE RANG, and the sound startled me

so much I yelped, drawing the attention of everyone in the room. Flushing, I snatched the device and checked the display, grimacing when my father's name showed. "I need to take this."

With the paperwork signed by me, no one needed me, so I stepped into the hall. As expected, Meredith trailed in my wake and stood guard nearby.

I supposed asking her to stick with Eva for two hours had tested her patience a little.

I answered right before the phone went to voice mail. "What's wrong, Dad?"

"That hyena went to the media, and as expected, she's spreading a cocktail of lies. I've done some preliminary work, including securing the security tape of her entering your bedroom with Donald for her tryst, much to your mother's dismay. I want your permission to leak it to the media along with an official statement that you'd claimed irreconcilable differences due to you directly witnessing her cheating on you."

"Do it," I ordered. "I'll get a verified statement about the situation from a truth seer and have it released to the media in the morning."

"Get your lanky ass home, Kel. You're going to need to be seen in public if you want this to work."

"All right. I'll be there by morning. I'm bringing an updated copy of the abdication agreement with me, signed and ready for your confirmation along with the congress's."

My father sighed. "Great. That's going to add fuel to the fire. Can we delay this?"

"No. The agreement includes a clause that upon marrying the woman of my choice, two days before spring, the abdication will be stricken assuming my health issues are resolved to the satisfaction of Montana's royal physicians."

"Say what?"

"I'm marrying someone two days before spring, and the promise to do so is written into the agreement that'll be signed by you, Mother, and the congress. It should take the wind out of Gail's sails. I'll authorize the agreement to be leaked to the media so they can have a field day with it."

"You're really going to marry that woman."

"We've already picked a wedding date, and we've already selected a wedding planner, so yes. I am. The agreement specifically mentions that I will have an unobstructed choice of wife. Dad, it's not a game to me. She's not the queen you want, but she's the queen I need. That's the end of the story. If you want me to be the king in your wake, you need to accept her or cut me loose. That's something only you can decide. But this agreement will ease concerns in the congress about the line of succession."

"But you have no proof she's your one, Kel."

"Dad, I don't care if she's not the one my talent needs. Bone marrow transfusions will buy me some time if necessary. With Eva's contribution of talents, we don't need a male heir. We just need an heir. Her talent is likely strong enough to classify as royal level without any contribution on my part."

"You're serious. You're really willing to accept suffering for the rest of your life for her."

"Yes, I am. I've spoken with His Royal Majesty of Montana about the issue, and he helped draft the amendments to the agreement. I'm expecting you to sign, and I'm expecting the congress to sign. If I die by age fifty, that's an unfortunate consequence of my choice. But I refuse to marry someone like Gail, who is attempting to coerce her way onto the throne. She does not nor will she ever love me. She's after a crown, Dad. Why can't you see this?"

"Oh, I see it. Your mother's beginning to see it, too. But your mother worries Gail is a better alternative to Eva."

"I've made up my mind, Dad. I won't change it. I'd like my engagement to Eva to remain a secret for as long as possible so she can enjoy her work in the RPS without interference. As such, I fully intend on discrediting everything else Gail has said and coming up with a suitable answer to the rest."

"Who will you use for the verification?"

"His Royal Majesty of Montana. If he's verifying the truth, there'll be no doubts. When you release the security footage, ensure both her and Donald emerge with their modesty intact, such that it is."

"I shouldn't give them that much. To think they'd do that in your bedroom."

"I told you, Dad. I told you there were circumstances ensuring I'd never entertain Gail as a wife ever again. I was serious."

"I see that now." My father sighed. "This is a nightmare."

"For Gail, yes. For me, no. While the health clause will still be within the contract, I will make a public statement that I'm working towards being able to resume my full duties within the next, say, three months. That'll give me time to work with my new RPS detail and be able to adapt to heightened security."

"I can work with a three-month window. What about Grégoire?"

"What about him? I'm going to evaluate his workload starting tomorrow, shift as much off him as possible, and return him to a supporting role. I won't be able to pick up much of the work personally, but at least I can better delegate so he won't smother as much. Montana's concerned, and that's my top priority. Once I've delegated the workload off him, send him to North Dakota for a while."

"I see you've been notified about his relationship with Abby."

"Dad, he's an Averett man. If he settles down with Abby, she'll find no better partner. A wolverine will be able to protect her, too. Until King Adam and Queen Veronica have a child of age, she's the next in line for the throne. She'll need someone like Grégoire supporting her."

"But Grégoire will be a miserable king."

"No. I disagree. He'll be a miserable king of Illinois. He works best in a supporting role. Abby would be the queen. He would be the husband supporting his wife in every capacity possible. When you put him in a supporting role, he shines. He can learn to be her consort, but he may never learn to be Illinois's king. Those are two different things. With luck, Abby will never have to worry about coming near a throne. Suggest he go to North Dakota for some time away from Illinois. With a little work and some help, I can manage without him. He's earned the break."

My father heaved a sigh. "Your mother isn't going to handle this well, Kel. She's going to handle this so not well. There will be screaming. She's going to have a meltdown. She's already well on her way to having a meltdown. She didn't believe Gail had cheated on you until she heard about the surveillance videos. Also, I might leak your request for them to take their debauchery to another bedroom so you could burn your sheets. That clip shows nothing, but both of their voices can be heard, and we can match the videos with them going to your bedroom and leaving their clothes all over your floor."

I'd be playing with fire, and inevitably, I'd get burned authorizing it, but I had little choice.

Gail would do her best to sabotage me. "Do it, but you're taking responsibility for the leak. I'm going to feign ignorance over the leak if asked."

"Very well. When will you be able to return to the castle?"

I smirked at the easy, obvious way to taunt my father. "I'll let you know when we're on route. I'll get the bear to fly us in to save some time."

My father groaned. "Please don't let him crash the plane. The last thing I need is for you to be involved in a plane crash today, Kel. Please."

"Despite appearances, the bear is a licensed pilot and keeps his plane in good condition, Dad."

"I know, but I worry."

"Him crashing the plane is the least of our concerns right now. I'll call you with an ETA. Expect a few hours. I have some things I have to take care of before I can leave."

EXHAUSTION HIT me at the same time I relayed my father's warning about Gail going to the media. His Royal Majesty of Montana pinched the bridge of his nose. "I was hoping for at least a day before this happened. Just one day."

"Gail isn't very patient."

"So it seems. Alfred? Get the plane ready. I'll go to Illinois to handle this issue personally. Arrange a pilot to return Mr. Averett's plane to wherever he stores it. I'll take them with me. We'll plan to leave so it appears I flew to the airstrip nearest to Mr. Averett's residence before flying us all to Chicago. That'll give us a few hours to make a game plan and deal with this issue."

Meredith cleared her throat. "With all due respect, Your Majesty, Prince Kelvin needs some rest. He's not going to be able to handle pulling an all-nighter plus a potential press conference in the morning."

His Royal Majesty of Montana looked me over with narrowed eyes before turning to his wife's security detail. "Geoff?"

"When you ask things of me, I become worried."

"Contact Dr. Hampford, get the appropriate dosage, and ensure His Royal Highness of Illinois enjoys a nice nap until we reach Chicago. I don't want to be murdered by one of my own physicians for putting her patient at risk."

Eva snickered, linked her arm with mine,

and held me in place. "Grab the other arm, Meredith. He's slippery, and he'll try to run."

"You don't have to sedate me," I protested.

"We don't have to, but we're going to. We'll have your wife keep an eye on you, but I know your type." William closed the distance between us and dropped his hand on my shoulder. "You'll do what I do, which involves running yourself into the ground, and you're not in a good place to do that right now. So, a drug-aided nap is our best option. Just go along with it. Some sleep will do you a world of good, and Dr. Hampford can meet us in Chicago and make sure you're properly on the mend. This has the added benefit of giving you an out from any press conferences. I'll handle it on your behalf, and I've already heard your side of the story, which I can verify as the truth. To add insult to injury, I'll call in another truth seer to verify that I'm telling the truth. This Gail woman won't have a leg to stand on when I'm done, and if she wants to pull any stunts, she's going to have to somehow convince you to forgive her. I wish her the best of luck with that by the time I'm finished. For the truth seer, I'll pick a New Yorker, because New Yorkers love nothing more than trying to catch me in a lie."

With no other choice, I surrendered with a weary shrug. "If you really think it's necessary."

"It's necessary." Eva gave my arm a

squeeze. "You've been on the run all day, and you'll stress over the preparations. Let us take care of everything, then you'll only have to worry about the mandatory stuff in the morning. It'll be all right. I'll make sure that piece of shit doesn't have a chance of sinking her claws into you."

"All right. I'm going along with this, but I'm doing so under protest."

William grinned at me. "Welcome to being a royal. Alfred and Geoff do the same thing to me for the same reasons. You'll get used to it."

"Like hell I'll get used to it!"

Eva laughed. "Famous last words, Your Highness."

"I promise you I have zero intention of getting used to being sedated to make the RPS feel better, Your Highness."

She tugged on my arm. "No, but you'll accept it because it'll make me feel better."

I'd been played, and damn it, she was right. I would. "Under protest," I repeated.

"He's lying, Evangeline. You've already won the war."

She had, and I looked forward to what the future would hold.

———✦———

HIS ROYAL MAJESTY OF MONTANA called my father on my behalf, as it took Geoff less than ten minutes to contact Dr. Hampford and acquire the appropriate sedative. I learned the hard way he was willing to cheat, and unlike the sleeping pills I was accustomed to, injected sedatives took less time to kick in. Within five minutes of being stabbed, I was down and out for the count and didn't budge until sometime after the plane touched down in Illinois.

It took smelling salts to drag me out of the drug-induced haze, and the bearer of the vile jar smiled unrepentantly. Dr. Hampton set the salts aside, sat beside me, and checked my pulse from my wrist, staring at her watch. "The plane landed an hour ago, but I ordered them to let you sleep a little longer. You needed the respite and time to get yourself together. I would've liked to let you fit in another hour, but you're going to be needed at the castle fairly soon."

A glance out the window confirmed we were at the Illinois royal airstrip, a safe haven where reporters were barred and royal planes could stay on the tarmac indefinitely without disrupting other flights. I stretched, bit back a groan as my sore muscles protested the movement, and wondered how I'd been suckered into accepting yet another sedation.

"Any problems?"

"None yet, Your Highness. His Royal Majesty of Montana is enjoying himself a little more than he should. As a fair warning, he brought the queen and princess with him. Agent Evangeline is currently assigned to the princess's detail, which puts her in a good place to observe the press conference. Agent Scarson is on the tarmac keeping an eye on things. Your parents are at the press conference, and it's going to be mass chaos if the rumors spreading around the castle are to be believed."

"In this case, the rumors are probably right. The castle staff is well aware of the situation with Gail, and there are those who've been waiting a while to see her get her due on the matter," I admitted.

"Take your time getting up. You're going to be wobbly for a few minutes while the rest of the sedative works out of your system. I've had breakfast prepared for you, so you should eat before joining the fray. You're not expected at the press conference, as His Royal Majesty of Illinois made it clear that you're still recovering."

I really didn't want to deal with my parents yet, especially my mother. Within the next few hours, I expected my relationship with my mother to take a deeper dive, likely right into the death zone. "How much of the press conference will my mother be handling?"

"None of it, per order of His Royal Majesty of Montana. They had a row, and he informed her that if she couldn't put her son in front of the picture-perfect image she wants to present to the world, perhaps she's unqualified to have children. He's cranky when he's suffering from a lack of sleep. He's next in line for a dose of sedative, but we'll wait until he's back in Montana before he's off to take his enforced nap."

"My mother likely didn't handle that well."

"She handled it better than anticipated. I believe she's starting to figure out she's made a severe miscalculation. She hadn't reviewed the videos yet. That's been rectified, and it's probable I'll be treating her for shock by the end of the day. I wouldn't worry too much about it, although I expect you'll have a row or two with her before she settles down. Your father's going to be the easier one to manage. He understands that he has to dance the right line with you or risk losing his heir completely. And as you've committed to a marriage, despite it being to someone they don't approve of, I believe they'll play along."

"It's not like they're the one who has to marry her," I grumbled.

"That argument was used, and your mother countered with a list of qualifications she feels is needed for a queen."

"Did she say that in front of Eva?"

Dr. Hampford grinned. "She did."

"Tell me," I ordered.

"Well, Evangeline began with the biological responsibilities of a queen, which involved maintaining good health to ensure the line of succession, and we were treated to a lecture about ensuring the health of the future king, as he has an equal contribution to the development of little heirs. After she informed the queen on the state of her ovaries and her reproductive cycle, she then went on a rather delightful rant about the practical responsibilities of a queen. It was then I realized we've made a slight miscalculation."

"A slight miscalculation? How? What are you talking about?"

"Evangeline knows far more about the internal workings of a kingdom than we anticipated. Some of her speech was dated, but that's no surprise, considering her disowning. You might want to look into her lineage yourself, Your Highness. She knows too much to be a fringe elite. Her family has ties to a royal family somehow. I expect His Royal Majesty of Montana will be looking into it more aggressively after her rather impressive and accurate speech regarding the duties and responsibilities of a queen. She also got some new barbs in about ensuring the health of the heir, too."

I chilled, sitting straighter in my seat. "Which royal family?"

"We're guessing Nevada. That's her kingdom of citizenship. It could be with another kingdom if she sought refuge following disowning, but we haven't found any evidence she transferred her citizenship yet."

I could understand how an elite could transform from prim and proper to a hellion with a foul mouth, and the idea she's grown from someone who had needed to know the intricate details of rulership and found her way in the world, transforming herself into a huntress.

How the puzzle fit together would shape a lot of the future, but I'd seen something in Eva when her family had been mentioned.

It bothered me she might fear anything.

"Please tell Meredith I'd like to see her," I requested, getting to my feet to work the kinks out. "Unless breakfast is something I can choke down in a hurry, I'll skip it until after this is dealt with."

"Oatmeal. Should be easy enough for you to shovel into you before you get carried away."

"I can work with that."

"Good. I'll fetch Agent Scarson, you get yourself presentable and walk out the kinks."

I inhaled breakfast, smoothed out the worst of the wrinkles from the flight, and wasted too much time wrangling my unruly hair into something almost presentable. When I finally emerged from the bathroom, Meredith waited with Dr. Hampford.

"What do you need?" she asked.

"I want you to look into Eva's background and find out what steps we need to protect her. Dr. Hampford expressed concern, and I want to make sure we won't have any surprises from Nevada or another kingdom. If Dr. Hampford's speculations are correct, Eva might have worrisome connections."

Meredith's grim nod warned me of trouble brewing on the horizon. "A wise precaution, Your Highness. His Royal Majesty of Montana is likewise looking into the situation. We may have miscalculated. Several of the sessions regarding your health were televised, and Evangeline was in several notable clips. If she has royal connections of any sort, I've no doubt word has spread back to her family. This could create issues later."

"Honestly, I don't care who her family is. I do care about what they might do once they learn how involved she is with me. I don't want to see her used as a pawn in a political game."

"Well, she's established she's not a scraping from the bottom of the barrel. While there's definitely a rift between her and your mother, she's established she knows a lot more about being a queen than anyone expected. Your father's expression was interesting."

"Interesting how?"

"He's figured out Evangeline isn't nearly as two-dimensional as he wanted to believe. I expect you'll have an interesting few weeks after you're done with your first wave of RPS training. Speaking of which, we're skipping a trip to the castle altogether. We're going to the training center, where we'll get you settled. If you want to watch the press conference, we'll have a recording available. Evangeline will come to the center once her other duties are completed."

"His Royal Majesty of Montana is trying

to use his baby to get her interested in having a baby, isn't he?"

I wasn't sure what I thought about that, but I looked forward to when I could find some time to be alone with Eva.

"You would be correct. It doesn't help she gets stars in her eyes whenever she goes near the princess. I'm concerned you'll be dragged into the nonsense between North Dakota and Montana."

"Alaska might become a contender, too. They wasted no time having a child," I muttered.

"The Alaskan monarchs claim they're having no more than three. I have my doubts they'll stick to their guns. They're both too smitten with each other and their firstborn. Royalty tend to be unreasonable when it comes to having large families, as you're familiar with."

"I literally lost count of how many sisters I have, Meredith."

"Don't be absurd, Your Highness."

"I'm being serious! After five or six, I stopped counting. I might remember their names with a little effort."

Meredith sighed. "Add in your cousins, and I suppose I can understand."

"They do blur together. At one point, I think there were twenty or thirty of us in the same room." I wasn't even exaggerating, either. "Okay, fine. I have twelve sisters. I think."

"I have some bad news for you," Meredith announced.

Damn it. Thanks to the Averett talent, once securely bonded, the women didn't age or go into menopause until late age, which left one viable option. "Well, that would explain my mother's determination to meddle in my marital affairs. If I end up with another brother, can I quit?"

"No, Your Highness. You may not."

"Seriously? Again? Aren't the fourteen other children she's had enough?" I sighed. "What other bad news are you going to give me?"

"She'll be announcing her pregnancy next week."

"Good. Maybe that'll distract from the mess. Can she move that up to this week? This week would be good. Today would be even better. Please tell me it's a boy."

"Your Highness."

"What? I just woke up to find out my mother's pregnant again. If you're expecting me to take this with grace, I'm going to think you've been snitching from my medications, Meredith."

"I was more thinking it might be nice to be happy for your mother."

"When she's happy for me for the choices I've made in my life, I'll be happy she has a functional reproductive system. Until then, let's just stick to neutral ground."

Meredith stared at Dr. Hampford. "This is going to be harder than I thought."

"What were you expecting, Agent Scarson? The entire Illinois royal family is populated with stubborn men and even more stubborn women. If he relented with just that, you'd need to use the smelling salts on me. Don't underestimate him. I expect he's the type to hold a grudge until he's satisfied there's no threats left to his peace of mind, and his piece of mind is named Evangeline. The only reason it's a problem is because His Royal Highness is so tolerant he's taken everyone by surprise."

When Meredith's gaze returned to me, I shrugged. "She's not wrong."

"This is going to be a problem, isn't it?"

"Only if she tries to come between me and Eva, Meredith. I might be stubborn and capable of holding a grudge, but I'm not asking for much."

"No, you're not," she conceded. "All right. I'll try to impress upon Her Royal Majesty that it might be wise if she concedes this battle. Though, after the press conference today, I think you'll find it much smoother sailing. The truth is a difficult foe to fight."

"That it is."

FIFTEEN

If I could go even an hour without trouble, that'd be wonderful.

I'D BEEN to the RPS training center before, but I'd never been there as the one about to be tenderized. For the next month, my home would be a small bedroom in a hive of similar rooms, and Meredith and Eva had rooms nearby, which offered a chance to have some quiet time with my new wife. Judging from Meredith's bemused expression, she anticipated what I had in mind, but the small shake of her head warned me I shouldn't get my hopes up.

Meredith's expression changed; her eyes narrowed, and I presumed she was listening to a message in her earpiece. "Your parents are on their way here, Your Highness. They already left, so they'll arrive any minute. As you can probably guess, the press conference is over. The delegation from Montana is settling in at the castle now. Evangeline is accompanying your parents here."

"If I could go even an hour without trouble, that'd be wonderful."

She offered me a sympathetic smile. "At least your training officially begins today, so they won't be visiting long. To begin with, I'll introduce you to two of your new agents. They'll be the foundation of your daytime detail. The other members of your detail will be operating the scenarios. For the first run, you'll keep the same daytime detail for two weeks. After that, you'll cycle through agents on a daily basis to acclimate you to a shifting detail."

"Will I at least get a chance to catch up on my damned paperwork?"

"Surprisingly, yes. Currently, we have you scheduled for half days of physical therapy, and to ensure you can do your paperwork, you'll be scheduled for office hours in the first half of the day. That'll be when you start adapting Agent Evangeline to her acting-as-principal role."

"I don't know what he's going to make me do with paperwork, but I already don't like it," my wife muttered. "Christian drives like a lunatic, Meredith."

Meredith checked her watch. "I'm going to have to talk to dispatch. That was not enough lead time."

"I tried to tell them, but they ignored me."

My parents lurked behind Eva, and I gave my mother a full dose of my worst glare. "Seriously? Number fifteen?"

"It's your father's fault."

"I'm pretty sure you hold equal blame in this, Mother. Are you finally satisfied Gail would've been the worst mistake of my life if I'd done things your way?"

She had the decency to wince. "I've been convinced she isn't as she seemed."

"And neither is Eva."

"I discovered that this morning."

"If you're going to start screaming, let's get it out of the way. I have several weeks of torture thinly disguised as physical therapy ahead of me sandwiched between catching up on paperwork. As I expect you'll never accept my choice of wife, let's get the unpleasantness aside; you won't be making that choice for me. I trust His Royal Majesty of Montana delivered the paperwork for your review?"

"After we're done here, we'll be heading to Chicago to present it to the congress for signing," she replied. "This could cost you your life, Kelvin."

"I'm aware of that more than anyone in this room, Mother. But it's my choice, not yours. It was never yours. I tried things your way once, and it resulted in Gail. Now we've had a press conference because she was pissy she wasn't picked after she cheated on me in my own bedroom. You tell me, Mother. Whose choice was inherently flawed?"

"I'll admit I never believed she would do such a thing."

"You still think she's innocent, don't you?" I clenched my teeth. "You're delusional."

Silence. My mother's mouth dropped open, she swallowed, and tried several times to say something before clacking her teeth together.

"Delusional is exactly what to call someone when her own son has it verified by the king of fucking Montana that his ex cheated on him in his bedroom. And you still side with her? Look. I get you prefer the perfect family image, but enough is enough. I don't want your version of a perfect family image. What happened to family loyalty?"

"How dare you!" my mother choked out.

"Are you really asking me that, Mother?"

My father cleared his throat. "He's not wrong, darling. You hate being wrong, and frankly, you're wrong. He's provided irrefutable evidence of what she's done, and after he rejected her unwanted advances, she began her attempts to manipulate the court against him. A manipulation you're currently supporting. I think you need to reevaluate where you stand. Unless, of course, you want us to lose our son to your need to be right all the time."

Ouch. Me yelling at my mother over Gail was one thing, but my father's ice-cold delivery entered a whole different realm of harsh. "Dad, let's be civil about this. I'm angry, but I'm not that angry."

"He's already gotten over the angry part of

things around the same time he skipped dinner with me and walked out the door and almost died," Eva muttered under her breath. She didn't do a very good job of muttering; I had no doubt everyone heard her.

"Agent Evangeline is absolutely correct. We're the ones who are in the wrong in this situation, and we have zero right to dictate anything to him regarding the relationship he wishes to form. He has provided, in writing, a wedding date. He doesn't need our approval. He needs the congress's approval, which he has. They don't care who he marries. They want to ensure the line of succession remains intact and he rules instead of Grégoire. He's an adult, and perhaps it's time we started treating him like one."

"He's making a mistake," my mother hissed.

"And it's his mistake to make. Not ours. We've already made more than our fair share of mistakes, and Gail is at the top of the list. She's trying to ruin him in the eyes of the Royal States. That's unacceptable. I don't care how damaged your pride becomes over this issue, but enough is enough. Leave him alone about it. Maybe you'll never approve or accept his choice, but you'll do your job as the queen to at least pretend. Dislike his choice of wife all you want, but in the public eye, they'll believe you couldn't possibly be happier about your son finding a queen. This is not about you. It's about what makes him happy, and if his talent continues to eat away at him, then damn it, let him be happy for however long he has left."

"You two act like he's hopeless." Eva rolled her eyes. "I'll put an end to this right now, if you please."

I blinked. "Eva?"

"Sit your lanky ass down and let a woman work her magic," she ordered.

Dad would call me whipped, Mom would be disappointed, but I sat my lanky ass down on the bed and watched her with wide eyes.

Eva closed the door, and in a low voice, she said, "I branded his ass the minute I saw him. I know what his animal is. I know who he is. Man and beast. I'm not into beasts, I'll admit. I'm definitely not interested in men who act more like beasts than men. But he is what he is, and I accept all of that. If he spends every spring as a beast, it is what it is. I've accepted that. Perhaps you need to, too. But, I know something you don't know."

Meredith sat beside me and chuckled before whispering in my ear, "Pay very close attention, Your Highness. This is far more important than you think."

I stared at Meredith. "You're crazy, aren't you? She's going toe-to-toe against a pair of stubborn monarchs and enjoying herself. Anyone with a pair of eyes should recognize I won't find a better queen in the Royal States."

I earned a brilliant smile from my wife. "Quiet, you nutter. I'm not finished here."

"Sorry," I replied, not at all sorry.

"Point one: I'm a probable leech, as is the mouthy Your Highness who forgot I control his physical therapy regime for the foreseeable future."

"Not one of my brightest moves, provoking the controller of my physical therapy regime," I admitted.

"Point two: Being disowned doesn't remove my talents. It's already been partially investigated, but I come from an elite family, a family I want no association with. I don't want them to contact me or find me. I've been on the run from them since I was fifteen. That's not your problem, but it is mine. I have the level of talent you need for your son, and I introduce useful abilities to your bloodline."

"I don't want you for your talent, Eva."

She sighed. "But that's the reality of being your queen."

"Bullshit. Mom's got a middling talent at best. Your talent has nothing to do with joining this royal family, no matter how much my mother likes to posture and pretend she started out as something more than someone from a lower part of the middle castes."

"Kelvin," my mother complained.

"Stop complaining when I tell the truth. You should value honesty a lot more than you do," I snapped.

"Kelvin!"

"Well, you should. It's not my fault you don't like hearing the truth."

Eva cleared her throat. "I wasn't done yet, Your Highness."

I shut my mouth.

"Point three: I'm the anonymous bone marrow donor."

If Eva was trying to shock the entire royal family into submission, she was doing a good job. I gaped at her, at a complete loss over her claim. I glanced at Meredith for verification, and she offered me a smile.

"With all due respect, Your Majesties, when you were scrambling worrying about your line of succession and what to do about your dying son, she was in surgery buying him time," the head of my detail confirmed. "She asked for the procedure to be anonymous, and it was sealed to the point only Dr. Hampford, myself, and the hospital staff handling the transplant were aware of her identity. This was done completely of her volition. She volunteered to be tested to see if she was compatible. She was not approached, she did not ask for anything in exchange, and she also volunteered to serve as a blood donor when he was initially hospitalized."

I struggled with what I was being told, and I swallowed, staring at Eva, uncertain of what to say. With another one of her brilliant smiles, so much like the sun peeking through stormy skies, she crossed the room to me and dropped a kiss on my forehead. "I knew your worth from the first time I saw you. It was the least I could do."

"You're the marrow donor?" my mother whispered.

"There's a massive stack of paperwork confirming it I can authorize to have released through Dr. Hampford to prove my claim. Agent Scarson can also provide the medical leave documentation from my recovery period, although she had me on light assignments as soon as she believed I could handle it."

Meredith nodded. "Considering the nature of his talent, her assignments were to stay in close proximity, as Dr. Hampford wasn't certain how the marrow transplant would interfere with his talent. As far as she can tell, it hasn't. There are concerns he may have additional talents that are surfacing due to the procedure."

"I have nothing to prove to you, Your Majesty. Frankly, I don't give a flying fuck if you don't like me or approve of me, but should your pettiness hurt your son, I'll show you exactly why I'm not afraid to face off against the bear. He'll never be the aggressive type, not in the way you likely hope. He's never going to take the offensive like a lion, wolves, or bears."

"Or lynxes," my father added.

"Or lynxes," Eva agreed. "But he is what he is, and if you're unwilling to look beyond your own desires to see his virtues, you're the only losers here. If I can see what he is at first glance, I question why you can't. His worth shouldn't be defined by the woman you think is better for him. She's a user. She's an abuser, too. She displays every behavior the RPS is warned to watch for."

"I'm the first to admit I'm not in the same class as the rest of the men in the family." I shrugged. "The type of woman Averett men typically need isn't going to work for me. Call it a genetic defect if you'd like, but I'm simply not going to be able to match anyone in our family in that regard. I don't want to, either. That also means I'm not going to be the type of ruler you want me to be."

My father snorted. "You're going to outclass us in that department, son. You took to it from day one. You enjoy the work. We don't. We'd rather be doing anything else."

Unsure of what to say, I shrugged.

My mother stared at Eva as though seeing her for the first time. "You donated, and you asked for nothing?"

"I asked for nothing. Someone had to donate, and I was there. I was willing. I offered to be tested." Eva's expression turned wry. "Had I known going in it would hurt like a bitch, I might've asked for more than a few days off for the procedure. Between the quantity of marrow required and the chain healing accelerations, it was not a comfortable procedure. Well, procedures. They needed a lot of marrow."

The truth of her words soothed me as nothing else could, and I marveled at her. I couldn't fathom why she would even consider donating marrow for my sake.

I'd been so busy wondering how I'd convince her to give me a chance that she'd gotten so far ahead of me I'd lost sight of her. I'd been so busy looking behind me, searching for ways to entice her into staying I hadn't noticed all the clues screaming she'd already decided to stay.

"They regenerated your marrow with magic?" I asked.

"Several times. They needed to because if they left any of your marrow intact, your immune system might not recover; they needed to replace the whole shebang with mine. Also, if I have to do this again in ten years, we're having a talk, Your Highness."

"I'll keep that in mind."

"Do. That's where things currently stand. I'm on notice to be his donor for however long he needs a donor, which means I need to stick around. I agreed to this in writing. Like it or not, you're stuck with me in some capacity." Eva's expression turned wry. "It's entirely probable I'd be kicked out of the RPS and assigned a limited detail because of my status as his marrow donor. Dr. Hampford can provide you with more information once I authorize the release."

"Meredith?"

"It's true. That's part of why we've been

really lax in how we're handling her position in the RPS. Because she's your donor, she needs to be close in case another transplant is required. I've had to cite exceptional circumstances more times than I care to think about. A marriage would simplify matters significantly."

Marriage did simplify things significantly, although I remained stunned I'd been so thoroughly tricked.

I'd blame Dr. Hampford's cocktail of medications I'd been drugged with for far too long on my inability to put the pieces together. I'd also take some time to figure out how best to thank Eva, which would take an entire lifetime.

Eva smirked at me before giving my mother her full attention. "I really don't expect you to like or accept me. But you will have to deal with me."

My mother frowned, refusing to meet Eva's gaze. "Agent Scarson, how difficult would it be to find a matching donor?"

Meredith snorted. "Dr. Hampford is the best person to answer that question, but she anticipated it and told me what to say. Finding a donor for your family is difficult at best. Typically, thirty percent of donors rely on a family member to donate, but that's not a possibility in this case; the testing confirmed that the defect exists throughout the family, and because it's paternally genetic and maternally inherited as a dormant gene due to how the talent works, you, his sisters, his brother, and other direct blood relations would only transplant faulty marrow. Because of the alterations to his biology due to his talent, finding an appropriate donor would require large-scale effort. We checked the bone marrow registries for candidates. We found no one compatible. That Evangeline is compatible indicates they're likely a bonded pair and she was already being subjected to his talent. Her biology was already overwriting elements of his. This factored into our decision to keep her within the RPS."

Yep. I'd been thoroughly tricked. "I see I was left out of a few important details."

"We felt it was best to let nature run its course, Your Highness. It's been going exactly as we anticipated, although we underestimated Evangeline's acceptance and interest in a partnership with you. The cursing and general posturing led us to believe, rather falsely, she viewed you as an annoyance."

"Oh, he's an annoyance, but he's my annoyance," Eva cheerfully replied.

Ignoring Eva, Meredith directed her attention to my parents. "We also underestimated how quickly she, with a very strong firebrand talent, would grow attached to him. Dr. Hampford thinks they're a little like magnets. She branded him, he displayed interest, and they locked onto each other from the start. Completely accidental, but it is what it is. Enter the possibility they're both leeches on top of her talent, and I suspect they had no choice in the matter."

"Is this bond breakable?" my mother asked.

"Sure, if you want to run the risk of killing them. Dr. Hampford instructed I answer that question as a no. Should one die, it's probable the other will as well. This is the same with every other couple in the Averett family as far as I'm aware. It was a primary factor in my decision to proceed with putting Agent Evangeline in a principal position until the wedding ceremony. If we lose her, we lose him, too. This information will not leave this room. Agent Evangeline has an advantage; she's very adept at self-defense. In that, His Highness is the weaker link, as he's behind the curve. This is why we're doing an intensive training cycle here. Frankly, if I could keep him on this schedule through the end of winter, I'd be much more comfortable. The RPS in his kingdom has failed him to shameful degree, essentially gambling with his life."

Eva grimaced and glanced at me. "I hadn't been told about the mutual death part," she admitted.

"I suspected that'd be the case, but I've been in the family long enough to see how things work. In good news, we're harder to kill than the average person," I replied.

"That's a concern," my father said, sitting on edge of the bed. I worried the damned thing would collapse under the combined weight of three people, but it held. "It's not something we want to experiment with. Very well. It is what it is, and you've been determined to have her, so have her. If she'll have you."

If Eva rolled her eyes any harder, I worried I'd be expected to catch her when she fell. "I volunteered to have a bunch of pushy doctors cut open my leg and withdraw bone marrow multiple times. I think we're a little beyond that."

"And arms," Meredith added.

"I was not thrilled with that part. I am impressed with the surgical team, though. I had no idea it was possible to do so many torture sessions back-to-back like that. Also, your lanky ass needed a lot of marrow, Your Highness."

"Thank you, Eva."

She smirked. "You'd already thanked me once without knowing it, but you're welcome. Let's try to avoid needing to do any sorts of operations again in the future."

"Agreed."

Eva locked onto my parents and narrowed her eyes. "Now, if you two will excuse us, he needs to get changed so we can start his physical therapy."

My mother's eyes widened. "You're really dismissing us."

"Damned straight I'm dismissing you. I have work to do to get this Your Highness healthy, and I will not tolerate unnecessary delays to my schedule. Out! My work doesn't involve sitting here getting all wishy-washy. You can get wishy-washy at dinner this evening after I've run him into the ground."

When my parents obeyed, I worried Eva might truly be capable of taking over the world while dragging me along for the ride.

IT OCCURRED TO ME, sometime after getting dressed in a pair of sweats and being chased around the RPS compound, I was married to a devil of a woman I hadn't even gotten to kiss yet. I'd have to work on that. I'd also have to work on escaping my wife so she wouldn't pound me into the ground.

Again.

Every time she caught me and tossed me like I weighed nothing, she laughed. I toed the line between a pricked pride and amusement she found my misfortune entertaining.

"If you don't want to be tackled, you have to run faster, Your Highness."

I stretched out on the hardwood floor and debated the pros and cons of staying where I was at. "Run faster and for longer," I corrected.

A curious audience of RPS members watched while Eva straddled my back and poked my shoulder. "Something like that. Catch your breath and try again."

"Has anyone told you that you're evil, Eva?"

"On occasion. Fortunately, evil is part of my job description. I requested it to be added to the fine print. You're not going to rebuild your endurance unless I push you to the limit, find it, and then shove you over for a while until you do better. You'll survive. Just remember, I keep track of every time you whine and add ten minutes to your workouts."

I groaned and went limp on the floor. "Mercy isn't in your dictionary, is it?"

"Not a chance. Walk it off, and when you aren't gasping for air, get on the move, Your Highness."

"Is this what the next month of my life looks like?"

"Oh, no. The next month of your life looks like you're going to be tossed around by other RPS agents determined to relocate you until you're exceptional at escaping any and all capture attempts. This is just a warmup."

"Just how many relocations are you talking about?"

"As many as I can fit in within a four-week period of time. I expect five or six attempts a day after your paperwork. Up, Your Highness. Walk it off and get back to running. You need to hit your quota of miles before you get a break." Eva got off me and nudged my side with her shoe. "And less groaning. You're not dying. You're not even hurt. You're a little tired. When I'm done with you, you're going to be exhausted. March!"

As I had no doubt she'd haul me to my feet and shove me along to get her way, I got to my feet, dusted off and walked at my most dignified stride until I caught my breath.

"Run, little prince," Eva whispered from behind me.

I obeyed.

EVA CORNERED me in a supply closet, not one of my better moves in my efforts to escape her, and after a glance over her shoulder, she shut the door behind her. "Good discovery of that security gap," she announced.

I doubled over, hands braced on my knees, and panted to catch my breath. "Say what?"

"There aren't any cameras in here, and I'm not sure the camera in the hallway has a good view of the closet. I could do whatever I wanted to you in here, and it could be a while before anyone thought to check in on us."

"Wouldn't it be obvious when we didn't appear in the other camera's frame?"

"Sure, if they go through the trouble of double checking." Eva smirked and patted my cheek. "I got three and a half miles out of you today. Better yet, you're still on your feet. You aren't winning any races, but at the bear's house, you were dying after a mile. That's good progress."

I did some basic math, forcing myself upright to confirm there weren't any cameras in the closet. There weren't. "I'm more interested in the 'whatever you wanted to do with me in here' part of this equation."

"You've been a good sport, so perhaps you need some encouragement to be chased around and caught. By me, of course."

"As if I'd want to be caught by anyone else."

"I'd gotten that feeling. Except that time. You went for my face. Twice."

"The second time doesn't count. You told me to hit you."

"A cute boop to the nose doesn't really count as a hit, but I'll let you have it. For the record, I was counting that as your hit for my terms, but I wanted to make you squirm before the spring. My plans changed."

"For which I'm grateful. I'd already had to ask Meredith to provide protection if I had to resort to planning ambushes to land a hit." I smiled at her. "I would've, too. It wouldn't have ended well for me, I expect."

Eva grinned at me, stepped closer, and shoved my hair out of my face. "Meredith told me. She recommended I show some mercy on you, as we didn't want you to stress and impair your recovery. Of course, I wasn't anticipating your mother's mulish pride ruining my fun."

"I'm sorry about her."

"Don't be. I expect she gives all your potential agents a difficult time. Now, there's an evaluation I need to do to check on your general health, Your Highness."

As Eva enjoyed catching me by surprise and putting me on the spot, I watched her warily. "What sort of evaluation?"

"Your mouth, my tongue."

I discovered a whole new appreciation for unmonitored supply closets. "You caught me. It seems unfair of me to deny you an opportunity to do an examination at your leisure."

She smirked. "I thought you'd say something like that, and we forgot in Montana. A foolish oversight on our parts. Who knows when we'll get a little quiet time alone for the next few weeks? We better make use of every single moment."

As I had no doubt privacy would come at a premium beginning tomorrow, I wasted no time wrapping my arms around her and taking the initiative, ready to prove I could be an instigator, too, if she took too long taking advantage of every opportunity.

IT TOOK the RPS ten minutes to contact Eva on her earpiece, puzzled over how we'd managed to vanish into thin air. While I caught my breath, she assured the RPS she had the situation under control, and that she'd allowed me a breather before my next run.

I admired how she told so many lies using nothing but the truth.

"There are security gaps in the camera feeds, so if you could kindly close them, it would be appreciated."

"Kindly?" I mouthed at her.

"I don't want fucking excuses, I want the gaps closed!" she barked, shooting a glare at me.

I grinned.

Tapping her earpiece to shut off the microphone, Eva shook her head, opened the door, and peeked into the hallway. "Surprise, surprise. It's clear. That's going to be our job for the rest of the day, identifying more gaps in the security system here. There's no excuse for this, not here. If this place is a disaster of gaps, what is the castle like?"

"Well, my bedroom is monitored more than I like, although there's a deliberate gap over the bed itself," I grumbled.

"Sound and video?"

"Yes, both. The outer rooms of each suite are monitored while the inner areas are recorded but not actively monitored."

"Royals do need some privacy."

"That was the logic behind the choice, yes. One I'm appreciative of. It's bad enough I can't walk through my own living room without knowing I'm being recorded."

She chuckled and snapped her fingers,

pointing down the hall. "Brisk walk, Your Highness. You're on a light schedule until after lunch, then I'm going to run you into the ground so hard you'll be half asleep during dinner. After dinner, you get to walk for however long it takes for you to pass out. During our walks, we'll be discussing basic protocol for relocations. There are some rules, as no one wants anyone to be injured running any scenarios. While you're expected to fight back and do everything you can to prevent a relocation, there are certain cues the agents will use. When you're hit with one of these cues, your job is to drop limp and play dead. Depending on the cue, you'll count to a certain number. That's how we'll mimic you being unconscious for a capture or simulating a fatal or critical hit."

"That sounds less than fun."

"Oh, it'll be fun. For us. You might even enjoy it if you like playing hide and seek. Try to think of it like a game, although it's a game that might save your life down the road."

And hers, which is why I'd treat it seriously. "I'll do my best, but don't get your hopes up too high."

"Your job is simple. Survive. You do that, and you pass with flying colors. This training is to help give you the tools to accomplish that goal. I'll be taking a walk in your shoes doing the same thing, but I'll be giving the agents more of a challenge because I'm skilled, good at evasion, and am much healthier than you are. Don't sweat that, by the way. It's going to be at least another month or two before you're closer to average. Dr. Hampford is hopeful you'll start bouncing back fast, but patients recovering from chronic illness often take longer to get back into shape."

"I'm honestly impressed I'm progressing as fast as I am."

"You're doing well."

I glanced her way. "Well enough for another adventure in a supply closet?"

"If we can find another one that hasn't been secured."

"I'm suddenly much more interested in this running and walking I have to do to earn lunch and dinner."

Eva arched a brow. "Of course you are, Your Highness. Typical, bird-brained man."

Only for her, but if she hadn't figured that out yet, I'd enjoy showing her the truth.

TRUE TO EVA'S THREATS, she ran me into the ground until dinner, but I was in such an exhausted daze I barely remembered any of it. I almost felt guilty over communicating with my parents in grunts and other forms of wordless communication. Instead of walking with Eva as planned, I staggered to my new bedroom for the next month, flopped, and passed out.

My day started at dawn, and a bright-eyed Eva woke me bouncing on the bed. "How the hell do you have so much energy?"

"I'm on your sleep schedule, so I get to sleep when you sleep, and since you wussed out on me yesterday, I got time off work. I'm refreshed and ready to go. How about you?"

"No." I rolled over, grabbed my pillow, and shoved it over my head. "No."

"No once was sufficient. You've been down for almost twelve hours. Rise and shine, sleepyhead. You need a shower, then you have a mountain of paperwork to tame. And it's a literal mountain. I watched a herd of people bring it in last night. There's a nice office filled with many papers waiting for your attention. Also, Grégoire will be arriving within the next two hours to help you with the transition."

"Get him to make a list of priorities he needs shifted off, then tell him to get his ass to North Dakota for a while."

"Isn't that a bit mean? He wants to help."

"He's covered my ass for months. My turn. Tell him to give me a list of the critical matters so I can deal with them. He deserves some time off, and Abby's probably itching to be going home by now."

"She is. Do you want to see her before she goes?"

"And delay her taking Grégoire out of the war zone? Hardly. Tell her I expect her to be at the wedding, though. I'll go to North

Dakota and relocate her skinny ass here if she puts up a fight about it."

Eva chuckled. "Is that a hint she should be in the bride's party? Mackenzie wanted names. She called me last night about it. I have a ten-page list of things we need to tell her so she can plan everything. It's on the list to be handled this week."

"I'll put her in my party if necessary."

"She's not a man."

"I don't see how this is relevant."

"Men go into the groom's party, women go into the bride's party."

"I see no reason why the bride can't have men in her party if she wants."

"I'm not sure that's how it's supposed to work, Your Highness."

"If it makes the stuffy royals feel better about it, we'll pick an equal number of men and women and assign them to sides regardless of why they're there."

"I'm pretty sure that's untraditional, but I like it. I guess the answer to 'Do you want a traditional wedding?' is no?"

I sighed, rolled out of bed, and grimaced that I'd gone to sleep still wearing my sweats from yesterday. "Unfortunately for the bride and groom of this wedding, there needs to be a Cinderella makeover for the bride, and the prince has to be even more princely than usual. Weddings are productions. I'll be contemplating escape before this is over."

"Well, you have plenty of time to worry

about it. Your shower situation is fringing on critical." To prove her point, Eva pinched her nose closed and pointed at the bathroom I shared with Meredith and Eva. "Please take a shower. Use extra soap."

"It's your fault. I hadn't thought you'd run me into the ground quite so literally."

"I underestimated the power of a food coma. And anyway, you seemed content and happy sleeping once you went down, so we decided to leave you alone. Try to stretch out the kinks so you don't get too sore being a desk slave for the morning."

"I'll try." Moving hurt enough to warn me I'd be miserable if I didn't heed her advice, and I checked the closet to discover someone had moved in most of my wardrobe. With a half day of work ahead of me, I selected a suit for the day, decided against the tie, and went to take the hottest shower of my life.

It helped some, but I'd earned a few bruises from my close encounters with the floor. I expected I'd have a lot more by the end of the day, but I refused to complain. If all went well, I'd have a real detail, as would Eva.

A few bruises wouldn't kill me.

Dressed for the work I knew best, I emerged from the bathroom to discover Meredith, Eva, and Christian having a discussion. Where Christian went, my father wasn't far behind, and I peeked through the open doors. "Where's the cat?"

"His Majesty is waiting in your temporary office, Your Highness," Christian informed me. "You're looking well."

"That's only because the suit hides the evidence of my latest beating."

"Physical therapy doesn't count as a beating," he replied.

"I may have tossed him around some to better motivate him. He wasn't running like he meant it. I figured if I took him down like one of those damned wolves after a baby deer, he'd run faster. It worked. I got an extra whole mile out of him last night through carefully timed takedowns."

Christian laughed. "Whatever works. How's the schedule looking?"

"He might be on track by the end of the month if there aren't any setbacks." Eva looked me over and nodded her satisfaction. "He has a lot of work ahead of him, but he's going to pick up a lot of it quickly. The offense will be a challenge, but I think I can I can bring him to tolerable levels on the defensive side of things. The morning paperwork will delay things."

"And you begin scenarios this afternoon?"

"Yes, we do. We're going to start him light with a few unconscious relocations. We're going to go through the cues and do a staged scenario so he gets a feel for how they work before we start him on the unexpected scenarios. Tomorrow, anything goes. If his paperwork schedule allows, we'll start him up on twenty-four-hour scheduling."

I wasn't the only one to grimace at Eva's enthusiasm, and I sighed. "I'd like to survive this."

Meredith offered one of her consoling smiles. "Agent Evangeline has a good eye for the training regime. It's harsh, it's more than a little brutal, but if we stick to her game plan, it'll be an effective way to bring you up to speed. His Majesty asked me to go over the strategy. He's concerned."

There were times I contemplated murdering my father, and I wondered if I'd get through the day without wanting to strangle him. "Why now?"

"Ironically, he's concerned you might be trying to hurry your recovery too much."

I blinked, furrowed my brows, and tried to think why my father would want my recovery slowed. "Say what?"

"He's concerned you're going to push yourself too hard and suffer a relapse or get sick. Mostly, he's concerned you'll get sick."

"Dr. Hampford checked him over last night after he went to sleep," Meredith announced. "He's fine. He'll be checked every night for any evidence of illness. Sore muscles and bruising is being ignored as long as they're within her level of tolerance. So far, Dr. Hampford is pleased with his progress. Muscle development is her primary concern, and while Agent Evangeline wanted him to fit in a little more exercise after dinner, he surpassed her expectations for the afternoon."

I hunted for my shoes, shoved them on, and searched the room for my briefcase, which was nowhere to be seen. "My briefcase wandered off again. Why does that damned thing keep wandering off?"

"It's in your office, worrywart. Your bedroom is a no-work zone, so your briefcase will stay in your office," Eva informed me. "Keys, wallet, and phone are in the nightstand drawer."

I retrieved them and put them in their proper pockets. "All right. I suppose Dad wants something more than have you poke your nose into my detail, Christian?"

"You grunted at him last night, Your Highness. You were so tired you ate some of your least favorite foods without even noticing. His protective instincts are going haywire. Reassure him you're fine, and he should go away."

"He better. I have a lot of briefings to read today, and if he doesn't get out of my hair, nothing will get done."

"He has to go to Chicago with Her Majesty to finalize the new set of paperwork you brought from Montana. The Montana delegation is going with them to ensure there aren't any mishaps."

That would keep them out of my hair for a while, much to my relief. "All right. I can take care of that."

"Good. If you need me to keep him busy because he's bothering you, tell Meredith. I'll take care of it."

Fighting against the urge to laugh, I arched a brow and glanced at Meredith. "Please contact Christian and tell him my father is bothering me."

"Christian, I've reason to believe His Royal Majesty is bothering His Highness, if you wouldn't mind dealing with it," she relayed.

Eva snickered, shook her head, and lifted her hand to her ear. "His Royal Highness is headed to his office."

"That's code for the interested agents to scatter so you don't feel like the latest addition to the menagerie," Meredith translated. "Everyone's eager to start the afternoon session, so there's been a lot of loitering. Most got a look at you yesterday, and after reviewing a truncated version of your medical file, they're impressed you're doing as well as you are. Everyone's been briefed about your physical limits, and they're getting a taste of dealing with an indisposed principal. I meant what I said before, Your Highness. The next three weeks will be an endurance test for you, and I fully expect you to try to run when you reach your snapping point. At no time are you to notify anyone you're about snap, either. Let it happen. I'm trained in dealing with the fallout, and your new agents need to experience it for themselves."

The thought of being pushed to the limit, especially when Eva would be involved, worried me.

My expression changed as Christian chuckled. "It's normal, Your Highness. We did it to your father. We did it to your mother, too. We've done it to every Illinois monarch since the founding of the RPS. The RPS shouldn't have delayed this stress test for this long, but without a stable team, it's difficult. Starting with a stress test is unusual, though."

"He can handle it," Eva promised.

I worried I wouldn't live up to her expectations. "All right. Show me to the office so I can handle the paperwork. It'll take me months to catch up, but there's no time better than the present."

IT WOULD TAKE months to dig out of the paperwork hell waiting for me; an unfortunate amount of the documents dealt with my absence. As I'd requested, Grégoire left a note with the critical matters listed in order of priority. My father watched me read over the letter.

"Hey, Dad?"

"Yes?"

"Make sure Grégoire doesn't come back to Illinois for at least three months."

"Isn't that a little excessive?"

"No. He can keep Abby company."

My father scowled. "What game are you playing, kiddo?"

"I'm not playing a game. I'm merely giving him a chance to convince Abby she should keep him. In North Dakota. Out of my hair for at least three months."

"Are you angry with him?"

I looked up from the note and snorted. "No. I'm thanking him for putting up with this shit on my behalf."

"I'll make sure he's aware his eviction from the kingdom is a gesture of good will."

"Tell Abby I'll call her after things settle down to plan a visit. Grégoire can handle all the kissy-kissy crap she likes so much."

"Kissing your cheek is hardly kissy-kissy crap, kiddo."

"It is when she does it to annoy me. The last time I let her, she licked me."

My father snickered, coughed to cover it, and then shrugged. "She has a sense of humor."

"She knows I head right for the bathroom to try to scrub the skin off my face, too."

"There is that. I'll pass along the word. Your mother and I are going to be in Chicago for the next few days. Will you be all right on your own?"

"I'll be fine. Please give my regards to King William and Queen Mackenzie."

"I will. If you need anything, give me a call."

"Dad, I'm at the RPS training compound

surrounded by RPS agents. I think I'll be fine. If there's anything the matter, I'm pretty sure one of the fifty-some agents loitering around here will notify you."

"Kelvin."

"Should I for some unfathomable reason require your assistance, I will call you."

"I raised a mouthy boy," my father muttered, heading for the door. "Call me."

I waited until he was out of earshot before I turned to Meredith and said, "The only way I'm calling him is if I'm somehow relocated, abandoned in the middle of the forest with my phone, and have absolutely no other choice. I really hope the RPS has similar feelings on this matter."

She chuckled. "I'll make certain that His Royal Majesty is only contacted should there be an actual emergency."

"Appreciated."

LUNCH SIGNALED an end of my return to familiar ground, and as soon as I'd eaten enough for Eva's satisfaction, she herded me to the compound's gymnasium where two younger men waited.

Meredith took over, and with a single nod of her head evicted my wife from the gymnasium. "Your Highness, this is Agent Barclave and Agent Ithaca. They'll be your primary detail. They have the best talents and skillset among the new recruits. While I'm briefing you on how scenarios will work, Agent Evangeline will be preparing to take a principal role so the teams will get used to protecting two people at once."

Agent Barclave looked me over, his dark eyes narrowing as he took me in, his gaze locking on my open collar with no tie. Something about the man put me on edge, and I assumed it had something to do with the challenge in his gaze.

Agent Ithaca flashed me a grin before resuming his stoic pose.

"Agent Barclave will be functioning as the head of your detail for the current exercises. Expect him to be with you at all times. Agent Ithaca is the footman of the pairing. Should your agents need to separate, Agent Barclave will stay with you while Agent Ithaca will be more mobile. The other agents assigned to your detail will be operating as actors in the scenario. After you're accustomed to how scenarios work, you will rotate through agents daily. This will give everyone a chance to work with you."

"Gentlemen," I greeted. "I expect we all have a lot to learn here."

With narrowed eyes, Agent Barclave looked me over, and I wondered what he was thinking. His expression led me to believe nothing good.

"His Highness's health condition made it difficult, at best, to undergo the training other principals enjoy. Now that his health is improving, he's ready to begin with relocation scenarios and learn the general ropes. He'll also be learning basic self-defense, as this was unfortunately neglected. This will make your jobs more difficult for the foreseeable future. While Agent Evangeline will be working with him on self-defense, you will need to do what he can't."

Both men saluted Meredith.

"All right. Your Highness, to begin this session, we're going to go over the cues you'll need to follow. Cues will be used for most physical interactions for the first few days. As you become more adept at self-defense, we'll remove cues for most things, requiring you to be handled rather roughly. Some cues—for dangerous maneuvers that could lead to substantial injury—will be used until the end of training. For example, should a would-be kidnapper attempt to hit you on the back of the head with a bat, we will use a hard swat to indicate you've been hit."

I winced at the thought of someone taking a bat to my head. "Is that even survivable?"

"Surprisingly, yes. It depends on how hard you're hit, if you receive medical attention immediately, and the talents of your agents at the time you're struck. Agent Barclave has a minor healing talent, which makes him ideal for this line of work. While he can't save you from catastrophic injury, he can buy you a few minutes for additional help to arrive. A severe blow to the head would test his abilities, but he's talented enough he can buy you time for proper medical care."

"Well, that's reassuring."

While grim, Agent Barclave smiled.

He reminded me of a shark on the hunt for his next meal. The prey instincts that kept me alive during the spring flared to full life, but in true turkey fashion, I stood my ground. I blamed my overactive imagination, the deluge of concern I'd meet an untimely end due to my lack of training, and my battered trust in the RPS for my hesitancy. Later, I'd need to ask Meredith about him.

"All right, Your Highness. The first cue will be the swat to the head. Any strike to your face or head essentially means the same thing. You'll drop to the floor and wait. How long you wait will depend on where you're hit. A strike to the face, for example, will only stun you for a few moments. You'll count to five. In this case, you don't have to necessarily fall to the floor. To a knee is fine." Meredith stepped to me, and with startling force, she slapped me. I staggered, blinking as the realization she'd hit me sank in.

When I didn't drop to a knee, she helped me along with a kick to the back of the knee. "I forgot to mention that if you don't drop on your own, you'll be helped down."

As my knee colliding with the hardwood floor hurt, I hoped I'd learn that lesson faster than the others. "I'm going to emerge from this holding bags of frozen peas to my face, aren't I?"

"Ice packs, probably. Why waste good peas?" Meredith replied. "If you're lucky, I'm sure Dr. Hampford would be pleased to help lessen some of the swelling should we do any damage to your pretty face."

Agent Ithaca coughed to hide his bemusement while Agent Barclave's smile widened.

One I liked, the other grated my nerves the wrong way. I'd learned from an early age there'd always be an agent I wouldn't like; my personal feelings about my detail were to be put aside if they did their job. Fortunately, part of my job was to pretend they didn't exist unless something was wrong.

What separated me from my parents and the rest of my family was knowledge. They knew what to do if something went wrong.

I didn't.

"So, standing shocked I just got hit in the face isn't a reasonable response? Because honestly, that's probably exactly what I'd do in a live situation." I held my hands up in surrender. "Unless I got hit so hard my ears rang, then I'd probably fall down without any help."

Meredith chuckled. "Assume that anyone who lands a hit on your face is trying to take you down, Your Highness. I just used enough force to catch your attention."

"Consider my attention caught."

"Again, but remember your job is to drop to the floor this time."

I got to my feet, braced to have the sense slapped out of me, and when Meredith cracked her palm against my cheek, I went down, careful to keep my knee from slamming into the hardwood floor. The blow stung, but I ignored the discomfort.

"Better. The agents will try to be gentler than that, but expect to get smacked around. In the midst of a scenario, everyone tends to get overly excited, so agents and principals alike tend to get roughed up. When you're in a struggle with one of the agents, put in your best effort. Obviously, we don't want anyone to get hurt, but our goal is to give you the skills you need to escape dangerous situations."

"What am I supposed to do after I count to the right number?"

"Escape. You're going to get taken out the first few times. You need more training, but this'll at least let you see how we work. It'll also let you be aware of ways someone might try to relocate you without your permission. By the time we're done, you'll have been manhandled so many times you'll go where we want you to go, learn how to escape dangerous situations and regroup with your agents, and work with your agents."

Any one of those things sounded like a challenge, and I was at a loss of how I'd accomplish any of them.

"For today's starting session, I'm going to be your assailant. Agent Barclave will be responsible for extracting you from the situation. Agent Ithaca will be assisting either side as the scenario requires. For our first run, we're going to go with the baseball bat assault. This is one of the more dangerous versions, as without the right talent, it's more likely to lead to death."

"Dying is definitely not on my schedule," I muttered.

"Good. Cue number one, a hit to the back or side of the head. You'll drop the floor, go limp, and count to five hundred. Take your time counting, and try not to react to anything. With a blow like that, it's probable you'll be unconscious long term, and if Agent Barclave and Agent Ithaca haven't recovered you by the count of five hundred, you're likely in progress of being relocated. The scenario ends, and your agents lose. In this case, a loss could be either relocation or death."

"Again, definitely not on my schedule," I replied wryly. "In application, couldn't a blow to the head stun rather than knock out?"

"Yes. It's possible. In live situations, you'll be expected to do what you can. For training purposes, we work with the worst-case scenarios."

"If you train me to handle the worst-case scenario, I should be able to handle everything else?"

"Exactly. Today, we'll give you a taste of them. Tomorrow, outside of the four hours you're in your office working, we'll be in full scenario mode. Anything goes, day or night. As soon as you're sufficiently caught up on work, we'll shift you to twenty-four hours."

I considered the head of my detail. "Is there a reason you can't shift me to twenty-four hours now? Because honestly, dealing with four hours of working uninterrupted on briefing documentations is not my idea of a good time. I'd view interruptions as rescue."

She chuckled. "I don't think you appreciate the respite I was offering, Your Highness."

"I don't need a respite. I need training. I understand that. The sooner I'm shifted to twenty-four hours, the faster I'll learn. I'll probably curse you every step of the way, but I see no reason to delay. Once I return to the castle, there's no such thing as a conveniently scheduled respite. I'm already used to that. I'm just not used to people actually taking advantage of the lackluster security. So, let's fix that."

"It's ultimately your choice. We'll try not to disrupt your work too much."

I doubted her definition of too much matched mine, but I remembered what she'd said. Within two weeks, if I wasn't trying my best to escape from my agents, I'd be surprised.

It would do.

THE NEXT TIME Meredith offered me a respite, I would listen. Not only would I listen, I would be grateful for her mercy. I'd even consider kissing her feet. She'd told the truth when she warned me I hadn't appreciated her offer.

When she said twenty-four hours, she meant it. I lost track of the days. I missed sleep. I missed Eva. She'd been assigned as a principal, but no one had told me I wouldn't see her often. The agents she worked with kept her busy, and unlike me, she put up a fight when they tried to relocate her.

I'd gotten a chance to watch once, and it had taken four agents to finally take her down. The demonstration left me conflicted.

I loved watching her. I loved how she defied four men stronger and bigger than her, holding her own for longer than I managed. However, the instant they put their hands on her and caught her, I wanted to tear them away from her.

It'd taken a few whispered words from Meredith to remind me it was nothing more than a scenario.

I still wanted to get involved, but I'd stood still and quiet, seething while they did their work and Eva played dead like she was supposed to. I'd never been the jealous type with Gail, but every day separated from Eva put me on edge. I suspected Meredith knew; I caught her smirking in my general direction, waiting for the moment I snapped.

All I wanted in life was a few minutes alone with Eva. A single kiss would work wonders for my mood. Hell, I'd forgo the kiss just to hear her grace the world with her colorful vocabulary. When playing the part of a principal, she'd used language royalty would approve of, which grated me almost as much as other men touching her.

It took a week for me to start plotting a relocation of my own with Eva as my target. Every time they started another scenario, I watched. Calculated. Wondered how they bypassed security while observing the way they moved to get behind me for the strike to the back of my head.

Meredith liked going for the back of my head, and I believed Agent Barclave let her get away with it more often than not.

I found that interesting, but I kept my misgivings to myself. I had no reason not to trust the man. Furtive looks didn't mean anything. Allowing Meredith to get close and whack the back of my head didn't mean anything, either. Together, they meant something to me, but I didn't understand what enough to ask Meredith about it.

Something about him grated, something that only manifested in the quieter moments before a scenario began. I'd learn to anticipate the scenarios from his reactions.

His expression always changed, growing colder than the façade he presented to his fellow agents. If looks could lie, his did.

I hadn't realized something as simple as a glance could tell truths or lie.

Two weeks and three days into the torture labeled as training, Agent Ithaca worked as my primary agent, supported by Agent Greene, a second-round pick, replacing one of the younger agents who'd discovered he didn't have a taste for disrupted hours, a stressful job, and the risk of putting up with me for extended periods of time. I liked the older man replacing the washed-out agent.

He reminded me a little of my great-grandpa, refusing to deal with unnecessary bullshit.

The morning went about as well as I expected. Every time I started to get somewhere with work, Meredith or one of the other agents would barge into the office, triggering mayhem. Meredith enjoyed it best when I got into a groove, sinking into the routine of work to the exclusion of all else.

The door banging open did a good job of notifying me I had company.

The first week I'd launched out of my chair.

I was too tired to launch anywhere, although I did raise a brow and glance up from my paperwork. Meredith had made it two steps into my office before Agent Greene had gone after her like a wolverine after lunch, and the two squabbled on the floor, vying for position. Of my agents, Greene enjoyed the sport of trying to best Meredith the most, and it would take them ten or twenty minutes of wrestling on the floor for one of them to win.

Agent Ithaca sighed, moved so he could get between me and Meredith as needed, and called in the scenario start on his earpiece, his tone resigned.

I returned to work with a shake of my head, filtering out the thumps, the occasional giggle Green evoked whenever he landed a hit on Meredith's ribs, and their grunts. Had the paperwork in question been important, I might've cared more, although I did need to fax the damned thing to my father.

My first edict as king would be to ban fax machines and buy good scanners so we had better digital records of paperwork moving through the government offices. Armed with the ten other sheets I needed to fax, I got up, stepped around the pair on the floor, and headed down the hall.

"That's the first time you've tolerated them doing that without doing more than looking eternally disappointed at the interruption," Ithaca murmured, keeping close. "I'm pretty sure you're breaking at least a few rules just wandering off."

"Agent Greene looks like he has the primary intruder in hand, and if she has friends, I'm sure you can take care of the rest. You did the call in for backup, so a little movement on my part isn't going to make much difference. I need to fax these."

Ithaca called in my destination, all of twenty feet away from my office.

One of my agents turned torturers made a run at me from behind the photocopier.

After two weeks of being slapped around, bonked in the back of the head, tossed over shoulders, dragged by my feet, and otherwise moved in humiliating fashions, I thought whacking him in the face with my paperwork was appropriate. "Hollacks," I greeted.

Like me, they had to play by set rules, and my agent went down to a knee, and I took the time to roll up my papers and whack the back of his head with them.

He played dead, although unconscious victims weren't supposed to laugh.

"It's a little like smacking unruly dogs when they won't stop bothering me," I observed, resuming my hike to the fax machine.

"In real situations, I'd be the one dealing with him," Ithaca replied.

"Well, you have time. You can take a turn with him if you want. Honestly, I just want to fax these papers and then take a walk. I'm not going to get much more done if Meredith put Hollacks onto the assault team. He's the one she sends in for extra bodies. Do you think Greene managed to subdue Meredith?"

"He'll keep her busy. Should I just notify the others you're about done with this for today?"

"And ruin their careful planning to make

me snap so you can see what I'll do? That would be inconsiderate of me."

Maybe if I got lucky, my walk could expose where Eva hid during the days so I could at least say hello.

When I got back to the castle, I'd have to ask my father how often he actually saw my mother during the day. If the rest of my life involved struggling to get five minutes alone with my wife, I really would snap. After I finished snapping, I'd rewrite the rules to mandate a minimum amount of time I got to spend with her.

I contemplated my options while I faxed papers to my father. By car, the castle was only five minutes away. After being run around the RPS compound most days, I could handle the hike there. I glanced at Ithaca. "Nothing in the rules says I can't just wander off if I take you with me, right?"

"It's technically not an escape attempt if you're accompanied by your active agents. Agents. That's plural."

"We'll have to rescue Greene, then."

"Yes."

I rolled up my newly faxed papers and marched to my office. Meredith still wrestled with Greene, and I waited for a good opportunity to beat her with my papers. "I'm going on a walk, and the rules say I have to take Greene with me, so you can't play with him right now."

Meredith sighed. "Please take the scenarios seriously, Your Highness."

"I've disabled two goons. I thought I was doing a good job." I offered Greene my hand. "I want to walk, and it seems I need to take you with me, so let's dump the body in a closet somewhere or something."

"How about under your desk?"

"Can we tie her up first?"

"That would waste time," he replied, accepting my help to get to his feet. "Rolled up papers are now your weapon of choice?"

"I'm thinking I need to invest in a spray bottle."

"You're in a mood today," he observed, grabbing Meredith's hands and dragging her around my desk. I pretended I didn't notice her helping him with shoves of her feet.

"I need a breath of fresh air. This paperwork has gotten on my last nerve."

"And here I thought the constant stream of scenarios would've done the job first."

I tossed the documents on my desk. "I'd ship them to my father, but he'd just ship them back and tell me I'm better at this shit than he is."

Meredith snorted from her position under my desk.

"Hey, Green?"

"Your Highness?"

"Smack the back of her head a few more times so she stays down long enough for us to take a breather without her pulling another scenario on me."

The agent chuckled, vanished behind my desk, and returned moments later. "We usually give you an hour, Your Highness."

I could think of four times yesterday I'd gotten less than ten minutes, and I ignored his attempt to lower my guard. If my luck held, they'd give me half an hour, and after escaping Meredith and Hollacks, they'd take me down before I realized I'd been hit.

They liked putting me back in my place after any form of victory.

Oh, well. At least I'd get a walk in before they returned to tenderizing me in preparation for life back at the castle.

SIXTEEN

You didn't kill him, did you?

I LEARNED from first-hand experience why the RPS considered a hard blow to the back of the head game over. The memory of being hit escaped me, but according to the throbbing in the back of my skull, I'd come a little too close to having my brains scrambled.

I'd thought having the marrow of my bones sucked out and replaced hurt, but I'd been mistaken.

Even breathing triggered bursts of agony, and each time the pain crested from the slightest movement, I sank back into unconsciousness only be to be ripped back to reality.

Had anyone had a smidgeon of compassion, I would've been put out of my misery, but no. The statistics proved true: royals were typically targeted for relocation.

Live capture and relocation took the top spots for my least favorite experience. I'd rather have another bone marrow transplant before being subjected to a hard hit to the head.

"You didn't kill him, did you?"

Gail. Her voice cut through the pain tearing through my skull, and I fought to remain conscious so I could get a better feel for what had gone wrong, how, and why. I expected to lose the battle, but every snippet I caught might help me solve the puzzle of where I was, what Gail had to do with it, and if I could raise my odds of surviving.

"Of course not."

Barclave.

If I ever had a bad feeling about someone again, I'd toss my hesitancies in a box and light it on fire. Had I listened to my gut feeling and gone to Meredith, I suspected things would've been a lot different.

But how were Barclave and Gail connected? Why?

Trying to think only made my head hurt more.

"He has a severe concussion. He's not dying. How many times do I have to tell you I'll keep him alive as long as necessary? Him dying ruins our plans, so stop worrying. I'm taking care of it."

"There's a lot of blood."

"That happens with head injuries. It'll keep him down longer. He's not in any danger at the moment. We can keep him here indefinitely. Just keep your cool and do your part. I'll do mine."

"And you're sure this will work?"

"I wouldn't have paid a band of mercenaries a fortune to grab him and expose the weak links in security at the compound otherwise. Stop worrying. You'll eventually get to be the queen just like you want. Our first move is to smooth feathers and rebuild your broken relationship. You've given me enough information about his personality I can handle taking his place. With the blow to the head, I'll feign amnesia, which will explain the differences in mannerisms. My talent will take care of the rest."

I didn't remember anything in Barclave's file that might help him pull off such a scheme. Why did he need me alive to do it?

Gail's desire to become a queen didn't surprise me. The lengths she'd go to accomplish her ambition did.

"What about that woman?"

"I've looked into her talent. The bindings I got have a suppressor designed to mitigate it. She won't be able to locate him even if she has branded him. I have my doubts she's done anything like that. It's a good way to get fired, and despite your opinion of her, she's good at her job. She's a scapegoat meant to drive you off and nothing more. I believe they've been playing you to buy him time to find a suitable wife before his marriage deadline. Anyway, I got the damned suppressors, so be happy. Those damned things cost us a fortune. A fortune we would've been better off using studying our target before acting."

"You said you could play the part after working with him at the compound," Gail snapped. "The deal was to get rid of that woman."

"Leave the woman to me. When she's discarded, there will be no doubt of your position. After you're queen, you can have her shipped off to some other kingdom. Killing RPS agents is a good way to heighten scrutiny and wreck the plan. That's why I told those I hired they needed to pull this off without fatalities. Once I'm in position, things will calm down, and the mercenaries will give the RPS a good run for your money."

"That woman's going to be in the way."

"A known challenge. Stop worrying about her. Worry about your role," Barclave ordered. "Did you do your part?"

"It's not finished yet. You know that."

"Then we'll leave him here for now. He's not going anywhere."

"You split open the back of his head. Shouldn't one of us be here in case his condition worsens? What if he dies?"

"I staunched the bleeding. The swelling in his brain will go down on its own in a few days. It's too late for cold feet now. I told you. I used my talent. He'll survive. Just make sure your project is done by the end of the week, or we did all this for nothing. We can't keep him here forever."

"It'll be done," Gail swore.

"Good. Stop worrying. We have a busy day ahead of us. Remember, stick to the script. If I accept you back too soon, people will get suspicious. And for fuck's sake, don't forget to act remorseful. Wait until you've secured the throne before acting like a bitch. It's a lot harder to revoke your position after you're been confirmed as the queen."

WHILE DR. HAMPFORD had made strides on learning more about my family's talent, no one really understood how it worked. One trait united every Averett man, and it was the bond shared with his wife.

Maybe I'd only stolen a kiss from my Eva, but either my talent viewed that as good enough or it'd changed its mind about killing me off. What triggered the shift remained a mystery, and transforming into a turkey did nothing to ease the pain in my head, but I was free.

I could work with free.

The blurred vision, sensitivity to light, the stabbing agony in the back of my head would cause me trouble, the kind of trouble that'd land me back in Dr. Hampford's care while she struggled to piece my skull back together.

At least Dad could afford the price tag associated with the sort of doctor required to restore a broken skull. While I had no proof my skull was actually cracked, I'd assume the worse. It felt like the bastard had smashed the bat into my head repeatedly, taken me to the brink of death, and hoped my brain would never properly recover so he could take my place.

If I saw Barclave again, I'd spur the fucker in the face, beat him with my wings, and give him a taste of his own medicine. Instead of clubbing him in the back of the head, I'd peck his eyes out.

Then I'd feed him to my great-grandpa.

It wasn't until I explored the hole I'd been dumped in, a literal one with a dirt floor and roots overhead marking where a tree grew, that I realized the fucker had stolen my clothes to help create his ruse.

Barclave was close enough in size to me to pull the trick off.

Unanswered questions and a healthy dose of desire for revenge motivated me enough to scramble up the incline, which opened up beneath a tree. A boulder helped hide the spot, making it ideal for their purposes.

Had I not shifted, but remained essentially helpless with a skull-splitting headache, I doubted anyone but Eva would've found me. I gave credit where credit was due; Barclave and Gail had made a good plan for getting rid of me. With the right talent, Barclave might've been able to fill my shoes. A lighter blow to the head, just enough to make him bleed and give him a concussion, would let him play my role well enough.

His scheming would fall apart the instant Dr. Hampford got a hold of him unless he somehow managed to completely duplicate my DNA and basic biology. Time would tell, assuming I didn't get to him first and expose the plot to put Gail on the throne with a traitorous fake RPS agent at her side.

How would the RPS handled an imposter? Would they identify he'd taken my place? If so, how long would they allow the ruse to go on? The RPS would go into a frenzy looking for me, assuming Barclave's ploy failed.

Handling an imposter hadn't been on the list of things the RPS had meant to shove down my throat during my crash course. The scenario work hadn't done me any good, either, although I found limited comfort in Barclave's declaration his goons had been ordered not to kill anyone. I liked Ithaca and Greene.

Hell, I liked most of the agents when they weren't trying to beat self-defense and preservation skills into me.

I wished I remembered what had happened. I remembered leaving my office after tapping Hollacks and Meredith, but everything after remained a big, black nothing. It reminded me of my hospital stay, but instead of a hard object scrambling my memories, Dr. Hampford had beaten my recollection abilities to death with a cocktail of painkillers.

I preferred the painkillers, and I hoped after I waddled my sorry, feathered ass back to civilization I could talk her out of some at the same time I asked her to check that I still had a brain.

Acid dumped into my cranium seemed more probable.

At least I had one thing going for me. Barclave and Gail hadn't made any efforts to cover their tracks, and I had no trouble following them, even with my blurred vision. My wallet, keys, and phone would've made me happier, but as long as I reached a road and could get my bearings, I'd manage without any help, assuming my brain stayed in my skull where it belonged.

I gave it fifty-fifty odds at best.

THE FOOTPRINTS LED to a pair of ruts weaving through the trees. At one point, several vehicles had been parked at the spot, the dirt freshly disturbed. Barclave's audacity astonished me.

Did he really think no one would follow such an easy trail through the woods? Did he believe no one would notice where he'd walked?

Something didn't add up.

The idea I dreamed up the whole thing worried me almost as much as the idea of Barclave impersonating me to take the throne with Gail. To land on the throne, he'd have to remove my father first.

How long would the pair wait before trying to remove other obstacles from their path? Would Barclave, pretending to be me, try to convince my father to step down? Doing so would trip my father's trigger; playing the amnesia card wouldn't change me that much, and a lifetime of dealing with paperwork had taught me to enjoy being next in line rather than king of the castle. Unless he feigned complete amnesia, in which case he'd learn my father wouldn't step down without ensuring Illinois wouldn't suffer.

He'd name someone else heir; Grégoire would be a better choice than someone with no memories of the inner workings of Illinois. He might even name one of his brothers heir to spare Grégoire. In either case, Barclave and Gail would discover a stumbling block in their plans.

For their plan to work, Barclave would have to become me in all ways, convincing enough to fool even my father.

They forgot a simple truth: there were those who could see through the lies, and my father would call for Montana's aid the instant he believed an imposter had taken my place.

I wanted to watch the fireworks, but for that to happen, I'd have to return to civilization. Walking hurt, but I trudged on, keeping a close eye on the trail.

A nearby growl froze me in place. A predator would enjoy an evening meal of turkey without much of a fight. Resigned to an early death more humiliating than being clubbed by a traitorous RPS agent, I turned to face my demise.

Coming beak to muzzle with one of my oversized wolf uncles startled an indignant squawk out of me before I did what any self-respecting turkey would do when staring down the throat of a large predator.

I attacked, pecked at his face, and battered him with my wings. When that didn't remove him from my personal space, I flapped my wings and took flight enough to rake my claws down his muzzle.

Since I liked my uncle, whichever one the asshole was, I avoided his eyes.

He yelped and retreated, his ears flattening while blood dripped from his nose. I'd preen over having scored a few good hits on him later, sometime after my head ceased its insufferable pounding. Fanning my tail, I rose to my full height, raising my head and stretching my wings in warning.

"One angry, white turkey with silver barring, check," Christian announced, stepping out from behind trees. "One bloodied wolf who was warned specifically against approaching the angry, white turkey with silver barring, check. I need to commend Agent Evangeline for her excellent skills when it comes to locating you, Your Highness. And no, the lynx may not pounce the turkey."

My father growled, snapped his teeth at Christian, and prowled towards me.

A good defense was a better offense, and I tensed, ready to introduce my spurs to his muzzle. Moving hurt, but if I let the lynx get a hold of me, he'd lick me into submission, which would hurt more.

"Your Majesty, I'd like to remind you of the probability of a severe head injury before you do something foolish. Your Highness, are you aware there's an imposter?"

Nodding would hurt, but without any other way to communicate, I bobbed my head.

"Your father knew the instant he smelled the imposter and notified me. The new agents haven't been taught the code words for this situation yet, so everyone but Agent Scarson and Agent Evangeline are in the dark. Agent Evangeline, you will be pleased to know, was immediately aware someone had taken your place. She notified Agent Scarson. She has been instructed to play along with the ruse to buy us time to locate you. The rest of your family is hunting the forest around the compound for you. In case you were unaware, we're about ten miles from the compound. Unsurprising, as it takes time to set up a plot like this one, and they wouldn't have been able to afford losing critical minutes relocating you, especially with a severe head injury. All of your agents have been accounted for. Agent Greene and Agent Ithaca are both in serious but stable condition. I thought you'd like to know. Both should fully recover."

I relaxed, sank to the ground, and stared at him.

Christian passed my father and my bleeding uncle, crouching beside me with no care for the mud. He frowned, pressed his hand to my beak, and turned my head. "The back of your head's a bloody mess. It looks like the concern that the imposter had accurately mimicked the severity of your injuries is warranted. Do you know who is behind this?"

I nodded, rose despite having just settled, and scratched Barclave and Gail's names in the mud with my claws. A chicken could've done a better job, and I sighed at my efforts, blaming my blurred vision and pain for my poor clawmanship.

"Agent Barclave and Gail. Your ex-girlfriend?" Christian growled a few curses, fetched his phone from his pocket, and sent a text message. "Do you know why? Then the problem is even worse than I thought; Agent Barclave was accounted for shortly after your disappearance."

I glared at him, unable to figure out how to concisely explain the situation. At a loss, I gave up, waddled to my father, and hunched over his front paws, settling my wings over my back.

"All right. Yes and no questions, then. Can you shift back?"

I went with no as I had no idea if I could or not.

"Do you have an idea of what they're up to?"

I nodded.

"Did they gloat in front of you?"

Since turkeys couldn't shrug, I nodded and shook my head in quick succession. I swallowed my complaints the movement worsened my headache.

"They thought you were still unconscious?"

I nodded.

"Good. We'll play along to learn their goals, identify any co-conspirators, and gather evidence."

The rumble of engines announced the arrival of two SUVs, and Christian waved one to come as close as possible before hurrying to it, opening the back door, and gesturing for me to hop inside. I made it to the vehicle, steeled my nerves, and took flight long enough to get inside, crashing to an undignified halt. My father joined me, shoving his nose under me and pushing until he had room to fit.

Before I had a chance to escape, my father wrapped his paws around me and pulled me against his chest.

At least he didn't lick me. I considered that a victory, and I used one of his big paws as a pillow and rested while I could.

TO CONTINUE the ruse that the RPS and my family were unaware of an imposter taking my place, I needed to venture into the castle with the escort of a slightly mangled wolf. Uncle Edgar stalked me, and I considered taking another run at him to add to his healing scratches.

"Both of you, behave," Christian ordered. "Dr. Hampford's already called in a trauma specialist from Montana, who'll arrive within the hour. He'll check over our imposter first, concoct a pretty story to make sure he stays put, then he'll check on you, Your Highness. We have not informed your mother of the development yet."

With one sentence, Christian added another layer of complexity and worry to an already murky situation.

My mother liked Gail.

Distrust made sense, but I struggled to believe my mother would betray me or my father like that.

My father's growled promised he didn't believe she would, either.

"Your Majesty, it is a possibility. Her Royal Majesty is one of the few people with access to the training schedule. Do I think she's involved? No. I don't believe she'd replace His Highness with a traitor. But do I believe she'd try to work Gail back into the royal family? It's possible. This isn't passing judgment, but something went catastrophically wrong, and it was well planned. Everyone with the resources to pull off the kidnapping and swap is a suspect." Christian hesitated. "Technically, even me."

My father bared his fangs but fell quiet.

"You need to pretend everything is normal, Your Majesty. This is critical if we want to get as much information out of them before we make the arrest. More importantly, we need to find out if they have any other targets."

Eva.

I fanned my feathers at the thought of anyone targeting her, and while Barclave had it out for me, he'd been careful about targeting an RPS agent. Even dazed, in pain, and barely conscious, I thought he'd spoken the truth.

There was no gain for him in hurting Eva, not when he believed she was part of some clever ploy to drive Gail away. The extra attention would hurt his chances of taking my place.

I almost admired Barclave for his cunning. Almost.

My father growled, but he nodded, relented, and jumped out of the SUV leaving me with my uncle, who stared at me down the length of his long, battered nose.

"Sir, please try not to traumatize your nephew any further. Until Dr. Hampford's associate is able to look him over, treat him as though he is more fragile than glass. He's your responsibility. Keep him mobile and conscious. Those are Dr. Hampford's orders. If he can't stay conscious, shift and get a hold of me immediately. We'll route him directly to the ER. Ideally, we'll avoid that, but when an injury like that survives transformation, it's a cause for concern."

My uncle nodded and draped a paw over my back, tugging me closer. Protesting would wear away the little energy I had left, so I shuffled to him to convince Christian I'd cooperate.

"Good. Remember, call me immediately if there are any problems. I'm toeing more lines than I like right now. Your Highness, if you think your condition is worsening, peck your uncle to call me."

I bobbed my head.

Christian sighed, bailed out of the SUV, and tailed my father into the castle. As sticking close to my uncle ensured I had at least one predator on my side, I waited for him to hop out of the vehicle before I followed.

Landing hurt, especially as I misjudged the distance thanks to my wavering vision. The temptation to crawl under the SUV to hide almost got the better of me, but my uncle shoved his nose under me and herded me towards the castle.

Agents from my father's detail watched me like hawks ready to swoop down and enjoy a fresh Thanksgiving dinner, likely at Christian's order. Their scrutiny woke the same nervousness that got me through each spring. Unlike in the spring, I had someone larger and more lethal to hide behind.

My uncle growled, showed off his sharp teeth, and matched my pace, an unfortunately slow wobble. As I couldn't seek sanctuary in my normal places, I headed for my father's office. Under his desk would make a fantastic hiding place, and no one would judge my uncle for invading.

All of my uncles and aunts invaded my father's office for no reason other than to annoy him.

I made it halfway to my chosen sanctuary before my uncle shifted, picked me up, and set me on the desk, which was the last place I wanted to be. Uncle Edgar shifted with his clothes, something I was more grateful for than usual, but I disliked how he grabbed my neck with one hand and examined the back of my head with the other.

"In good news, Christian is overreacting. You have mud on your head." While still holding my neck in a firm grip, my uncle snatched a tissue from my father's desk and wiped it over my head. "Well, mostly mud.

There's a small cut. I expect that's where you were hit. Head hurt?"

He eased his grip enough I could nod.

"No surprise. When Christian tells me my job is to keep you awake, that's exactly what I'm going to do. I'm also going to start giving you your first lesson on how to transform to human without getting help from someone. And yes, we can help each other transform, but it's unpleasant. I expect you transformed when you were unconscious?"

Startled, I peered at him with an eye.

"We all start out that way, kiddo. We usually don't figure out we can shift outside of our season unless something goes wrong. Your father fell off one of the castle walls and about broke his neck. He panicked. Fortunately, he's a cat, so he landed on his feet, but it surprised the hell out of him. He bolted right back to your mother and hid under her chair until our father had a chance to coax him out."

Once I returned to my human form, I'd have to ask a great many questions about the time my father hid under my mother's chair, as he was a rather large lynx and I couldn't imagine him fitting under any chair in the castle.

"The basics of shifting is figuring out which parts of you are man and beast, separating them enough to pick your shape, and making your talent do as you wish. We theorize that securing a bond allows our talent to develop enough to control the shapeshifting. In the spring, you'll find it's easier to shift to your beast but harder to become human. You'll manage, though. Lord knows you're stubborn enough to fight the magic. But this? Extreme fear or severe injury is what triggers our ability to shift. Well, in your case, unconscious but out of season ability to shift."

He released my neck and grabbed more tissues, rubbing away as much of the mud from my head as possible. I stood still for him, as I worried he'd shift to his wolf form and use his tongue.

"In good news, there's limited blood. I'm concerned about the severity of it before you shifted. Lethal, probably."

I nodded to acknowledge him.

"We'll be able to use a truth seer to verify how the family talent works and confirm an attempted regicide count in addition to kidnapping and general assault. I'm sure Christian and Meredith will enjoy adding charges to the list." My uncle growled. "I'll help."

In his case, I suspected 'help' actually meant 'rend flesh from bones.' Inflicting bodily harm on someone was more of a predator's inclination, but I'd make an exception myself if an opportunity presented itself.

At the minimum, I wouldn't interfere with my family when they dealt with Barclave and Gail.

"You'll be pleased about your Evangeline's reaction to your disappearance."

I lifted my head and gave him my undivided attention, and when he didn't continue, I gobbled my demand for details.

His grin oozed smug wolf. "First, she was the first to know something was wrong. Evangeline called in an unknown threat. She had your complete schedule so knew there wasn't supposed to be a scenario going on, and she'd known the scheduled scenario had already ended. Second, she was able to pinpoint the exact location where the attack happened, but she said something disrupted her brand on you. Third, whatever you do, don't make that woman angry. I'm not sure you'll survive it. Someone suggested she was hallucinating the whole thing, and she told him if he dared to doubt her judgment when it came to you again, she'd be delivering his body in a coffin tin. She was a little upset over your disappearance." Leaving me on my father's desk, my uncle closed the door, went to the closet, and retrieve a pair of sweats from the top shelf. "Let's try to get you shifted. I'm not sure Dr. Hampford or her associate would appreciate treating a turkey, and honestly, transforming should help you heal faster."

Becoming human would make my life much simpler, although it'd be a lot harder to hide from the rest of the palace staff. I wondered if word was already spreading someone had used magic to take my place.

My uncle didn't give me long to think

about it. He dug his fingers into the feathers of my chest and secured a hold on me.

The next time anyone suggested I be helped through a transformation, I would fight to my last breath to prevent it. Only an idiot would consent to being turned inside out, stabbed with a thousand, invisible tiny blades, and subjected to the agony of broken bones.

I would've preferred the headache.

Mercifully, I hadn't had anything to eat or drink, so while my stomach heaved, I was spared from the indignity of vomiting. Coughing, I struggled to catch my breath.

"Better than I thought. When your grandfather forced me through my first change, it was ten minutes of that. You didn't take long at all. Perhaps an unexpected benefit of your transfusion? You are in dire need a shower. I'm so glad the architects thought it'd be wise to have a bathroom adjacent to your father's office." My uncle grabbed my elbow and dragged me across the room. "Shower first, and don't fall on your ass. Hell, don't even try to stand. Sit your ass on the tiles. I'll help you wash your hair so we can get a better look at the damage without shaving your head."

Any other day, I would've bristled over my uncle joining me in the shower, but between general exhaustion and the persistent throb in my head, I cooperated without a fight.

He dealt with my hair first, poking and prodding where I'd been struck. "Well, transforming helped. I can see where you were cut and hit, and while you've gotten one hell of a bump, it doesn't feel like your skulls in pieces. But I'm not a doctor."

"It doesn't feel as bad as before," I admitted.

"Good. Any nausea?"

"Not like before."

"You're ahead of your old man. It took him months to shift without throwing up. It takes a lot of transformations to adapt to it. Once you do, you'll hardly notice it."

"That's something."

"It's going to take forever to get all this mud out. What'd they do? Dump you in a hole and shovel dirt all over you?"

I sighed. "That's not far from the truth. I think they used an animal's den maybe? They talked about making a long-term solution."

"They wanted to keep you alive?"

"As far as I could gather. Barclave seemed confident his talent would keep me alive despite a head injury."

"He sounds delusional to me. What do they want?"

"Gail wants to be queen." I resisted the urge to shrug. "I guess Barclave liked the idea of becoming a king, too. He'd have to take my place to make Gail the queen."

"Unless they have no idea how the succession works here, which I'm thinking is a possibility. Gail wasn't the type to look into the actual duties of being a queen, only the prestige of the position," my uncle muttered, and he dumped more soap on top of my head before rubbing it in. "There wasn't much blood on you as a turkey, but it's all caked in your hair, kiddo."

"I bet this wasn't in your job description as an uncle."

"Beats what the rest of my brothers are having to deal with. I get to stand guard duty and keep people away from you while they handle the imposter. They have to hide their fury and instinct to eliminate a threat. Killing either one without sufficient evidence would cause a great deal of trouble for the royal family. No, we're going to let them live, and we'll make sure they're ruined before they rot in prison for a long time."

"Without maiming them?"

My uncle grunted, digging his fingers into my hair to work the soap in. "Maiming is up for negotiation."

"Gail wanted to go after Eva. Barclave didn't want the RPS looking closer at him, which is what would happen an agent is attacked. I'm concerned Gail might've made plans to get rid of Eva."

"After you're clean and changed, I'll notify Christian and see what we can do to get security increased around her. It might take a while; with this incident, your detail's going to be shuffled and everyone reverified. It might take a while to go through the interviews. His Royal Majesty of Montana can't be everywhere at once, and we're not the only kingdom having problems right now."

"Do I want to know?" I hesitated. "You know what? I'm pretty sure I don't."

"There are some issues about California's line of succession."

That surprised me. "Why?"

"Well, the heir is refusing any matchmaking ploys by his family, citing North Dakota's situation as he's an unbonded leech, and he'll probably get ideas from you if he's not allowed to do as he wants to find a partner. That leaves his brother, also an unbonded leech, who is utterly unprepared for ruling. While the rumor mill has been going strong, I doubt the younger brother has any idea he might become king."

"Another Grégoire situation?"

"Not entirely. The prince is likely unaware of the situation. The rumor started in New York last week."

I groaned. "New York is starting even more trouble? Again?"

"New York is developing a bad habit of producing queens. I think His Royal Majesty of California was hoping to find a woman his son might accept."

"How?"

"I haven't figured that out, truth be told. I was still stuck on California going to New York in the first place. I would've paid good money to be a fly on the wall during that meeting. So, you'll want to watch California in the near future. There's going to be drama."

"We should just rename the Royal States to the Drama States. It'd be more accurate."

"But we're royally dramatic, kiddo. Just take a look at you. You've been the undisputed king of all things drama for several months now. There are entire websites dedicated to speculating on what you'll do next. Word's already spread you've set a wedding date without announcing the woman you intend to marry. Your father and mother aren't telling us, but we have a pretty good idea who she is."

"I'm sure she'll notify you herself should she desire."

"With or without her charmingly extensive vocabulary?"

I chuckled. "I have no idea what you're talking about."

"How's your head doing?"

"Better than earlier, much to my relief. I've got a headache you wouldn't believe, but it's tolerable. Earlier? Not so much."

"Transforming isn't a cure-all, but it helps a lot. Let's get the rest of that muck off you so you can enjoy a soak. I expect they'll be dancing around that imposter for a while trying to get as much on him as they can before making the arrest."

"After the day I've had, so help me, if Barclave sleeps in my bed tonight, I might kill him myself."

"And if he does, it's for good reason. You can't kill him, kiddo."

"That's not at all fair. He got to hit me. I should get to hit him back."

"It's doubtful he personally hit you. He probably hired someone to hit you, and until we figure out the money trail, you might need to disappear in the castle for a few days while the imposter settles."

"He should have to go to the RPS compound and stay only in the secured sections."

"But then he'd have to share a suite with Eva and Meredith."

I grimaced at the thought of him being anywhere near Eva. "If I asked Meredith to kill the bastard, do you think she'd do it?"

"You're even more bloodthirsty than I am right now. No, kiddo. There will be no acts of premeditated murder."

"Why not?"

"Because no matter how satisfying it would be, it's still wrong."

DR. HAMPFORD INVADED my father's office, and an old man with jet black hair and stress lines across his brow followed. The pair locked on me faster than I could blink, and I grimaced at their scrutiny. Had I been wise, I would've stayed in the tub for longer rather than moving to my father's couch and toweling my hair dry while wearing his sweats.

"No one told me he'd transformed back," Dr. Hampford announced, annoyance sharpening her tone.

"He's fine. It helped the headache, it let him get the blood off, and he was covered in mud. Let the kiddo have some of his dignity back."

"This is Dr. Thorton. He's the best Montana has to offer for trauma care. How bad do you think the injuries were, Mr. Averett?"

"He was unconscious when he involuntarily shifted. That's a good indicator of lethal damage. We may not have the best talent but it's useful in a pinch. The way he was behaving in his animal form supports the damage; he still had injuries to his head although it'd stopped bleeding. Christian mistook his natural coloration and mud for blood."

"And now?"

"They left him in the mud covered in blood, which had caked in his hair. It took me almost an hour to get that crap out. There's no bleeding, but he's got a bump he's not going to forget anytime soon. In good news, his headache has improved."

"Your Highness?"

"My uncle won't let me kill them," I complained.

"It's prudent to allow them time to identify if there are any co-conspirators," my doctor replied, and she offered me a smile. "Good work rescuing yourself. Let Roger have a look at you, and we'll figure out how best to care for you."

"And the imposter?"

Christian slipped into my father's office and took a seat beside the door.

"I assigned him to bedrest for the next forty-eight hours with careful monitoring. He's not to be left unattended at any time," Dr. Thorton announced.

"Christian? What about Gail?"

"She's been thanked for her contribution in helping with 'Prince Kelvin's' recovery and sent home. She's also going to be monitored. I sent a pair of RPS agents home with her, and she'll have a pair with her at all times. I picked the pair from His Majesty's detail, and they're aware she's a conspirator in this situation. They'll be recording her every word."

I almost felt sorry for her, but then I remembered she'd almost gotten me killed with her greed. "And Eva?"

"Agent Evangeline has been temporarily relieved of duty. She was relieved upon confirmation of your disappearance. I thought you'd be happier about the situation that way. We're still hammering out the details of how to hide your presence, but honestly, it's not going to stay a secret long. We've already put out the code there's an imposter in the castle, so the entirety of the permanent staff knows. All cameras are recording, and we have a full staff evaluating every word the imposter says. We're doing a comprehensive background check on Agent Barclave. As per protocol, all of the newer agents have been temporarily relieved of duty while the circumstances of your kidnapping are being investigated," Christian announced. "Agent Barclave's impersonator will be given an assignment at the RPS training compound in secured areas so we can monitor him."

"I assume to identify any gaps in the talent allowing them to pull this off?"

"Exactly."

I gave my hair a final rub with the towel and tossed it in the direction of my father's desk. "I've tracked enough mud in here to make people question if they come in here."

"I'll take the blame for it, kiddo. Everyone saw me tracking mud in here with my new pet turkey."

"Ah, yes. About that. Sorry, Your Highness, but your secret is no longer secret. Gossip spreads even faster than bad news around here, and as your uncle got snarly with anyone who even thought about getting too close to you, there was no hope of hiding it."

I bowed my head and sighed. "It couldn't be avoided."

"It really couldn't."

"And my mother?"

"There's no evidence of her involvement. Your father will handle briefing her later tonight, but for the moment, it works to our advantage having her react naturally. Your father is having difficulty reining in his temper. He's needed to be pulled aside several times and given a reminder his job it to help incriminate them."

"This is a disaster."

"Only for your pride, Your Highness."

Dr. Thorton cleared his throat. "If you don't mind, I'd like to begin my examination. You can discuss this all you want after I'm convinced His Highness shouldn't be on route to the nearest hospital."

Silence answered the doctor's request, although Dr. Hampford directed a scathing look at the head of my father's detail. Christian held his hands up in surrender.

As I had no idea what to expect from Dr. Thorton, I tensed, watching him with wide eyes.

"You have nothing to worry about, Your Highness. While I have no objections to the creative rearrangement of bones belonging to interfering RPS agents, I take my patient's health seriously, and I'd rather not see Dr. Hampford's hard work undermined."

That made two of us. "What do you need from me?"

"How would you rate the severity of your headache?"

I liked he jumped to the obvious conclusion I had a headache. "It's manageable. I wouldn't say no to a handful of those little white pills Dr. Hampford used on me, though."

"How does it compare to when you first regained consciousness?" The way Dr. Thorton watched me gave me the impression he was doing more than asking me questions, but I couldn't tell what. "Use a number scale if you'd like, but your pain levels can help me determine how the injury has progressed."

"When I first woke up, it was like I'd split my skull open. I guess I'd describe it as pulsing waves of pain. The worst of it would knock me back out again, then the pain would lessen, but it'd wake me up again. I would've preferred another marrow transplant."

Dr. Hampford cringed. "He was off the scales on the pain chart for the transplant, Roger."

"How is your vision?"

"Better than before, but it blurs some still. It's okay right now. It was worse before I took a shower."

"Dizziness?"

"Some."

"Pain anywhere else?"

I shook my head.

"All right. I'm going to have to touch where you were hit, and it's probably going to hurt," Dr. Thorton warned, sitting beside me. "Mr. Averett, should he fall unconscious, your job is to catch him."

My uncle nodded. "Understood, Dr. Thorton."

"I will be using my talent on you. This

comes with a few inherent risks, including a temporary bonding should your injuries be severe enough. I've been informed you already have a life bond, so this risk is mitigated. However, I am a strong generalized leech, and in order to better evaluate your health, I will forge a temporary connection with you. While this connection is active, I will be able to get a look at your physical condition and judge the severity of your injuries. It also enables me to manipulate cells in your body. If there is excessive pressure in your brain, I can take steps to make sure you arrive at the hospital without your condition worsening. Depending on how your body has healed, I can also get a sense of the initial injury."

The disclosure startled me, and I glanced at Dr. Hampford, who smiled and shrugged. "There's a reason he's the trauma specialist. I'm more of a generalized physician, although I've found I've been doing some more specialized work than normal with you. You won't notice anything from his connection with you, and it'll fade on its own in a few days. He's very experienced."

"All right, Dr. Thorton."

"Just be patient. This will take some time, as I intend on addressing any problems I can during the examination."

He touched the back of my head, and the constant throb I'd endured since waking up died away. I closed my eyes and breathed a relieved sigh, not caring how long it took him if it meant I could enjoy the respite for a while longer.

I DIDN'T SLEEP, but my attention wavered, making it difficult at best to follow the conversation around me. The little I picked out boded well for me, although I believed everyone else in my father's office drove Dr. Thorton to the limits of his patience.

No matter how many times he repeated himself, no one believed my less than coherent state was due to the absence of severe pain. I rested, and my dazed state made his work easier.

I found the whole thing amusing, which made it easier to ignore my uncle and Christian, the two worst offenders.

"If this takes much longer, my brother's going to come in here ready to rampage," my uncle warned in a growl.

I realized I had gone beyond a dazed stupor into sleeping territory.

"Good job, Mr. Averett," my newest doctor growled back. "You woke him."

"His eyes are still closed."

"He's awake now. He just hasn't gotten himself together enough to open his eyes and evaluate the situation. Give him a few minutes. He's still dazed, which is to be expected."

"Does that mean you'll tell us what's

wrong with him? You said you would after he woke up."

"Mr. Averett, if you'd let me work without interrupting, I'd be finished faster. If you can't do your job without complaining about it, I'll replace you."

I decided I liked Dr. Thorton. Any man with the courage to face down a grouchy wolf deserved respect. "Why are you whining, Uncle?" At first, my tongue fought me, and I gave it even odds anyone understood me.

"You've been down and out for two hours. That's why I'm whining. I was supposed to keep you awake."

"Until the doctor arrived," I corrected, cracking open an eye to discover I'd been moved so I stretched out on the couch, and my uncle held an ice pack against my forehead. "Your job is to hold ice?"

"He claims his talent can raise your internal body temperature, and his solution is to keep the front of your head cold. I gave up trying to understand what he's doing. How's your head doing?"

I thought about it. "It doesn't hurt."

"And it won't until I stop working, and when I'm done working, you should be left with a mild headache, which I'll have Dr. Hampford drug into submission while you rest." Dr. Thorton rubbed the back of my skull with a finger. "Feel where I'm touching?"

"Yes, I do."

"That's the impact point. I've been rebuilding your skull here. Your uncle's speculations of the severity are correct. Your skull was shattered here. Frankly, I'm astonished you weren't killed instantly. Something protected your brain. I've sufficient evidence from my talent to confirm the lethality of the blow. It could be from the work Dr. Hampford had done; if I recall correctly, she had some fairly advanced protective talents being used to get you through the marrow transfusion."

Dr. Hampford sighed. "That's correct. The skull itself lacks bone marrow, but because of the talents we were using to eliminate and replace all types of your bone marrow, we needed to do some extensive work with your skull to protect it from being targeted. We also put in some protections around the brain to protect unaffected cells. I opted to have those protections to wear off naturally. The estimate was three to six months."

"Well, your decision likely saved his life. Something buffered his brain from the blunt-force trauma. It didn't protect him completely, but enough to buy him time. His familial talent did the rest of the work. I can see where the transformations helped fuse the skull. He's exceptionally fortunate. The fusing allowed room for the swelling, which prevented additional damage. That's part of why this is taking so long. I have to relieve the pressure and bruising so I can rebuild his skull to its appropriate shape. The bone was thinned and expanded to give extra room for the swelling. Frankly, I've never seen anything like it, but it's why you're still alive, Your Highness."

"I'll view this as compensation for needing a bone marrow transfusion."

My uncle laughed and flicked my hair out of my face. "Well, your sense of humor is still intact. I'll take it. Dr. Thorton, how much more work do you have to do before he's out of danger?"

"He's out of danger now, but it's best to finish this work now while his skull is still soft. It'll be a lot harder to fix it later. Be patient. Doing everything at once also will help with the trial. Dr. Hampford will need to get a comprehensive file on the protections used during the bone marrow transplant to assist."

"Easily done," she replied.

A knock at the door ended the conversation, and Christian held up his hand, cracked open the door, and peeked out. A moment later, he let my father and Eva in. "Your Majesty. Agent Evangeline."

"How is he?" my father demanded, closing the door after Eva.

I lifted my hand and waved. "I'm feeling great. Dr. Thorton probably won't be feeling so great by the time he's done."

"Perceptive," the trauma specialist muttered. "Your Majesty. I expect another hour of work before I'm finished. I'm almost done reshaping his skull, then I'll be fusing and strengthening the bone."

My father's expression turned carefully neutral. "How bad was it?"

"Your heir is exceptionally lucky to be alive right now. Ah. This is his bond?"

Eva straightened, and red flushed her cheeks.

"She is," my father confirmed before she had a chance to speak. "I borrowed her, claiming I needed her reinstated temporarily as an agent as my 'son' needed a few of mine."

"All right, lady. You take Mr. Averett's place. Your job is simple. Apply ice packs to his forehead and face to keep his temperature down. Increased body temperature isn't uncommon during a procedure like this. How much feedback did you get when he was hit?"

Eva glanced at Christian, who nodded. "Enough."

Dr. Thorton sighed. "Well, he'll be fine. Come reassure yourself; if you're worried, it might feed back to him. If your brand was interfered with, now's the time for you to reestablish it."

Eva's eyes widened. "You found my brand?"

"Don't be alarmed. I found it because I've been evaluating him from head to toe. I noticed it had been disrupted, but I didn't want to remove the remnants, uncertain what would happen."

"They had a suppressor meant to block it. A specialized one."

"That would do it. I'm impressed any of it survived. Just don't forget to keep his head cool while you work your talent, ma'am."

"Eva," she corrected, and she used her foot to shove my uncle out of the way and take his place. "It's all right to restore my brand?"

"As long as you can do so without inflicting any actual injuries on my patient, do so."

Eva twisted around and shot a glare at Christian. "Told you."

I reached out and brushed Eva's hair away from her face to draw her attention back to me. "I'm sorry I worried you."

"You're sorry? What the hell do you have to be sorry about, you fucking nutter? You got jumped by a bunch of dumb fucks out to make a quick buck led by a goddamned traitor!"

"Well," my uncle said, making distance from my wife. "I can say I've had a taste of her temper and vocabulary now."

"You're one of the fucking wolves." Eva looked my uncle over, and I wondered if she was debating the best way to cook a wolf. "You haven't seen even a hint of my temper yet, wolf."

The door cracked open and my great-grandpa leaned inside. "Indoor voice, Evangeline. I could hear you snarling from in the hall. There's quite the party in here. Also, you need to get your office soundproofed. Everyone's going to know the kiddo is in here if you don't keep it down."

My father sighed. "Noted. Come in. Anything new?"

"Are you sure I can't shift and resolve this problem now? Your brothers are about ready to go hunting, and I already had to tell your father he needed to restrain himself. I believe your father intends on terrorizing the imposter as a lion."

"I'm sorry you're being exposed to this idiocy, Eva," I muttered.

"I'm sure I'll find an appropriate way to chastise you for this travesty later."

"If you could please wait an hour until you have your family chat, I'd be appreciative," Dr. Thorton announced. "This is not nearly as easy as it looks."

For the first time in my life, my family shut up without argument.

EVEN WITHOUT INTERRUPTION, Dr. Thorton wasn't happy with my condition for another two hours. When he finally stepped away from the couch, wiping sweat from his brow, the promised headache didn't come. "Dr. Hampford, try to keep him somewhere quiet for the next two to three days. The groundwork's finished, I've eliminated the swelling, but that could change with too much stress.

Keep his bond nearby, and make certain things remain relaxed for her as well. He should be fine, but I'd rather be safe than sorry."

Dr. Hampford sighed. "Still. It took you four hours."

"That's what happens when I have to reassemble the fragmented ruins of someone's skull."

I glanced at my father and prepared for the explosion.

"Fragmented ruins?"

Eva locked onto my father, got to her feet, and waved her ice pack at him. "I called dibs, feline. I get to deal with that pair."

"You get to stay with Kelvin and keep him happy, calm, and safe," my father replied. "Non-negotiable. However, I'll allow Meredith to deal with them on your behalf."

"I'm not convinced arrest is the right solution to this."

"Arrest is what you're both going to have to accept unless there is any evidence of another attempt. Christian, as Meredith can't leave her post to maintain the ruse, I'm leaving arrangements to you. Where should we take him until this is resolved?"

Christian turned to Dr. Thorton. "Is he cleared for air travel?"

"Yes, he can fly."

"We can smuggle him to the royal airstrip and take him to one of the residences until this settles down. That'll make certain he's inaccessible."

My great-grandpa shook his head. "I'll fly the plane, but not my place. Gail knows how to get there, and I'd rather not take chances."

My father paced, clacking his teeth together. "That eliminates any of my properties."

"Why not just arrest the bastard? We have the evidence we need." I rolled my shoulders, and my joints creaked. "While I'd enjoy showing up, I have no idea if he has offensive talents, and there was nothing in his file about abilities letting him take someone's place."

"It'd be safer to eliminate the threat," Christian agreed. "I'm concerned he has contingency plans in place. Or that Gail does."

I scowled. "Because Gail wants to get rid of Eva. To Gail, Eva's a threat."

"And rightfully so." My wife flicked my hair with a nail. "I'll be on guard, don't worry."

"I'm going to worry."

"Well, your rooms in this mausoleum will need to be decontaminated, so we should find some empty bedroom to claim as ours and let the on-duty RPS agents figure out the best way to deal with those two. And if anyone asks why I'm with you, I'm your detail until your detail is properly returned to you."

I could work with that.

"How about the main guest suite, Christian?" my father asked.

"I like it. It's already wired to be easily defended, and we can run a ruse easily enough that we invited the Montana doctors to stay there to be close. We'll open up one of the other suites for Dr. Hampford and Dr. Thorton. The palace staff will play along. The guest suite is far enough from the royal wing that things should be quiet for them, too."

"That works for me. Just take care of this. There's no need to dance to their tune, not now."

"It'll be dealt with by morning," Christian promised.

I could work with that. "All right. By morning, then."

SEVENTEEN

When given an entire suite to share without supervision, a wise couple takes advantage of it.

IT TOOK Christian one order and ten minutes to have the palace hallways cleared, implementing a temporary lock-down situation so I could walk to the guest suite without having to deal with anyone. At Christian's direction, I engaged the deadbolt and used a door jam to keep everyone out.

If the RPS wanted in, they had ways of getting in, but any unwanted parties would have to make a lot of noise to break through the door, which would buy Eva and I time to prepare or make a quick escape through one of the secret passages few in the castle knew about. It was a last resort for the royal family, added during the war in case the castle faced assault.

Outside of training and maintenance, no one used the passages.

If I really wanted, I could reach my bedroom in stealth and unleash Eva, but I thought better of it.

She might kill Barclave, which would complicate matters for everybody.

"You look dead on your feet," Eva said, shucking off her suit jacket and tossing it on the nearest chair. "Which is much better than dead."

"You won't hear me arguing with you over that. I'm also going to loudly protest relocation scenarios for the next while."

"And we're going to have to adjust how we do them in case someone touching the back of your head causes issues. It very probably will. I've been told you don't remember what happened?"

"I don't. The last thing I remember was a scuffle in my office with Meredith and Agent Hollacks. Next thing I knew, I had the worst headache of my life and was lying in a dirt dugout under a tree and rock."

"It was a clean hit. In and out, done by a professional unit. I'm surprised they used lethal force on you when they used non-lethal force on your detail. There's something fishy about that. They won't let me see the limited footage. It seems Meredith believes if I get a look at any of your attackers they won't live long enough to be brought in for questioning, and she's of the opinion I have a strong enough talent I might be able to track them by appearance. I've never done something like that before, but I'm game to try. I told her I'd stick to non-lethal force if she let me be on the team."

I chuckled and crossed the room, heading for the primary bathroom, which had a jet tub large enough for two. "You have other work ahead of you."

"Like what?"

"Taking a bath with me. That's just for starters. When given an entire suite to share without supervision, a wise couple takes advantage of it. The bathroom and bedroom will be unmonitored, but if we're particularly noisy, there won't be any hiding our activities."

Eva chuckled and joined me. "I see someone wants more than another kiss."

"I think I've earned at least a kiss."

"You survived and found your way out of trouble, so I'm inclined to agree with you. And from what I've been told, you and your detail were caught blindsided, so it's not like you could've done anything to prevent it. Meredith wouldn't lie about that, not to me. Not about this."

"Not when your life is equally at risk."

Eva sighed and nodded. "Well, any doubts about our status as a bonded pair has been laid to fucking rest, that's for certain."

"Gail's going to go after you."

"Not from prison she's not."

"She's a lot of things, but I really don't doubt she's already paid someone off to deal with you. You're a threat to her plans, and that she was willing to go that far tells me you're just a loose end for her, but one that could cost her the throne she wants."

Eva sighed and shook her head, closing the bathroom door behind us. "I'll be careful, but if she hired the same people, it's going to be tricky to catch them. However much I fucking don't want to admit it, the fuckers have skills."

"Barclave told her it was a bad idea to go after an RPS agent. I think he planned to ship you out of kingdom after he secured his hold."

"What a fucking moron." Eva narrowed her eyes to slits and looked me over. "You have two choices, Your Highness. We can keep talking, or you can fill the tub and we can stop talking. Make bubbles and turn the jets on. Warm water, but I don't feel like becoming a fucking lobster today."

Relaxing, I went to do as ordered. "You're all right?"

"I'm fine. I wasn't the one hurt, although if your father is to be believed, I'm currently classified as delicate. I couldn't even bring myself to beat him to make him stop hovering, either. He's figured out what you've been trying to tell him all along. As long as I stayed up and kicking, you were alive somewhere. Don't expect me to cut that nutter slack often, but consider playing nice with him and your mother for a while."

"Considering that your typical response is

to knock sense back into people, I'll take that under advisement. Anything else I need to know?"

"Yeah, there is something you need to know."

I tensed. "What is it?"

"There might be a reason that woman wants to get rid of me. And she's right. I am a threat to her."

I frowned, considering Eva and biting back my initial impulse to tell her she'd done nothing wrong to deserve being in Gail's sights. For me, being born had been enough to turn me into a target. Secrets had a way of haunting those who kept them, and I wouldn't make assumptions about Eva's secrets. "Beyond being a skilled woman with a terrifying amount of courage, how are you a threat to her? Oh, and being my wife. That part's important."

Then, afraid her secret could be something that could put her in the sights of my psychotic ex-girlfriend, I held my breath and waited.

"My uncle is a king."

I choked on my own spit. "What?"

"My uncle is a king."

Fuck. I hadn't misheard her the first time. "You're part of a royal family."

"Technically not. My uncle cut ties with my mother because my mother's an asshole who married another asshole, and the royal family didn't want that pair polluting their bloodline. She was evicted from the royal family because she's that much of an asshole. I'd just been born when she was evicted from the family, so I guess my uncle didn't want me to suffer by completely revoking her rank. She was granted elite status for my sake. That doesn't change the most important part, though: the royal family didn't want her in it." Eva hesitated and shrugged. "For just cause. I'd evict her from the family, too, in his shoes."

"You're King Jacques's niece."

"Yes."

"And you've been on international television about my abdication."

Eva's eyes widened. "Well, yes."

A mountain of problems and challenges rose before me, and if I screwed up anything, Eva would pay the price for them. "Gail is the least of your problems right now, Eva. What sort of resources does your family have? Would they try to take advantage of our relationship? Or will they use the publicity to find you? You didn't want them finding you."

"I don't know. I left at fifteen. They wanted to marry me to an old man. I refused. Then I ran."

Of the challenges I faced, Eva's parents marrying her off to an old man took top spot as the one I'd address first with extreme prejudice. "Did you sign anything?"

Eva's face flushed. "No. I didn't even sign any disowning paperwork. I refused. I didn't trust them to not attempt to sneak in marriage documentation in on it."

"Wise. All right. So, if Gail did background research into you, what are her chances of discovering this?"

"I don't know. I've told Meredith and Christian my familial name, which is different from my uncle's. I don't know how hard it would be to find the connection."

"But if she did find your connection to King Jacques, she'd consider you a threat for certain." I kept an eye on the tub, dipping my hand in the water to confirm the temperature before turning on the jets and hunting for shampoo or bubble bath to fulfill her every request. I found a bubble solution in the closet and added too much, resulting in a cascade of foam on the tiles. "She'd definitely want you out of the picture. If she found out about this attempted marriage, what is the possibility she might go to your family to have you relocated back to Nevada? Or have you assassinated?"

The assassination part worried me almost as much as the relocation element. If someone kidnapped her, she could be rescued.

If she died, I died. If I died, she died.

"I don't know. I didn't stick around to find out how determined they were to have me marry the old fucker."

"Any chance he's dead? I'd be all right with that."

"I don't know. I'm sorry."

"Don't be sorry. Fuck, I'd run, too. I should've left Gail long before I found out she was cheating on me. But unlike you, I'm an idiot."

"You're not a fucking idiot. You had good reason to try to make it work. Your life depended on it. Literally."

"Well, it would've been a very short and unhappy life if I'd continued trying," I replied, yanking my father's sweatshirt over my head. "We'll call it even on circumstances, and I'll pay King Jacques a personal call to handle this. And don't bother arguing with me on this one. This is a fight I refuse to lose. There are ways to handle situations like this, and I won't leave you unprotected. If your family discovers your worth or wants you to continue with that old marriage proposal, I need to solidify your position here and in Nevada. King Jacques is typically reasonable, and he likes me."

"You're the one Your Highness almost everyone likes. It's actually disturbing how many people like you."

I shot her a look. "What do you mean by that?"

"You're insufferably nice, considerate, and handsome. All around, you're the sort of prince kings and queens use as an example for their younger princes. I've been treated to the lecture numerous times as a result of going to watch those damned sessions in

Congress. I swear, if another one of those obnoxious senators attempts to flirt with me, I'll hit them."

"They're probably trying to earn your favor because you have a connection with me, Eva."

"You mean they don't want me for my beauty?"

I laughed and winked at her. "I want you for your beauty, but you're going to laugh at me and tell me I'm blind because you don't think there's anything beautiful about you. But I doubt it. They want me for my beauty, and they want to flatter you because they're terrified you'll beat them up."

"I think we've done enough talking for one day, Your Highness." To make sure I understood what she wanted, she stripped out of her shirt with admirable speed and tossed it at me. By the time I'd escaped the white, silky fabric, she'd escaped the rest of her clothes, leaving me with a glimpse of tanned skin before the bubbles blocked my view.

I gave credit where credit was due; Eva outclassed me in the game of seduction, and she watched me with a bright smile, which promised she'd enjoy every moment I spent undressing for her entertainment.

I took my time to indulge her. She'd more than earned it.

A PERSISTENT KNOCK at the door woke me, and while loathe to leave Eva, I muttered curses, grabbed a bathrobe, and hurried across the suite so they wouldn't wake her. I peeked through the hole to discover Christian and my parents in the hall. I muttered a few of my wife's curses, moved the jam out of the way, and unlocked the door. "Shh. Eva's sleeping."

"Good. She needs the rest," Christian replied, leading the parental invasion force. "We come bearing a gift of news, and breakfast will be along for you both."

They also came with a gift of Meredith, who carried a metal briefcase, and I smiled at the head of my detail. "Meredith."

"You're looking good for someone who dodged death by a hair."

"How are Greene and Ithaca doing?"

"Dr. Thorton's attending to them both, so they'll be fine. Dr. Thorton was concerned you'd stress over their condition, so he invaded the hospital two hours ago to make certain their recovery went smoothly and without impairment."

I closed the door behind everyone, locked it, and headed for the loveseat in case Eva woke up. "Have Barclave and Gail been dealt with?"

"Both are in custody along with the man who'd taken Barclave's place. We've already started the process of going through their financials to find out as much as we can about their plot." Meredith took the seat beside me, set the briefcase on the table, and opened it. "We have some cause for concern. Both have made substantial payments to a mercenary firm, and your ex-girlfriend made some additional payments to an outfit in Nevada."

"She's trying to get rid of Eva, and she's likely going to try to bring Eva's family into it," I speculated. "Protecting Eva is my primary concern."

"We do believe she's going to be a target, but I have reason to believe it'll be a live capture."

I could work with a live capture; it protected her. I wondered where things had gone wrong with my capture, but I had my suspicions, and they involved a vengeful ex making an additional payment to override Barclave's planning. "What are our chances of getting a confirmation of the plan out of Barclave's replacement?"

"Good. He's already singing like a canary, and we've already pinpointed a few key discrepancies."

"Gail paid the mercenaries extra to make sure I didn't show up again?"

Meredith shot a glare at me. "Did you sneak out of here and eavesdrop on our work?"

"No. I'm just picking my worst-case scenario guesses and rolling with them."

"Well, your worst-case scenario guesses are accurate so far. There is good news: the outfit they used has no problem killing royals, but they won't kill registered RPS agents. Some of their members are former agents. Some want revenge against royals, but they are hesitant to attack active agents. That's what spared your detail's lives during the attack."

"That explains why they were able to infiltrate the compound."

"Yes, that's what we believe. Agent Evangeline should be safe enough. Our canary won't talk about the outfit itself, but he's vocal enough about the plans they'd made. It's a good strategy on his part. We're getting good intel out of him; it won't lead us to the outfit, but it will help us firm our security at the compound and the castle."

"The mercenaries will walk?"

"Unless we get lucky, yes. But he's informed us they won't hit Illinois again, not for a long time. It's a good way for them to get caught, and most of the outfit has already bailed."

I eyed Meredith's briefcase, wondering what she'd brought with her. "And you believe him?"

"We have reason to."

"Truth seer?"

"Among other reasons." Meredith popped open the case and pulled out a stack of papers. "The preliminary trial is tomorrow, but we're confident none of the accused will be granted bail, not with the overwhelming evidence of guilt, and due to the nature of their crimes, they'll be kept in maximum security with prison-grade suppressors until the completion of the trial."

Some viewed the suppressors as a form of cruel and unusual punishment; when worn for too long, they carried a chance of nullifying the wearer's talents. "An understandable precaution with his illumination talent. But does Gail's talent warrant it?"

Meredith pulled out a sheet of paper and handed it to me. "Gail's been aiding the scheme with a mutated illumination talent of her own, unregistered. That's why they were working together. It was her talent that was boosting his."

The sheet confirmed the presence of a mid-strength illumination talent verified by a truth seer as being capable of creating convincing illusions. "Barclave's talent was the one capable of tricking the cameras?"

"Correct, Your Highness."

"What do you need from me in the meantime?"

"You'll have to stand witness, but honestly, you remember so little your session won't last even an hour. Dr. Thorton's testimony will cover the physical reasons for your memory lapse from the event. He's going to have a model made of your skull to show the work he had to do, so you'll need to go in for imaging before the trial. The discovery phase of the trial will take several months due to the volume of information and the severity of the case."

While relieved I wouldn't have to be part of the trial for long, I didn't look forward to the months of research and questioning I'd endure to ensure Barclave and Gail stayed behind bars where they belonged. "All right. I need a favor."

"What is it?"

"I need to make an unofficial trip to Nevada to speak to King Jacques personally." I shifted my attention to my father. "Can you make it happen?"

He crossed his arms over his chest and glared down his nose at me. "Why?"

"Because he's going to be brought into this mess and deserves a fair warning, as it will inevitably involve his court."

My father's eyes widened. "What do you mean?"

Meredith chuckled. "Figured it out, did you?"

"He didn't figure it out," Eva announced, emerging from the bedroom wearing the other bathrobe. "I told him. You're a pesky Your Highness."

I grinned at my wife. "Did you really think I'd sit around and do nothing?"

"I was fucking hoping you would. Why can't you be a lazy nutter about this?"

"I don't want to, that's why. You're not stopping me, not this time."

"Oh, you're being assertive." She smirked

and perched on the arm beside me. "I'll have to thank Dr. Thorton for making some adjustments while he was working on you yesterday."

"I'm not a car," I complained. "He didn't make adjustments. This is just something I can do, so I'm going to do it."

"Do you think it's necessary?"

"Without doubt."

Eva scowled, then she sighed and shrugged. "All right. Do you want me to go with you?"

"No. I'm not going to create a security gap. You can keep my parents company and keep them out of trouble."

"You're asking for miracles today."

My conversation with Eva earned us both glares, and I grinned at having nettled my parents. "What?"

My mother flung her hands in the air. "How can you be in such a good mood?"

My father arched a brow and stared at my mother. "I think it's obvious. Someone had a nice evening."

Nice was one way to describe it, and Eva snickered. "Damn straight we had a nice, quiet evening."

It was my turn to arch a brow. "Quiet?"

Eva narrowed her eyes and poked me in the chest. "Hush, you."

My mother sighed and pinched the bridge of her nose. "I regret having asked. I don't want to know."

My father's grin promised trouble. Sometimes, my father abandoned every self-preservation skill he'd learned over the years hoping to infuriate my mother, and suspected I'd be crowned king a lot sooner than anticipated. "I do, especially if it involves grandchildren in the near future."

Yep. My father was going to die at my mother's hands. "Before you kill him, Mom, Dad can you wrangle me an invite to Nevada?"

"I'll get on the phone with Jacques and make it happen. Getting you out of the kingdom for a few days and under their security might help, too. That'll give Meredith time to shuffle your detail."

"If you think I'm allowing him to leave the kingdom without me, I'll call Dr. Thorton in to give you an examination, Your Majesty."

"Meredith goes with His Highness," Christian ordered. "With Meredith's leave, I'll handle the detail shuffle with Evangeline's help. That'll keep her busy and as safe as we can possibly make her. We'll have security gaps between here and the compound, but it should be safe enough, especially with her self-defense skills. If they go for live capture like we believe, she should be safe enough."

"All right. I'll get that started. How long do you think you'll need for this business?"

"I'm not sure," I admitted. "It could take an hour, it could take several days. It really depends on him. I'd like to be back as soon as possible."

"I'll take care of it. How are feeling? Any headaches? Dr. Thorton said we were supposed to call him immediately if you develop a headache."

I gave it a few hours before I'd need the trip to Nevada to dodge my parents and their concern, no matter how justified their concern was. "I'm fine. Really. If I get a headache, I'll let someone know right away. But I feel fine."

"I can't believe she'd go that far," my mother whispered.

"Well, she did. And she might go after Eva."

"I'm seeing that now. I should've trusted you."

It was as much of an apology as I'd get, which I accepted with a nod. "Now you know. I'm trusting you with Eva while I'm gone, so make sure she's comfortable. I trust you'll make sure the bear will make himself available when she needs to take her temper out on someone."

"For the record, the number two lure of marrying into this family? Beating on that bear." Eva smirked at me.

I'd ask her about the number one lure when we were alone.

"Perhaps you two should delay making any heirs until after the wedding?" my mother begged.

Eva's smile did wonderful and terrible things to me. "No, I don't think so."

My father laughed so hard he doubled over. "Darling, leave the love birds alone. If they want to grace the kingdom with a future heir, I certainly have no problems with her wedding dress accommodating her pregnancy. Give Kel some credit. He doesn't mess around when he makes up his mind, and heaven knows his choice is certainly better than ours. Let them make a family if they want. It won't be the first or last time a royal pair got hitched after their firstborn was already on the way. No one cares."

My mother's mouth dropped open, but she closed it with a faint click of her teeth.

It would do.

The good humor fled from Eva's expression. "I meant what I said. You don't have to like me. You don't have to get along with me. You don't even need to give me the time of day. But you have to put up with me. I'm not leaving, and I'm not going to let you push either one of us out of this relationship. It's not your choice. At all. You get zero say in if we have one child, three children, or even twenty children."

"Considering I lose count of how many sisters I have, I don't think twenty is a good idea," I muttered.

Eva shot a glare in my direction. "If we want twenty kids, we'll have twenty without the Her Royal Majesty over there adding her input. If we only have one, then we only have one. Without the Her Royal Majesty over there adding her input."

My father chuckled. "You're not winning this one, darling. She's a mountain you can't climb, so give up now. And Kel, stop being mean to your sisters. You haven't lost count of them."

I felt my face grow warm, and I turned my head so I wouldn't have to look either of my parents in the eyes.

"He totally has no idea how many sisters he has," Eva announced, and she ruffled my hair. "He works too much, gets too involved with his paperwork, and doesn't see them often enough. And, judging from how waspish Her Royal Majesty is, you're likely adding another to the fray, so perhaps you shouldn't talk smack about us having children."

"She's waspish because someone tried to kill our son."

"Oh, no. That's definitely not someone tried to kill my son waspishness. She'd be turning that rage on the ones who tried to kill her son rather than the one who helped you locate him. She's totally pregnant."

With Meredith seated behind me, I couldn't flop across the loveseat and hide my head under the throw pillow, so I covered my face with my hands. "We're going to have to talk about subtlety, Eva."

"She who lives in a glass house shouldn't

throw rocks at me. I throw rocks back, and I don't give a shit if I break fucking windows. I can take care of myself, and I don't need some man protecting me from his mother."

I laughed, shrugged, and said, "I'm okay with admitting I need a woman protecting me from my mother."

"Kelvin!" My mother's shoulders slumped. "It's not like that."

"Oh, it is. It really is. I've been so pliable most of my life you have no idea how to deal with me now that I'm saying no and putting my foot down. I'm not very good at it yet, but you're just going to have to get used to it. Sure, you have the status quo to maintain, but I have everything to lose, including the only woman I want for my wife. I don't want this to become a choice between you and her, but you're not going to like my choice if you force me to make it. I'm not asking you two to go do your nails at some parlor, but try to get along."

Meredith coughed, Eva burst into laughter, and my parents both sighed. Christian smiled, which worried me most of all.

"What?"

"You're being assertive," Eva replied as though explaining everything.

I didn't understand. "I've been assertive before."

"You're being assertive without accepting any other options. They're probably considering if they need to ask Dr. Thorton there was brain damage he hadn't repaired."

Eva teased me, and I'd enjoy teasing her back in private the first time I got a chance. "There are no other acceptable options in this situation."

"While I agree with you, they're not prepared to handle you being assertive and refusing to consider other options."

I worried Christian would choke if he continued to smother his laughter, and I sighed at the head of my father's detail. "Christian, it's not that funny."

According to the faint snort from the RPS agent, it was. "Your Highness," he replied, and I marveled at how calm his tone sounded despite looking like he wanted to run out the door so he could laugh without anyone witnessing.

"If His Highness will be making a trip to Nevada, I need to know a rough timeline for departure," Meredith announced. "Then I can get the required signatures for investigation. Christian, when you're assigning Agent Evangeline's detail, account for potential separation anxiety. We're not sure how they'll react. Should she show symptoms, make arrangements for her to go to Nevada with a double detail."

"Easily done. I'll set a double detail from the gate so we won't have to shuffle shifts in case she needs to go. And frankly, with their luck, I'd almost suggest sending them both."

Meredith frowned, her eyes narrowed as she considered his words. "Evangeline?"

"If you double a detail on me, and I'm with him, he's better protected. But I won't promise it won't create problems. Technically, I'm probably barred from going anywhere near the palace grounds in Nevada."

"I'll make sure there are no problems," my father said. "Would it be better if we went, too?"

The RPS agents stared at each other, and I marveled they could hold a silent conversation without me being able to guess what went on between them.

In the end, Meredith shrugged.

Christian remained silent, his expression flitting from intense concentration to resignation. "It might leave an odd impression."

"But it would elevate Nevada's relationship with Illinois, as it gives the Royal States the impression we've selected their kingdom as a temporary haven while the RPS infiltration is handled," my father countered. "I'm okay with this if Jacques agrees to it."

"Meredith, are you willing to handle four principals?"

"You handle matters here, I'll take care of the visit to Nevada. I can call in trusted support if it's required, but Nevada's team is solid, and I've trained with many of the senior agents there. I don't foresee any problems as long as we give them advance notice we have a targeted principal in the delegation."

"That role's going to fucking suck," Eva muttered.

"There is a bonus: you get to share space with me as it's easier to protect two in the same room. Right, Meredith?"

"I'm not getting involved with your attempts to flirt, Your Highness."

"I wasn't flirting. I was just telling her it's safer if she stays in my bed. You should be happy you have one less thing to worry about."

"He has issues right now," Eva said, and she reached over and ran her fingers through my hair. "Let the clingy Your Highness here have his way. Otherwise, he's going to become annoying. He hasn't computed he's the one we're fucking worried about. He's gotten the feather-brained idea his sole duty in life is to make sure I don't stub a toe."

I wasn't worried about her stubbing her toe, but as she boiled the situation down nicely on my behalf, I saved myself the trouble of correcting her and nodded. "That about sums it up."

"Your species explains so much, though," my father admitted. "No wonder you've been skulking around and refusing to show off during the spring. You do realize you would've been surrounded by entire packs of overprotective predators willing to maim on your behalf, right?"

"Damn it, Dad."

"A turkey," my mother added, sniffing. "I really hope this doesn't mean we'll be stuck with ham on Thanksgiving and Christmas."

"You stick me with ham on Thanksgiving and Christmas, and I'm staging a revolt."

"Then we're good. Although I find it slightly disturbing my son has no scruples about eating his mundane counterparts."

I stared at my father and willed him to go away, but he ignored my unspoken command.

"From the reading I've done, turkeys are highly aggressive when defending their turf, although this Your Highness here is monogamous rather than polyamorous," Eva announced. "I've been doing my homework so I know how to appropriately care for my turkey."

"I wish you the best of luck," my father admitted. "He'll forget to eat if anyone takes their eyes off him for extended periods of time. You might want to take control of his feeding schedule, because he'll forage."

"I'll make sure he eats. I need him healthy for my various plans. I'm going to have to accept hunting the other members of your family first, as I suspect he'll need some extra time being conditioned for being my prey, but a pack of wolves, a lion, and lynx, and a big teddy bear should keep me amused for a while."

My father sighed. "You forgot the wolverine. I'll do the rest of my family a favor and warn them to avoid revealing their animals to you."

"There's even more of you? Excellent. Anyway, I didn't forget the wolverine. He's exempt until he's no longer at risk of requiring a bone marrow transfusion like the Your Highness over here. I like hunting, but let's not stress the sickly beasts. If he's bored during his season and wants me to hunt him, that's different."

"You're marrying a strange one, son," my father muttered.

I snorted. "Birds of a feather flock together. From where I sit, she's perfect."

"If you're going to impose on Nevada, Your Majesty, perhaps you should go to your office and call to make arrangements," Christian suggested.

"My office is currently being cleaned because of an unusual volume of mud and blood."

"The blood wasn't mine."

"I still don't want my brother's blood in my office, Kel."

Christian sighed. "Then call on your cell phone, Your Majesty. Please. Preparing is much easier with a flight authorization, and Meredith has a lot of work ahead of her."

I hoped the head of my detail wouldn't try to kill me for the extra work I was about to give her. "Meredith?"

"Your Highness?"

"We're going to need some paperwork from Montana, if you'd put in the request, please."

"I'll take care of it," she promised.

"What paperwork?" my father demanded.

"The paperwork I'll use as a weapon if King Jacques doesn't give me what I want," I replied.

"That's concerning."

"You can thank Eva for my newfound ability to be assertive later, Dad. Am I cleared to go back to my room? I need to pack."

"Your clothing was already brought back from the RPS training compound, and it's still packed, so you don't have to worry about that," Meredith replied. "Agent Evangeline will require appropriate clothing, but I can make arrangements."

"Or I can just wear my RPS attire. It won't offend any delicate sensibilities."

"Her work attire's fine. It'll save time. If she needs more clothing, we can shop in Nevada."

"They'll only need a few minutes to be ready to leave, then," Meredith announced. "As soon as I have the order to obtain the flight authorization, I can have it within an hour. Fifteen minutes if it's preauthorized over phone and Nevada handles the first stage of the paperwork."

"I'll have Jacques handle the paperwork on his end. He'll be willing to do it once I fill him in on the entire situation."

"Then, assuming the call goes well, Evangeline can leave within an hour if that's enough time for you, Your Majesties."

"It'll be enough time," my mother promised, and she headed for the door. "Evangeline, please send me your dress sizes. One of my daughters must have something that'll fit you in a closet somewhere. I'll handle your evening attire for the visit."

I leaned towards my wife and whispered, "Accept the peace offering for what it is, please. You can beat me with the dresses later. Consider them loaners, although my sisters won't notice they're gone."

"Thank you, Your Majesty," Eva replied. Then she elbowed me in the ribs hard enough I sucked in a breath through clenched teeth.

My mother huffed and marched out of the suite.

"We'll meet back here before we leave for the airport, so you two might as well relax until then."

Meredith waited for my father and Christian to leave before shaking her head. "I'll make sure your breakfast isn't forgotten. I expect everyone will get carried away."

"It's a bad habit here," I admitted.

"I know, which is concerning. At the rate this is going, I'm never going to be able to leave."

"Such a tragedy," I replied.

Meredith bowed her head while Eva laughed.

WHILE I WAITED to find out if we'd be going to Nevada, I ate a breakfast so healthy I suspected my doctors had threatened death on the kitchen staff if they gave me anything appealing. I choked down the oatmeal to keep Eva happy, and I used my laptop to catch up on the news. Word had already spread throughout the Royal States about my kidnapping, near-fatal injury, and the attempted replacement, and the media locked onto Gail's portion of the story.

I was starting to believe there was something to Eva's claims that I'd become one of the most-liked royals. The media had no mercy on Gail or her reputation.

"They're a little vicious," Eva said, pointing at a paragraph in the article I read describing Gail as ruthless and conniving. "I'm pretty sure that's the nicest thing anyone's said in any of the statements you've looked at so far."

"I get she could be a bit standoffish at times, but this is excessive."

"She was caught red-handed in an attempted regicide attempt with the end goal of becoming queen using an imposter to do it. The court of public opinion is going to tear her apart. It's unavoidable. Anyway, because of her machinations, you almost fucking died, so don't you fucking dare feel sorry for her."

I held up my hands in surrender. "I don't

feel sorry for her. Honestly, I was considering sneaking out last night and encouraging you to commit murder while I watched. Sorry is not the word I'd use right now. I'm startled the media is diving in like this, though. I've been hiding for months."

"Due to severe health concerns, and just as you were on the mend and about to resume your full duties, you had your skull caved in."

"Were they reporting about my progress?"

"Of course. Your parents are doing their best to make sure you come out of this shining. They've been doing controlled releases of information about your recovery to keep the public happy. It's worked so far, too. The wedding announcement started a storm of speculations and gossip, though." Eva smirked and shrugged. "Some of them have figured out I'm a likely candidate, which is driving Meredith insane because they've identified me as someone associated with the RPS, but since she refuses to talk about it for the reporters, they don't have any juicy details to work with. I've been enjoying the news portion of my mornings. Meredith seems to think she can ease me into my responsibilities by exposing me to politics via morning television."

"Well, you're more with the times than I am right now."

"I also hadn't had my skull caved in."

"You're not going to let that go anytime soon, are you?"

"Not a fucking chance in hell."

"All right. I'd say I'm sorry, but I don't have anything to be sorry for except for letting a band of mercenaries get the jump on me. I mean, I'm definitely sorry I got hit. I'd like to go the rest of my life without a repeat of that."

"Agreed. And there really wasn't anything you could've done to prevent it."

"And if what I've been told is true, there's nothing you could've done to prevent it, either. That's probably what has you so cranky about this whole thing, I bet."

"That's an unfair usage of your deductive reasoning, Your Highness."

"We're in agreement. I'll stay out of trouble, you'll stay out of trouble, we'll live happily ever after. I'll also avoid having people beat me in the head, and you won't get nabbed by vengeful parents attempting to sell you to some old fart. For the record, I may need you to teach me some basic offense so I can beat the fucker if he even looks at you."

"I can get you a picture and show you a few offensive moves, but I'll tell you a little secret you'll appreciate."

"What?"

"That bastard's afraid of birds."

For the first time in my life, I was happy I'd drawn the short straw and could shift into an oversized turkey. "How afraid are we talking here?"

"He pissed his pants once because a pigeon got too close to him. I was fourteen, and my parents were introducing us for the first time. I knew then I wanted nothing to do with such a sniveling coward. It was a pigeon!"

It took colossus effort, but I kept from laughing. "What do you think an oversized turkey will do to him?"

"Give him a heart attack, I hope."

"Well, if a close encounter of the avian kind doesn't do that, I'd be happy to give my best shot to spur and peck him in the face for you."

"You're such a sweet talker. Beat him with your wings, too. I've first-hand experience on that one. Those wings hurt, Your Highness."

"You tried to skewer me with an arrow," I reminded her.

"I'm going with accidental injury during self-defense on this one. You tried to break my face with those wings of yours. Obviously, the only solution was to skewer you, brand you, and make you mine as payback."

I held my arms out to her, and without any other coaxing, she sat on my lap. Resting my head against her shoulder, I hugged her close. "I'm okay with that."

"Do you think we're going to have to hide in closets moving forward to spend time together? Because seriously, I was considering relocating you myself," she confessed.

"I had similar thoughts. I was about ready to make a run for the border. I could deal with the ridiculous schedule, but only getting to see you when you were being run through scenarios was driving me insane."

She laughed. "Your expression at the last one was priceless. I could see you calculating how you might be able to get away with murder. None of them even bruised me, so you have nothing to worry about. I rather enjoy some of those scenarios."

"I didn't like them manhandling you."

"You're going to be ridiculous about this, aren't you?"

"Maybe."

"How about this? Next time, you can be on the capture team. You'll have fun with it, we'll get to face off, and it'll add to the challenge."

"I'm pretty sure I'm a disadvantage to the capture team, but it's probably a lot more fun being on the capture team than it is being the principal."

"You rolled up your papers and beat Agent Hollacks and Meredith with them. You were starting to figure it out. She'll want to do a repeat of the stress test after you've had a chance to settle down, but I expect she'll be careful with how it's done. It depends on how you handle the taps we use."

"I'm game, except I'm going to need you to be more readily accessible for my plans to run away."

Eva laughed and rewarded me with a kiss. "I'm going to be the one running away with you if I have to resort to a closet again to get even a kiss."

"Then we're in agreement. If we have to resort to closets, we're breaking out and running away."

"Why do I have a feeling we're going to turn Meredith's hair prematurely gray?" Eva freed herself from my arms and smoothed her clothes. "Let's get ready to go; I expect as soon as arrangements are made, the entire looney bin is going to fucking barge in here."

I read between the lines, amused over what Eva thought the looney bin might be interrupting, but I didn't question her choice. Given a chance, I probably would put us in an awkward situation and leave no doubts as to the state of our relationship.

EIGHTEEN

Sedation might help with that.

NEVADA AGREED TO HOST US, both to my dismay and relief. If Meredith wanted to do a stress test on me, all she'd need to do was pop a balloon. I'd be halfway across the kingdom before I controlled my flight instinct or someone caught me. Training with the RPS had given me a better idea of what could go wrong, and I lacked the skills needed to protect Eva.

That scared the hell out of me.

Time hadn't been on my side, and I recognized I wouldn't have a chance to learn until I finished climbing other mountains first, which didn't help my mood at all. I remained tense from the instant my father returned to the guest suite confirming we'd be leaving for Nevada within the hour until we boarded the royal plane.

Had I known the trip would become a family affair, I would've insisted on going alone. My great-grandpa sat behind Eva and kept poking my wife in the ribs. "I get to be your bodyguard for the duration of this trip. I've been informed I count as two guards. My whippersnapper of a son will also get to be one of your bodyguards. I'm not sure if I should count him as two bodyguards or zero. Lions can be lazy."

My grandfather chuckled, following the head of his detail onto the plane, an older man a few years shy of retirement. "I heard that, Father. I count as two, thank you. But we really know I'm here so you have access to Seb."

The head of my grandfather's detail sighed and sat across the aisle from Eva. "My apologies, Your Highness. They're excitable today."

"Sedation might help with that," I suggested.

"They wouldn't do you any good as bodyguards if they're sleeping on the job."

"They'd be a lot less annoying."

He chuckled and buckled in. "I'm afraid you're going to have to suffer for the next few days. Be grateful you don't have an entire pack of wolves to contend with. The wolves are handling matters here for the duration of the trip."

"What's the pecking order of RPS agents for this visit?"

Seb pointed at Meredith. "We're all taking orders from her. Consider us standard members of your detail until we're back in Illinois."

"I'm pretty sure having members of the royal family acting as a detail for another member of the same royal family breaks RPS rules."

"I think we've accepted we're going to have substantial breaches in RPS assignment protocol for the next few weeks. We may as well openly embrace it. In good news, it will leave no doubt that the Illinois royal family sticks together. We're confident we can mitigate the fallout, although I expect every member of the royal family will be fired officially and told to keep their noses out of the RPS's general business." Seb stared at Eva with an arched brow.

"Unlike the other dipshits on this plane, I have a special exemption." Lifting her chin, Eva faked a sniff. "I'm a trainer. Who has been acting as a principal. My job security is better than yours right now."

I wouldn't remind Eva she'd been temporarily reinstated and had zero security in the RPS although her future prospects looked good in my opinion.

Meredith's laughter proved Eva's job wasn't as secure as she'd like, although when I finished in Nevada, there'd be a good reason for that.

When my parents found out we'd eloped in Montana, there'd be a bloodbath: mine.

Would they forgive me if I sent them an invitation to our public wedding?

"Hey, what's that supposed to mean?" My wife twisted in her seat to face Meredith, kneeling for a better look at the head of my detail. "That's not funny."

"You know exactly why I'm laughing, Agent Evangeline. Fight it all you want. It'll amuse me probably as much as it'll amuse His Royal Highness. Also, I'd like to remind you that the RPS immediately puts any pregnant agents on paid leave or assigns them to desk work."

Eva stiffened and her face flushed. "Meredith!"

As I liked everything involved with the idea of Eva and children, I listened to the discussion with interest. I'd been unaware of the pregnancy clause, although it made sense.

RPS agents had dangerous, stressful jobs. "I didn't know that. At what stage of pregnancy are women put on leave in the RPS? Fully paid leave?"

"They can remain on duty throughout the first trimester. The beginning of the second trimester is when agents are suspended from field duty and put on either paid leave or transitioned to a desk job until the child is born. Currently, the RPS allows six months of paid paternity and maternity leave that can be spread out over the first two years of the child's life. We just ask for forty-eight hours notice if an agent needs to take time off work to care for their child. Emergencies being exempt, of course."

"I've learned something new. Interesting. How does that rank against standard employers? I'll admit, I've never looked at it closely."

"Well, that makes sense, Your Highness. It hasn't been relevant to your interests until now. The RPS is a leader in maternal and paternal leave. Being an RPS agent is dangerous, but we try to accommodate families as much as possible."

I eyed Eva and smirked.

"Don't you even think about it, Your Highness."

"You only have yourself to blame, Agent Evangeline." My smirk grew into a grin. "I'm just considering the best ways to use this to my advantage."

"What's going on in here?" my father demanded, boarding the plane and glaring in my direction. "What trouble are you causing now?"

"I've been informed it's probable I'll get Eva fired."

"Maybe in a few months. You have to get to the wedding first, kiddo."

Eva arched a brow, staring at me in silent questioning.

Unable to do anything else without revealing the truth, I shrugged.

"You're not supposed to master the art of silent communication until at least a year after your marriage, kiddo."

"I can't help it you're a slow learner, Dad."

"You're obviously feeling fine. You're getting mouthy." My father claimed the seat in front of me, and my mother joined him. "Darling, he obviously got this from you. I can't claim any responsibility for the way this child of ours turned out."

"Like hell you can't, you flea-ridden cat."

I expected Dad would be sleeping on the couch. "So, would you be on paid leave yet or not, Mom?"

"Kelvin," she warned.

"I'm just wondering if I should expect another sister in six months."

"Fine. Seven."

I glared at my father. "Aren't you too old for this? Really?"

"I commend you for avoiding making that comment to your mother, as I'd rather not bury my son today. And no, I'm not. It's a perk of dealing with the inconveniences of our talent."

A suspicion sank in, and I gave my great-grandpa my undivided attention. "Could you still have children?"

"Maybe. We do make an effort to avoid adding to the insanity. Your father has added enough to the insanity for the rest of the family, and don't even get me started on his brothers."

"Do you think all my relatives would fit in the main audience chamber if we tried to cram everyone inside?"

"No," my great-grandpa replied. "They wouldn't."

I spent the rest of the flight wondering how I'd be able to go a hundred years with Eva without having twenty children. I'd have to budget for a lot of birth control.

Then it occurred to me neither one of us had given as much as a second thought to birth control last night.

I wondered if Eva would kill me, if my mother would kill me, or if Dr. Hampford would kill me.

I found it ironic I'd survived so much only to throw it all way being a thoughtless idiot. I gave myself low odds of surviving the next few days.

EVA LOCKED onto my worries like my uncles did when they spotted a wild rabbit, and she waited for everyone to file off the plane before she pounced. "What has you worked up? You've looked like you swallowed a lemon the entire flight."

I decided to accept my approaching death with grace. "I forgot birth control, and I forgot to ask you if you were on birth control."

"You use the word forgot like it is important."

"It's not a do and ask for forgiveness later type of situation."

"It's a 'there's no problem' situation." Eva rolled her eyes, unbuckled her belt, and hopped to her feet. "Boy meets girl. Girl brands boy's ass to keep him around. Girl lures boy into nearest empty closet. Boy lures girl to nearest empty bed. Nowhere in this progression is there a detour for birth control. That's what pregnancy tests are for in a few weeks. If we didn't get the result anticipated when boys lure girls to the nearest empty bed, then we'll just have to try again later. Has that offered you any clarity of my opinion on this matter?"

Huh. I blinked, unbuckled my belt, and considered her with newfound appreciation. "We're one of those couples, then?"

"One of what couples?"

"The kind who loses count of the number of children we have because we have issues with luring each other to the nearest empty bed without any care if birth control is used?"

"We can discuss if we want to limit the number of children we have after the first one. I figure if we have more than a hundred years to put up with each other, we'll get the first kid out of the way early so we can uphold the family traditional of abdicating as quickly as possible and dumping the problem of ruling on our child's lap."

I loved the way Eva thought. "I still should have thought about it."

"I consider it a compliment, as I'd enticed

you so much your common sense dribbled out of those pretty ears of yours."

"I'll claim a temporary lapse of common sense due to head trauma and a beautiful but impatient woman."

"See? There you go. All covered. We'll blame Dr. Thorton should anyone ask why there's no evidence of birth control in use."

"For the record, I really will run away if we have to resort to closets."

She laughed.

My father poked his head into the cabin. "Are you two coming or not? King Jacques is waiting, and he seems confused by why you're not out here yet. As a reminder, you can't join the mile-high club when the plane is grounded, so you have no excuse for delaying."

"We're coming," I replied, getting to my feet.

"Your father is much more casual about our relationship than your mother is," Eva observed.

"Are you ready to see Jacques?"

Eva shrugged. "He won't even recognize me. I only know who he is because my mother liked to rant about how he cruelly evicted her from the family. Maybe if she hadn't been an asshole, she wouldn't have gotten kicked out."

I could think of a few circumstances a king would be pushed to remove a member of the family from the picture. "She wanted to become the queen."

"It's like you've been paying attention to current events."

"I love that sarcastic mouth of yours."

"That surprised me," she admitted, gracing me with one of her smiles. "You liked me for who I was from the very beginning, foul mouth and all."

"Especially because of that foul mouth. You haven't been using nearly enough of your favorite words lately. Sprinkle them in, please."

She took a few steps and waited to make sure I followed her. "I figure the more I curse, the less people will want to do with me. That obviously didn't work on you."

"I'm afraid to inform you that your efforts to remain a loner failed spectacularly. I'd also like to remind you that you cursed more without an audience."

"Well, sometimes cursing is just fucking fun."

"If you're not ready to face King Jacques, you're welcome to hide behind me."

"Will that increase the odds of you beating him with the paperwork you asked Meredith to acquire?"

"I honestly have no idea. I suppose it depends on what he does if he recognizes you."

"Reminder: you can't attack a king."

"If he raises a hand against you, I'm attacking him."

Eva laughed. "That's just a disaster waiting to happen. You're really not good on the offense. I'm going to be spending years trying to make you adequate."

"Daily lessons?"

"Don't sound so hopeful about being invited to your own beating, Your Highness."

My father bellowed, "Move it, kids!"

"He's impatient," my wife complained.

I nudged her into the next row of seats so I could pass her and shrugged. "He's edgy with good reason. He wants to parade me in front of the cameras to verify I'm still alive, and Nevada likes taking pictures of everything. We're giving them something to gossip about."

"Would me grabbing and kissing you in public give them reason to gossip?"

"Yes, and I'd probably like it. But realistically, we should wait for that until we find out if I have to use paperwork against His Royal Majesty of Nevada."

"Spoilsport."

I laughed and slipped through the door, taking my time on the stairs so I wouldn't fall and earn the wrath of my doctors for trying to break my skull again. At the bottom, King Jacques waited with his wife.

Anyone with a pair of eyes would recognize the family resemblance between him and Eva, and the instant Nevada's king caught sight of her on the stairs behind me, his eyes widened.

"Prince Kelvin. You're looking well," His Royal Majesty of Nevada greeted, his gaze locked on my wife.

"Your Majesty," I greeted.

"Evangeline," King Jacques greeted.

Eva stumbled on the last step behind me and collided with my back, and I turned on the step, offered my arm to support her, and waited until she regained her balance. "Your Majesty."

For the first time since meeting her, Eva kept her eyes on the ground, and she stood tense.

"I see there's a lot more to discuss than I initially thought. If you'd like to join me, Your Highness? Evangeline?"

My wife gulped but jerked her head in a nod.

I stepped away from the staircase and kept a hold on Eva until certain she wouldn't hit the ground. While hesitant to relinquish my hold on her, I released her and tailed after Nevada's king while the rest of my relatives joined Nevada's queen heading to a second vehicle.

Meredith flanked me, and she held my most potent weapon, my first and last resort, in a silver briefcase.

King Jacques's RPS agents held open the limo's back door, and I slid inside after the king. When Eva joined us, I snagged her hand and directed her to sit beside me with a single tug, which put her directly across from her uncle. "Thank you for seeing us on such short notice."

"I'll admit, you've gotten my attention. What's going on that'd have your father itching for a meeting?"

"I have reason to believe that my ex-girlfriend has paid someone in Nevada to deal with Evangeline, and as this could cause you substantial problems, I wanted to give you adequate warning."

"You have my attention."

"The papers, Meredith?"

The head of my detail sat beside King Jacques, buckled in, and put the briefcase on her lap, popping it open. Without fanfare, she handed Nevada's king a single sheet of paper.

He read it, his eyebrows inching upwards. "I understand how this could cause me problems should there be a plot. I also see congratulations are in store. You've picked well for yourself, Evangeline."

My wife's face flushed red, and she spluttered something incomprehensible. To spare her from further embarrassment, I reached across her, snagged the seatbelt, and buckled her in before doing the same for myself. "I may have underestimated how flustered she'd become."

"No doubt. It puts everyone in an awkward position," King Jacques replied. "Seeing this was issued in Montana and witnessed by His and Her Royal Majesty along with a few other interesting choices, your marriage is a secret?"

"For now. We've already set a wedding date, but I wasn't taking any chances with her, not when there are potential concerns with the matter of her disowning."

"I may have gotten a rather stern letter from His Royal Majesty of Montana advising me what I'd do if I had any integrity. I was rather annoyed with you for putting me in that position, I'll confess, but considering the latest developments, I see the reasons behind it. Were the severity of your injuries overplayed in the media?"

"Want to field this one, Meredith?"

"Of course, Your Highness. The media reports are accurate. It took Dr. Thorton of Montana four hours to reconstruct the damaged parts of his skull. His Highness's familial talent spared him from death, but when he transformed to preserve his life, his skull was essentially reshaped to account for the swelling in his brain. Prior medical procedures had left enough latent magic in the brain, meant to protect it from the transfusion process, to prevent lethal damage from the blow. His assailant meant to kill him, of that we have no doubt."

"When it takes Dr. Thorton four hours of work, I think that counts as serious. Do you have any impairment?"

I walked on thin ice, as I had no doubt King Jacques would spread word around the

Royal States the instant I headed home. "I have no memory of shortly before the attack, and my memory is patchy in places up until Dr. Thorton did his work," I replied.

That would cover me for the important bits and hopefully keep curious people off my back for a while.

"I certainly wouldn't remember much if I'd gotten hit in the head like that. If you don't mind me asking, how extensive were the injuries, really?"

Eva glanced my way, and I nodded to her. "Go ahead. Say what you want, Eva."

"The fuckers shattered his skull like an egg tossed out a window at highway speed."

I flinched at her description. "That's graphic."

"You said I could say what I wanted."

"That I did. Next time, I'll remember you're more creative than I'll likely anticipate."

"And the procedure was for what?"

Meredith retrieved several more sheets of paper from her briefcase and handed them over. "This should explain the situation nicely. This is the initial medical report along with a handwritten note from Dr. Thorton."

King Jacques read it, and his eyes widened. "Have you looked at this, Agent Scarson?"

"I have."

"And you, Prince Kelvin?"

"When I wasn't having the pieces of my

skull put back together in the proper order, I was sleeping."

Granted, some of that sleep wasn't exactly restful, but it'd done me a world of good.

"Dr. Thorton wrote a letter informing me he'd rather work on jigsaw puzzles in the future."

"I expect having to reshape someone's skull isn't exactly easy."

"From fragments."

Eva grunted, and I wondered how long it would be until the edge wore off of my close brush with death. "I got exceptionally lucky."

"I think this is going to put to rest any doubts about Illinois's talent line." King Jacques flipped through the papers. "No, it definitely does. This is impressive and horrifying."

"I've been told to misplace those documents in Nevada in a safe location," Meredith announced. "His Royal Majesty of Montana thought it best you be the one to handle this small issue with Evangeline's status."

"Well, there's only one thing I can do, and in light of the situation, I have no trouble doing it. I doubt I'll have any difficulty passing it through my congress. Evangeline, reinstatement to the royal family will mean a full and official disowning from your mother and father, I hope you're aware."

"I'm already disowned."

"Not officially. I've looked into the matter. The paperwork wasn't submitted correctly. I believe it was done so intentionally, too, likely to coerce you into something you didn't want to do."

Evangeline tensed. "Yes, a marriage."

"They attempted to forge your signature, but it will be easy to override, as Montana has already submitted legalized documentation confirming you have only entered into one marriage, the one with His Royal Highness of Illinois. Officially, you'll have to be brought in as my daughter, but as you're of the royal bloodline to begin with through my sister, that won't be an issue. It's a matter of willful disowning and adoption into my family. It's unusual, but it's legal. As an added benefit, His Royal Highness will get to wed the princess he rightfully deserves."

"I'll make a terrible princess," Eva muttered.

"You'll make a lovely princess and an even better queen, Evangeline. I've seen parts of your file, courtesy of the Illinois RPS."

Meredith closed her briefcase and stared out the window, the faintest of smirks gracing her lips.

"That was very sneaky of you, Meredith."

She smiled in earnest. "The wellbeing of my principal is my top priority, and my job is to manipulate the situation however needed to ensure the best outcome for my principal."

The women in my life were tricky, and I wondered when my mother would start meddling again. I gave it several hours before I needed to start worrying about her, too. "How long will it take to handle this? Without knowing who is coming after Eva, I want to get as many protections on her as possible."

"Of course. It can be taken care of today. I'll call an emergency session of the congress to ratify my decision and get the necessary signatures. I'll also deal with your parents, Evangeline. I'll make it clear if they are involved in a plot dealing with you that it's in their best interest to abandon it. I'll also have a warning issued that any outfit found to be attacking Illinois's interests at this time will be met with lethal force. Nevada is an execution kingdom for attempted regicide, and I have no problems putting out a kill order to protect members of my family."

If it came to that, I expected a bloodbath. "Is there any chance we can find out who accepted the payment from my ex-girlfriend?"

"Do you have the financial paper trail?"

Meredith popped open her briefcase and handed over a few more papers. "We do, Your Majesty. These are all of the account numbers we've found so far."

"I'll have a warrant issued and get these numbers run as soon as we arrive at the castle. Mercenary outfits don't tend to target royals in Nevada, as the punishments are exceptionally harsh, so I expect the payments are to individuals. It could also be a payment to Eva's family trying to secure her in Nevada. That wouldn't surprise me."

"That's what I'm afraid of," I admitted.

"Now, all that said, if you don't mind, I'd like to have one of my royal physicians have a look at you, Prince Kelvin. I'd rather make certain the flight didn't create any unexpected problems."

"Of course. What's one more doctor in my collection of them?"

"Have you found a permanent physician yet?"

"No, not yet. Dr. Hampford of Montana has been on call."

"Well, I might be able to help with that. We have several new royal physicians, so some of the more senior of our staff are looking to try new waters. They've served Nevada well over the years, and Illinois would make an excellent place for them to prepare for retirement while training new doctors. If you'd like to meet them, we can make that part of your visit."

"I recommend you accept his offer, Your Highness," Meredith ordered, and her tone allowed no argument.

"I'd greatly appreciate that, Your Majesty."

"Excellent." King Jacques glanced at Evangeline. "Dr. Pemland is one of them."

Eva's eyes widened. "She is?"

"She is."

"Who is Dr. Pemland?"

"She's a royal pediatrician, and while I removed my sister from the family for her crimes, I pulled some strings to make certain

Evangeline was seen by Dr. Pemland when she was little."

"I last saw her right before I ran," she admitted. "She'd come to my school and pretended she was the school nurse so my parents wouldn't find out about it."

"At the risk of bringing up a sore point, what were the charges against Eva's mother?"

"The official charge is conspiracy to take the throne and planned regicide. I'd ordered a stay of execution on grounds of Evangeline's birth, with strict conditions for her parole."

"I take that to mean Eva's mother might work with mercenaries to retrieve her?"

"I have no doubt of it. I have connections with the underground network. I'll put out a notice that any outfit cooperating will find itself on the wrong end of the regicide laws in Nevada, and we have extradition treaties with most of the Royal States."

I wanted a lot more, but it would have to do until I had some time to find a better way to protect Eva. "All right. Thank you, Your Majesty."

"Now, if you don't mind me asking, how on Earth did you two meet? Evangeline, you're an incredibly difficult young woman to find; your parents have been trying to retrieve you since you wisely ran away. You could've come to me. All you needed to do was tell Dr. Pemland about the situation. She would've made arrangements."

"I didn't think I could," Eva admitted. "As

for the rest, I found a wild animal, and I decided I liked him. I branded his ass so he couldn't escape me. The fucker escaped me anyway, so I had to hunt his ass down again. That's when things got weird."

King Jacques chuckled. "It sounds weird from the start. Also, we're obviously going to talk about the appropriate branding of people."

"I appropriately branded him. Permanently. He's mine."

I smiled, shrugged, and said, "I'm certainly not going to argue with her about that."

"Yes, but I doubt your mother warned you about the consequences of our brands. You're better off sticking with the basic flameweaver portion of our talent, Evangeline."

Meredith chuckled. "I wish you the best of luck convincing her to remove her brand from His Highness. The fastest way to stir her ire is to suggest it be removed, and when someone disrupted the original brand, let's just say her reaction was not positive. They're already bonded for life, Your Majesty, courtesy of His Highness's talent. They're also both suspected leeches, and in the unlikely event that bond hasn't already taken, the additional bond from Agent Evangeline's brand won't hurt either of them. We're going to be monitoring the development of their talents and nurturing any fledgling bonds. All things considered, it's easiest to let her use her talent and keep monitoring him. It proved useful when he was taken. Her ability to pinpoint his location on a map through her brand is spectacular. At distance, she has a quarter to half a mile accuracy."

"That good?" King Jacques chuckled and held his hands up in surrender. "As long as they're both aware of the risks."

"She's already life bonded to him, Your Majesty. There's nothing we could do to prevent it at this point. If her talent hadn't bonded them, his would have. I have the appropriate paperwork if you need to see it; Dr. Hampford thought it would be wise to have their bond officiated in case of future incidents."

"At the castle," he ordered. "Anything else I should know?"

"She has a temper, and the fastest way to provoke her is to threaten him, so I'd be aware there might be incidents if anyone gets too close to him right now," Meredith reported.

"Understandable. I'll make certain the RPS is aware of the situation and ensure things are kept as quiet as possible. Anything else?"

"Should he develop a headache, we're to contact Dr. Thorton and route him to the nearest hospital, but he believes His Highness is fully out of the danger. He doesn't like taking any risks with his patients, but this was too important to delay."

"I'm seeing that. Securing a kingdom's line of succession is critical, and Illinois has had a few uncomfortable years wondering what would happen with the succession. It's rare for an heir to have as much support as you do."

"I've always taken my job seriously."

"And you have a knack for it, which your cousin doesn't. With all due respect to your cousin, of course. But the real question is this: how will you pick your successor with the introduction of my family's talent to your line?"

"While I still need to discuss this with Eva, I expect we'll ultimately decide on our heir's ability to rule," I replied. "Should we have more than one child, I'll spit the duties between them and see who handles it the best. I'd rather not repeat the issues my father has had with Grégoire with my children. And Eva's contribution to the family should ultimately allow Illinois to pick a boy or a girl, although I anticipate the congress will want to continue the tradition of naming an heir with the family talent. I look forward to watching Eva battle the congress over it."

"I'll enjoy it." My wife smiled. "They're scared of me."

"That's because they're wise," I muttered.

Eva jabbed me with her elbow. "What does that make you?"

"Happily married and prone to fits of jealousy. If they're scared of you, they're not getting too close to you."

With a laugh and toss of her head, Eva

shrugged. "He's still cranky the training RPS agents were tossing me around during scenarios. They were just doing their job."

Meredith joined in the general laughter. "I was honestly hoping that'd snap him during the stress tests. I'm not looking forward to repeating the stress test, although the training agents were starting to get a feel for you, Your Highness."

"Can we do the next stress test at the castle?"

"We'll discuss it in Illinois."

By discuss, she meant dictate, which meant I'd be back to the RPS training compound until I snapped like a twig and did my best to run for the border. "I'll just accept that as a no and save you the trouble."

"It's nice when the principals understand their place in the hierarchy."

Eva leaned close and whispered, "If we start planning our escape from the start of the stress test, we might be able to pull it off after the first week, but we'll probably have to make use of some closets until we flee their clutches."

"It seems only fair we test every closet for security breaches," I whispered back.

"I don't know what you two are whispering about over there, but the answer is no," Meredith announced.

I exchanged looks with Eva, and we burst into laughter.

NINETEEN

I'm such a good influence on him.

HAD I known I'd go from lively to lethargic without warning, I would've given myself at least a day before imposing on King Jacques. By the time we arrived at the castle, I wanted nothing more than to find somewhere to sleep.

"Perhaps I should show His Highness to his suite and give him a chance to settle while I handle bringing you back into the main family, Evangeline. There'll be paperwork you need to sign, but I can bring it to your suite. Agent Scarson, I'll have the head of my detail assign a group to help with your duties, although I expect His and Her Majesty are sufficiently protected with the team you've brought in. While rather untraditional, only a fool would try to attack them under my roof."

"That would be appreciated, Your Majesty. Thank you."

"It'll take three or four hours, but give me your phone number so I can contact you if the estimate changes. I'd rather keep this off the network until everything is finalized. Is it a safe assumption you're planning a detail for Evangeline?"

Meredith gave Nevada's king her phone before saying, "She's been training with them, although I expect a few will be startled to discover she'll be their permanent principal. In good news, they won't stress nearly as much as your detail will, Your Highness."

I scowled, took a page out of Evangeline's book, and flipped the head of my detail my middle finger. The look Meredith shot me promised retribution in some form at a later time, which I assumed would happen during the stress test she'd see finished come hell or high water.

Eva tossed back her head and cackled. "I'm such a good influence on him."

"Well, it's definitely the most casual I've ever seen him around RPS agents, so I'm inclined to agree with you." King Jacques opened the door, a signal to those waiting outside he was ready to begin officially welcoming us to Nevada. "We're keeping things low-key today, but expect the usual pomp and circumstance tomorrow. They like when we put on a show, and I have a few ideas of how to make both of you shine for the public."

I groaned. "You're not going to the long-lost princess route, are you?"

"For your sake as much as hers, yes, I am.

And considering the evidence I have, some I've gathered myself and some provided by Montana, I'll be able to weave quite the story for the crowd. You can consider this an early wedding gift."

Exposing Eva as a princess of any sort would create a frenzy in the media, and once word spread she was marrying me, the frenzy would escalate to pure insanity. The other options, including hiding and becoming a hermit, wouldn't protect her as well as integrating her into Nevada's royal family before I publicly claimed her as my wife. "Thank you, Your Majesty."

"I've put your parents in the main guest suite while I've made arrangements for you to stay in one of the ambassadorial suites. That'll give you a little distance from the rest of your family and make it easier to identify if anyone is overly interested in you." King Jacques led the way into the castle, which I'd always found to be pretentious. The architect had tried to outshine Buckingham Palace, and in some ways, had succeeded, but doing so with a modern flair I expected of Las Vegas.

Inside and out, the place oozed extravagance, making me long for the more practical stone halls of home, built to withstand war rather than display the kingdom's riches. Did the trappings make the constraints of rulership easier to bear?

I doubted it.

King Jacques fulfilled his duties to my parents first, guiding them to the suite they'd share, slowly dispersing members of my family in the visitor's wing before taking Eva, Meredith, and I across closer to the administrative wing of the palace. "The suite has two bedrooms, but I expect most will assume you ladies will be staying together. They'll be corrected soon enough. Evangeline, I'll have a proper room in the family wing of the palace opened for you, and you can move Prince Kelvin into it at your leisure once the paperwork is signed. Agent Scarson, I expect you'll enjoy having the ambassadorial suite to yourself."

"Thank you, Your Majesty."

I waited for him to leave before debating if I wanted to flop on the couch or attempt to find the nearest bed.

Evangeline linked her arm with mine and pulled me across the room. "Meredith, I'll get sleepy here vertical, then we can make a game plan. While I expect my uncle means well, let's not take any chances."

Amused by her determination to take care of herself and too tired to protest, I went along with her wishes, not that I stood any chance of resisting her. I barely managed to kick off my shoes and plop onto the mattress before my worn body gave up the ghost and clocked out.

"I'M PRETTY sure he's done for today," Eva said, which woke me enough to listen in on the nearby conversation. "I called Dr. Thorton, and he wasn't surprised. He had some medical term for it, which I couldn't pronounce if I tried. He said to just leave the Your Highness here to sleep it off and keep tomorrow as quiet as possible."

"Tomorrow's going to be anything other than quiet," King Jacques warned.

I foresaw King Jacques testing Eva's patience, Eva's patience snapping, and a brawl breaking out between the pair. "I'm awake." I rolled over, hit the edge of the bed, and would've smacked into the floor if Eva hadn't intervened.

"You are for now. If Dr. Thorton's is to be believed, you'll last an hour before you pass out again. He thought you'd do better, but then you crashed and burned on us." Eva made me sit on the edge of the bed, where she helped me out of my suit jacket. "I wanted to get you out of that, but you refused to fucking budge, and you weigh a ton for someone so scrawny. It's all wrinkled now."

"Sorry, Eva. What did I miss?"

"Your parents had an epic fucking meltdown when my uncle decided he was going to yank custody from my parents and adopt me back into the royal family. You would've fucking loved it. Every last one of your mother's excuses for disliking me, gone in the blink of an eye. Your father melted down because he gets a princess for a daughter-in-law rather than a hooligan. It seems he'd embraced the idea of a hooligan marrying into his family. Honestly, I can't tell if he was thrilled, disappointed, or both. Meredith recorded it for your enjoyment. Do you think you're up for dinner? The royal pains in my ass are going to blow gaskets if you're not up for dinner."

"I'll have to be, won't I? There were no issues with your congress, Your Majesty?"

"There were no issues. I've sent copies of the documentation to Montana along with the formalized adoption papers. They'll take care of the legalities on their end. I've already put in a court order and have a warrant out to deal with the fraudulent marriage certificate. However, the supposed groom has requested an audience with me."

That announcement woke me up, and I removed my tie, tossed it onto the night table, and considered Nevada's king. "If possible, I want in on that audience."

"Why?"

"I have it on good authority he's afraid of birds."

King Jacques gaped at me. "Pardon?"

Eva snickered. "I'll get you a change of clothes while you two discuss this."

When she left, I appreciated the skip in her step. "I'll probably have to ask my father for some help with the transformation, but I'm of the avian bent. When I inform him he won't come anywhere near my wife if he wants to enjoy his old age, should he protest, I will give him one good reason to stay away from her."

"I was going to inform him he was going to be investigated for fraud and attempted enslavement of a child, but I suppose having you witness can be arranged, and if he's unreasonable about the edict, it's only natural steps would have to be taken to prove our sincerity. He has a lot to lose pushing me."

"Eva's terrified of him," I whispered, hoping my wife wouldn't overhear while she hunted for something I could wear in a bid to give me time to talk to Nevada's king alone.

"Yes. Agent Scarson was astounded. She's going to look into options, as she's convinced it's a form of PTSD. Expect therapy sessions, and you'll probably be asked to attend to make it easier on her."

"She wasn't acting like herself on the tarmac, either."

"We're aware. She'll be fine. The RPS has training in handling situations like this. I recommend approaching North Dakota for general advice. King Adam has a full team helping the royal family. Also, I wanted to mention your kingdom did well by Princess Abigail, especially with the rumors of a potential match between her and Grégoire. An entirely unexpected match, but one worth watching. Your agent has been doing a stellar job at information releases. Sending him to North Dakota was a stroke of brilliance."

"Was it? I was more thinking he was about to go right off his rocker, and we've always been close to Abby. I missed her entire visit, though."

"Well, you can visit her and make up for it later. The few times Princess Abigail has been cornered by the media, she's been with your grandmother and looking happier than anyone has seen her in months. You're getting the credit for it, as certain elements of the visit were your responsibility before you became ill. I had several physicians check on you while you were resting, by the way. They all came to the same conclusion. I'll have to plan tomorrow to give you chances to rest between events, but I think we can manage. I've been informed my head will be served on a silver platter if I even think about suggesting stimulants, and you're barred from coffee for the near future."

"Coffee would result in someone needing to peel me off the ceiling, I'm afraid. They like limiting my coffee intake for some reason. I think I was close to convincing them I really need it to survive."

Eva laughed from the other room. "I'm so looking forward to when you're cleared to have coffee again. And you were barred from coffee because you being wired during scenarios would result in even more mayhem than usual."

"I'm writing into any future contracts I need coffee to put up with scenarios."

Eva poked her head into the bedroom. "Next, you're going to ask for sugar, then hell really will break out. You just want to turn the scenarios into a party. Meredith's still trying to figure out how to get you drunk without you complaining about having to drink."

"She'll give me booze but I can't have coffee? I cry foul."

Eva tossed a suit bag onto the bed. "Evict the king, get dressed, and come to dinner, you nutter."

King Jacques chuckled and headed for the door. "If it makes you feel better, dinner is a private affair; we'll be discussing plans for tomorrow, which will be more formal."

I could work with a planning session. Nevada's king closed the door behind him, and I got changed, swallowing several yawns. I emerged from the bedroom with my untied tie dangling over my shoulders, debating if I wanted to bother with it.

Eva pounced, and I lifted my chin so I wouldn't get in her way.

"Is this a hint I should leave the ties to you?"

With a faint snort, she gave the silk a tug. "We'll be late if I let you fiddle. You'll play with that damned tie for an hour until you're happy with it. I practiced on your herd of relatives to spare us from your fiddling."

Meredith strode in through the front door, looked up from the papers she read, and chuckled. "Good evening, Your Highness. She was going stir crazy waiting for you to wake up, so I recruited some men to stand still while she learned how to tie ties properly. I'm not going to have to work hard to do a stress test on her. If anything, I'm going to be working hard to make sure she waits until we're back in Illinois to snap. I'm slightly concerned she'll attempt to relocate you at her leisure."

"I'm already plotting how to run away when you start your second stress test, Meredith. I'm obviously going to need a lot of time to plot if I want any hope of escaping your clutches."

"You're such a flatterer. How are you feeling?"

"I'm fine. No headache, just tired."

"Well, I come bearing good news."

"What good news?"

"Dr. Hampford and Dr. Thorton got into a spat over your fatigue, and after said energetic spat, I've been authorized to give you some stimulants to get you through the remainder of the visit. Your Majesty, Dr. Thorton requests you loan him one of your physicians to make certain there are no issues."

"Of course."

"I like Dr. Pemland," Eva said.

"Evangeline, the other physicians aren't

going to bite you or Prince Kelvin, I promise," King Jacques replied, his tone exasperated. "Dr. Pemland is a pediatrician."

"Per Dr. Hampford's instructions, he'll get to enjoy that cup of coffee he's been whining about with dinner, and we'll see how it goes from there. She expects he'll enter orbit for a few hours and then crash out again for the night. Then we'll mainline coffee to get through tomorrow. You're going to be jittery, Your Highness, but jitters are better than the alternatives, and she'd rather not use a prescription stimulant if coffee will suffice."

As I had everything to lose by disagreeing, I offered Meredith my best smile. "I like coffee."

"If your wife is done with your tie, you need to review these papers," Meredith announced.

Eva huffed but released me, making space for the head of my detail. Taking the sheets, I skimmed them to discover I held a copy of Eva's adoption papers, a certified copy of our marriage certificate, and a letter from King Jacques granting me his permission to marry his niece turned daughter. I arched a brow and pointed the papers at the king. "Cute."

"If you want the woman, you need my permission. You're just lucky I like you, or I'd make you work a lot harder for it."

Eva sighed and bowed her head. "I'm sorry this created so many problems."

"Eva, you haven't done anything wrong,

although I'm slightly concerned we'll have to fight off an invasion of new relatives in the near future."

"We'll wait until you're fully recovered before we stage any invasions. Have you put in any thought into your wedding plans?" King Jacques smirked at me.

"Montana is handling the preparations. Or, more accurately, we're wisely getting out of Queen Mackenzie's way."

"Queen Mackenzie is planning your wedding?"

"Your Majesty, a pregnant queen wants to plan our wedding. I'm not brave nor foolish enough to tell her no."

"She's really pregnant again?"

"Don't get me killed spreading the news if they haven't announced it officially. Please," I begged.

"Everyone thinks she is anyway, so it's not a big deal. I'd be more concerned if she wasn't, as every time I've seen them together lately, Her Royal Majesty has been licking her lips and looking at her husband like he's the most delicious treat she's ever seen in her life. Now that's what men should aspire to for their woman, Prince Kelvin. When your woman looks at you like that, you know you're doing something right."

Eva's face turned red.

"I like when mine curses and can kick my ass at her leisure. She need not look at me like I'm the main course."

"I'm just saying that's a life goal to work towards, and a good way to figure out if you're on the right track."

If Eva's face reddened any more, I worried she'd drop into a faint, and to spare her from further embarrassment, I tucked the papers under my arm, put my hands on her shoulders, and turned her towards the door. "I think we're fine. After all, she branded me for her permanent enjoyment the moment she laid eyes on me. I'm sure we can figure it out without having to resort to Montana's tactics for raising the birth rate of an entire kingdom without help."

King Jacques chuckled. "It's a genetic flaw in your family line, Prince Kelvin, and I need a lot of babies to spoil. My other kids refuse to have more than two each."

"Don't listen to him, Eva. Monarchs have a basic genetic defect resulting in them becoming overly interested in the private matters of other people. You'll get used to it. It'll just become meaningless babble you have to politely tolerate in limited quantity. And when you get tired of it, you'll just mention someone else who will be having a baby soon, and then everyone's attention will fixate on them. If you really want the conversation to stop, you'll mention the latest political drama and start an argument. Sprinkle in a few of your charming curses, I expect people will leave you alone most of the time. I'll hide behind you, so they'll leave me alone, too."

"What have I gotten myself into?" she lamented.

"A royal mess," I informed her, pushing her through the door.

MY PARENTS STARED at me with matching expressions of parental disgust and disappointment. "Someone told them about the marriage certificate."

"You've been most thoroughly busted, Your Highness."

I was going to need a lot more than coffee to get through dinner. "Remember about that whole no alcohol thing?"

"You're not getting any alcohol, Your Highness. I'm sure you can handle dinner like a mature adult. All you need to do is explain you had just cause to worry about someone coming for her. They'll understand. They're just wanting to hear it from you."

I suspected King Jacques wanted to torture me, as I was directed to sit beside my father. Then, to add insult to injury, he claimed Eva and herded her to the other side of the table. As a consolation prize, Meredith sat beside me.

"What, they don't have you by the door today?"

"I've been forced off duty for dinner, and honestly, I wouldn't miss this for anything."

"You're an evil woman, Meredith."

She smiled.

As delaying would only add to the misery, I turned to my parents and said, "I'm sorry I didn't tell you, but with the risk of someone taking her from me, I wasn't taking any chances."

My parents sighed.

"Kiddo, you're going to give us both gray hairs. I told the congress you were going to get married, not that you were already hitched and whipped."

"I'm sure the congress can handle my marriage to a freshly minted princess."

"Now that surprised me. I'd wondered why she knew so much about basic protocols," my father confessed. "Now I know. No, we're upset you didn't tell us, as we'll have to smooth feathers in Congress, but we're pleased you can handle your own problems like an adult at least some of the time."

"Thanks for such a backhanded compliment, Dad."

"That's for making us smooth feathers with Congress again."

"I could go smooth feathers myself. It'd be dictatorial style, but I could do it."

"That's exactly why you're not going to do it. You're entirely unreasonable when it comes to your newly fledged princess, so let's keep the internal conflicts to a bare minimum. Nice job picking Montana as your conspirators, however. I'm giving you a full passing grade for that one. I've also heard some rumors you're planning assault while in your shifted form?"

"Maybe."

"I've already agreed to help you perform the assault but only if there's any actual evidence of threat to your princess."

"You're going to call Eva a princess as many times as possible to drive us both insane, aren't you?"

"It's in the parenting handbook. Also, I'm pushing her buttons to see how long it takes for her to go on a profanity-filled rampage. Your mother misses the profanities already."

"I do not."

"Your mother is also a little cranky the doctors didn't warn her you'd be taking unplanned naps."

"That part is true."

"I don't think the doctor really knew, Mom. Anyway, I'm feeling fine, and I'm finally getting to enjoy coffee."

My father chuckled. "They've been rationing coffee like it's an illegal drug around you. You're going to be wired."

"Wired is better than sleeping until we're through this."

"That's true enough. Alright, kiddo. Why are you plotting assault, and why did your agent barge in and inform me I'd be cooperating with your attempted assault? You're not a fighter. All that's going to happen is that I'm going to have to shift and do the fighting for you."

"The man Eva's biological parents attempted to fraudulently marry her to is afraid of birds."

"I take back everything I just said with the exception of having to shift and help you with the fight. I'd been briefed there was an illegal certificate, but I hadn't gotten all of the details. Wouldn't a warrant for his arrest be better? She was a minor when the forgery occurred."

"I see no reason both can't occur at the same time. I'll just helpfully accompany the arresting officers. I like that idea. King Jacques informed me the bastard requested an audience."

"Yes, he did. And yes, I'll grant the audience, which is when he'll be arrested. Evangeline has already agreed to be present for the audience, as we want to record his reaction to her presence. Initially, the plan was to have the audience after dinner while you were still sleeping, but as you'll be awake, we'll make some adjustments for your inclusion. This could be a political disaster for Nevada, so it'll be addressed immediately. There's another concern we'll need to address as well."

I considered the worst-case scenarios, grimacing at the severity of each one. At the top of my list was a violation of parole terms, which could easily lead to the execution of Eva's mother. While my wife had been on the run for years, I wasn't sure how she'd handle the news.

Some things remained a mystery with my wife, and I looked forward to long years of solving them.

"Does this incident violate parole terms?"

"Yes, it does. While evicted from the royal family, the parole terms state that she must obey all of Nevada's laws. Nevada doesn't have stellar protections in place for children of marriageable age, but forgery and fraud are illegal, as is offering and accepting money for a child's hand in marriage. Dowries have been barred in Nevada; the laws were put into place before they attempted to marry Eva off. We have uncovered documentation and financials proving they'd arranged her marriage for direct profit. While evicted from the royal bloodline, my sister has a strong talent. It's stronger in Evangeline. Evangeline's talent is likely on par with mine, although we'll want to do proper evaluations after everything has settled. I'm not convinced she has adequate control over her talent." King Jacques stared at my wife, and she bristled, matching him glare for glare.

"Just curse him out, Eva. He already signed the paperwork, as did his congress. If he wants to disown you, he'd have a hefty battle ahead of him. I think your talent is perfect as it is, so don't worry what he thinks about it."

"You're both fucking nutters."

"The nice thing is that you get to come home with me and you don't have to see that fucking nutter unless you want to. You're stuck with this fucking nutter, though."

My mother's pained sigh made me unreasonably happy.

My father drummed his fingers on the table. "You're going to be using her favorite words trying to give your mother and me more gray hairs, aren't you?"

"Good idea. Thanks for the suggestion, Dad. Being serious. When is this audience, should I wait to have my coffee until right before it to ensure I don't miss out, and at what stage can I be involved?"

"It'll be right after dinner. I've already issued the royal summons, which he won't ignore as he put in the request to be summoned. I expect he'll contrive some bogus accusations regarding Evangeline's involvement with the assault at the training center. Be prepared for that, Your Highness. While everyone at this table knows that's a lie, he'll be convincing. This man's a snake and has been the entirety of his time in my court, but he's a cunning snake who hasn't done anything I've been, until now, able to prove."

No matter how many obstacles came between me and Eva, I'd tear them down so she could have a safe, stable, and comfortable life, one where she wouldn't have to run from her past. I couldn't protect her from everything, but when she faced her demons, I'd face them with her. I glanced at her before giving King

Jacques a long, serious look. "If he raises a hand against her, I make no promises I won't kill him."

My father raised his hand like he was a little kid in school rather than a king. "I'll be helping him."

A gusty sigh exploded from my mother, startling us all into staring at her. "I'm inclined to agree, but I'll have to keep my contributions purely magical. I don't want to break a nail on a worthless piece of slime."

The rest of my family, scattered around the big table, snickered.

"This is the problem with inviting a bunch of predators into my house. There's inevitably bloodshed."

"The Your Highness over there isn't a predator," Eva said, pointing at me. "First, he's too pretty to be a predator. Second, actually, I don't need a second. He's too pretty to be a predator."

"Predators can be pretty," my father protested.

"Predators exist to be trophies in my photography collection, Your Majesty."

"Do you take requests?" my mother asked. "Would you pose your prizes in certain ways? Do you do group hunts for trophies?"

"If you're asking if I'll tag and bag multiple members of your family, your husband and king included, we can discuss the details."

"Is a pile of unconscious predators with a

lively white turkey on top displaying his feathers feasible?"

I liked the idea enough I leaned forward for a better look at my mother. "You have my attention, Mom."

"I thought that would. Evangeline, I've lost count of the number of times those freaks have paraded around the castle in the nude because they couldn't wait to shift until they returned to their rooms like civilized beings."

Ah. Having heard the complaint my entire life, I accepted it as a long-standing grudge an incriminating photograph would help soothe for a while.

"The problem here is that you view them as civilized beings, Your Majesty. If you don't train the beasts appropriately, they'll do things like run around the castle in the nude. I recommend a training regime. Poor behavior can result in a trophy-hunting session. I think we can work the initial hunt as a sneak peek of what they'll face if they can't moderate their nudity to tolerable levels." Eva smiled. "I promise you my Your Highness will not be walking around any castle in the nude. I don't share."

"This is where the pretty part of the equation comes into play, I see," King Jacques murmured. "Could you two possibly be any more possessive of each other right now?"

"No," Eva and I chorused.

"It's going to be a long night," Nevada's king predicted.

AS WARNED, the coffee had its way with me, filling me with restless, jittery energy. All in all, I preferred it to needing an immediate nap, but if I didn't find something to do with myself while waiting for Jerome Dansen to arrive, I'd lose my mind. The man, aged seventy-nine, bothered me in more ways than I could count. Even his photograph managed to give me a serious case of the creeps, as he leered for the camera without even bothering to hide his disgusting tendencies.

He'd been married and divorced six times, and not a single one of the women had been over the age of twenty-one. Had he succeeded in his plot with Eva, she would've been his youngest victim.

The file did a good job of riling up every member of my family, but my mother's determination to get in her hits worried me. If Dansen even looked at my mother, my father would rip him to pieces, resulting in a lot of ruined carpeting in the king's personal office and cranky RPS agents. Because my father would be doing the killing, he wouldn't even attempt to cover up the murder.

He'd own it and use it as an example of what would happen if anyone tried to hurt his wife. Then, because he was my father, he'd lay out the various crimes the old man had committed, including the attempted theft of my wife.

I'd need a lot of coffee to get through the next few days.

"I'd be a lot happier if you avoided transforming," my father grumbled, taking over King Jacques's couch with my mother, leaving my great-grandpa, as a bear, to decorate a corner while I stood off to the side with Eva.

Eva shifted her weight from foot to foot, and at a loss of how to ease her anxiety, I wrapped my arm around her waist and pinned her to my side. It didn't stop her from fidgeting, but it offered me the illusion she wouldn't fidget her way through the floor or otherwise escape me.

A knock at the door ended the conversation, and one of Nevada's RPS agents stepped inside. "Your Majesty, Mr. Dansen is here to see you."

Showtime.

I tightened my hold on Eva, keeping her nestled to my side. I recognized the move for what it was, purely possessive and territorial, but she pressed against me. I couldn't view her as weak.

No, my wife wasn't weak, but the fear lurking under her skin and reflecting in her tense expression made me want to put a quick end to the man who'd terrorized her since she'd run away too many years ago.

"Show him in," King Jacques ordered, and he sat on the edge of his desk, casual and composed. My father used the pose sometimes when he wanted to trick people into relaxing their guard. A king behind his desk intimidated. A king perched on his desk seemed more approachable.

Anyone who thought so knew nothing of the game of politics.

King Jacques prepared to wage a quick and vicious war.

After, I'd need to sit him down and have a talk with him, as behind the desk was a great deal safer than on it when my family expected bloodshed. Then again, he'd learn the truth soon enough, around the time he had to replace his pale carpeting because blood often left stains most cleaners couldn't handle. I supposed magic might clean the mess.

My father typically replaced the carpet in a new color and called it a day.

Dansen stepped into the king's office, his leer in place, his hair so grayed it fringed on white, and eager enough I wanted to fist my hand and knock the pride out of him. I'd seen his expression before in my father's court.

He believed he'd won, that he would get exactly what he wanted, and what he wanted was my wife.

"Your Majesty," he greeted, dipping into a bow.

Had the man bothered to acknowledge anyone else in the room, he might've noticed Eva, although she shrank against me and trembled. A quick glance at her face eased most of my concerns.

The fear had made way for rage, and she

wasn't shrinking against me, she prepared to do battle, and I expected I'd become a launching block for her assault if he crossed any one of her lines.

Was I better off restraining or encouraging her?

"I hope you have a very good reason for interrupting my time with Illinois's delegation."

"I wish to lay charges of kidnapping and conspiracy against our sovereignty, Your Majesty."

"Against whom?"

"Illinois."

My father snorted, and then he laughed. "You win that bet, Jacques. And here I thought only one of my court would have the audacity to try such a foolish thing."

As it happened so often with men utterly convinced of their superiority, Dansen woke to the fact he hadn't walked into a private audience with his king. He turned to face my father.

Something about the motion, something about the way he dared turn his back on me, who stood to lose the most from his interference, infuriated me. My blood rushed in my head, my heartbeat pulsing in my ears and throat.

"Kelvin," Eva whispered in my ear. "Don't do anything stupid."

Protecting her would never be stupid, but I stood still, watched, and waited despite wanting to wade in and teach the old man a few lessons about terrifying young women.

"You," Dansen spat.

"Me," my father cheerfully agreed, and he took his time wrapping his arm around my mother and holding her the same way I held Eva, possessive. "It's considered rude to try to take another man's woman, Mr. Dansen. It's even ruder to attempt to rob a kingdom of its future queen. It's downright criminal when a man attempts to force himself upon a little girl."

Eva stiffened at my father's description of her.

To my father, to most in my family, fifteen was little, a child in all ways, and little more than an infant in arms, albeit a mouthy infant prone to fits of independence. I reined in my temper and sighed, my turn to do the soothing. "They're old men who look young, Eva. To them, we are babies."

She grunted but stayed put.

"Excuse me?"

I considered banging my head against the wall but thought better of it. Instead, I lifted my free hand and rubbed my brow, convinced I'd contract a migraine due to Dansen's general ego and stupidity before he was dealt with and arrested.

"What part was incomprehensible for you? Did you really believe the forged documentation would hold up to scrutiny?"

"How dare you accuse me! My papers are accurate and legal."

"They're a confirmed forgery." My father rose from the couch, crossed to the desk and picked up one of the papers. "This claims you married one Evangeline Estrin two days after she turned fifteen." He picked up another piece of paper. "This document is a visa application, submitted in person, for a ninety-day visa to remain in Texas signed the day before your so-called legal documentation was signed." My father snatched a third piece of paper. "This is a confirmation of asylum in Texas signed on the same day in Houston. Please explain to me how a little girl on the run in Texas, seeking asylum to get away from you, can sign a paper in Nevada."

Uh oh. I heard the fury in my father's voice, and I wondered if Dansen would make it to trial.

"This is preposterous! Those documents aren't real."

"Oh, they're real," the voice of Montana's king said from the phone, and everyone save King Jacques jumped. My heart skipped a few beats, and I wondered how King Jacques had put through the call without any of us noticing. "Allow me to introduce myself. I'm King William of Montana. I've been brought in to verify the truth of your words, and you, Mr. Dansen, are aware the documents you claim are real are a forgery. Also, Your Majesty, congratulations on your adoption.

You're wise to bring such an accomplished woman directly into your royal bloodline, and I'm glad we could see eye to eye on this matter."

Talent? A clever RPS agent tapping into the phone lines? A sneaky use of computers? No matter how the pair of monarchs had pulled it off, I was grateful I wouldn't have to call in for a truth seer to put the man's lies to rest.

I forced myself to relax, although I kept a firm grip on Eva.

"Adoption?" Dansen blurted. "What adoption?"

"As my sister and her husband are obviously incapable of caring properly for a little girl and filed an incorrect disowning to terrorize her and coerce her into a marriage, I've decided to ensure the disowning was properly finalized, as we have confirmation Evangeline was informed she was no longer a part of the Estrin family. This is to protect her from men like you, who believe little girls should be the property of the wealthy. This is also to protect the interests of Illinois, who wisely chose my new daughter to be their future queen."

Eva did her best to hide behind me, and I preferred her embarrassment over her fear. I made enough space she could cram her face against my back.

Dansen's gaze flicked to me, and his eyes widened. "You're supposed to be dead."

I raised a brow. "Haven't you been watching the news?"

"What? No. I don't need to watch the news. You're supposed to be dead."

My father stilled, and he locked onto Dansen, a low growl slipping out of his throat. "Your Majesty?"

"He speaks the truth," Montana's king reported. "As does the money trail, which indicates he helped pay for the unpleasantness in Illinois. Answer me true, Mr. Dansen. Were you involved with the plot to murder Prince Kelvin of Illinois?"

Hatred twisted Dansen's leering face into a repulsive mask. "What is it to you? Things would be simpler without a defective prince around."

Defective? I supposed requiring a bone marrow transplant due to the family talent did count as defective, which made it easier to shrug off the insult.

"Answer the question, Mr. Dansen."

Something in King William's voice changed, as though he'd become a thunderstorm poised to break overhead and fling the terrors of nature down on our heads.

"Yes."

"Truth. There's your confession, King Jacques. Do with him as you please. Should you give him to the lynx, I recommend you make him take his prey outside first, as I doubt you'll be able to get the bloodstains out of your office no matter how hard you scrub."

A click and dial tone announced King William's departure from the conversation, and King Jacques reached across his desk to hang up his phone.

"I'm not going to allow His Royal Majesty of Illinois to kill you, however satisfying it might be to watch you be ripped limb from limb so you won't bother anyone ever again. No, I'm going to do something far worse. I'm going to ruin you, Mr. Dansen. Everything you have ever built will be torn down, and I will give His Majesty the pleasure of exposing your every crime to the public. You'll get a trial, and it'll even be a fair one, overseen by truth seers to ensure you'll never see the light of day ever again. Your conspirators will pay a similar price. I've already ordered for them to be apprehended and imprisoned for their crimes. Within twenty-four hours, you will be remembered as nothing more than a filthy, disgusting excuse of a human, one who preyed on little girls to enjoy their terror. But, you won't escape this room unscathed."

King Jacques circled his desk and sat, and his grim smile chilled me. "Your Majesty, Mr. Averett, please give him a taste of what it is like to be truly afraid."

"Oh, no. The best person for that would be my son," my father announced, crossing the room towards me, pausing long enough to snarl at the man who'd caused Eva so much anguish. "Evangeline, with your leave?"

My wife released me. "Do I get to hit him, too?"

"If he as much as lifts a hand against Kel, you may do whatever you feel is necessary to eliminate the threat," my father promised. "Try to leave something for me when you're finished."

With Eva's blessing, my father took hold of my arm, gave a nod, and induced my transformation.

THE INSTANT DANSEN SPOTTED ME, wings spread, tail fanned and whistling my intent to spur a few years off his life, he screamed. My father got out of my way, and I hopped forward, flapping my wings and slashing my talons in Dansen's direction.

The man scrambled backwards to escape me and bumped into my great-grandpa, who roared his displeasure and, with a single swipe of his paw, batted the old man in my direction. Dansen hit the ground hard, and I pecked at him, grabbing his hair in my beak and yanking on it.

While I didn't count incoherent screaming and flailing his arms as a threat towards me, Eva dove into the fray, shunted me aside, and went for his throat. Her first blow caught him in the cheek, and she struggled to get a hold on him. Had she been thinking, she would've taken him out within a few breaths, but her fury had come back in full force.

She just wanted to hit him.

Heaving a sigh, my father grabbed Eva by her waist, stood straight, and pulled her off while she spewed more profanities than I'd ever heard come out of her mouth at one time. She strained to reach Dansen, howling threats, curses, and promises of violence the instant she got her hands on him.

"Easy, Eva. Kel's fine. That was incoherent terror, not an actual attempt to hurt him."

Eva struggled, slashing her hands at the target of her fury. "He almost died because of this fucking waste of air!"

"He's right there, safe and sound," my father promised. "However much I'd like to kill him, too, what your new family has in mind is far worse than a quick out. I know you're upset. I am, too. But you need to let this go."

We all did, but it didn't stop me from darting in and spurring the bastard's face for daring to hurt Eva as he had, forcing her to run, inflicting terror on her so intense she hopped from kingdom to kingdom seeking asylum so she wouldn't become his victim.

My grant-grandpa grabbed me in his huge paws and lifted me off while I squealed my protests.

"And now there's blood in my carpet," King Jacques complained. "Thank you, Mr. Averett."

Meredith stepped away from her post behind King Jacques, shook her head, and sighed. "What happened to not shifting, Your Highness?"

I gobbled more protests at the head of my detail, wishing I could tell her she'd stood still and watched the entire squabble without lifting a finger.

Meredith grunted, lifted her hand to her ear, and said, "There's a gentleman in the king's office requiring immediate arrest and minor medical care."

Her order brought several of the Nevada RPS, who hauled Dansen to his feet and dragged him from the room, droplets of blood staining the pale carpet in his wake.

"Well, that was an entertaining end to the day," King Jacques declared, rising from his chair. "I think this calls for a stiff drink and celebration, don't you? As soon as my sister and her husband are apprehended, notify me immediately," he ordered his RPS agents, who seemed as resigned to the situation as my agent.

With my target gone, I waddled to my father, who still held Eva captive, and pecked his shins and battered him with my wings until he let her go. She straightened, dusting herself off. "You should've let me beat him for a while longer."

"If I let you two beat on him a little longer, the RPS would've been carrying him out of here in a body bag. Be grateful we have sufficient evidence of psychological strain to cover why you'd both go after an old man. In good news, in the worst-case scenario, provoked assault is a minor fine." My father nudged me with his shoe. "Time to get you back to your suite and shifted back. While you, lucky little brat you are, shifted with your clothes, I expect you'll want some private time with your wife. You both need a chance to relax before someone gets hurt because you're both on short fuses and ready to blow."

As I had no problems with spending some time alone with Eva, I headed for the door at my fastest run and waited in the hall for the slow-poke predators to catch up.

EVA'S biological parents evaded arrest for a full forty-eight hours, and to encourage the public to aid in their capture, King Jacques went to the public with the entire story, beginning from Eva's flight from her family to the day she'd met me, although some of the details remained private. Montana contributed to Nevada's efforts, releasing parts of my medical file with my blessings. Eva's contribution also went public.

And, protecting my family's dirty little secret, while our status as a life bonded pair was shared, the media spun it in ways only the media could. Rather than a consequence of my talent, Eva's selfless donation of her bone marrow took the blame for our bond. Specialists confirmed what I'd heard, and it bothered me how painful the procedure had been for her, too.

In the time we waited, Eva had been given a room of her own in the palace, I'd been relocated to it by the grizzly, who treated it like a scenario right down to tapping the back of my head to get me to play dead. The first tap had shocked me into staring at him. The second, a little more insistent, had reminded me it was a scenario move, and the third had annoyed me into going for his throat.

He'd smacked me around more enthusiastically until he'd knocked the breath out of me before grabbing my foot and dragging me across the palace.

Watching Eva go for the bear's throat would be one of my favorite memories for the rest of my life.

"Do you think that's it?" Eva asked, returning me to the present, which involved a lot of waiting, most of our time spent on the couch watching the news or in bed without sleeping a wink. I wasn't sure what King Jacques and my family were up to, but we hadn't been invited. Guards at the door, under orders to lock us in her room until they were finished, ensured our good behavior.

"It better be. I'm not sure what else we can do to put an end to it. The mercenary outfit's out of Illinois. They aren't in Nevada as far as we can tell, and if they're wise, they'll lay low. With your parents behind bars for more crimes than I care to count, as far as I'm concerned, this mess is over. We just need to worry about preventing Queen Mackenzie from turning our wedding into a complete zoo."

As I already knew there'd be horses involved in some fashion, it would be a zoo, although I hoped Eva would like the surprises I had in store for her. Add in the various predators in my family, and I expected pure chaos.

"Do you think King Jacques is going to fight Montana for the right to meddle with our wedding plans?"

"It's okay to call him your uncle or your father. Whichever you're comfortable with. One of your new uncles is also a king, and you'll find he's pretty relaxed about titles."

"South Dakota?"

"Yes."

"Did Her Majesty of South Dakota wade knee-deep in cow shit, too?"

"I believe so. The entire family had to work hard to get by, although their situation changed once my aunt married."

"Huh. That could be entertaining. Does your aunt bristle as much as your mother?"

"If you join forces with my grandmother, I think you'll find new and interesting ways to drive my relatives to the brink of insanity."

"I'll keep that in mind."

"My grandmother specializes in relocations."

Eva grinned. "Think she'd help plan our escape from stress-test hell?"

"I think she'd be delighted to assist our efforts to escape from the RPS and get in some serious rest and relaxation before we're cruelly forced to attend to our duties as the future monarchs of Illinois."

"Paperwork, children, or both?"

"Probably both," I admitted. "Children seem to be one of the early consequences of being royal. But there's a lot of paperwork."

"Does my percentage of paperwork go down as the number of children go up?"

Did it? As children hadn't been part of the equation before, I hadn't thought about it. "There must be some sort of mathematical equation that determines how much paperwork the mother of my children has to do, which is directly related to the number and age of our children."

"Despite my tendency to curse whenever the fuck I want, I do like children. I just..."

"You just didn't want them with a sick old pervert."

"Right."

"I'm no longer sick, I'm definitely not old, but I'm probably tamely perverted."

She smirked, an expression I loved almost as much as her tendency to curse when stressed, annoyed, or desiring space. "We'll have to work on that, Your Highness, but don't worry. I think I can work with you. It might take a lifetime to train you, but I'm sure I'll enjoy it even more than you do."

I got up, made sure the door was locked, engaged the deadbolt, and considered jamming a chair against the door to ensure we weren't disturbed. "Then let's begin, shall we?"

BONDS IS the next novel in the Royal States series. Continue reading for a sample.

About Susan Copperfield

SUSAN COPPERFIELD is the royal romance, urban fantasy loving alter ego of award-winning and USA Today best-selling novelist RJ Blain.

Want to hear from the author when a new book releases? Sign up here! Please note this newsletter is operated by the Furred & Frond Management. Expect to be sassed by a cat. (With guest features of other animals, including dogs.)

For a complete list of books written by RJ and her various pen names, please click here.

Under the super not-so-secret identity of Susan, the Royal States of America is explored, where the work of sixteen founding royal families preserved the United States from destruction and civil war when magic swept over the world.

In the Royal States, life, love, and magic always finds a way.

RJ BLAIN suffers from a Moleskine journal obsession, a pen fixation, and a terrible tendency to pun without warning.

When she isn't playing pretend, she likes to think she's a cartographer and a sumi-e painter.

In her spare time, she daydreams about being a spy. Should that fail, her contingency plan involves tying her best of enemies to spinning wheels and quoting James Bond villains until she is satisfied.

RJ also writes as Susan Copperfield and Bernadette Franklin. Visit RJ and her pets (the Management) at thesneakykittycritic.com.

FOLLOW RJ & HER ALTER EGOS ON BOOKBUB:
RJ BLAIN
SUSAN COPPERFIELD
BERNADETTE FRANKLIN

From Bonds

In the Royal States of America, magic rules all, but life—and love—always finds a way.

When a sinking oil tanker threatens to destroy the picturesque coastline of France, search and rescue diver Jack Alders and his waveweaving talent stand between France and a record-breaking oil spill.

But what Jack finds on board the dying ship will forever change the course of the Royal States and puts him in the sights of a royal tyrant out for blood.

CHAPTER ONE

One day, I might understand why I enjoyed

jumping out of helicopters during squalls. I checked my harness for the third time since strapping in. As soon as I was a safe distance above the water, I'd release my line and go for a swim. Had the weather been better, we would've used the nearby rescue ship as our base of operations. Too much could go wrong, and the rescue team on board already had their hands full tending to the crew of the oil tanker that had run aground on rocks off the French coast. The sheen of oil on the waves below complicated the already complicated rescue.

My first job would be to plug the leaks and keep the tanker from polluting even more of the water. Once I had the holes plugged, I'd board and check for any missed crew on the floundering ship.

The ship listed enough she'd go under in time; the rocks, a well-charted menace the captain should've avoided in the first place, kept them afloat. With each wave threatening to tear the monster vessel from its haphazard perch, I wouldn't have much time to work.

I hated when my magic became the first and last defense during a dangerous rescue. The storm darkened the afternoon sky, and it wouldn't be long until I was forced to use my magic to illuminate our efforts.

I wanted to give the captain a piece of my mind for endangering the crew and the rescue team stuck bailing their irresponsible asses out.

I eyed the water again while waiting for the pilot to get the helicopter into position, close enough to the ship I'd be able to work my magic but far enough away a rogue wave wouldn't smash me into the hull. Any other dive, I would have worn flippers into the water to make swimming easier, but if I needed to board the ship, they'd get in the way.

I missed my flippers already.

With so much crude in the water, without my magic protecting me, my gear and I would be in serious trouble. Crude oil could be volatile in many ways, depending on the type. I wouldn't know if I dealt with tar-like sludge, lighter crude, or refined gas until I got into the water.

To add to the fun, a single spark could ruin my day—and light the nearby ocean on fire.

I'd gotten that lecture a few times already. Under normal working operations, fire risks on a tanker were low, but once oxygen in the air mixed with the crude's fumes, things could go wrong in a hurry.

"I'm in position. Ready, Jack?" the pilot, Louis, asked, his French accent so thick I struggled to understand him. My French was so bad everyone on the team took pity on me, using English when they needed me for something.

The rest of the time, I pretended I understood what the hell they were saying.

Learning more languages was on my to-do list, but every time I settled in to learn something, someone needed me to jump out of a helicopter to rescue a floundering vessel.

Most of the time, I loved my job. I loved knowing I saved lives. I even loved flinging myself out of various aircraft.

Today, however, I wanted a new job. No one sane wanted to enter oil-polluted waters with monstrous white-capped waves ready to pound me into a smear against the hull of the dying ship.

Then again, if I quit my job as a search and rescue diver, I'd have to return to the Royal States of America, which was on the top of my 'over my dead body' list.

It might really be over my dead body if I didn't do everything just right when I entered the water.

I checked my mask again. If I lost it, I wouldn't be able to communicate with the helicopter and the rest of the rescue team. Once certain I wouldn't lose it along with my oxygen tank, I replied, "*Oui.*"

My limited French usually made the team laugh. Beyond a basic yes, I could cuss like a champ and ask where the bathroom was. After trying to order a drink and getting a fish instead, I'd given up pretending I had any idea what I was doing.

A rapid conversation conducted in French filled my ears, but I'd been on enough dives with the team to know the pilot was giving the basic instructions to the rest of the team, who'd handle the wench and be prepared for when I released the line and went into the water.

The first time I'd released my line and dove into stormy seas with a small oxygen tank, the entire crew had about shit their pants until they remembered I used a blend of illumination and waveweaving magic. Unless knocked unconscious, my chances of drowning were slim to none. Add in my minor airweaving talent, which allowed me to refresh my oxygen tank without needing to surface, and I made the perfect rescue diver.

No one needed to know I wasn't actually a borderline elite. Borderline elite put me one step below the elite class, and I'd made certain to leave the Royal States before I could be evaluated again.

Being above average worked well for me.

My real rank, elite class or better, would've dumped me directly into a political nightmare. Before I could get sucked into worrying about what would happen if I had to return to the Royal States, the rest of the team finished their final checks and gave the okay for me to slide out of the helicopter.

I descended until I was only a few feet from the crashing whitecaps. After eyeing the roll of the waves, I lifted my hand to indicate I was ready, released my line, and plunged into the water.

More French, probably confirming I was in the water, blasted into my ears. I ignored the chatter and submerged, swimming for the ship. In the eyes of most, my illumination talent wasn't worth writing home about. Unlike the truly powerful illuminators, I couldn't become a living lighthouse capable of guiding ships safely to harbor.

I could, however, flood the ocean with a gentle light, which worked well for my needs. My magic exposed a gaping hole in the vessel.

"The breach in the hull is at least ten meters long, starboard stern," I reported before approaching, eyeing the ship until I found a suitable handhold. "There's enough crude leaking out I need to get it back in the ship before this shit hits shore."

We'd gotten lucky; the waves were mostly keeping the oil near the ship, but it would be a matter of time before the rocks and the ship itself no longer protected the rest of the ocean from the mess. I closed my eyes so I could concentrate, getting a feel for the churning water and the crude polluting it.

If we got lucky, it'd be a lighter gas, which would evaporate quickly and do minimal damage to the environment. Light gasses and oils registered as an oily warmth feathering over my skin, expressing its more volatile nature.

The cold, sticky sensation clinging to me promised I had a heavier, toxic crude on my hands, and I'd be pushed to the limits of my skill dealing with it. Worse, it was a mixed blend, and at first glance, it hadn't been blended well. On second thought, I suspected the tanker carried at least two crude batches, one possibly partially refined. It was also possible it was just one of those batches of oil that couldn't quite decide if it was a heavy or a light crude. That left me with one viable candidate for the origin of the oil: OPEC liked trying to control the market, and its suppliers, mostly from the Middle East, would often flood the market with their crude if gas prices got out of hand to make certain demand didn't die out due to price increases.

It just wouldn't do if safer, cleaner alternatives were pursued due to economic factors.

"Likely an OPEC Basket mixed shipment," I finally reported. "It's a huge spill, so I'm going to get as much of it back in the tanker as possible and plug the hole. Flag the wreck as critical. This shit is toxic."

"How toxic?"

"It's toxic. It's heavy enough if I don't get this back into the tanker where it belongs, say goodbye to France's nice beaches for a few years."

A chorus of French curses blasted my ears, and once they started chattering to each other, likely cursing the Middle Eastern oil trade, I began the tedious and exhausting process of pulling the crude oil back to the ship where it belonged. At the same time, I began encasing the tanker's hull and the rock it perched on in ice.

The ice might help keep the ship afloat for a little while longer. Maybe.

We'd find out soon enough.

Lightning Source UK Ltd.
Milton Keynes UK
UKHW011302180620
365213UK00003B/536